Aunt Phil's Trunk
Proudly Presents

Where the Sun Swings North

Written by
Barrett Willoughby

Edited by
Laurel Downing Bill

Alaska's First Official Author
By Laurel Downing Bill

Originally published 1922
By A.L. Burt Company, New York
Under agreement with G.P. Putnam's Sons

Reprint from Public Domain 2018
by Aunt Phil's Trunk LLC
Anchorage, Alaska
www.AuntPhilsTrunk.com
ISBN: 978-0-9849494-7-2

Cover art: Flickr.com/24873512149_b28483723e_0

Alaska author Florence Barrett Willoughby.

To

My mother, who can make a tent in
the wilderness seem like home.

"In this book I write of my own country and its people as I
know them – not artfully, perhaps, but truthfully."

– Barrett Willoughby
Katalla, Alaska

TABLE OF CONTENTS

TABLE OF CONTENTS

VOCABULARY NOTES

When Florence Barrett Willoughby wrote *Where The Sun Swings North* in 1922, some words and terms that referred to minorities were acceptable that today are not. In fact, a few words from that era continue to cause pain.

To be sensative to changes made over the years, and still share this wonderful story of adventure, Aunt Phil's Trunk edited some of the original verbiage while striving not to affect the integrity of the original work.

Also during this time period, people used a wide variety of vocabulary words that are not in common use today. Following are definitions for some of the words found in this tale.

Ablution – The washing of one's body

Bannock – A flat cake

Bidarka – Skin boat

Billow – A great rolling wave

Cad – One who behaves in a dishonorable way toward women

Carousal – A merry drinking party

Cheechako - Newcomer

Chemise – A loose-fitting, shirtlike undergarment

Cleft – A space or opening made by or as if by splitting

Depreciatory – Belittling

Espying – Seeing at a distance; catch sight of

Gloaming – Twilight, dusk

Hootch – Distilled alcohol drink

Imprecation – Curse, swear

VOCABULARY NOTES (Continued)

Inchoate – Not yet completed or fully developed; rudimentary

Indissolubly – Firmly

Invidious – Calculated to create ill will, discontent

Kustaka – Ghost (Tlingit word, pronounced Kus-ta-ka)

Letquoan – The Snow People (white people)

Limned – Outlined

Misogynist – A person who dislikes women

Outside – Name by which the contiguous United States is designated in the North

Pareu – A wraparound skirt, loincloth

Perturbation – Mental disquiet

Plaint – Sad cry

Potlatch – A Native festival

Potvaliant – Brave only as a result of being drunk

Prodigiously – Extraordinary in size

Querulous – Full of complaints

Serrulated – Notched, scalloped

Shaatk' – Unmarried young woman (Tlingit word)

Soliloquies – Talking to oneself

Squattering – To go along through or as if through water

Stygian – Of or relating to the river Styx or to Hades; dark or gloomy

Susurrous – Full of whispering or rustling sounds

Tatterdemalion – A person in tattered clothing; shabby person

Troglodytic – A prehistoric cave dweller

Vehemence – Fury

Woof – Texture, fabric

PART I

1

THE WHITE CHIEF OF KATLEEAN

It was quiet in the great storeroom of the Alaska Fur and Trading Company's post at Katleean. The west sun streaming in through a side window lighted up shelves of brightly labeled canned goods and a long, scarred counter piled high with gay blankets and men's rough clothing. Back of the big, potbellied stove – cold now – that stood near the center of the room, lidless boxes of hardtack and crackers yawned in open defiance of germs. An amber, mote-filled ray slanted toward the moss-chinked log wall where a row of dusty fox and wolverine skins hung – pelts discarded when the spring shipment of furs had been made because of flaws visible only to expert eyes.

At the far end of the room the possessor of those expert eyes sat before a rough homemade desk. There was a rustle of papers as he closed the ledger in front of him with an air of relief. He then clapped his hands smartly. Almost on the instant the curtain hanging in the doorway at the side of the desk was drawn aside and a small, brown feminine hand materialized.

"My cigarettes, Decitan."

The man's voice was low, with that particular vibrant quality often found in the voices of men accustomed to commanding peoples deemed inferior on the far outposts of civilization.

The curtain wavered again, and from behind the folds a brown arm, bare and softly rounded, accompanied the hand that set down a tray of smoking materials.

With a careless nod toward his invisible servitor, the man picked up a cigarette and lighted it. He took one long, deep pull. Then tossing it aside, he swung his chair about and faced the open doorway that gave onto a courtyard and the bay beyond.

He readjusted the scarlet band about his narrow hips. Flannel-shirted, high-booted, he stretched his six-foot length in the tilting chair and clasped his hands behind his head. The movement loosened a lock of black hair, which fell heavily across his forehead. His eyes – long, narrow and the color of pale smoke – drowsed beneath brows that met above his nose. Thin, sharply defined nostrils quivered under the slightest emotion, and startling against the whiteness of his face, was a short, pointed beard, black and silky as a woman's hair. When Paul Kilbuck, the white trader of Katleean, smiled, his thin, red lips parted over teeth white and perfect, but there was that in the long, pointed incisors that brought to mind the clean fangs of a wolf dog.

He closed his pale eyes now and smiled to himself. His work on the company's books was finished for the present. He hated the petty details of account keeping, but since the death of old Add-'em-up Sam, his helper and accountant, who had departed this world six months before during a spell of delirium tremens, the trader had been obliged to do his own.

Queer and clever things had Add-'em-up done to the books. The directors of the Alaska Fur and Trading Company down in San Francisco had long suspected it no doubt, but it was not for nothing that Kilbuck was known up and down the coast of Alaska as the White Chief. No other man in the North had such power and influence among the Tlingit tribes. No other man sent in such quantities of prime pelts; hence the White Chief of Katleean had never been obliged to give too strict an accounting of his stewardship. Taking what belongs to a company is not, in the elastic code of the North, considered stealing. "God is high above and the Czar is far away," said the plundering, roistering old Russians of Baranoff's day, and the spirit in the isolated posts had not changed, though Russian adventurers came no more to rape Alaska of her riches, and the Stars and Stripes now floated over the old-time Russian stronghold at Sitka.

Kilbuck had been the agent of the company for eighteen years. In trading posts up and down the coast, where the trappers and prospectors gather to outfit, many tales of the White Chief were afloat: his trips to the Outside; his lavish spending of money; his hiring of private cars to take him from Seattle to New York; his princely entertainment of beautiful women. There were women in every story told of Paul Kilbuck. Sometimes they were white, but more often they were dusky beauties of the North.

Among the several dark-eyed Tlingit women who occupied the mysterious quarters back of the log store, there was always rejoicing when the White Chief returned from his visits to the States. He was a generous master, bringing back with him many presents from the land of the white people – rings, beads, trinkets and yards of bright-colored silks. The favorites of his household fondled these gifts for a time with soft, guttural cries of delight and gentle stroking of their slim, brown hands, and then laid them away in fantastically Native-carved chests of yellow cedar.

Perhaps the strangest of these gifts had been a pair of homing pigeons, which had thrived and multiplied under the care of Add-'em-up Sam. A fluttering of wings now outside the doorway bespoke the presence of some of them. Kilbuck stirred in his chair and opened his eyes.

He had been many hours alone in the store, but he had been prepared for that today. The entire post of Katleean was getting ready for the potlatch, a Native festival, scheduled for the near future. For this occasion, Kayak Bill – in his carefully secreted still across the lagoon – had completed a particularly potent batch of moonshine, known locally as hootch. The arrival earlier in the afternoon of the jocose old hootch-maker with a canoe load of his fiery beverage had been a signal for a gathering at his cabin across the courtyard. From the sounds that now floated out on the late afternoon air, he must have already distributed generous samples of his brew.

The White Chief rose from his chair and reached for another

cigarette. As usual, he tossed it away after one long, deep inhalation. Before the smoke cleared from his head, he was crossing the storeroom with his easy panther tread – the result of former years of wearing moccasins.

He paused in the open doorway, leaned against the portal and hooked one thumb beneath his scarlet belt. His narrow eyes swept the scene before him. Across the bay, between purple hills, a valley lay dreaming in rose-lavender mist. Blue above the August haze was a glimpse of a glacier, and farther back, peaks arose tier upon tier in the vague, amethystine distance.

Suddenly the quiet beauty was shot through with the sound of loud voices and snatches of song issuing from the cabin of Kayak Bill. The trader listened with a smile that was half a sneer. He himself never drank while at the post, deeming that it lessened his influence with the Natives. But among the secrets of his own experience were memories of wild days and nights aboard visiting schooners, at the end of which – prone in the captain's bunk – he had lain for hours in alcoholic oblivion.

The voices from the cabin ceased abruptly. Then, like the bellow of a fog horn on a lonely northern sea, came Kayak Bill's deep bass:

"Take me north of old Point Barrow
Where there ain't no East or West;
Where man has a thirst that lingers
And where moonshine tastes the best;
Where the Arctic ice pack hovers
'Twixt Alaska and the Pole,
And there ain't no bloomin' fashions
To perplex a good man's soul."

There was a momentary pause, followed by a hubbub of masculine voices apparently in a dispute as to how the song should run. High above the others rose a squeaky Scandinavian protest.

"By yingo, ven ay ban cook on *Soofie Suderlant* ve sing it so dis vay –"

"Close yore mouth, Silvertip." As a whale would swallow a minnow, so Kayak Bill's drawling tones engulfed the thin, high accents of the one-time cook of the *Sophie Sutherland.* "I ain't no nature for Swedes a-devilin' o' me. I been singin' that song for nigh on to ten yars, and by the roarin' Jasus, I reckon I know how to sing it. Come on boys – now all together!"

Joining the again raised bass of Kayak Bill, several voices took up the rollicking strain, among them the high, easily recognizable tenor of Silvertip, and the voice of another, a baritone of startling mellowness and purity, having in it a timbre of youth and recklessness:

"Up into the Polar Seas,
Where the Inuit maidens be,
There's a fat, bright-eyed va-hee-ney
A-waitin' there for me.
She's sittin' in her igloo cold,
Chewing on a mukluk sole,
And the sun comes up at midnight
From an ice pack round the Pole."

At the sound of the baritone, the White Chief hitched his shoulders with a movement of satisfaction. Add-'em-up Sam's successor, the bookkeeper, was bidding fair to follow in the sodden footsteps of his predecessor. Given a little more time, this baritone-singing cheechako would be where the White Chief need have no anxiety as to the accounts rendered the company's new president, whom Kilbuck had never seen. A little more time, a little more hootch, and he also would have settled the case of Naleenah.

The thought of the Tlingit girl's soft-brown eyes brought a momentary pang. The white plague permitted few Native women to become old. Twice now Naleenah had lost her voice, and only last night he had noticed behind her soft, her singularly beautiful little eyes, the peculiar drawn look that to his practiced eye spelled tuberculosis. She

THE WHITE CHIEF OF KATLEEAN

would last two years more, perhaps, but in the meantime he must protect himself. He stirred uneasily. The bookkeeper must be made to take her off his hands. His musing was broken into by another burst of song.

"Oh-o-o-o! I am a jolly rover
And I lead a jolly life!
I have my hootch and salmon
And a Native gal to wife."

Simultaneously the door of Kayak Bill's cabin opened and the owner, a tatterdemalion figure, stood for a moment on the doorstep. Stretching his arms above his head, he yawned prodigiously, and then, espying Kilbuck, sauntered across the courtyard toward him.

An old sombrero curved jauntily on red-grey hair that was overly long. A wavy beard of auburn-grey spread over the front of his blue flannel shirt. Hanging loosely from his shoulders a hair-seal waistcoat, brightly trimmed with red flannel, served as a coat above faded blue overalls. And from the knees down, Kayak Bill was finished off with rubber hip boots, the turned-down tops of which flapped with every step, lending a swashbuckling air to his rolling gait.

He seated himself leisurely on the steps below the platform in front of the trading post door.

"By hell, Chief," he drawled as he drew a huge clasp knife from his pocket. "I been grazin' on this here Alasky range nigh on to twenty yars, and so help me Hannah, I never did find a place so wild or a bunch o' hombres so tough but what sooner or later all hands starts a-singin' o' the female sect." With a movement of his thumb, Kayak Bill released the formidable blade of the knife and nonchalantly, dexterously, began using it as a toothpick.

"Yas," he said slowly, in answer to the other's silence. "A-talkin' and a-singin' o' women and love. ... Now, I hearn tell a heap about love and women in my time, but neither o' them things has affected my heart ever, though one time a spell back, tobaccy did. Still, Chief, with all respects to yore sentiments regardin' them Chocolate Drops what inhabits yore harem ... still, it sort o' roils me up to hear a white man a-talkin' and a-singin' o' takin' a Native girl to wife."

There was an involuntary contraction of the hand that was hooked under Kilbuck's belt. Not another man from Dixon's Entrance to Point Barrow would have dared to hint at the White Chief's domestic arrangements in that gentleman's hearing, but there was something in the soft twinkle of Kayak Bill's hazel eye, something in the crude, whimsical philosophy distilled in the old hootch-maker's heart, that amused while it piqued the trader at Katleean. He sat down now on the steps beside his visitor.

"Kayak," he said, almost gently. "When an old fellow like you begins to talk about Native maidens I have to smile. A man past sixty! But how about twenty-five years ago? ... What's a man going to do when he finds himself on the edge of the wilderness and he wants a woman?" Kilbuck's voice rose slightly, his black brows drew together over the pale, unseeing eyes that sought the distant peaks, his thin nostrils quivered. "It's a wild country up here, Kayak. Makes a man hunger for something soft and feminine – and where's the pale-faced woman who would follow a man into this. ..." He finished his sentence with a wave of his hand. "That is a woman one would marry," he amended. "The average female of that country down south has no spirit of adventure in her makeup."

Kayak Bill closed his clasp knife, restored it to his pocket and slowly drew forth an ancient corncob pipe.

"Wall, Chief," he drawled between puffs, "I ain't a-sayin' yore not right, seein' as you've had consid'able more experience with petticoats than me; but one time I hearn a couple o' scientific dudes a-talkin' about females and they was of the notion that sons gets their brains and their natures from their mammies."

Disregarding the contemptuous sound uttered by the White Chief, Kayak's slow tones flowed on.

"And I'm purty nigh pursuaded them fellows is right. ... Take it down in Texas now, where I was drug up. I'm noticin' a heap o' times how the meechinest, quietest little old ladies has the rarin'est, terrin'-est sons, hell-bent on fightin' and adventure. ... Kinder seems to me,

Chief, that our women has been bottled up so long by us men folks they just ain't had no chance to strike out that way, except by givin' o' their natures to their sons. You take any little gal, Chief, a-fore they get her taken with the notion that it ain't ladylike to fight, and by hell, she can lick tar outen any boy her size in the neighborhood. Same way with she bears, or a husky bitch. Durned if they don't beat all get-out when it comes to fightin' courage!"

Kayak Bill drew once or twice on his pipe with apparently unsatisfactory results, for he slowly removed his sombrero, drew a broom straw from inside the band, extracted the stem of the corncob and ran the straw through it. The immediate vicinity became impregnated with a violent odor of nicotine.

The White Chief, however, musing close by on the steps, seemed not to notice it. His eyes were fixed on three canoes being paddled in from the lagoon across the bay that now was taking on the opalescent tints of the late Alaska sunset.

"What I been a-sayin' goes for the white women, Chief. As for them Chocolate Drops – wall, I ain't made up my mind exactly. 'Pears to me if I ever went a-courtin' though, it would be just like goin' ahuntin'. No fun in it if the end was certain and easy like. Barrin' the case of Silvertip and Senott, his woman, it's like this: you say 'Come,' and they come. You say 'Go,' and they go. Now, a white woman ain't that way. By the roarin' Jasus, you never can tell which way she's goin' to jump!"

Kayak Bill held the stem of his pipe up to the light and squinted through it, fitted it again into the bowl and gave an experimental draw. "But everybody to his own cemetery, says I."

"Bill, you old reprobate, you have an uncanny way of picking the weak spots in everything. There's some truth in that last – Gad, I'd like to get into a game of love with a woman of my own blood up here in the wilderness! There's never been a white woman in Katleean. It would be great sport to see one up against it here, eh, Kayak?" The White Chief turned, smiling, and the light in his pale, narrow eyes matched the wolfish gleam of his sharp teeth.

The face of the old hootch-maker was hidden in a smoke cloud, but his voice drawled on as calmly as ever.

"Wall, from what I hearn tell when I'm over at the Chilkat Cannery, Chief, you may get a chance to see a white woman at Katleean purty soon. There's a prospector named Boreland a-cruisin' up the coast in his own schooner, the *Hoonah*, and from what I can make out he's got his wife and little boy with him."

The trader turned sharply. Like a hungry wolf scenting quarry he raised his head. There was a keener look in his eye. His thin nostrils twitched.

"A *white* woman, Kayak? Are you sure?"

Before Kayak Bill could answer there came an extra loud burst of song from the cabin across the courtyard. The door had been flung wide and in the opening swayed the arresting figure of the leader of the wild chorus.

Early trading posts in Alaska carried a wide variety of goods, as seen in this store near Bethel in 1902.

THE WHITE CHIEF OF KATLEEAN

2

THE CHEECHAKO

He was young and tall and slight, with a touch of recklessness in his bearing that was somehow at variance with the clean-cut lines of his face. He stood unsteadily on the threshold, hands thrust deep in the pockets of his grey tweed trousers, chin up – tilted from a strong, bare throat that rose out of his open shirt. As the singing inside the cabin ceased, he shook back the tumbled mass of his brown hair and alone his mellow baritone continued the whaler's song:

"Up into the Polar Seas,
Where the greasy whalers be,
There's a strip of open water
Reaching north to eighty-three."

The White Chief, with his eyes on the singer, spoke to Kayak Bill.

"Our gentleman bookkeeper takes to your liquid dynamite like a Native to seal oil, Kayak. He's been at Katleean three months now, and I'll be damned if he's been sober three times since he landed. Seems to be hitting it up extra strong now that the potlatch is due." Then Kilbuck lowered his voice. "I want nothing said to him of the prospector and his white wife, *understand*?"

At the dictatorial tone flung into the last sentence there came a narrowing of the old hootch-maker's eyes. It was seldom that Kilbuck spoke thus to Kayak Bill.

The singer was crossing the courtyard now with steps of exaggerated carefulness. Suddenly he paused. His dark eyes, in vague, alcoholic meditation, sought the distant peaks stained with the blush-rose of sunset. The evening purple of the hills fringed the bay with mystery. Gulls floated high on lavender wings, their intermittent plaint answering the Native voices that drifted up from the beach where the canoes were landing.

Kayak Bill moved over on the step, indicating the space beside him, and called. "Come along side o' me, son, and get yore bearin's!"

"Yes, Harlan, stop your mooning and come here. I want to talk to you," added Kilbuck.

Gregg Harlan turned, and the smile that parted his lips, though born in a liquor-fogged brain, was singularly winning.

"Chief," his words came distinctly but with careful deliberation, "an outsider would think that I am a fellow of rare judgment and s-sound phil-os-ophy from the way you're always wanting to talk to me."

He advanced and seated himself on the steps near the base of the flagpole, leaning heavily against it. The gay recklessness that is the immediate effect of the fiery Native brew of the North was evidently wearing away, and preceding the oblivion that was fast coming upon him – stray glimpses of his past, bits of things he had read or heard, and snatches of poetry flashed on the screen of his mind.

"It doesn't go with me, Chief. Don't bring on your little forest maiden Naleenah again. Tired hearing about her. Know what you say: Up here my people never know. Me a shaatk' man – Lord! What do I want with a Native maiden?" He laughed as at some blurred vision of his brain. "It's not that I'm so damned virtuous, Chief. But I'm fas-fas-tid-ious. That's it – fastidious...."

Kilbuck's eyes flashed a cold steel grey. "We'll see how fastidious you'll be a year from now." His lip lifted on one side exposing a long, pointed tooth.

"That'll be enough, now, Harlan."

"Sure, 's enough for me, Chief," admitted the young man with drowsy good nature, as his tousled head sought a more comfortable place against the flagpole. "Pardon casting aspersions on your taste in women, Chief. Wouldn't do it if sober. Hate to be sober. Makes me feel re-responsible for so many things. ... Hence flowing bowl. 'Member old Omar – unborn Tomorrow and dead Yesterday. ... Why fret 'bout it if ... if today be sweet." His voice trailed off in a murmur and his boyish chin with its look of firmness despite his dejection, sank slowly on his breast.

The canoes had made a landing. A dozen or more Tlingit women came straggling up the beach, laden with the fruits of their afternoon labors – gay-colored baskets of wild strawberries, red and fragrant from the sand dunes along the lagoon. From the Native village, a short distance down the curve of the beach where the smokes of evening fires were rising, a few young Native men came to accompany the softly laughing young women.

Slightly in advance of the shawled figures moving toward the group on the steps walked one whose slenderness and grace marked her from the rest. A scarlet shawl splashed the cream of her garments. Unlike the other women, she wore no disfiguring handkerchief on her head. Her face, oval and creamy brown, was framed by two thick braids that fell over her shoulders. In the crook of her arm rested a basket of berries. At her side, rubbing against her now and then, came a powerful husky, beautiful with the lean grace of the wolf and paw playing as a kitten.

"Mush on, Kobuk! Mush you!" She laughed, pushing him aside as she advanced. When she smiled up at the white men, her face was lighted by long-lashed childish eyes, warm and brown as a sun-shot pool in the forest.

The White Chief rose. With an imperious gesture he motioned the other Natives back.

"*Ah choo*, Naleenah! Come here." In rapid, guttural Tlingit he spoke to the girl, pointing from time to time to the now unconscious Harlan. As she listened, the smile faded from her face. Her smooth brow puckered. She turned troubled eyes to Kayak Bill, sitting silent, imperturbable, in a cloud of tobacco smoke, his interest apparently fixed where the slight breeze was ruffling the evening radiance of the water. Still mutely questioning, Naleenah glanced at the figure of the young white man, slumped in stupor against the flagpole. ... A look of unutterable scorn distorted her face. Then she looked up at the White Chief shaking her head in quick negation. At her rebellion, Kilbuck's voice shot out stingingly like the lash of a whip. With a hurt, stunned expression, the girl shrank back. Her shawl shivered into a vivid heap about her feet. The basket of berries slipped unheeded to the sand, their wild fragrance scenting the air about her. While he was still speaking, she started forward, her wide, idolatrous eyes raised to his, her little berry-stained hands held out beseechingly.

"No – no, Paul!" Anguish and pleading were in her broken English. "No, no! I cannot do! Too mooch, too mooch I loof you, Paul!" Brimming tears overflowed and rolled slowly down her cheeks.

Kayak Bill rose hastily and stalked across the platform into the store. The White Chief turned away with tightening lips, but there was no softening in his smoke-colored eyes. It would be to his interest to have his bookkeeper take Naleenah off his hands. The old Hudson Bay Company factors had proved the advantage of having their employees take Native wives. For his own health's sake, he must get rid of her. The tubercular girl would live longer in the house of a white man than with her own people, where he would soon be forced to send her. He was, therefore, doing her a kindness in turning her over to Harlan.

He lighted a cigarette, inhaled a deep draught, and tossing the scarcely burned weed away, crossed deliberately to the huddled figure of Gregg Harlan. He shook him by the shoulder.

"Wake up!" he ordered, "Go to your bunk."

From Kayak Bill's cabin doorway several men drifted curiously toward the store steps. The Natives gathered closer. The bookkeeper raised his head and passed a slow hand over bewildered eyes.

"Beg pardon, Chief," he said quickly, as he rose on unsteady legs, "making sleeping porch of your steps ... awf-lly tired." Wavering, he clung for support to the flagpole. With a peremptory gesture, Kilbuck motioned to Naleenah.

"Take this man to his cabin," he snapped. "And," he paused significantly, "remember what I have told you."

The girl came forward with drooping head and listless arms. She paused dully beside the flagpole. The trader placed the arm of the stupefied young man across her slim shoulders. Obediently she led her charge away in the direction of the small cabins across the courtyard.

Though the eyes of the spectators had been intent on the drama of the steps, only Kayak Bill, perhaps, knew its real significance. The old man now stood in the doorway of the store, his sombrero pushed to the back of his head, a pair of binoculars held against his eyes. From around the point beyond the Native village and into the bay, a white-sailed schooner had drifted. As it advanced there was wafted across the water a faint and silvery fragment of melody, which endured but a moment and was gone. The White Chief turned his back on the courtyard, and for the first time, noted Kayak Bill's attitude. He followed the direction of the old man's gaze and beheld the incoming vessel just as the white men and Natives behind him broke out in a babble of interest and curiosity. There floated inshore the rattle of the windlass letting go the anchor chain. On the deck of the schooner men ran about as the sails were lowered. The vessel swung gently until the bow headed into the current of the incoming tide.

"Get out the canoe, Silvertip," ordered the trader, turning to his henchman. "And take Swimming Wolf with you. Find out who's ..."

He broke off, wondering, incredulous, for at that moment across the water came the golden singing of a violin. Wonderfully low and tender it began. Swelling, it rose and soared and trembled, then with lingering, chorded sweetness died away like the exquisite music of a dream.

The listeners on the shore stood spellbound. Gregg Harlan, swaying in the doorway of his cabin, steadied himself while the silvery harmony stole into his clouded senses.

"Strange – strange," he muttered. "A violin playing like that in

Katleean. Dreams ... more ... dreams." He stumbled into the room and the weeping Native girl guided his footsteps to the narrow bunk in the corner.

In the after-sunset light that precedes the long Alaska twilight there is some rare quality that seems to bring nearer objects on the water. Kayak Bill, in the doorway, took another long look through the glasses, then stepped down to the White Chief's side. His voice was the first to break the enchanted silence that followed the strains of the violin.

"That windjammer's the *Hoonah* I been a-tellin' you of, Chief," he drawled, holding out the binoculars. "There's two women aboard o' her, instead o' one. 'Pears to me like one o' them's purty young, and it's her that's standin' in the stern a-playin' o' the fiddle."

Courtesy Alaska State Library

The *Hoonah* many have resembled the schooner *Helga Caroline*, seen here near Juneau in 1894.

3

THE LITTLE SHAATK' WITH WHITE FEET

The morning after the arrival of the schooner, Gregg Harlan awoke with an aching head and trembling limbs. As he sat on the edge of his bunk holding his fingers against his throbbing temples, he made a mental vow that he would drink no more of Kayak Bill's liquor; that today he would settle down to the business that had brought him to Katleean.

He had made the same vow every morning since his landing – made it earnestly, intending to keep it, but there was something in the air of the trading post that made irresistible the reckless camaraderie engendered by the hootch cup; something that emphasized that very quality of gay irresponsibility he had come North to lose. The stale, close air of his little cabin sent waves of nausea through him.

Hatless and coatless he sought the open air. He turned his steps instinctively toward the point beyond the Native village. On the other side, screened from sight of the post, he was accustomed to take the daily plunge in the bay that enabled him to throw off the immediate effects of his hard drinking. As he stumbled along, his lackluster eyes rested but a moment on the schooner in the bay. He had not been long enough away from the world to be other than faintly interested in the arrival, and his recollections of the night before were nil.

The tide was low. The fresh, keen scent of seaweed came up from the Point refreshing his sickened senses. Noisy gulls wheeled and tilted over the brown, kelp-covered rocks and on the ridge back of the Native graveyard, ravens answered the gull cries with raucous soliloquies.

He was nearing the Point when his eye was attracted by a splash of white among the boulders. Something peculiar in its outline drew his inquiring steps. At the sound of crunching gravel under his feet a great husky dog rose almost from under him. The young man sprang aside with a startled exclamation. Against the wet sand the dog's dark coat had been practically invisible.

"Heavens, Kobuk, old boy – I thought I was seeing things!"

He passed a damp hand over his brow. The dog, strangely undemonstrative, advanced and placed a sleek head against Harlan's knee, its pointed muzzle down, its tail hanging dispiritedly. Vaguely wondering what the trader's favorite lead dog was doing among the boulders on the Point, Harlan patted the animal's broad back and turned to the object that had attracted his attention. What he had at first taken to be seaweed was a mass of long, dark hair. Beneath it, a damp, clinging cream-colored garment outlined the dead body of a Native girl.

"God!" came Harlan's awed whisper, as he bent above the pitiful little heap. "The White Chief's Naleenah ... poor little devil!"

Steadied by the tragedy he did not understand, he stooped and gathered up the still form. He started back to the trader's quarters, little dreaming that the last earthly act performed by those small hands, now so still, had been for him. But if Kobuk, following close at his heels, could have spoken, he would have told of the manner of her going the night before.

The trading post of Katleean had lain wrapped in moonlight and slumber when Naleenah, after obeying her master's instructions to the extent of making the drunken young white man comfortable, crept from the doorway of Harlan's cabin. Kobuk, waiting outside for the mistress who had fed him since puppy days, pressed closely to her side as she crossed the courtyard. At the beach line, where silvered rice grass grew tall among the piles of whitened driftwood, she paused, looking with wistful eyes toward the Native village cuddled in the crescent curve of the beach. The weird, ghostly totems of her people rose above the roofs, catching the moonbeams fearfully on their mystic carvings. Stern and forbidding they seemed, as if guarding the quiet shelters at their feet against one who had forsaken them for the more luxurious cabins of the white man. Slowly she turned from the tribal emblems of her clan to look back at the log trading post, dim and softly grey and splashed with shadows.

So still she stood, and so long, that the dog grew restless and rubbed his cold nose against her hand. She sighed, a tired, quivering sigh like that of a child who has been hurt, and with bowed head, stumbled along the trail that led down to the water.

Over a dark line of hills glowed the glorious red-gold orb of *Sha-hee-yi*, The Moon When All Things Make Their Winter Homes. Unbelievably large and round and clear it stood out against the night blue, throwing a path of shimmering gold across the bay to her little feet. With eyes raised to its splendor, she waded out slowly, steadily, into the moonlit, whispering waves.

Kobuk settled on his haunches at the edge of the beach, watching her with questioning, side-turned head. He whined uneasily. The scarlet shawl slipped from her shoulders and floated off behind her ... the water crept above her waist ... her shoulders. Her wide-eyed, frightened face caught the light. Then the ripples closed above her head. A moment later, her long hair, loosed from its braids, swayed on the amber-lighted surface like seaweed, then the moon path lay quiet as before.

On the shore Kobuk waited, his slant eyes blinking at the moon. Occasionally he raised his pointed nose and uttered a muffled whine that ended in a short, querulous yelp. Hours passed. The tide began to ebb, leaving a dark line of sand at the edge of the water. After a long while Kobuk went in search of his mistress, and having found her, watched beside her until Harlan came and bore her away.

As the young man ascended the steps to the store platform, he was dimly aware of encountering a tall, dark stranger, who afterward proved to be the owner of the schooner that had come in the evening before. Shane Boreland, whose figure was blocking the doorway, stepped aside to let Harlan pass into the building with his burden. From about the stove, where several men were already gathered, came low exclamations, and the White Chief, who had been following Boreland to the door, stopped suddenly at the sight of Harlan. His face went as cold and emotionless as that of the dead girl.

"Take her in to Decitan," he said shortly, with a gesture toward his quarters back of the store. Turning on his heel, he walked out to the platform where Boreland stood waiting.

"A damned sad ending to their little domestic difficulty," he murmured softly, as befitted one with a large heart and a kindly understanding of the follies of youth. "But young Harlan, my bookkeeper, hasn't been long enough in the North to appreciate the intensity of these little hot-blooded savages. I told him, when he took Naleenah…." The Chief, as if he had said too much, let his sentence trail off into silence. He shook his head in apparent sorrow, but his eyes were fixed on the schooner that rode at anchor in the bay.

"But don't let this incident mar your arrival, Boreland," Kilbuck went on, and then, with the frontier heartiness he knew so well how to assume, he set about tendering Boreland the hospitality of the post, urging the prospector to bring his family ashore for a visit during the time of the coming potlatch.

This was a festival, he assured the master of the *Hoonah*, which could not fail to interest Mrs. Boreland and her younger sister. Even as the trader planned for the reception of the white women, the Native women who had borne him children were preparing the body of little Naleenah for its resting place below the ridge where the grave houses and totems of the Tlingit dead huddled among the wild celery bushes. Quietly that night, just before moonset, she was laid away so that her funeral might cast no sadness on the coming visitors. On the grave, the silent women of the household placed the treasures that had been dear to the heart of the White Chief's favorite: a string of cheap beads, a scarlet shawl, a gaudy painted cup and two dead pigeons, progenitors of the flock that now cooed and fluttered in and out of the high wire enclosure back of the store.

A week later, on the ridge above the new-made grave of Naleenah, a white girl stood talking to a small boy by her side. Above the amber-freckled nose of the youngster wide grey eyes were raised in eager coaxing to her face. From the crown of his bare head, a lock of dark-red hair trembling with absurd earnestness stood up from the mass of its fellows.

"Oh, Jean! *Don't* put on your shoes and stockings just yet. Let's have one more story before we go back to the post. P-l-e-a-s-e, Auntie Jean!"

Jean Wiley dropped to the ground a bundle made of her discarded footwear. Earlier in the afternoon her nephew's barefoot enjoyment of the beach sand had enticed her to remove her own shoes and stockings, and delighting in the feel of the cool earth against her pink soles, she had not replaced them when they decided to follow the trail to the ridge. She tossed her head, and even in the sunless afternoon, the dark mass of hair that tumbled down her back seemed shot through with glints of copper.

"*I* wouldn't mind going without them always, Loll," she said, holding out a slim foot and contemplating the freedom of her five, wriggling, perfect toes. "But," the foot took its place beside its stationary twin, "you see, little man, it isn't done at my age, even in Katleean." Her long-lashed hazel eyes, full of the dreams of eighteen happy years, laughed down at the boy, and her slender fingers, that could coax such tender harmonies from the strings of a violin, busied themselves with the ribbon that bound the hair at the back of her neck. It was one of the lavender dream days peculiar to the late summer of the North. Faint wisps of colorful mist clung to the pickets of the small fences in the Native burial place below them. The totems and the windows of the tiny grave houses were filmed with it, and through the dim glass appeared vague glimpses of the kettles, blankets and provisions inside the houses of the dead – material comforts that the Tlingit people provide for the departed soul's journey over the Spirit Trail to the Ghost's Home. On the quiet bay below, the *Hoonah*, blurred in mist, tugged gently at her anchor. Some hundred yards to the left, smoke from the trading post rose above the alder bushes.

"This is a dandy place for storytelling, Jean. See!" Little Laurence Boreland pointed to the dim-limned schooner. "The *Hoonah* looks like a ghost ship out there. Listen – I'll tell you the story Kayak Bill scared me most to death with last night. Ugh ... it's spooky, Jean!" The boy's eyes were round and his voice had lowered at the remembered thrills of terror. He tugged at the girl's skirt, until she sat down beside him, tucking her slim bare feet beneath her as she prepared to listen. A raven, weird epitome of Tlingit myth and legend, croaked spasmodically from the white branch of dead brush behind them. The damp air had in it the freshness of new-cut hemlock boughs, a wild, vigorous fragrance that stirs the imagination with strange, illusive promises of the wilderness.

"And the door of the dead house slowly opened," Loll ended his tale, pointing to the graveyard below for local color, "and the door s-l-o-w-l-y opened and a long, white finger – a *bony* finger – beckoned...."

He broke off with a gasp of astonishment and terror, for above the rank growth of native celery in front of the lonely grave house door, there was a sudden, unmistakable flutter of white. So thoroughly had the little fellow lost himself in the weird mysteries of his own creating that panic took possession of him and communicated itself to the girl beside him. They sprang to their feet, and with one accord raced toward the trading post. Near the courtyard their footsteps slackened, and as Jean began to recover, she remembered her shoes and stockings left behind on the knoll. She became suddenly ashamed of her headlong flight, precipitated, as she now saw, by the first breath of afternoon breeze as it came in from the sea and fluttered a piece of weather-bleached canvas nailed over the grave house door.

"Goodness, Loll, you frightened me nearly to death with your wild imaginings," she said with a laugh. "Let's run back now and get our shoes and stockings."

The youngster laid a detaining hand on her arm.

"But, Jean," his shrill voice trembled, "didn't you see it – the long, white skeleton finger?"

"Nonsense!" Jean stood a moment pointing out the reason for the flutter of white. As she did so, a group of Natives that had landed from canoes on the beach came up the trail toward the post.

Curiously and quickly they gathered about the strangers. Many of them had never before seen a white girl or boy, specimens of the strange Letquoan, the Snow People from that faraway land of the White Chief. Solemn, black-eyed little toddlers peered cautiously out from under their mother's shawls. Pretty young maidens with dark handkerchiefs over their heavy hair jostled one another to get a better view, and at the sight of the white girl, the young men of the tribe straightened their shoulders and shifted their rifles to a jauntier angle.

In low, throaty tones, punctuated with long-drawn "Ah-a-a's" and occasional explosions of laughter, they talked among themselves, pressing closer each moment. From time to time a brown finger pointing at Jean's bare feet evoked a general shaking of dark heads and more "Ah-a-a's" of wonderment.

Perhaps because of the apprehension in her heart, Jean held her head high and looked fearlessly into the brown, apparently menacing faces about her. She glanced out over the dark heads hoping to see some member of her own race; but the post, for the moment, seemed deserted by the whites. She reached for her nephew's small hand and held it tightly. Among the Natives the talking ceased suddenly. A sense of expectation emanated from the group. There was a shifting of positions as a tall Tlingit, whom Jean had heard the White Chief call Swimming Wolf, stepped toward her, his red-bordered snowy blanket trailing majestically from his shoulders. He stopped, bent his stately form, and looked long and earnestly at her bare feet. Before the girl knew what he was about he had wetted his finger in his mouth, rubbed it along her foot, and scrutinized it gravely. He glanced up, his teeth flashing at her in a pleased smile.

"Ugh! Ugh!" he marveled in his best English. "Little shaatk' with white feet!"

The smile ended in an involuntary grunt, for Loll with the fire of wrath in his eye had leaped at the investigator, and with all the strength of his eight years, had planted both fists in the stomach of the unprepared Native.

"*She's* not a shaatk'!" shouted the outraged little fellow, making ready for another attack. At the same moment Jean, her face burning and her hazel eyes two points of fire, landed a stinging blow on the surprised Swimming Wolf's ear.

Straightening himself, he sidestepped, flinging his white blanket over his shoulder with a sheepish grin.

"Fierce little shaatk' with white feet," he chuckled admiringly. With loud laughs of amusement the others backed away. The circle broken, the indignant Jean caught at the hand of her small protector and fled away in the direction of the store. Angry with herself, and thoroughly mortified by what she considered the insulting familiarity of the Native, she ran heedlessly. She rounded the corner of one of the little courtyard cabins with reckless haste, and before she could check herself, had collided smartly with the dejected figure of a young man. The impact sent her staggering backward, but at the stammered words of apology that accompanied the steadying hands he reached toward her, she looked at him with angry scorn.

"It's a pity you white men are never around when you're needed," she stormed at his surprised face. "But men who take Native wives, I suppose, are always busy driving their wives to suicide!" She flung the last words at him and fled across the courtyard. At the moment she was out of patience with the entire population of Katleean. As she disappeared into the store with Loll, she left Gregg Harlan gazing after her perplexedly, wondering at her last sentence. It was his first actual meeting with either of the white women from the *Hoonah*. Because of their advent in Katleean, he had remained sober for several days, but for some reason he did not understand he had not yet been given an opportunity to meet these women from his own world. He turned from his contemplation of the empty doorway and walked back to his own cabin, his head bowed in thought.

4

BAIT

While Jean and Loll were pursuing their adventures about the post, the White Chief was entertaining his other two guests in his low-ceilinged living room, dusky and pleasantly scented from logs of yellow cedar burning in the fireplace. He was posed in his favorite attitude, half-sitting, half-reclining among the cushions on a low couch of red fox skins. But while he told tales of the country to the interested Boreland, his narrow eyes watched the play of the firelight on the softly massed golden-brown hair of Ellen, Boreland's wife, who sat knitting in the glow. Life, for the trader, had taken on a new zest this past week. Long years of acting a part – the part of a great white chief, mysterious, all knowing, all powerful in the eyes of the simple Natives of the North, had made him fully alive to the dramatic possibilities of playing host at Katleean, and he was not unaware of his own semi-barbaric attractiveness in these surroundings. It had been easy to induce Shane Boreland, for the sake of his wife and young sister-in-law, to spend a few weeks in the quarters back of the store, where they were ministered to by the silent, dark-eyed women whose status they did not understand.

The trader's heart was stirred with interest and expectancy. Here at last was an auditor worthy of his best efforts – a white woman, not too young, fair-faced and gentle, yet with the courage to follow her man into the wilds of a new country. A woman, who, he had learned, could unfailingly put a shot in a bull's eye at twenty paces and handle an oar in a small boat, yet a woman who could look sweetly domestic as she knitted on a garment for her small son. To Paul Kilbuck, as to all domineering men who scoff at matrimony, there was something irresistibly appealing in the "sweetly domestic" woman, something suggestive of that oldest occupation of woman – the business of ministering to man's physical and temperamental needs, the duty of making his body and his egotism comfortable. He watched her in covert approval. How soft and white her throat appeared above the open neck of her blouse – soft and white with a tiny hollow at the base where a man might leave kisses … or the print of his teeth. What little hands she had, white with nails of rosy pink. Little white hands! The words kept singing through his consciousness. So long had brown hands done his bidding up here in the North that he had nearly forgotten that a woman's skin could be so white. To have those little white hands just once, softly feeling, caressing, losing themselves in the blackness of his beard....

The White Chief sat bolt upright to shake off the mad, sweet pang that had thrilled him. The voice of Boreland brought him back from the land of forbidden thought.

"You say this Lost Island is nothing but a myth, Kilbuck?" The prospector had evidently been thinking of the White Chief's last story as he sat rubbing the head of Kobuk, the husky, who had placed his muzzle on Boreland's knee.

The trader lighted and tossed away a cigarette before he answered.

"Just how much truth there is in the tale of the Lost Island I can't say, Boreland," he said slowly, with a care to his English. He shifted his position until his eyes could no longer rest on the white woman in the fire's glow. "It has come down from the days of the Russian occupation of the Aleutian Islands far to the west. Our Tlingits, you know, got it from the Natives of that section and the story runs that an Aleut and his wife were banished from their village for some crime, set adrift in a bidarka, a skin boat. Instead of perishing, as their kinsmen intended, the pair turned up a year later with a tale of a marvelous island many days' paddling to the east. On this island, they said, the sun shone warmer and the flowers grew larger and the snowfall was lighter than anywhere else in their world; and there was some queer story, I don't remember the details exactly, about an underground passage and sands flecked with shining metal, the stuff that trimmed up the holy pictures the Russian priests brought over from Russia."

"Gold!" interrupted Boreland. "It must have been gold!" His brown eyes glowed and the White Chief noted that an eager alertness lighted his lean tanned face.

"The exiles decided to let a few of their friends in on the island proposition and set out at the head of several bidarkas. According to the story, they knocked about up and down the North Pacific from Kodiak to Sitka for several months – but they never found their island. Neither did the Natives of later years who went in search of it from time to time."

Boreland pressed the White Chief for more information.

"But the Russians, Kilbuck, didn't they ever try to find the place?"

The trader, pleased at the interest his story had aroused, laid back once more against his cushions.

"Possibly they did," he went on easily. "But it's likely they were satisfied with the wealth of furs their Aleut hunters brought them. Those were great old days for traffic in furs. The early Russians were, for the most part, a lazy, rum-drinking lot, you know. To them riches meant sea otter skins, and they managed by various devilish methods – I can't say more about them in your presence, Mrs. Boreland – to enslave the entire Aleut nation to do their hunting. They gave them a little – and a mighty little – trade goods in return."

By the inflections of his voice, the agent of the Alaska Fur and Trading Company sought to convey to his listeners the impression that the policy of those early companies was against *his* principles, although the books, so carefully kept by Add-'em-up Sam, might have told a different story.

"And it's possible the Russians thought the yarn to be merely another Native fairy tale," continued Kilbuck, waving a careless hand. "As I said, there may be no other foundation for it. It has come down now for over two hundred years, and you may be sure when a Native tells a story it loses nothing in the telling."

The drowsy crackle of the flaming logs filled a short interval. Boreland sat lost in meditation, his hand resting quietly on the dog's head, his eyes a dream as with visions of the golden sands of the Lost Island. His wife glanced up at him, uneasily, almost apprehensively it seemed to Kilbuck, who was again watching her. Never in all his varied amorous experiences had a woman's eyes held such a look for the White Chief – a look in which there was a protecting tenderness, comradeship and something more. He settled farther back in his cushions, his eyes narrowing. Love had yet some new delight to offer him. His virile years were slipping by – he was surprised and disturbed how often this thought had been with him of late. Should he grasp the opportunity offered? There might be a way up here in Katleean, where his word was law ... perhaps....

Kilbuck brought himself up with a start. Ellen Boreland had dropped her knitting and had crossed to her husband's chair. Her hand rested on his broad shoulder and there was a wistful little twist to her smile as she shook him gently to rouse him.

"He's forever dreaming of the gold that lies beyond the skyline – this man of mine – and always going to find it," she said fondly. "So please, Mr. Kilbuck, don't get him interested in any mythical island. We've been gone from the States six months now, and I want him to go back for the winter." There was a half-playful, half-earnest note of pleading in her voice, but the White Chief noticed that her eyes did not fully meet his.

During all her thirty years, doubtless, Ellen Boreland had looked a friendly world in the eye. She was that sort. He saw that she was troubled now at not being able to do this in the case of the trader of Katleean. Probably he himself was not attractive to her – perhaps he was even fascinatingly repellent with that electric and disturbing and promising quality that drew almost irresistibly. There were women who, under that impulsion, had been moved to come close and gaze into his pale, black-lashed eyes. It was an impulse akin to that which urges people to fling themselves from great heights; to peer into abandoned, stagnant wells. He had an idea that she knew he saw this, for he had watched her face flush under his glance as though at the thought of having dishonored herself by sharing with him some guilty secret. He saw that she was uncomfortable in accepting his hospitality. Twice during their stay she had entreated her husband to leave Katleean, or at least go back aboard the schooner for the remainder of their visit.

But Shane Boreland, clean-hearted adventurer, to whom the vagaries of a woman's mind were a closed book, had only laughed at her request, retorting that life aboard the *Hoonah* had made her into a little sea dog and a few weeks ashore with such a host as the White Chief would do her a world of good. The host now lighted one of his short-lived cigarettes. In his mind was forming a plan suggested by Ellen Boreland's words. He might develop it later, and again he might not, but it would not be amiss to prepare the way.

He tossed his cigarette into the fireplace, slipping without effort into the part he had assigned himself.

"Dreams are the things that make life worth living, Mrs. Boreland." His low, vibrant tones sounded pleasantly in the dusky room. "Boreland here has his dreams of a mine of gold, but I ..." he hesitated, his voice taking on a whimsical softness, "but I, in my northern solitude, have my dreams of a heart of gold." His look was designed to leave no doubt in Ellen Boreland's mind that it was a feminine heart of gold that he sought.

There was a pause during which the charred logs in the fireplace dropped down, sending up a brighter flame.

"But you mustn't be too sure that the Lost Island is a myth." He spoke briskly now, as if putting aside deliberately his own longings. "In this part of the country some say that the Lost Island is that of Kon Klayu."

As Shane Boreland looked up questioningly, the White Chief continued.

"Of course, it does in some ways answer the description. It is ninety miles off the coast here. Cape Katleean is the nearest land.

The Japanese currents give it a milder climate, and we know that the beach sand carries gold – a little gold."

"Anyone living there?" interrupted Boreland eagerly.

"Not a soul. The Alaska Fur and Trading Company did send a party out there some years ago to start a fox farm. That's how I got my information. They were a hootch-drinking, lazy lot and the farm wasn't a success. But Add-'em-up Sam, a bookkeeper I used to have, spent a winter there. He told me many things about the place." The White Chief paused a moment. A new idea had just come to him. "Silvertip, who used to be on the whaler *Sophie Sutherland*, has stopped there for water, too."

Boreland, rising from his chair, thrust both hands into his pockets and began to pace up and down the room.

"By thunder, Kilbuck, I'm interested in that island, whether it's the Lost Island or not! Kon Klayu ... Kon Klayu." He repeated the name thoughtfully. "Seems to me that's Tlingit for ruby sand, which in itself suggests possibilities. Ruby sand is a gold carrier." There was a note of enthusiasm in Boreland's voice, but as he noticed the look on his wife's face, he crossed to her side and put an arm over her slender shoulders. "But we'll talk that over some other time, Chief. I don't want to bore Ellen with too much mining."

Boreland's speech was cut short when an indignant little boy flung open the store door and burst in on them.

"Mother! Mother!" he shouted. "That big old Indian, Swimming Wolf, called my Auntie Jean a shaatk'!"

Jean, following close on the heels of her nephew, stopped before her sister.

"And the wretch put his hand on my foot, Ellen!" Jean told her sister as she clenched her slim hands. Each outraged shake of her head loosening the ribbon that bound her hair. "I hate this place, Shane!" she cried, turning swiftly to her brother-in-law. "I wish we were all back aboard the *Hoonah*!" Her voice trembled with unshed tears of mortification, and both her sister and Shane started toward her with exclamations of sympathy and alarm.

The White Chief regarded the attractively disheveled little figure with appreciation, but he realized that something had happened that endangered the stay of his visitors. He rose to place a chair for her. When he spoke, his voice – the voice that had charmed many women – soothed while it promised.

"There now, Miss Wiley, things may not be so bad as you think. Sit down and tell me all about it, and I'll see what can be done."

Disregarding the proffered chair, the girl launched forth with the story of her encounter with Swimming Wolf. Above her flushed cheeks her eyes flashed and the unruly cloud of hair, freed at last from its ribbon, fell about her shoulders. As she told of the slap on Swimming Wolf's ear, the pale eyes of the White Chief glowed. Truly, as Kayak Bill had said, one could never tell about a white woman. Here was a situation he would have to handle with care. Here was a time when his knowledge of Native nature, gained during years of association with them, stood him in good stead.

"Miss Jean," he said. "Just a moment. I think I can explain Swimming Wolf's extraordinary action." The White Chief measured her with an air of understanding that, he could see, made an impression on the girl in spite of herself. "First, the word shaatk' means young woman in Tlingit. Second, a Native, you know, never really grows up. Even though he has the body of a man, he still keeps the heart of a child. Now when you were little, Miss Jean, don't you remember the first time you saw a person with dark skin? Didn't you wonder, while you looked at his face and his hands if he could possibly be dark all over? Be honest now, didn't you?"

Loll, who had settled himself on the floor with an arm about Kobuk's neck, sprang up and stood beside his aunt.

"Yes, I did, Chief," he interrupted, with eager, nodding head. "And I asked him about it, too. I did!"

Jean's face was clearing. She inclined her head in faint affirmation.

"Just so," the trader went on. "When Swimming Wolf saw his first white woman, no doubt in his simple heart he wondered, too, and so did the other Natives who gathered about you – children, all of them. Swimming Wolf had no English words to ask you about it, so he took the simplest way to find out whether or not the white came off."

A shadowy smile began to twitch at the corners of Jean's mouth. Seeing it, the White Chief was encouraged to go on.

"The inquisitive rascal is really one of our bravest hunters, and a man of tall totems and many blankets. He would feel astonished and *kush-i-a-tu* – very sad – if he knew he had offended you. As a matter of fact," the trader said with a laugh, "the Wolf admires you and in his primitive way has paid you a great compliment. I wasn't going to mention it, but since this has come up, perhaps it will help explain."

Jean looked up inquiringly.

"Up here in the North, Miss Jean, it is the custom of the young men to buy any little girl who takes his fancy. He pays for her while he is strong and a good hunter, you see. When the girl grows up, he takes her for his wife."

There was a gasp of astonishment from Ellen and her sister, but Kilbuck continued.

"One hundred dollars is a mighty good price to pay for a wife, but Swimming Wolf, my little lady, came to me yesterday with four black fox skins, which are worth perhaps $3,000. He wanted to know if I would arrange with the Big White Man – your brother-in-law – to take them in payment for the *shawut clate*, the White Girl Who Makes Singing Birds in the Little Brown Box."

Jean lifted her chin with a laugh, in which amusement and embarrassment were equally mingled.

"How quaintly ridiculous, Ellen, to describe my violin playing in such a way. But mercy," she added, after they had all laughed over the incident, "I must run away upstairs and put on some footwear. If I had kept on my shoes and stockings, as I should have done, Swimming Wolf might not have called me little shaatk' with white feet!"

Kilbuck, satisfied with himself, had settled back once more against his cushions, and as she turned to say a parting word to him, was regarding her with half-closed eyes. The firelight played on her slim, white ankles and soft little feet. He surveyed her with a look that slowly, appraisingly, stripped her body of its garments and swept her from her bare feet to her face and back again. The girl caught it. Conscious, for the first time of him – his savage reality as other than a middle-aged man – of her own womanhood, she flushed violently. Shrinking back, she reached for Loll's hand, and stammering an incoherent excuse, ran from the room.

Ellen, unconscious of what had happened, measured off a row of stitches in the knitting she had again taken up.

"Jean certainly seems to be tumbling in and out of adventures," she remarked. "Sometimes, Shane, I wonder if we did right in bringing her with us."

"Nonsense, Ellen," her husband said. "A year up here will make a different girl of her – help her break away from the cut and dried sameness of school life. Darned if it doesn't make me tired to see all the young women turned out of the same mold."

As Boreland spoke, the door leading into the store opened slowly and into the room sauntered Kayak Bill. He seated himself in silence, tilting his sombrero to the back of his head – the only concession to convention he ever made, since Kayak had never been known to remove that article of apparel until he sought his bunk at night.

"I just been mouchin' round down in the village, Chief," he drawled, "seein' if there was anything a-doin' in the way o' local sin, and they tells me that the funeral canoes is a-comin' in tonight."

Courtesy Alaska State Library

Alaska Natives decorated canoes to attend funeral potlatches and other events, as shown in this photo of canoes arriving for a 1904 potlatch in Sitka.

5

THE FUNERAL CANOES

Ellen glanced up at the old hootch-maker sitting serenely on the other side of the fireplace. Some time during the day he had put on tall leather boots, but having neglected to lace them, the bellows-tongued tops stood away from his sturdy legs and the rawhide laces squirmed about his feet like live things.

"The funeral canoes?" she echoed, wonderingly.

Kayak Bill turned to her with a sort of slow eagerness, as if he had been awaiting an excuse to look at her

"Yas, Lady. They're a-bringin' in the ashes o' their dead kin from up in the Valley of the Kag-wan-tan."

Ellen's mind reverted to the many strange things she had heard during her short stay in Katleean concerning the coming potlatch of the Natives. This land and its people were new and mysterious to her. These primitive Tlingits, descendants of the fiercest and most intelligent of all the northern tribes, were a fearful people living in a world of powerful and malignant spirits that frowned from the rocks, glittered from the cold, white mountains and glaciers, whispered in the trees and cackled derisively from the campfires; a world of hostile eyes spying upon them in the hope that some of their weird and mystic taboos might be broken, and of sly ears listening to avenge some careless remark.

A childlike people they were, who spoke kindly to the winds and offered bits of fish for its favor; who begged the capricious sea to give them food, and who spent most of their lives working for the comfort of the dead – the Restless Ones – who sweep the winter skies when the day is done, beckoning, whispering. The Northern Lights the white men call them, as they leap and play above the frozen peaks, but the Tlingits know them to be the spirits of the dead, homeless in space, but hovering confidently overhead until their relatives on earth can give a potlatch for their repose.

Running like a black thread through the woof of the spirit tales was the mention of witchcraft – witchcraft with which Kilbuck was now preparing to deal; not because he hoped to benefit the Natives and free them from the curse of superstition, but because owing to a belief in the black art, the Natives of Katleean were not bringing in the amount of furs expected, and this meant a loss of money to the Alaska Fur and Trading Company.

Ellen recalled the superior air of amusement with which the White Chief had told of the dominating belief in demons.

"When one of the beggars wants to cast a spell," he had said, his lip curling in a sardonic smile, "he takes a bit of cloth from some garment his enemy has worn and at the hour of midnight slinks into a graveyard and digs down until he finds a body. If he wants to cripple his enemy's hand, he puts the cloth in the fingers of the corpse. If he wishes his enemy to lose his mind, he puts it over the skull, and if he wants him dead, he places the cloth over the heart in the coffin. Oh, they are a sweet outfit, I tell you!" The Chief had laughed as if these things were merely amusing.

Then he had gone on to explain that across the Bay of Katleean, in the shadow of the great blue glacier that was discernible on sunny days, there had been a lonely Tlingit graveyard. Because of its isolation, this burial place had been so riddled with reopened graves and so much killing, torturing and fighting had ensued among the Natives in their efforts to detect and punish so-called witches, that he, their White Chief, had been obliged to interfere. He had put an end to the reign of sorcery in that particular graveyard rather cleverly, Ellen was forced to admit, by having all the bodies exhumed and cremated on the spot.

"They'll bring the ashes over here where I can keep an eye on them and prevent further 'witching,'" the trader had finished. "And after the potlatch, we'll have a little peace in the country, I hope. I never interfere with the potlatches. They make good business for the company, for the brown heathens believe the spirits are really feasting and rejoicing with them." Kilbuck laughed as at some recollection. "The company sends in hundreds of blankets every year for dead Natives. Whenever a potlatch blanket is given away, the name of a dead man is called and he receives it in the spirit world. Whenever a little food is put on the potlatch fire, a dead man's name is mentioned and he gets a square meal up there in Ghost's Home. Altogether the Alaska Fur and Trading Company does a lively business with the dead!"

As Ellen thought on these things, there crept into her mother heart a feeling of pity for these simple, trusting people who sought the protection and guidance of this white man only to have their beliefs and superstitions laughed at and exploited for the benefit of his company. She was beginning to feel, dimly, what every reader of the history of exploration knows: drunkenness, fraud and trickery are among the first teachings the white man's civilization brings to the tribes of a new country.

A tinge of sadness and foreboding darkened her thoughts.

Kayak Bill, who had been drawing contentedly on his corncob pipe, rose suddenly through a low-hung cloud of tobacco smoke, and taking up an old almanac from the table, began fanning the air clumsily. His slow drawl, with a suspicion of haste in it, broke in on her meditations.

"By hell, Lady," he apologized earnestly, "excuse me for creatin' of such a blamed smudge!"

Ellen looked up from her knitting.

"Oh, I don't mind a little smoke, Kayak Bill." She smiled at the concern in the old man's voice. "You see, Shane smokes a good deal, too." She nodded toward the couch where her husband puffed on his pipe as he plied Kilbuck with questions about the island of Kon Klayu. "I was just thinking about the funeral canoes and the potlatch."

"The beginnin's of the potlatch will be pulled off tomorrow, Lady, but tonight ...," Kayak stopped fanning and leaned closer to her. Then with a glance in the direction of the White Chief, he lowered his voice. "Tonight, when the funeral canoes come in, I'd aim to gather in the young sprout, Loll, and that little gal sister o' yourn. We're purty civilized here in Katleean, but – wall, there ain't no tellin' what a Native will do after he's taken on a couple o' snorts o' white mule – or a white man, either, for that matter. O' course, I make the stuff myself, and a mighty hard time I have, too, to keep shut o' these pesky dudes o' revenue officers that's all the time a-devilin' o' me. But I don't recommend it none a-tall."

Kayak Bill, with his bootlaces snaking along behind him, shuffled over to his chair once more and settled himself for conversation, which Ellen had learned meant a monologue. The edge of his sombrero backed his busy head and kindly face like a soiled grey halo. His low voice, never rising, never falling, droned on.

"Yas, I don't drink none myself, bein' weaned, as you might say, when I'm but a yearling'. But I make it for those as likes it, and I makes it good, for it's everybody to his own cemetery, I say. No, I don't join no temperance union or nothin,' but one time, when I'm a real young feller, I'm off on the range for a spell down in Texas, and I ain't no nature for shavin' or none o' them doo-dads, and besides I don't have no razor or no lookin' glass. Wall, six months or so goes millin' by and finally I comes down into San Antonio one Sataday night. And right away, havin' at that time what you might call an eddycated taste for whisky, I makes a charge for the nearest bar and takes on a dozen or so good snifters, likewise some beverages they calls mint julips. And dum me, Lady, if in no time everything in that place ain't a-whizzin' past me like the mill-tails o' hell!"

The old-timer shifted in his chair and then continued his tale.

"But I gets my bearin's after while and lays my course for a door to get some fresh air. Just as I reaches this here door, Lady, a big, swaggerin' rough lookin' hombre with a red beard starts to come in. Wall, I looks him over careful. He likewise gives me a nasty look. Then polite-like, I steps aside waitin' for him to come through. But he don't come none, havin' stepped aside, too. ... Wall, by this time I'm feelin' purty groggy and I makes a bolt for the door again, aimin' to get through quick; but blamed if that durned son-of-a-gun don't do identical! Then back I sashays once more and my dander sort o' riz up in me. 'By the roarin' Jasus,' I yells, 'you lay offen that monkey business, you consarned whiskery cuss, or I'll fill you so full o' holes yore own mammy won't know you from a hunk o' cheese. Just one more crack like that out o' you,' I says, 'and down comes yore meat house,' I says. ... Wall, I got started through the door again, and by hell, Lady, in spite o' my warnin' o' him, he comes at me again."

Kayak Bill paused a fraction of a second; then his voice went on with its accustomed languor.

"So I just whipped out my little old .45 and shot him."

Ellen gasped, her big blue eyes opening in horror as she looked into the serene face of the self-confessed murderer.

Kayak Bill, apparently unconscious of her regard, droned on.

"Yas, I charged full tilt into him shootin' as I went, but instead o' him a-fallin dead, I finds myself in a shower o' glass, and all the boys is a-dancin' round me and likin' to die o' laughin' at me. ... You see, Lady, that door happens to be one o' them long mirro's saloons has, and not havin' no acquaintance with myself in a beard a-tall, I pots my image! Ha! Ha! Ha!" Kayak Bill's laugh gurgled out slowly like mellow liquor from a wide-mouthed bottle.

"Wall, after I got done a-payin' for the mirro' and a-settin' 'em up for the boys, and a-payin' for a saw bones to fix me up – me bein' conside-ble carved by glass – I don't have no more money than a jack rabbit. So I says to myself: 'Bill, you ol' jackass, you got to reform, that's all there are to it. We can't have the whole durned world laughin' at you when yore in yore liquor', I says. ... And I did reform, Lady. So help me Hannah, I did!" said Kayak Bill, with an air of conscious virtue, and then filled his pipe again.

While Ellen gathered up her knitting, the corners of her mouth were twitching with amusement.

"Kayak Bill," she said as she shook her finger at him playfully, "you surely have an effective way of making a confession. I don't really know whether to praise you for your sobriety or scold you for horrifying me a moment ago."

Ellen heard the old man's chuckle as she arose. Her face went sober, however, the moment her eyes sought the couch where her husband sat still engrossed with the White Chief. Though she lingered, Shane did not turn her way, and she finally moved toward the door through which her sister had gone an hour earlier.

"Thank you for telling me about tonight, Kayak," she said as she passed him. "I'm going up now to warn Jean and Loll, but ..." she hesitated, "I wish more of the men in Katleean had been 'weaned' as you were." She saw approval in the slow softening of his hazel eyes, and as the door closed behind her, she caught a remark the old hootch-maker addressed to the dog at his feet.

"By hell, Kobuk," he pronounced earnestly, "that little lady's husband has sure fell into a bed of four leaf clovers!"

She stored this quaint tribute away in her mind and told it to Jean that evening after she had repeated for the second time Kayak's warning regarding the arrival of the funeral canoes. But Jean, determined not to miss any detail of the strange Tlingit festival, watched till an opportunity presented itself, and then, disregarding Ellen's advice, slipped away to the beach to a pile of silvery drift logs that lay at the edge of the rice grass, where she knew she could not be seen except from the sea. The girl settled herself comfortably among the logs just as the long day was waning.

She noted that here, as everywhere else in this northern land of exquisite, fleeting summers, the sunset colors came on gradually, increasing in richness of tone and fading through several hours. The mist of the afternoon had scattered before a faint sea wind, and settled wraithlike in the hollows of the hills across the bay. Violet now in the gloaming, it melted into the lilac shadows at the base of the range that needled the sunset sky.

There was something like promise in the wild beauty of the evening time; something in the clean night scent of the sea and the grass and the trampled beach weed that awakened in Jean a sense of expectancy. She breathed deeply, conscious of a keen delight in doing so. As she waited, the rose and amber tints died on the white peaks at the head of the valley, the flaming orange behind them turned from clear gold to vermilion, from rose madder to an unearthly red that glowed behind a veil of amethyst while the twilight deepened.

Suddenly she caught her breath. Out of the powdery, purple gloom across the bay floated a long line – the funeral canoes. In the blurred distance they took shape one by one, the paddles dipping in solemn rhythm. Nearer they came, and nearer. Then over the darkening water drifted the plaintive rise and fall of the funeral lament, faint and eerie as voices from the spirit land.

Jean, thinking to linger but a moment before returning to the store, was spellbound by the mystery and loneliness of the scene. All at once, as she watched, a line of silent, blanketed figures from somewhere behind began to slip down past her hiding place. Looming weird and tall in the dusk, they halted at the water's edge. Softly, almost imperceptibly, these waiting ones took up the mournful plaint, sending it floating out thin and high in answer to the approaching bearers of the dead.

While she listened, awe and wonder began to give way to something that tantalized her with a fleeting familiarity – a near understanding. Long lost memories of primeval things that eluded her when she strove to vision them mocked her with an indefinable yearning to pierce the ages of oblivion that separated her from other nights, other scenes, other chants like these. She longed for her violin. If she could but feel the loved instrument beneath her chin, her fingers drawing from its vibrant lower strings the mystery music to supplement the weird dirge, these primitive things hidden in the dust of the past might be revealed to her.

Suddenly she became aware that one of the tall figures had stopped in the trail beside her pile of driftwood. In a tone singularly pleasing, he was humming the air of the funeral lament, fitfully, experimentally at first, then as the haunting monotony of the strain became familiar, with a certain easy confidence. Jean forgot to be afraid. Almost unconsciously she found herself humming in unison with the motionless figure. Even when the man faced her and she saw in the dim light, not a Native, but the young white man, Gregg Harlan, she did not cease. She was conscious of a feeling of companionship. Night had gilded the wilderness with a primordial beauty and made her kin to all earth's creatures. She moved slowly from her pile of driftwood and stood beside him for a moment in the trail watching the incoming canoes. It was a moment of simplicity and unconsciousness of self such as might have been in the dawn of civilization when conventions were unknown. She hummed, cradling in her heart impressions of the night so that later she might awaken them through the music of her violin. The man in the trail continued his wordless song.

The crunching of leather soles on the gravel behind them startled Jean. She and her companion turned simultaneously to find themselves face to face with the trader of Katleean.

"Well, well!" The sarcastic voice of the White Chief shattered the sweet, wild moment like an invidious thing. "You two seem to be getting uncommonly friendly." His red lip lifted on one side into a cynical smile that suddenly infuriated Jean, implying, as it did, that he had caught the two young people in a compromising situation. She took a hasty step toward him, looking with fearless eyes into his face.

"How dare you slip up behind us this way!" she flashed, stamping her foot and flinging out her hands in a short, angry gesture. A moment longer she looked at him as if he were an object of scorn, then turning to the young man, said quietly, "Good night, Mr. Harlan."

The next instant she was walking up the dusky trail to the post.

Kilbuck watched her go. Accustomed to commanding all situations at Katleean, he was for the moment nonplused by the quickness and vehemence of the girl's retort, rather than by what she had said. He had expected to place the two at a disadvantage. Finding the tables turned, a momentary and unreasoning desire to cover his own discomfiture by hurting someone took possession of him.

"I say, Gregg, I'm rather surprised to find you at this time of night alone with Miss Wiley. I don't think her sister would approve, exactly. Since your affair with Naleenah, you know," he finished the sentence with a depreciatory shrug.

"*My* affair with Naleenah! What do you mean?" The young man took a quick step toward him.

"Oh, now, don't get excited, Gregg. You were drunk, of course, but you must remember she took you home and spent the last night of her life with you. The whole post saw you two go off together the night the *Hoonah* came in. Boreland has heard the talk, of course. Too bad, my boy," the Chief said as he put his hand on the astonished young fellow's shoulder. "Too bad, I say, that after all your fastidious virtue you have the reputation of being a cad, a womanizer." Kilbuck laughed his short, sardonic laugh.

"*She* thinks I'm a cad?" Gregg indicated the disappearing figure of Jean. His voice was sharp with hurt amazement, indignation, and the grasp of his hand on the Chief's arm made that gentleman wince.

"All of them do, my boy. *All* of them. But ..."

"Now I begin to understand," Harlan broke in bitterly. With a muttered imprecation he turned on the trail and walked toward the courtyard where a light shone palely from Kayak Bill's window. The White Chief looked after him until he vanished. Harlan had been sober for a week now, but if Kilbuck was any judge of indications, the bookkeeper's sobriety was at an end. As the trader turned toward the beach and walked to the canoes now landing in the dusk, he smiled to think how neatly he had nipped in the bud any possible romance between Gregg and Jean.

Two hours later, in the loft above Kilbuck's living quarters, Jean was kneeling at a tiny window looking up at the ridge where dark spruce trees peaked a line against the night sky. It was a strange guest chamber pungent with a faint, unforgettable odor from fox pelts dangling from the rafters, bear hides tacked to the slanting roof and rows of smoked salmon and dried cod hanging from lines along the sides. Loll lay fast asleep on his small floor pallet, his face half-buried in his pillow, his mouth reverted to the pout of babyhood. The door leading to Ellen's room – the only real room in the loft – was partly open. Jean rose and closed it, took up her violin from her own floor bed and returned to the window.

Courtesy Alaska State Library

Music was a welcome break to long days and nights in Alaska's wilderness.

Softly fingering the strings, she picked out the notes of the Native lament that kept repeating itself in her mind. She was possessed by a desire to express in music the mystery of the wilderness afterglow – the wild, illusive feeling that had touched her. She longed to use her bow freely on the strings of her violin until at one with the instrument she could lose herself in the ecstasy of creation. She reached for the bow that lay on the floor beside her. Perhaps, if she played very softly, she might not disturb anyone.

Up from the courtyard, as if a door suddenly had been opened, came startling sounds – short yells, Native war whoops and the maudlin singing of white men. The mournful, prolonged howl of a dog drifted in from somewhere. And down in the direction of the Native village half a dozen shots were fired in rapid succession.

Jean's heart beat oddly. Katleean was beginning to celebrate the potlatch in the singular way of the male, who, since time immemorial, has made a holiday an occasion for carousal. The girl sighed and placed her violin gently on the floor. With her chin in her hands, she took her former position at the window and listened.

Somewhere near the store a trio began singing. The blended harmony of men's voices as they sang in the dusk had in it a peculiar stir. Jean found herself, head up and shoulders swaying, responding to the lilt and swing of the air.

"Hear the rattle of our windlass
As the anchor comes away;
For we're bound for Old Point Barrow
And we make our start today."

Rollicking, devil-may-care, the whaling song went on through long verses. Many of the words she could not distinguish, but throughout the singing she was aware of a feeling that these singers were men who had cast aside the restraint of conventions, even in a way, responsibility for conduct, and were exulting in their freedom.

Thinking the song finished, she turned away at last. But the movement was arrested by the sound of a lone baritone taking up the chorus again.

She leaned over the sill to catch the words, for in the voice she recognized her companion of the drift logs.

"Up into the Polar Seas
Where the greasy whalers be,
There's a strip of open water
Leading north to eighty-three,
Where the frisky seal and walrus
On the ice floes bask and roll,
And the sun comes up at midnight
From an ice pack round the Pole."

Apprehension in the girl's heart vanished. She drew a deep breath of the night air and turned reluctantly from the window.

"There's a strip of open water leading north to eighty-three," she hummed. The words stirred in her dim, venturesome imaginings. She felt suddenly on the threshold of adventure beyond which might lay the fierce, wild things of romance that only men have known. It alarmed, even while it exhilarated her. She felt afraid, yet daring. She was beginning to feel the lure of Alaska – the vast, the untamed, the inscrutable, the promising.

She thought of the young white man as she slipped between her blankets. Cad he might be, and a drunkard, but he had the heart of an adventurer ... he was young ... and he could sing.

6

THE WHITE CHIEF MAKES MEDICINE

Sunless and softly grey morning came to Katleean. The water, smooth as satin, stretched away to the mist-shrouded hills. Owing to some odd, mirage-like condition of the atmosphere, trees bordering the lagoon across the bay stood high and clear above a bank of fog. The liquid music of the surf was hushed as if to give place to a new sound that pulsed unceasingly on the quiet air – the strange and thrilling boom of Tlingit drums. Up from the great potlatch house in the village floated the savage resonance, adding a barbaric note of announcement to the placid beauty of the scene. Above the roofs of the Native houses and straight between the totems of the Thunderbird and the Bear rose the black smoke of the potlatch fire.

Though it was early, the double doors of the trading post stood open, for the White Chief had been up for several hours. After a night of revelry in Katleean, there were always knife wounds to dress, battered heads to bind up, bullets to extract and even broken bones to set. The nearest doctor was five hundred miles away and Kilbuck, often the only sober man at the post – with the exception of Kayak Bill – performed these services.

Some said that he had learned all he knew of medical science from the row of gold-lettered volumes tucked away in one corner of his dusky living room; others claimed that a great eastern medical college had known him as a student in the far-off days before Alaska took him for her own. Whatever was the source of his knowledge, he did his work with a degree of rough skill, and humanely, using as an antidote stupendous quantities of the very liquor that had brought about his patients' troubles to ease the pain he inflicted during these operations.

Among the Kagwantans of the Tlingit people he had been given the rank of shaman, or medicine man. To further his own ends, and to keep his hold on the Natives, he had always donned the robes that went with this conferred honor and had taken an active part in the potlatch ceremonies. As the years went by, and with only four steamers a year to disturb his voluntary exile – and but a waning interest in anything south of Dixon's Entrance – he had grown to have a real enjoyment in these affairs. They served to banish any lingering inhibitions imposed by civilization.

As he walked across the courtyard toward the little cabin of Silvertip and his woman, Senott, there were thoughtful lines in the White Chief's brow. Today he would have an opportunity to impress the white women with his importance among the wild people of the North. Today Ellen Boreland should see him as the great chief and shaman, banisher of Tlingit sorcery. But how far might he go in this character without running the risk of becoming ridiculous? Never before had such an audience taxed his powers of discrimination. True, by subtle speeches, he had prepared his visitors for anything that might happen, and he knew they would excuse much that was bizarre on his own part because of his explanation that such ways were necessary in handling a primitive people. But he also knew that there is but a thin dividing line between savage pomp and ludicrous ostentation.

As he neared Silvertip's door he raised his head decisively, mounted the steps and entered without knocking.

His glance swept the small room with its snowy sand-scoured floor, its rectangular box stove of sheet iron, and two corner bunks, one above the other.

"Well, Silvertip, you and Harlan are the last ones on my list," he told the wan-looking man in the lower bunk. "I can't find *him* any place, but I see you've come to anchor all right. What's the matter with you?"

A long-drawn sigh quivered up from the blankets, and with a shaking hand, the Swede indicated his head.

"My ol' ooman (groan) ... lick hal outen me ... (groan)!"

Kilbuck bent down and parted the fair, blood-matted hair on the side of his patient's head.

"Oh, you're not much hurt, man. You and Senott ought to learn to take a little drink together without beating each other up this way," Kilbuck said with a laugh, as he made ready to cleanse the cut. "May I inquire where the lady is this morning?"

Between groans, the injured husband profanely unburdened himself.

"She go down de tam Injune house vit dat tam Injune hunter, Hoots-noo!"

"Trouble with you, Silver, you're too good to women. Now, instead of using the iron hand on them, you show the yellow streak."

"Me – jallow streak?" The indignant Swede raised his battered head to glare into the eyes of his satiric physician. "Vy, tammit, Chief, ven ay ban cook on *Soofie Suderlant* ay ..."

"That reminds me, Silvertip," interrupted the White Chief. "You remember telling me about stopping for water on the island of Kon Klayu when you were whaling? Yes? Well, while you are lying here sobering up, I want you to think about that island, Silver. I want you to remember every little thing about it that you can, and after the potlatch I'll be in to talk to you ... perhaps. I'll go and hunt up Harlan now. Damned fool! He raised hell last night ... something started him off. No doubt he's down around the Point swimming it off now. Queer how that fellow loves water ... on the outside of his skin."

The trader left the cabin and started across the courtyard. It had gradually filled up with multicolored, grotesque figures that might have stepped from the pages of some weird, fantastic fairy tale. The never ceasing beat of the potlatch drums made a throbbing, low accompaniment to their guttural tones and laughter. They stalked about wrapped in heavy broadcloth blankets adorned with designs and borders made of white pearl buttons – thousands of buttons – a style that had come in when the white traders came to Alaska. Many wore the Native Chilkat blanket of ceremony made of the hair of the mountain goat. These were marvels of savage embroidery done in conventionalized designs that might have startled a Cubist painter had they not been woven with the softest-toned native dyes – yellow, pale blue, green and rust. Huge, fierce detached eyes, the Tlingit symbol of intelligence, glared from some. Mouths with queer, squared lips and large teeth grinned from others. A school of killer whales with dorsal fins aloft disported themselves in rectangles of black on the back of another. From the bottom, a two-foot fog-colored fringe dangled about the wearers' legs.

Above the fantastic robes, black eyes looked out from painted faces rendered fearsome by red, blue and green designs representing mythical gods of the clouds, waves, and beasts, fish and birds. Heads were crowned with the skulls of grizzly bears and small whales. Pelts of animals disguised a few figures, but instead of paws, huge wooden hands with fingers more than a foot long dangled from the forearms.

Swimming Wolf, brave in a dance blanket that bore the wolf emblem of the Kagwantans, held his head proudly under the sacred hat of Kahanuk, the Wolf. On his face, in red and blue, was the *Kia-sa-i-da* – the red mouth of the wolf when the lips are retracted.

As the White Chief made his way through the throng, he noted with satisfaction that Ellen Boreland and her sister were standing spellbound in the doorway of the trading post watching the primitive masquerade. He watched as a creature broke suddenly from the crowd and rushed toward them, half-running, half-flopping like a wounded bird. To one side of its face half a moustache was attached. The other cheek was adorned with red and blue paint. The hair was twisted into a high peak and further decorated with the wings of a seagull. The creature wore a man's hair-seal waistcoat trimmed with red flannel that hung from the shoulders, and from this streamed yards of brilliant-colored calico strips an inch wide.

As the figure reached the platform, the two white women shrank back in the doorway. The half portion of the moustache was raised in a delighted grin.

"Heavens, Ellen!" gasped Jean, clutching her sister's arm. "It's that jolly little Senott, Silvertip's woman. The one that brought us strawberries the other day."

Senott, proud in her potlatch finery, came close and gazed with friendly eyes at the white visitors.

"Ha! Ha!" she laughed. "You not know Senott? Senott all same *kate-le-te* – all same seagull!" She threw out her arms and raised them up and down and lifted high her feet to represent a seagull alighting at the edge of breaking surf.

"Bime-by you white 'oomans come along Senott," she said and pointed in the direction of Kilbuck's living room windows under which he had caused a great grave to be dug. "You come. Senott show you t'ings."

With a wide smile and a wave of her hand, the gay Senott, apparently forgetful of the white spouse at home nursing the broken head she had given him, flapped away to join her Native lover, Hoots-noo, Heart of a Grizzly, the handsome young husband of Old Woman Who Would Not Die.

By noon, every soul in Katleean had assembled in front of the trading post. The boom of drums was louder. There was a feeling of expectancy in the air. The few whites, with the exception of Kilbuck, sat on the platform in front of the store. The Natives formed a shifting, motley crowd in the courtyard. Kayak Bill, sitting next to Ellen, smoked his pipe as he contemplated the scene.

"Wall, Lady," he drawled, leaning toward her. "I seen a heap o' this sort o' jaberwocky doin's in my time up here, and it used to make me feel like as if them Injines had a tank full o' doodle-bugs under their hair, but I don't know … take us white folks down in the States now, when we're a-celebratin' o' Decoration Day without our speeches and our peerades and our offerin's o' posies and such. It's the sarne principle exact."

The old man ceased speaking abruptly. Out of the door behind them and down the platform steps walked the White Chief of Katleean and the little Tlingit woman, Decitan. About her shoulders was draped a fringed black and yellow blanket of wondrous design. On her dark, thick hair she wore the crest of the Eagle clan – a privilege accorded only to a chiefess.

The waiting Natives stood back from these two principal figures in the courtyard and Kilbuck, with the Native woman beside him, turned to face the white woman on the platform whose favors he hoped to win.

He felt himself splendidly barbaric in the costume of a shaman. The greens and blues and yellows of his royal Chilkat blanket and dancing shirt set off his dark beard and dead-white skin. Carved wooden eagle wings on each side of a tall hat crowned his hair. Below this emblem of the shaman spirit, the Unseeable, his eyes, narrow, pale and dangerous, sent straight into those of Ellen a look that might have come down through the red pages of history.

She turned her face away with a frightened quickening of the pulses.

The White Chief and Decitan took their places at the head of the Native procession that had been forming, and the long, fantastic line wound about the courtyard and down the trail that led to the village. Before the graveyard, with its totems and curious architecture of the dead, they stopped and began a mournful ululation. The wailing gradually gave way to the potlatch songs in honor of the deceased – songs of curious rhythm and halting cadences; songs with a haunting plaintiveness that floated high above the throbbing of the drums.

On the platform, the white inhabitants of Katleean waited in silence until the procession came back once more to the courtyard. Then one by one they attached themselves to the line.

The funeral party halted around the excavation under the windows of the White Chief. Kilbuck, his handsome, barbaric head towering above all, spoke to the Natives for a few moments in Tlingit. Then one by one the small boxes containing ashes of the dead were handed to him. He lowered them into the grave. As the last one

THE WHITE CHIEF MAKES MEDICINE

settled on the bottom, he stepped back, flinging one corner of his fringed blanket from his shoulder. He exulted in the sense of power such an occasion gave him. He liked to feel that in the hollow of his hand he held every soul in Katleean.

Perhaps in his heart there still lurked some faint respect for the dead. Perhaps he merely intended to impress the white women in his audience, as from under the bizarre robe of his heathen office he produced a prayer book, and in the voice he knew so well how to modulate, read the service for the dead. At the close, he swept the gathering with an inclusive glance. First in Tlingit, then in English, he addressed his listeners.

"People of the Kagwantans, of the Wuckitans, of the Yakutats and the Ganahadi," he said, his voice making music of the Native names. "Listen to the talk I make and remember. Always, while I am the White Chief and medicine man of the Kagwantans, I will watch over the ashes of my brown brothers and sisters. Always, when the nights of the Big Snows come to Katleean and the spirit lights whisper in the North in the moon of Kokwa-ha, I, the Unseeable, will watch.

"Always, in the moons of the Big Salmon run, the Hat-dee-se, when there is no darkness in the nights of the North, I, the Unseeable, will watch ... I, who have brought you the great white medicine of the Letquoan, the Snow People, I make the big medicine now ... I make it with the sacred book of the White Shamans." He held one corner of his Chilkat blanket tightly against his breast with the prayer book, and with the other stretched out at arm's length, he swept the fringes slowly back and forth over the grave. "I make the Big Medicine ... my brothers and sisters may rest in peace at Katleean, for no witch can dig down into the grave below to work evil spells ... I, the White Chief, the Unseeable, I am always watching."

The solemn old Natives of the tribe nodded their masked heads approvingly and gave grunts of satisfaction. Kilbuck turned away as if a bit weary of his role and walked toward the trading post. The white members of his audience followed him.

After the departure of their foreign visitors, the Natives assumed an alertness strangely at variance with their usual stolid demeanor.

Kilbuck, with his white guests, watched them from his living room windows.

Blanket after blanket was spread over the boxes of ashes in the grave. Bolt after bolt of bright calico was torn into streamers and flung into the open space. Cooking utensils and food came next; then trinkets of every kind that might cheer the souls of the departed on their journey over the Spirit Trail. At the very last, Swimming Wolf, who had heretofore taken little part in the ceremonies, stepped forward with a tiny phonograph, a rare possession since it was the only one in the village. The Native carefully wound it up and lowered it into the hole. There was a craning of masked heads ... a period of grunting approval ... and then faintly from below came a whirring, a sputtering and a high, cracked voice of announcement.

The White Chief's face wore its sardonic smile as the gravel was being shoveled into the grave – the little tin phonograph was playing "There'll be a Hot Time in the Old Town Tonight."

Courtesy Alaska State Library

Many cultures, including the Native people of the North, have designated shamans, like this man pictured here in Yakutat during the late 1890s, to be their intermediaries to communicate between themselves and the unknown spirit world.

7

THE POTLATCH DANCE

Evening found the Boreland family, attended by Kayak Bill, taking the beach trail to the village. It was well past nine o'clock and the twilight had merged into the soft, luminous duskiness that would continue until the sun came up at two-thirty in the morning.

In the gloom, a hundred blanket-covered canoes lined the crescent beach that sloped gently upward to a strip of gravel before the row of Native houses. The totems of the Thunderbird and the Bear stood out high against the sky. Before the potlatch house a dog – small, coyote-like – yelped shrilly as he tugged at the rope that fastened him to a stake. The air throbbed to the incessant beat of drums and the muffled chant that rose and fell inside the meeting place.

The potlatch house, older than the oldest Native at Katleean, had been built before ever a white man had set foot on the beach of the village. The low building, more than sixty feet square, was made of huge, hand-hewed yellow cedar planks standing vertically.

The gable ends faced the bay, and all across the triangular space above the eves was painted the startling conventionalized head of a wolf. The ears rose weirdly from the gable edge of the roof. Two monster eyes glared through the twilight above a grinning, squared mouth twenty feet across. On either side of the oval door stood a totem, hollow at the base and containing the ashes of long-dead chiefs. The corner posts were carved into life-size grotesque figures of men.

Kayak Bill sauntered between Ellen and Jean. Their half-fearful looks at the potlatch house were inspired by the stories he had told, with a certain grim amusement, to these two fair women of the South. They were stories told to him over the hootch cup by the wicked Old Woman Who Would Not Die; tales of the long-ago heathen times when the potlatch house was erected and dedicated with human sacrifices; when for each of those carved corner posts a slave had been murdered and placed at the bottom of the hole that was to receive it; tales of scores of slaves who had been slaughtered upon its completion; tales of animal-like orgies – those walls had seen cannibal feasts, torture of witches and fiendish carousals about the burning dead.

Tame, indeed, in comparison were the potlatches of this day, even when the savage spirit was stimulated by the white man's firewater. And tonight there could be none of that. In honor of the white women, Kayak Bill was keeping drink from the Natives this one evening.

Ellen looked at Jean apprehensively as they pressed closely on the heels of Shane Boreland and followed him through the low, oval door of the potlatch house.

The air was thick inside with the smoke of many pipes. Through the haze, the wall lights burned dimly. All about the sides of the great room squatted Natives in their potlatch finery. At the farther end sat the drummers beating in booming rhythm on war drums made of hair seal stretched over rings from hollowed logs. Never during the three days of the potlatch did those drumbeats cease.

Near the doorway was a small, slightly raised platform. On this, in his shaman robes, sat the White Chief of Katleean. As they ascended the step, he rose ceremoniously to greet them and indicated some chairs near him that had been placed in anticipation of their coming.

When the white visitors had seated themselves, the drumbeats took on a quicker staccato rhythm. There was a craning of necks toward the doorway. Another moment and the chief dancer of the potlatch entered the oval.

Dancing in backward, so the decorations on his blanket were displayed to the best advantage, he sang a halting Tlingit song and scattered the down of eagles about him. In the middle of the room, he whirled, and Ellen recognized Swimming Wolf.

"If the feathers fall on you," said the White Chief as he leaned toward her, "you'll have good luck all the year."

Other dancers backed in and took their places about the drummers. As Swimming Wolf stepped forward, the drumbeats died to a muffled softness. The dancing sticks beat the floor in a low, sensuous syncopation that stirred the blood. The long-fringed blanket lent a wild grace to the Native's swaying, stamping figure. His crouched steps seemed part of his faint, humming chant.

Curious at first, and a little apprehensive, Ellen looked on, her hand clasping that of her husband. After a while, the steady pulsing of the drums banished that something faintly like foreboding with which the civilized woman looks for the first time on primitive ceremonies; it even stirred in her something that she seemed once to have known and forgotten.

By the time Swimming Wolf had finished his steps, she had withdrawn her hand from that of Shane and was anticipating with eager interest what was coming next.

She had not long to wait, for the oval door swung on its peg and into the room lumbered a huge brown bear so true to life in form and gait that both she and Jean gave a startled gasp. The White Chief smiled as he leaned toward them.

"It's only Hoots-noo, Heart of a Grizzly, dressed in a bear hide."

Hoots-noo must have spent many hours studying the actions and habits of his ferocious namesake, for in the pantomime that followed he gave a perfect imitation of the great bear of the North. After shambling down toward the center of the floor, he paused. Striking a pose, he made a motion as if jumping into a river to catch a salmon. With a floundering of his ungainly body, he brought the fish up on the bank of the stream. He turned his uplifted muzzle from side to side, as if scenting danger, and then proceeded to tear the fish into pieces, his head continually moving as though looking and listening for the hunter's rifle.

Hoots-noo's performance was followed by other clever impersonations and by more solo dances of blanketed Natives. All the dances, the White Chief told Ellen, were taken from the movements of the wild things of the North – the slinking of the fox across the tundra, the leaping of the king salmon in the river, the flight of the eagle over the fishing grounds.

When the general dance was announced, every unmarried Tlingit man sprang to his feet and sought a partner of the opposite sex. About the room in a circle the fantastic figures leaped with savage abandon. When tired couples sought resting places against the walls again, each young man gallantly presented his partner with a small bag of raisins – a custom introduced by the enterprising white traders.

Faster and more softly came the boom and thud of drums and dancing sticks, until the urge of them caused even Ellen's feet to beat time to the primitive music. She glanced at her sister. Jean's eyes were sparkling. Her lithe body was swaying and her hands moving in rhythm with the Tlingit's dance.

"For two cents, Ellen, I'd dance with my admirer, Swimming Wolf!" she said with a laugh in her sister's ear. "I feel the stir of the blood of our remote ancestors who must have stepped it off in some such manner as this. ... Look at your son, El!"

Loll, by now regarding every Native as his friend, was standing before Senott. That dusky belle was resting after a mad, joyous whirl with Hoots-noo, Heart of a Grizzly. The boy's head was nodding with earnestness as he talked to her, and he was playing with the dozen gold and silver bracelets that adorned the gay one's shapely arms. Suddenly, with a laugh, Senott rose from the floor, grasped the boy's hands and began to circle about the room with him. The drummers and holders of the dancing sticks showed their white teeth in delighted grins and quickened the rhythm of their music.

"By ginger," said Shane, his lean face alight with interest. "I'd like to shake a leg myself. Ellen –" he turned to his wife – "what you say?"

Ellen shook her head, smiling. "Take Jean, dear. She's wild to dance."

Shane turned to his sister-in-law. Laughing, she gave him her hand and the two stepped down and joined the bizarre throng. The smiling Natives paused a moment to watch as the white couple improvised steps to suit the music, then the dance went on as before.

The drumbeats grew wilder, more stirring. The room grew more wane and the lights burned dimmer. Kayak Bill, sitting between Ellen and Paul Kilbuck, attempted a monologue, but finding no listeners, gave it up to puff contentedly.

The fumes of Kayak's pipe seemed overly strong to Ellen. She began to feel the need of fresh air. She glanced at her sister and her husband as they passed her, laughing over an intricate step they told her was the "Bear Paw." Kayak Bill and the White Chief seemed buried in their own thoughts. Ellen rose, looked about her a moment, and then slipped quietly out of the oval door into the cool, star-spangled night.

After the close air of the potlatch house, it was good to draw in the freshness outside. The two tall totems framed a golden naked moon that hung above the hills across the bay. The shimmering path from its glow threw into silhouette the prows of the big canoes drawn up on the beach. Ellen walked down the sandy path toward them. Pausing, she leaned against one and gazed idly out across the water.

For the moment, the chanting of the Natives had ceased and the drumbeats sounded muffled and soothing. Weird and lonely from a distant ridge came the faint call of a wolf, presaging, though she did not know it, an early winter. She became aware of the aromatic savors of the wild sea smells, the forest breath, the tang of camp smokes. She was beginning to like these things.

There was a sense of dreamlike unreality about the night – about her whole life at Katleean. Sometimes she caught herself marveling that she was not more startled, more surprised at the new ways of life that had come to her, for it is only the seasoned traveler in the little-known places of the world who ceases to marvel at the adaptability of man to new and strange environments. Alaska, especially, Ellen thought, seemed to work strange spells on those who came to dwell within her borders. What would be considered melodramatic and foolish south of 53, became somehow, natural and fitting above the line.

Her drifting thoughts were suddenly checked by the sound of soft footsteps in the sand behind her. She turned swiftly. Her dreamy, contemplative mood changed to one closely akin to panic; as out of the shadows tall and dominant in his potlatch robes, the White Chief stalked toward her.

She had no tangible reason for fearing to be alone with the trader of Katleean, and she despised herself now for the impulse that urged her to run as fast as she could from the man. Mentally upbraiding herself for her foolishness, she forced a smile of greeting – and in her haste to say something that would put the meeting on a commonplace basis – she burst out with the inane and obvious.

"Isn't it a beautiful night, Mr. Kilbuck?"

The White Chief stopped beside her and flung back the blanket from his shoulder. There was a lawless gleam in the narrow eyes he turned on her and she was not unaware of a certain savage, picturesque appeal in him. She felt again a strange, undesired impulse that had troubled her ever since her first meeting with the man – the urge to go close and look deep into his pale, hypnotic eyes.

"On nights like this, Mrs. Boreland," he said, his tones low, almost caressing, "I always think of those lines – perhaps you know them ..."

"Press close, magnetic, nourishing Night!
Night of the South Winds! Night of the few large stars!
Still, nodding Night. Mad, naked summer night!"

Despite herself, Ellen thrilled under the magic of his voice and listened intently as he continued.

"It's the memory of such nights that bring me back to this country year after year, and then ... when I return ... there is only the mocking beauty of their loneliness."

Ellen knew but little of the "good, grey poet," but at the incongruity of his quoting she gazed with a new curiosity at this tall figure in the heathen splendor of a Tlingit witchdoctor.

"To be satisfying," he said softly, "beauty like this must be shared with a loved woman." His sweeping gesture indicating the moonlit bay of Katleean. "You are the first white woman to share it with me."

He stepped closer to her. Though there was three feet of distance between them, she felt his presence as a tangible thing. She stirred uneasily. The dull throb of the drums filled a moment's space.

"I have loved many women," his low voice went on. "Women of a sort, but never anyone like ..."

There was something tenderly personal in the omitted word. "Sometimes ... I wonder ... if I might not be a better man if I had someone like you to stand beside me when winter nights come, and watch the Northern Lights."

Kilbuck looked dreamily away toward the peaks raising their subtle loveliness to the stars. Doubtless he must have said the same things slightly varied to many women in the States, but never before had Nature provided such a setting for his posing. Doubtless it had always made a favorable appeal, for Ellen knew that man, though doing exactly as he pleases, is ever holding out his hand to woman to be uplifted, and the mother instinct in the feminine heart seldom fails to respond.

Ellen felt suddenly that the situation was getting beyond her. As she leaned against the canoe she tried in vain to think of some ordinary thing that would change the current of the White Chief's thoughts and enable her to get away to the potlatch house without his becoming aware of her perturbation. Fumbling uneasily with the handkerchief in her hand, she dropped it. As she stooped to pick it up an exclamation escaped her. She had been resting her head against the upcurving prow of the canoe, and now, as she moved, she became aware, by a sharp painful tug, that her hair had become entangled in some torn rivets embedded in the tarpaulin.

Instantly Kilbuck was behind her, reaching across her shoulders to release the strands. They refused to come away.

After a moment of ineffectual tugging, Ellen removed a pin from the soft, thick coil. Loosed by their efforts with the tangle, her hair shook down and tumbled in a lustrous mass below her waist. She felt Kilbuck's fingers working at the strands about the broken rivet.

Suddenly he was still, his hand grasping a long strand of the mass.

"Mrs. Boreland, there is a superstition among the Tlingits to the effect that whenever a man carries a lock of a white woman's hair he is protected from any kind of violence – no matter what he may have done to deserve punishment. Your hair is of such a rare shade and texture, there would be no mistaking a lock of it, would there?"

With a swift movement his hand slipped beneath the Chilkat blanket. There was a glint of steel, and the next moment he had severed the lock from the shining mass. Ellen started back, snatching up her hair to wind it into its accustomed knot, but before she could utter the words that sprang to her lips there was a sound of running footsteps.

"Ellen! Ellen!" Jean called as she sped toward them down the pathway. "I've been looking everywhere for you!"

She glanced at the White Chief with surprise, suspicion and disapproval succeeding each other in her eyes. She made no effort to conceal her dislike of the trader of Katleean.

"Come, Ellen. Let's go back to Shane."

Jean took her sister's hand, and the White Chief watched their retreating figures for several moments. Then from beneath his blanket he drew the long lock of hair he had stolen. One hand passed gently, caressingly along the length of it. It clung softly to his finger like a live thing ... the hair of Native women was long and thick, but coarse, and even after long residence in the trader's quarters seemed to hold the faint salmon tang of the smokehouse. But this ... his lip lifted in his wolfish smile. It would be difficult, very difficult indeed, for a wife to explain his possession of such a trifle.

He held it against his mouth. The faint perfume of the white woman thrilled him. His nostrils twitched. He felt his eyes grow narrow as when he sighted game on the trail. Suddenly, as if in decision, he turned and walked rapidly up the beach toward his quarters at the trading post.

In his living room, dark now except for a few dull embers in the fireplace, he lighted a candle and crossed to the corner beneath the high shelf of books. He drew aside a large, Native-made hair-seal wall pocket and fumbled a moment. Finally a small door swung open revealing a hollow in the log wall.

Very carefully the White Chief wrapped the lock of hair in a handkerchief and laid it away in the hiding place. Just as carefully he drew out a small moose-hide poke, and putting the candle on a nearby table, sat down before it. He removed the tag attached to the top and read the inscription: "Eldorado Creek gold." Then he loosened the string.

On the wall behind the man, weird, gigantic shadows, born of the flickering candle flame, leaped and danced. In the crude light and shade his barbaric gorgeousness became doubly sinister as he pushed the strange shaman headdress farther back on his dark head.

He wiped an ashtray carefully and poured the contents of the poke into it. Beautifully yellow and gleaming, it fell in a golden stream – perhaps two ounces of gold dust. With a satisfied nod, he poured the dust back into the poke and put it into his pocket. A few minutes later, he stepped out into the night.

The sound of drums and dancing came up from the village as he crossed the dim courtyard toward the light that shone palely from Silvertip's window. As he entered the cabin, the Swede – still nursing the broken head that kept him from participating in the potlatch festivities – groaned dismally in greeting.

There were a few perfunctory words, then for half an hour Kilbuck talked earnestly. Silvertip protested; he whined; but he listened. There was mention of Boreland and beach sand; of gold dust and Kon Klayu. And after much persuasion, Silvertip consented to do what the White Chief outlined.

Kilbuck held out the small bag of gold. The pale-eyed Swede reached for it and put it away under his pillow.

The trader rose to go. As he draped his robe about him, his eye caught a movement among the blankets in the top bunk. He started.

"God, you fool!" he whispered, leaning down and grasping Silvertip's arm. "Why didn't you tell me you had someone here. Who is it?"

The Swede groaned. "By yingo, Ay plumb forget about te tam jung yack-ass Harlan. He coom in har dis noon time drunk like hal, wit t'ree bottle of hootch. He tal me he iss lonesome. He iss drunk now, Chief. He can't har not'ing."

Kilbuck drew down the blankets from the head of the man in the upper bunk. The boyish sleeping face was flushed. Dark matted hair clung to the damp forehead and there was a sickening odor of vile liquor in the air. A long moment the trader looked to see if Harlan would open his eyes. Then, with a contemptuous laugh, he flung the blanket over the lean young face.

"Nothing to fear from him if he drank three bottles of Kayak Bill's brew."

Kilbuck then stepped out of the door into the courtyard, adjusted his headdress, and humming a dance hall ballad swung down the beach path toward the village.

Courtesy Alaska State Library

Potlatches are a long-held tradition among Alaska Native tribes. These are social gatherings that strengthen spiritual, ceremonial, social and cultural aspects of communities. Potlatches, which can last for several days or go on for months, are held to celebrate births, marriages, funerals and other significant events.

Festvities include serving traditional Native foods, giving gifts and dancing. Singing also plays an important role in these events. During funeral potlatches, songs about the person who died are written and sung.

Native potlatches were outlawed for a time by the U.S. government in the early 20th Century after missionaries pushed for their elimination. Religious groups saw them as direct threats to their efforts to reshape Native culture.

Potlatches had resumed by the time *Where The Sun Swings North* takes place.

THE POTLATCH DANCE

8

THE OUTFIT

A week later, in the snug little cabin of the *Hoonah*, Ellen Boreland sat opposite a folding table, where her husband, humming contentedly, was adjusting a gold scale. Ellen's hands were busy with mending, but her brow puckered anxiously and her eyes had purple shadows beneath them.

From the moment she had realized the loss of her lock of hair, her conflicting impressions of the White Chief of Katleean had crystallized into a certainty that he meant no good to herself or to her husband. That he desired her she now had no doubt, and while she knew in her heart that she was in no way responsible for this, she felt more keenly than ever that baffling sense of guilt that had attached itself to her since her first meeting with the man. It seemed some loathed feeling shared with the man and more gripping because of words never spoken.

Another thing troubled her. Because of him she had told her husband a lie – the first during her ten years of married life. Her mind went back again and again to the scene. They had come back to their room at the post the night of the potlatch dance. Jean, full of enthusiasm over the events of the evening came in from her loft room to talk it all over with her sister. Little Loll was solemnly practicing the bear antics of Heart of a Grizzly over in a corner of the room. Shane Boreland, as was his custom, sat watching his wife comb out the long beautiful tresses that were his pride.

Suddenly he rose from his chair. "By ginger, El!" he exclaimed. "What have you done to your hair? Looks as if you cut a chunk out of it!" There was concern in his face as he picked up a handful and pointed out the severed portion to his sister-in-law.

Ellen's blood seemed to turn to water. Her heart fluttered in her throat. What explanation could she give this chivalrous, hot-heated Irishman who loved her, and who, she knew from past experience, would shoot a man for less than the Chief had done? She valued above all things the trust and loving companionship that had blessed her married life. She hesitated, desperately seeking some plausible explanation that would approach the truth. Shane, she imagined, was looking at her keenly now and there was a curious light in Jean's frank eyes.

"I ... I cut it, dear," she stammered, hiding her face under the veil of her hair. "I cut it to send to mother in the next mail."

The instant the lie was out she would have given a year of her life to recall it. She realized, too late, that it but opened the way for other lies. It placed her in the position of one obliged to carry indefinitely an unexploded bomb, which the least jar might set off causing who could tell what destruction.

The next day she had insisted, with more than her usual vigor, on returning to the schooner. Shane had consented reluctantly, but he would not for the present accede to her wish to leave Katleean. He was stubborn in his determination to learn all that was to be known about the island of Kon Klayu.

Ellen recalled the events of the week, including her husband's enthusiastic reports of the island gold, his talks with the carefully noncommittal trader and the thin-nosed, shifty-eyed Silvertip, and finally his decision to spend the winter on the island in search of the precious metal. Shane was sitting now at the table pouring some shining dust into a saucer and studying the "colors" as it fell.

"The lure of raw gold, Ellen," he mused, and then looked up at her with glowing dark eyes. "There's no greater magnet for a man in the world, little fellow – except the love of a woman," he added softly with the smile that had won his wife's heart ten years ago and made her happy in sharing his shifting fortunes.

"But if I make a go of it this trip, Ellen, I give you my word that I'll go back to the States and settle down somewhere – any place you wish. Look at it … just look at it, El!" He held the saucer so that it caught the sunlight streaming in through the round cabin window.

"By Jove, it ought to go eighteen dollars to the ounce! It's clean as a dog's tooth. Silvertip says he and some of his mates panned it one day at Kon Klayu while the *Sophie Sutherland* took on water. Of course, the party sent over by Kilbuck's company didn't find much, but from what I hear they were a hootch drinking lot who knew nothing of mining and thought only of drawing their pay and keeping drunk. You can see for yourself, Ellen, what this northern hootch does to a man – young Harlan is a good example. Gone to the dogs in three months, though I can't help liking the fellow."

He shifted the gold dust again, and then bent his head to peer at it through a small microscope. During the moment's silence came the lap of the incoming tide against the hull of the schooner.

"That reminds me, Ellen," Boreland went on. "The Chief received word yesterday from a trading post down the coast that a revenue cutter is bound this way on a tour of inspection. Kayak Bill's going to hide his still and go into retirement until the cutter has finished investigating. Seems they're always suspecting him of making hootch," Shane said and chuckled with amusement. "Funny old devil, Kayak Bill – I like the old cuss. I've asked him to come over to the island with me for a couple of months until the Chief brings the *Hoonah* with our winter outfit."

At the mention of the *Hoonah*, Ellen glanced about the snug, cheerful cabin that had been her home for many adventurous months. This staunch little schooner had brought her and her loved ones safely over hundreds of miles that separated her from her home port. Thoughts came to her now of wild, stormy nights when she had awakened in her reeling bunk to the scream of wind in the rigging, the roar of waves, the tramp of hurried feet overhead and the shouting of voices. At those times she knew Shane stood at the wheel in the drenching rain giving his orders for the reefing of sails. During the first days of the voyage the awakening in a gale had always filled her with a great fear – a fear not for herself but for her family, her little son. She would clasp the sleeping boy more closely in her arms and lie with straining muscles, waiting, listening, every sense painfully alert and her eyes hypnotically watching the garments on the opposite wall swing out and back with the roll of the ship. Gradually, as the schooner righted itself after every roll, Ellen's nerves would relax. Unclasping her arms, she would snuggle close to the back of the bunk, the few inches of the *Hoonah's* hull that separated her and her loved ones from the black, bull-throated billows that sought to swallow them. The feel of the cool wood brought a sense of safety, a certainty that with Shane's strong, thin hands on the wheel the *Hoonah* would bring them all safely through any danger of the sea. Then bit by bit approaching sleep would dim the fury of the gale until at last it was but a lullaby zephyr wafting her, like her little son, once more into the harbor of dreams.

She had not realized how dear the schooner had grown to her until she had signed, against her better judgment, the bill of sale that transferred the vessel to Paul Kilbuck. On the reef-sown coast of Kon Klayu it appeared there was no harbor where a ship might find shelter, and Shane needed money for his winter outfit. Half the purchase price the trader had paid down – the other half was to be given Boreland when Kilbuck took the remainder of the outfit to Kon Klayu later in the fall.

Ellen aroused herself from her reverie. Shane had been speaking some minutes and his first words had been lost to her. He was quoting:

"One more trip for the golden treasure
That will last us all our lives!"

Life to Shane was a sweet and wonderful thing. Though there had been years of hardship and struggle, and often failure in the mining game, he still retained an eager joy in existence, a faith in men and women and something of the wonder of a boy. Perhaps it was because the place of his questing always had been the forests, the mountains, the clean, unpeopled places.

His present life of a prospector, sailing his little schooner boldly across dangerous reaches of ocean, through the intricate lovely waterways of Alaska's inland sea, poking her prow into hidden crescent coves, trying his luck with a gold pan on unknown streams, always sure that the next shift of the gravel in the pan would reveal a fortune. All this made life fascinating for Shane Boreland. No matter how far short realization fell, he always was ready with another dream, always eager when a new adventure beckoned.

And now it was the mysterious island of Kon Klayu.

Stripped of the golden glamour with which Shane had invested it, Ellen knew it to be an island but five miles long and a mile and a half wide, which lay out in the North Pacific ninety miles from the nearest land; an island uninhabited and completely surrounded by dangerous reefs and shoals; shunned by ships and spoken of as a death trap by sailors. But one tree, other than alder and willow, grew upon it. Three hundred feet above sea level on the high, flat top, a lone and stunted spruce rose from the tundra and breasted the heavy gales that swept the ocean. For firewood there were but the drift logs of the beach. There were no animals of any kind. The foxes and a pet cub bear taken there by the Alaska Fur and Trading Company, at the time of the fox farm experiment, had been killed off by passing whalers who were sometimes forced ashore for water.

Shane had entertained no idea of allowing his wife and family to accompany him to the island. All his powers of persuasion had been used to induce Ellen to stay at Katleean with her sister and Loll as guests of the White Chief until the fall steamer going south should take them back to the States. The trader, Ellen knew, had taken this arrangement for granted and she was certain she detected something of baffled rage in him when she informed him on her last visit to the shore, that since she could not dissuade her husband from going to the island of Kon Klayu, she and her family would accompany him.

It was in vain the White Chief pointed out to her that there were not provisions enough at the post to supply Shane with a complete winter outfit. He must sail at once for Kon Klayu in order to prepare for the winter's work, and the autumn steamer bringing more supplies was not due for six weeks. It was in vain Kilbuck assured her that he, himself, would take her to the island later on when he went over with the remainder of Shane's outfit after the arrival of the steamer. Ellen was obdurate in her decision, and once having committed herself, she became a different woman. Whatever misgivings she held in regard to the enterprise, she kept to herself. She plunged wholeheartedly into the preparations for the journey, becoming at once the practical director of the commissary. She looked carefully over the stock of goods at the trading post and obtained far more in the way of supplies than the easy-going Shane, inclined to trust to the trader's judgment, would have done. And Kilbuck, for some reason, seemed disinclined to furnish even as much as his stock would allow.

For the past week Ellen eluded every effort made by the White Chief to see her alone. Since the night of the potlatch dance she had talked with him only in the presence of a third person. Strange to say she found now that she could look him squarely in the eyes, but when she did so it was as if steel met steel. The feeling that she was playing a game of wits against the autocrat of Katleean was not without its interest for her. It was impossible entirely to conceal her growing hostility toward the man, and she knew that Kilbuck felt her wordless antagonism. To her anxiety she knew also that instead of diminishing his appetite for her, it increased it. She was growing eager to be away.

The outfitting went forward daily. Jean and Loll spent many hours ashore exploring the vicinity with Senott or Kayak Bill. Sometimes the visitors caught a glimpse of the tweed clad young man who seemed so quiet and aloof, and who, even when not drinking, avoided them all. Ellen observed a certain interest in him growing in Jean. A tentative question or two put to Kayak Bill revealed this, though it availed her nothing. The old hootch-maker, muttering something about "everybody to his own cemetery," had branched off to relate something he had "hearn tell" when he was "a-punchin' o' cows down in Texas."

Ellen, as well as Jean, wondered at the presence in Katleean of such a man as Harlan, and the reason for his connection with the dead Naleenah. Understanding of another's lapses comes with years and

Jean, Ellen knew, was too young fully to realize what this young man's dissipation portended.

Ellen kept a sharp eye on Harlan. Though she herself shared Jean's mild curiosity and faint pity, she managed to keep her sister at a safe distance from him. She intended very carefully to guard Jean.

Sometimes, in the evening, when the girl stood on the afterdeck of the *Hoonah*, her violin tucked beneath her chin, her eyes on the dreaming radiance of the sunset, Ellen studied her as she played. She wondered, if in her heart, the young girl played to him, and if he heard. And once, to her anxiety, as she sat listening to the silvery music floating out over the water, she had caught a shadow moving on the shore – a figure that moved stealthily down a hidden trail to the Point beyond the Native village and laid behind a great boulder, listening....

The outfitting for the island was nearly complete now. Each of the new acquaintances at Katleean contributed, with friendly intent, to the preparations of the departing travelers. In the cabin of young Harlan, which had been the home of the deceased Add' em-up Sam, were shelves laden with dusty books, old magazines and piles of ancient newspapers. At Kayak Bill's suggestion, the bookkeeper had packed the best of these into a box and the old hootch-maker had borne the package to Jean, remarking that "readin' matter might come in mighty handy on the island." The box was placed with Shane's outfit stacked in a corner of the store.

Ellen and Jean were looking through the collection one afternoon, judging the departed Sam by his taste in literature – which they found to be surprisingly good. As Jean turned the pages of *Treasure Island*, a paper fluttered to the floor. The girl picked it up, reading aloud the caption over a crude, penciled map: "The Island of Kon Klayu." She unfolded the paper, smoothing out the creases that she might better study the drawing, when Loll came running in from the platform in front of the store. His freckled face was puckered with suppressed grief, his grey eyes abrim with the tears he was too proud to shed.

"Mother – Jean – look at poor Kobuk," he told them, with a gulp that threatened to send the teardrops tumbling over his brown cheeks.

Kobuk, the big husky, had wagged himself into the hearts of every member of the Boreland family. Ellen knew that Shane had offered the White Chief a good price for the animal, but the trader had refused to part with his lead dog. Even when it was discovered that the husky had developed mange, Kilbuck would not give him up, though he did nothing to relieve him. Shane, busy with his outfitting, found time to take care of Kobuk, rubbing him every day with a mixture of sulphur, lard and carbolic acid until he was practically cured. Jean and Loll had attended these treatments taking turns holding the bowl of sulphur salve and encouraging the restive Kobuk to be a good dog and take his medicine. Now it was with the utmost pity and concern that they beheld him slinking to his corner in the store, for he had been out on a porcupine hunt and his nose and head were literally bristling with needle-like quills.

Ellen had seen irate dog owners spend hours with a pair of pincers removing quills from their animals, and she knew that even one of those tiny needles, if overlooked, could work its way straight through Kobuk's body. If it struck a vital organ, he would die.

The dog eased into his corner and tried to rest his head on his paws. The quills under his muzzle stabbed him and he cried out with a sharp yelp of pain. Jean and Lollie sprang toward him with expressions of sympathy and endearment. The dog whimpered, raising his soft, dark eyes to their faces as if begging for help in his trouble. Jean, on the verge of tears, sank down beside him, but Ellen, thinking to relieve him, ran to the living quarters back of the store to get a pair of pincers from Decitan.

When she returned, she stood a moment half concealed by the curtain in the doorway. Jean was soothingly stroking one of Kobuk's big paws. Near her stood the White Chief, who evidently had just come in. Both thumbs were hooked beneath his scarlet belt, and he was looking down at the dog. Kobuk at that moment lowered his head and tried to work himself farther back in his corner, but the effort brought out another yelp of pain.

The man's eyes became mere slits.

"Ah, damn you, so you've done it again, have you?" he said, with softness that in some indefinable way chilled the blood. "Well, this time we'll let the quills work through your brainless skull – or here, Hoots-noo," he said as he turned to the Native who was entering the store. "Take this cur out and shoot him. I'm tired of having quills yanked out of him."

With a cry of protest Jean came to her feet.

"Oh, no, no! Please!" Apparently forgetful of all but the safety of the dog, the girl clasped both her little hands about the man's arm. Her hazel eyes pleaded. Loll, too, was clinging to the trader's other hand, stroking it and looking up beseechingly into his bearded face.

"Oh, Chief, please, *please* don't shoot Kobuk. We want him. We'll take care of him!"

The White Chief paid no attention to the boy, but he looked down into the face of the girl and laughed unpleasantly.

"The little shaatk' with white feet can be very nice to me when she wants something," he said. "What are you willing to give me for Kobuk, my little lady?"

At his tone, the girl shrank back, but Loll, sturdily refused to be ignored and interrupted hastily.

"*She* ain't got nothing you want, Chief." He began tugging desperately at a string about his waist that bound to him his most cherished possession – an old broken revolver bestowed on him by Kayak Bill.

"Here, I'll give you my pistol for Kobuk!" The earnest little fellow held out the weapon with an air of certainty that indicated there could be no refusal of such a treasure.

The White Chief sat down leisurely on a box of pilot bread as if to better enjoy the situation.

"No, my boy," he said with another laugh. "Your disdainful aunt is going to pay me for Kobuk in coin, which you will learn more of by and by." He turned to the girl. "I'm not such a bad fellow, Jean," he continued, with an attempt at an ingenuous smile. "Come, kiss me once and the dog is yours."

Over Jean's face swept conflicting emotions of disgust and contempt for the man and pity for the moaning dog, whose life depended on her decision. The Native, stolid and unseeing, had already laid a hand on Kobuk's collar.

Ellen, unable to remain silent longer, started forward unnoticed by the others in the tenseness of the moment. But before she had taken two steps, Loll had taken charge of the situation.

Going close, he rested a hand on either knee of the trader and looked up earnestly into the man's pale eyes.

"Chief," he said, half-apologetically as man to man. "You see, Jean," he indicated his aunt with a tilt of his head. "Jean doesn't like to kiss strange men – but I don't mind." And before anyone realized what was happening, the boy had taken Kilbuck's face between two small hands and pressed cool, childish lips to the man's forehead.

Jean caught her nephew in her arms.

"You darling!" Half laughing, half crying she buried her face in his neck. "You darling!"

"Well, that's settled," said Loll in matter of fact tones as he wriggled to free himself. "Kobuk's ours now. Thank you, Chief. I'll have ...," he broke off with a shout to welcome Ellen, whom he had just seen. "Hey, Mother! He's ours now. Gimme the pinchers!" He took them from Ellen's hand and started toward the quill-filled Kobuk, who, sensing perhaps a change in his fortunes, had risen expectantly to his feet.

Shane, entering the doorway at that moment, was apprized of the addition to the family. The Borelands spent the next two hours extracting quills from the repentant Kobuk. For the first time in his life, perhaps, the pain-racked animal was soothed and cheered during the hated operation by quaint old Irish terms of endearment, punctuated with advice.

"But there'll be no more porky hunting for you, me lad," Shane assured the dog as he pulled the last quill. "For the very first fine day we have we're off for the island of Kon Klayu and devil a thing you'll find there to chase but sand fleas!"

9

HARLAN WAKES UP

Gregg Harlan had watched with interest the Boreland's preparation for departure to the island of Kon Klayu. For the first time in his life, he was doing some serious thinking – and ever since the potlatch, he had been seeing himself in no complimentary light.

His chief source of self-disgust was his way of taking the information that the Borelands, including Jean Wiley, thought him a cad. In his dejection, his thoughts went back time and again to those few moments of silent companionship when he had stood beside the girl in the dusk and watched the funeral canoes come in. Why hadn't he, after the White Chief told him of his reputed connection with Naleenah, why hadn't he followed Jean and explained? True, the shock and surprise of the thing had momentarily swept him off his feet, but why had he, in foolish reckless resentment against unjust circumstances, rushed off instead to the cabin of Kayak Bill and taken glass after glass of the stuff that had put him in such a state of oblivion that he was unable to take any part in the potlatch festivities? Since then he had been too ashamed to approach either of the white women. He felt that he must first do something to win their respect.

Harlan had been a drifter along the pleasant ways of least resistance during his twenty-five years. This was, perhaps, because he had never been called upon to shoulder responsibility. Six months before, because of this tendency more than because he had been in love, he had found himself involved in a foolish but unpleasant financial tangle brought about by a plump, perfumed, pleasure-loving little blonde. This small person from an eastern state had made his former knowledge of the hectic nightlife of San Francisco seem but a tuning up of the orchestra before the overture. After the inevitable parting of the ways, he had found himself obliged to call upon his irate and disgusted father for financial assistance. He had done this often before – so often that this last episode, more scarlet than any of the others, brought about a crisis. Later, penniless, but debtor to his father only, he had departed under a cloud of paternal disapproval to take the position of bookkeeper at faraway Katleean. It was then that he decided he was through with women.

At the time he believed it, as all men do who make a similar decision, but up here in the North he found that a white woman meant more to men than in the States. After three months in Katleean, a white woman had come to stand for the cleanness and the decencies of life. He found himself longing to be near and speak to these two visiting women of his own kind. He had heard of the "woman hunger" of Alaska and recognized in himself the symptoms of that state that causes even the most hardened misogynist to travel a hundred perilous miles merely to look on a white woman's face and hear her voice.

And music – the music of Jean's violin drew him like a magnet. Every evening when she played on the afterdeck of the *Hoonah* he slipped down to the Point beyond the Native village and listened – listened hungrily, with a longing to join her and explain his stupid innocence in connection with the dead Naleenah. His youth called to hers, and he wanted this clean-hearted girl to think well of him.

His drunkenness – but of course there was no excuse for that. He despised weakness in a man, and he had thought a good deal about his own of late. The episode of Naleenah had brought him face to face with the grim realities attending his drifting.

Sometimes when he looked at Silvertip, lolling brutish and drunken on the blankets of his bunk, Harlan had wondered what alcohol did for him. Once he had tried to outline to the one-time cook of the *Sophie Sutherland*, the beauties, as he saw them, of getting drunk. He recalled now his sensations from the moment the alcohol began creeping through his veins, softly, warmly, creating a glow about his heart.

Vistas then opened up before him. Romance and adventure beckoned him. Later, when the stimulant reached the centers of his brain, like the sentient fingers of a musician touching the keyboard of his soul, it produced golden harmonies from those keys whose tones are love, rhythm, color, appreciation of the beautiful. Inhibitions melted away in the amber light that enfolded him. Lovely things he had read or seen or thought and kept to himself for lack of expression formed themselves into words of exquisite simplicity that were to his ear as pastel shades to the eye. He could sing then, as he never sang at other times. Music that was felt, rather than heard, swayed him, and his feet, his hands, his whole body longed to dance and interpret this rhythm of the universe.

Afterward came oblivion, a sweet forgetting of all unpleasantness, a divine sense of mingling without responsibility with the elements.

But lately, he admitted reluctantly to himself, even in his moments of keenest alcoholic pleasure, he had been aware of an under thought that his exalted mood must pass leaving him more colorless, more listless, more inclined to drift than before. It took more of Kayak's whisky to produce an effect now than it had in the beginning. Perhaps, in time, he might even grow to be like Silvertip. He shuddered at that thought. It sickened and dismayed him to realize how the pale liquor had already enslaved him – to what it might lead him.

Another thing troubled him also. Ever since the night of the potlatch dance, which he had been too intoxicated to attend, something vague but insistent at the back of his consciousness strove to make itself remembered. Something he had heard in a half-drugged sleep. Something about gold and Kon Klayu. An idea persisted that on him depended some grave issue, but strive as he would he could not remember what it was.

Once, as he swam in the dawn below the Point in an effort to clear his cloudy brain, he prolonged his course until he found himself close to the hull of the *Hoonah*. It gave him satisfaction to find that despite three months of heavy drinking at Katleean, his daily plunge in the sea had kept him physically fit. He looked at the trim little schooner cradling her sleeping crew. Green wavelets lapped against the clean white side, and below the waterline the red of the bottom glimmered. Her upcurving prow seemed to urge to sea adventures. He wished he might go with Boreland to spend the winter on the island of Kon Klayu. But this, he knew, was not possible. He had work to do at Katleean, and it was time he was beginning it. And Ellen Boreland – he was not unaware that she disapproved of him and did her best to keep her sister from friendship with him.

But he might make the trip to the island and back to help Silvertip, whom Kilbuck had detailed to pilot the *Hoonah* to Kon Klayu. Silver was not fond of work. He would welcome the extra help in bringing the vessel home again from Kon Klayu – Kon Klayu! The words tantalized him afresh with his failure to remember the thing he should. Perhaps the sight of that mysterious island, though he had never seen it, might bring back to him the memory he sought.

He suddenly made a decision. When the *Hoonah* sailed for the island of Kon Klayu, he would be aboard – even though he had to go as a deckhand.

10

THE PIGEON

A morning came favorable for the departure of the *Hoonah*. Sunshine flooded the peaks, the hills and the trading post of Katleean. A stiff easterly breeze ruffled the bay into pale golden-green, and overhead long, white, scarf-like clouds streaked the blue. "Mares' tails," Kayak Bill called them, as he stood on the beach shifting his sombrero forward over his eyes so that he might better engage himself in what is known in Alaska as "taking a look at the weather," a proceeding that becomes second nature to those who live in the North where travel depends on wind, tide and atmospheric conditions.

The time for saying goodbye was at hand. Silvertip, with one of his countrymen and Gregg Harlan, were already aboard the schooner. The White Chief stood on a drift log watching Boreland load the last trifles into a whaleboat some hundred yards below him. One hand was hooked beneath the trader's scarlet belt, and the other held an unlighted cigarette. The wind ruffling the long, dark hair on his bare head gave him a lean and savage look.

Kayak Bill, who had been unusually silent all morning, left off searching for weather signs and sauntered over to him. His eyes narrowed slightly as he looked keenly into Kilbuck's face.

"Chief," he said nonchalantly, as he drew his pipe from the pocket of his mackinaw, "you and me's grazed conside'able on the same range. We ain't never got in each other's way. There's some things about you I ain't no nature for a-tall – but you been purty square with me. Likewise I'm not goin' round tellin' all I know about you. Everybody to his own cemetery, I say." The old man took his pipe from his mouth and faced the trader again.

"But before I go a-rampin' off on this vacation o' mine, I want to say this, Chief: I'm not knowin' nothin' but hearsay about this island o' Kon Klayu ... but yars ago I lost out in the matter o' family and I'm thinkin' a heap o' this Boreland outfit now. I'm trustin' to you, Chief, not to ring in no cold deck on 'em – or me. I'm figgerin' on seein' you at the island o' Kon Klayu in about six weeks with the balance o' the grub."

"You needn't be so all-fired serious about it, Kayak," Kilbuck said. "I'll take care of the grub all right. You say yourself that I've always played fair with you."

"Yas, Chief," drawled the old man. "But they ain't never been no women in the game before. Women and dogs is hell for startin' trouble. I ain't blind, Chief. I can still see offen the end o' my nose."

The trader laughed abruptly.

"Well, old-timer, you seem to be seeing off the wrong side this time. Don't you worry, Kayak. I'll be along and get you about the middle of October. Your revenue cutter friends will be gone by that time."

Kayak Bill was silent for a moment. Then, with seeming irrelevance, he slowly said:

"One time ... a long spell back ... I knew a woman ... and a man. He cheated her, and – wall, I shot him dead. . . ."

"Hey, there, Kayak!" came Boreland's shout from the whaleboat. "Come lend a hand here a minute, will you?"

Kayak Bill waited a moment. Then shaking the ashes from his pipe, he restored it to his pocket and plodded down to the boat.

Farther along the beach a little group of Tlingit women had gathered about Ellen and Jean to bid them goodbye. Senott, self-appointed spokeswoman for her shyer sisters, was shoving forward a plump, good-natured looking woman, who handed Jean a pair of hair-seal moccasins and a small Native basket.

"She potlatch you," explained Senott, supplementing her words with eloquent eyes and hands. "She like you, Girl Who Make Singing Birds In Little Brown Box. She Add-'m-up Sam 'ooman. She go Kon Klayu long time ago. She sorry you go. No river on dat island. No salmon, no tree, no mans. Only b-i-g wind! B-I-G sea! She sorry you go." The plump widow stood by shaking her head and making soft clucking sounds in her throat.

Leaving Jean to thank their Native friends, Ellen slipped through the circle. Her conventional training evidently asserted itself, for she turned now and went to say a few words of goodbye to their host.

She looked small and attractive as she stood before him, her blue eyes raised to his face, the sea wind blowing her hair across the pink of her cheeks. The trader stepped down from his log to greet her.

"I wondered if you would say goodbye to me without the presence of your whole family," he said softly, bending his head. Many a woman in Katleean, after incurring his displeasure, had seen the same expression in his eyes just before he struck her in the face with the flat of his hand. "One might almost think you are afraid of me. But ... though you will not stay at Katleean, I'll always have something to remind me of you." He slipped a hand into the pocket of his flannel shirt and the sheen of Ellen's stolen lock of hair caught the light for a moment before he buttoned the flap over it again.

Ellen, with a few stammered words, was backing away from him, her wide, fearful gaze fixed on his face, when he reached out, and as if merely to shake her hand in farewell, laid his iron fingers over hers in a grasp that made her wince.

"Just a moment, my frigid little Lucretia," he said. "I'm letting you go now because the time is coming when you'll want me. When you get aboard the schooner you'll find I have presented your son with a pigeon. Take good care of it. It was hatched here – and it's your only means of communicating with the mainland."

The White Chief then leaned down and whispered into her ear.

"And listen ... when I want a Native woman, I get her. When I want a white woman, I get her. Remember the pigeon. You'll want me. The pigeon, loose, comes back. I shall understand."

He then laughed, as if sharing with her the humor of some vile joke as Ellen shrank back, her face flushing with outraged helplessness and shame. She wrenched her hand free.

"All aboard! All aboard for Kon Klayu!" The cheery voice of her husband rang out. She turned from the White Chief and ran.

The Natives came forward in a crowd. Jean free stepping, wind-ruffled, met her halfway, and seizing her hand, the two hurried down to the whaleboat. Friendly Native hands shoved the boat off amid shouts of good will and goodbye.

The rattle of the anchor chain sounded as they boarded the *Hoonah* and made the towline of the whaleboat fast to the stern. The sails were hoisted and a moment later the little craft listed slightly as she caught the breeze. The entire population of Katleean waving farewell followed along the beach past the Native village and down to the Point.

"Goodbye! Good luck!" shouted the few white men on the shore. *"Tay-a-wah-cu-sha! Tay-a-wah-cu-sha!"* echoed the plaintive Native voices.

The Borelands waved back from the top of the cabin as the *Hoonah* rounded the wooded point that shut out even the smoke from the trading post.

Seagulls, white as the bellying sails, tilted against the wind in the sunshine. A wedge of wild geese honked high on their way to southern lands. Countless puffins, which some call sea parrots, scattered away from the schooner's path, dragging their fat, black bodies in splashing clumsiness across the water. The wind freshened and the rigging strained and creaked as the *Hoonah* swung to the long, wrinkled swells of the open sea. Driven ahead by the breeze she dipped and splashed sending showers of whitened water away from her prow and leaving a wake of foam laces behind her like a veil.

Already the adventurers had left behind the creatures of their kind, for Silvertip at the wheel was headed out into the lonely North Pacific, laying his course for the island of Kon Klayu.

PART II

11

THE ISLAND OF THE RUBY SANDS

Next morning the schooner was rolling easily on a long swell. Through the open hatchway the sun streamed down into the hold where Harlan lay, and as he awoke, the appetizing fragrance of boiling coffee drifted in to him from the cabin in the stern. Above the calls and the sound of feet on deck came a thin wild chorus that he had learned to associate with the island nesting grounds of thousands of seabirds.

Hastily slipping into his clothes, he climbed to the deck and looked about him. The *Hoonah* was riding at anchor ninety miles out at sea.

The morning air of sea-swept spaces filled his lungs with freshness. On three sides the sun-silvered green of the ocean fairly sang to the eye as it rolled away to meet the far blue of the horizon. Half a mile off the starboard bow, edged by lines of breaking surf, sand dunes topped with green merged gradually southward, into strange jade-green hills, low and soft as brushed velvet in the distance. To the North, the dunes tapered to a long, narrow shoal over which, as far as the eye could reach, swells of clearest emerald broke into a splendor of flying spray.

Above this sand spit thousands of gulls flashed, skirting and screeching in the sunlight, their weird, thin calls mingling with the diapason of the surf that boomed against the beach and the hundred reefs of Kon Klayu. Overhead a constant stream of gulls and sea parrots plied between their fishing grounds and the south end of the island where they had their young.

"By Jove, it's a regular little island paradise!" Harlan called to Kayak Bill. "How comes it that everyone is afraid of such an inviting looking spot?"

Kayak, who was picking his way forward to where Boreland was already busy with the outfit, paused and leaned a moment against the main mast. His eyes with one slow glance took in land and sea.

"Wall, son, I reckon she's somethin' like a pussycat. She's a-smilin' and a-purrin' in the sun today, but I'm thinkin' when it blows up a sou'easter, with nothin' in God's world a-tween here and Honolulu to stop the sweep o' it, she shows every one o' her reefs like a cat barrio' her claws."

Kayak Bill looked about him once more before striking a match to light his pipe. Then drawling something about the "ox-wee-nee-chal" gales, he passed on to the bow of the schooner, leaving Harlan smiling.

Silvertip and his mate were kneeling in the stern, both busy with the pulley blocks that held the steering cable of the *Hoonah*. Their low tones did not carry beyond a few feet. Silvertip slanted uneasy glances in the direction of the foaming shoals that ran far out into the sea. His helper, evidently disagreeing with him on some point, shook his head. Harlan caught something about fog and getting off the course in the night.

At last the man burst out.

"By yingo, I tank we are on wrong side of ..."

"Shut up, you tam square head," snapped Silvertip, with a glance in Harlan's direction.

The man made a gesture as if he washed his hands of the whole affair, and then raised his head to look about him. A dark streak far toward the southern horizon indicated a breeze from that direction.

"I guess we haf a beam wind home," he announced.

"Yas, tank God," assented Silvertip, with a last look at the rudder cable. "Ant as kwicker ve leaf dis de'th trap, as better for me. She blow up gale har in turty minutes. Ven Ay vas cook on *Soofie Suderlant* ..."

"Breakfast is ready, men!" interrupted Ellen's clear voice from the cabin hatchway.

The Swedes came to their feet, and after a moment of whispered conversation, joined the others in the cabin.

Half an hour later, when Boreland and Silvertip came on deck again, the breeze had freshened slightly and the sailor looked about him in a restless and worried manner. His glance finally lingered on the sand spit.

"Borelant, Ay tank ve lant you har right avay kwick. Ay tank she blow by an' by like hal."

Shane, glancing at the clear sky and the sun-kissed waves, laughed.

"Nonsense, Silver! The island's got you buffaloed, just as it has all the sailors in this section. But it's up to you. I'm ready to go ashore any time you say. The sooner you land me and show me our cabin, the better I'll like it."

The whaleboat at the stern of the schooner was drawn alongside, and another that had been carried on the forward deck was lowered.

The first one loaded, Kayak Bill and the two Swedes climbed down into it and shoved off from the side. Boreland and Harlan, loading the second one, stopped in their work to watch them.

Tossing up and down on the long, green swells, the moving boat drew nearer and nearer to the foaming lines of surf. Presently they were in the welter of white. Once when the little craft went completely out of sight behind a monster swell, Loll, watching from the cabin top, shouted in alarm, but yelled again in delight as it rose high on the same billow.

Silvertip and his mate bent to the long oars. In the stern Kayak Bill, hatless and wind-blown, steered wisely over the rollers that threatened to break on them any moment.

In profane admiration, Boreland watched. "It's the ninth wave," he shouted. "Kayak'll take her in on that one. ... By thunder!" he broke out as the boat rushed toward the shore in a smother of foam, and landed well up on the beach. "If that old cuss could rope a steer as well as he can land a boat in a surf, I wonder that they ever let him out of Texas!"

The work of landing the outfit went steadily on, and with each trip to the beach Silvertip urged more haste. Tides, currents, quick-rising fogs and gales, and the extreme danger of the anchorage were the burden of his conversation. Since he was the only one in the party who had been on Kon Klayu before, they were obliged to accept his reasons without argument.

Despite haste, however, it was late afternoon when the last boatload went ashore. Turning from his contemplation of it, Gregg Harlan looked down ruefully at the water blisters that decorated the palms of his slim hands. He was spending the most arduous day of his life. He was tired. Every muscle in his body ached from the heavy work of handling the outfit, and in his mind was weariness slightly tinged with bitterness.

It was not until he saw Ellen and Jean in the departing whaleboat that he realized how much he had counted on the few hours of their companionship aboard the *Hoonah*. With Loll he was on friendly, almost brotherly terms, because of his sincere appreciation of Kobuk and the boy's new pigeon. But as for anything else – he smiled now a little bitterly as he recalled Ellen's polite but wary treatment of him, and the seemingly casual way in which she managed to prevent any interchange of thought between himself and her young sister. He fancied Jean felt this also and resented it, for several times during the day, across the confusion of the deck, her eyes had sought his and in the meeting there was a warming sense of intimacy.

But she was gone now. He would never see her again. He had handed down her violin as she reached up from the tossing whaleboat to receive it. He remembered her firm, boyish handclasp as she said goodbye to him. Was there regret in her eyes at the separation, or had he imagined it?

Gregg leaned wearily against the cabin looking toward the shore. Everything seemed to have gone wrong for him today. He had intended going in with the last load for an hour's stay on the island, but Silvertip, fearing that the wind might grow stronger, had insisted on his remaining behind to watch the schooner.

Through the glasses he could see Loll and Kobuk racing up and down the beach now.

Jean and her sister sat, somewhat forlornly he thought, on part of the outfit piled up on the sand. The men had gathered about the whaleboat, which was to be left on the island, and were drawing it up higher on the shingle.

It would be an hour or more before the Swedes returned to the *Hoonah*. Harlan looked out across the rolling, endless ocean. Although the sun was yet shining brightly, there was a feeling of evening coming on. The cries of the gulls seemed to have taken on a tone of infinite sadness. All at once, for some inexplicable reason, he was overwhelmed by a sense of the futility of life – of living. No quest seemed worth pursuing. No dream worth dreaming. He had often felt this way during the past three months, and when he did, he drank. He longed, with sudden intensity, for a bottle of Kayak's clear, white brew. Alcohol was the magic brush that transformed the monotone of life into shades of wondrous hue.

His dejection was deepened by the fact that ever since leaving Katleean he had been trying vainly to recall that thing he should remember. While he strained and sweated over the loading of the outfit, his mind had been busy seeking, searching and trying to pierce the curtain of oblivion that separated him from that subliminal self who knew the thing he wanted. He felt as though he were being tantalized. It was almost the same feeling he remembered having in boyish dreams that came during examination time, when the answers to dream questions flashed in his mind for a moment then diabolically faded before he got them down on paper.

After a while his unseeing eyes left the water. He gingerly felt the blisters on his hands and shook his head with a half-contemptuous, half-humorous smile at himself. Then restlessly he began to pace the deck. If only he had something stinging – something stimulating to drink! But the White Chief had seen to it that there was nothing intoxicating aboard the *Hoonah*. It would be eighteen hours at least before he could hope to be in Katleean where Kayak Bill had left a generous supply of hootch stowed away in the top bunk of his cabin. In the top bunk. …

He stopped short. From some remote corner of his brain there had come to him one of those inexplicable flashes of memory that revealed, unbidden, the thing he had struggled so hard to remember. In a moment, he was back in Silvertip's top bunk the night of the potlatch dance. The voice of the White Chief came back arguing, commanding, threatening. The whine of Silvertip protested, and finally assented. As a realization of what this conversation portended dawned on him, his blistered hands clenched. Curs! Cowards! To lend themselves to such a work of deception! The aroused young man tossed back his wind-ruffled hair and squared his shoulders. He must reach Boreland immediately. He must tell him what he knew before the Swedes left the beach of Kon Klayu.

He sprang to the starboard side of the schooner and trained the glasses on the shore. The men were gathered about the whaleboat talking. He could see Silvertip's hand emphasizing some statement as he pointed to the hills. Harlan knew that once the Swede left the beach, he would never return to it. He had landed his party and his work was done.

Desperately Harlan longed for some kind of craft in which he might reach the shore before the sailors left it. There was none. For a moment he considered waiting until they came aboard. But could he, single handed, force them to return for the Borelands? No, the outcome of such a course was too uncertain. Something must be done at once.

There was only one other way in which he could get word to the adventurers. His eye measured the heaving, foam-streaked distance between him and the beach. Could he make it? A year ago in the States, before drink had gotten such a hold on him, that half mile would have meant nothing to him – but now … temperature, unknown currents, undertows must be reckoned with here. Again returned the intolerable craving for a drink, shaking him with its intensity.

His eyes once more swept the long line of breakers. If he was to warn the Borelands, he must do it at once. He must make that half-mile before Silvertip left the beach. He would do it!

Even as he decided, he had torn open the front of his shirt. Swiftly he stripped to his underwear and the next instant had dived over the side of the schooner.

He came sputtering to the surface. Contrary to expectations, the water was much warmer than that at Katleean. With a feeling of relief, he struck out for the beach.

He had not gone thirty yards when he became aware that a strong current was carrying him toward the south end of the island. Desperately he put every ounce of his strength into his shoreward strokes. The buffeting of the running chop sea began to tire him. He was becoming winded. He was losing his sense of direction. After ten minutes he realized, with alarm, that he could never make a landing, near Boreland's outfit. Five minutes more and he knew he would be lucky if he made any landing at all. The current was sweeping him on toward the cliffs at the south end of Kon Klayu where black reefs bared their fangs in a welter of foam. Even in the smother of the chop he was aware of the increased roaring of the breakers.

He made one mighty, but ineffectual, effort to reach the shore. Then with a feeling of baffled despair, he turned his back on the breaking surf and began to fight his way, inch by inch, back to the safety of the *Hoonah*.

12

THE LANDING

The last sack and box had been carried up the beach to a place selected by Silvertip as being above the high-tide line.

"Well, old man, I think we'll take a stroll around and see where that cabin is located," said Boreland cheerfully. "It can't be far from the anchorage here."

"No, no. Youst a little vay. Youst a little vay," answered Silvertip, as he waved an indefinite hand across the dunes. "You'll find it so easy you don't need me. Ay tank she makes a big vind in the sout'vest, so Ay go before a heavy sea coomes."

They talked about the island anchorage for a few minutes. Boreland insisted that the breeze would die down at sunset, as is often the case during good weather, but Silvertip persisted in his determination to get away from the island at once.

Finally Shane turned to Kayak Bill with a somewhat contemptuous laugh.

"What do you say, Kayak? This fellow seems scared to death to stay here any longer. I reckon we can get along without him now, don't you?"

Kayak Bill spat meditatively at a knot of brown kelp.

"Wall, we *mout* be a-makin' a false play, but durn the critter anyway, Shane – he ain't got no more backbone than a wet string!

He's been in a hell of a stew ever since we got here about this storm a-brewing and it's beginnin' to roil me just havin' him pesticate around. Let him go."

During the conversation Silvertip's pale eyes had been shifting back and forth between Boreland and Kayak. If he resented Kayak's disparaging remarks, he made no sign. When the old man finished, he began moving swiftly toward the whaleboat where his mate was adjusting the oarlocks.

Five minutes after a last hurried discussion relating to the location of the shelter, he and his partner were making their way out over the breakers to the *Hoonah*.

Shane and Kayak started out at once to look for the cabin in which they intended to sleep that night. As they left, they called cheerily to the women standing on the beach, but Ellen hardly heard them.

As the distance between the shore and the moving whaleboat lengthened, she felt a growing depression, a sinking of the heart. She was filled with a vast loneliness. All about her and above her was illimitable distance – ocean spaces green and rolling; sky spaces far and wide and blue; spaces through which the winds of the world swept unhindered; spaces filled eternally with the sound of the sea. She was awed and silenced by the immensity, the impersonality of it all.

Jean, too, was silent and meditative. Ellen wondered if she were thinking of young Harlan. That problem at least was solved, she thought with relief. The girl came close and placed an arm about Ellen's waist as if for the comfort her physical presence might bring.

Together they looked on while the *Hoonah* got underway. Flying before the wind it grew smaller and smaller in the distance. The awe in Ellen's heart gradually gave place to an acute homesickness for the comfort of the little craft that would be her home no more. Time passed, and as she watched the topmast sail going down on the horizon she realized, as never before, that the fate of herself and her family was dependent solely on the White Chief of Katleean. His word was law, his power absolute. She was aghast at her blindness in permitting the shaping of such a situation. Blaming herself, she went over the events of the last two weeks step by step, perceiving too late what she would have done, what she should have said to dissuade her husband from this last mad venture.

She turned her eyes from the sea at last, resolving to shake off her depression. She must prepare to meet the future. Jean had left her some time before and was busy tucking her violin away more securely in its wrapping of silk. Lollie, kneeling before the cage in which his pigeon fluttered experimentally, was trying to force bunches of wild peas through the bars. Ellen went close to the cage and looked down at the bird.

There was something sinister in the gleam of the bright, beady eye it turned up at her. The words of the White Chief came back to her. *You'll want me ... The pigeon loose, comes back. I will understand ... You'll want me.* What had he meant by that? The pigeon – she looked down at it again, thoughtfully. That afternoon, in lowering the cage from the deck of the *Hoonah* into the whaleboat, the fastening had slipped and it had fallen into the sea, but Silvertip, by a quick movement, had grasped it before it sank. Suddenly Ellen found herself beset by two conflicting emotions – one moment she wished it had gone down into the depths, and the next she felt that she must let nothing happen to this last, this only connecting link with the mainland.

She was brought back to her surroundings by Jean's call, as the young girl hailed Shane and Kayak Bill, who were coming toward them through the tall rice grass.

The faces of both men wore looks of unusual seriousness and there was no answer to Jean's greeting until they stopped beside the piled-up outfit.

"Oh, Shane, you didn't find the cabin?" Even as she asked the question, Ellen knew the answer.

"No, dear. It doesn't seem to be at this end of the island at all. But ...," noting the dismayed faces of those about him, "we needn't worry about it. We'll put up the tents here for the night and make an early start in the morning."

Loll had left his pigeon and was listening, wide-eyed and serious.

"But what if there is no cabin, dad?" With childlike directness he voiced the question that was uppermost in the minds of every other member of the party on the treeless island of Kon Klayu. In the momentary silence that followed, a gust of wind stirred the rice grass into questioning sound as the coarse blades swayed together.

"Oh, I know!" the boy answered himself enthusiastically. "We'll find a cave, of course, and live in it like Robinson Crusoe."

"Right-o, boy!" Boreland assented with a cheerfulness that did not escape being forced. "But just now we'll get busy making camp for the night."

Two tents were pitched in the rice grass at the edge of the beach. On a foundation of stones was set the small rectangular sheet-iron stove that every gold trail in Alaska knows. Within the hour the shiny new pipe was carrying a gay plume of smoke, and with the cheery crackling of the flames, the spirits of everyone rose; for the adventurer may wander where he will, but when he builds a fire – whether it be of coconut husks on the rim of a South Sea atoll, or of driftwood on the beach of a northern sea – there comes a sense of home and comfort.

Boreland, unpacking what he called the "grub-box," volunteered to get supper for the hungry band while they went in search of more driftwood for the fire.

Leaving him busy with the frying pan, they headed northward toward the long sand spit that pointed like an accusing finger in the direction of the mainland ninety miles away. Above the high-tide line the sand dunes were as powdery blue with lupine as the April fields of California, and Loll's whooping investigation revealed patches of wild strawberries larger than those found at Katleean, where acres of them grow on the low sand hills along the sea.

Jean and Lollie lay flat on their stomachs filling their mouths and grass-lined hats. The bouquet of sun-warmed strawberries and the perfume of flowering lupine were wafted across the dunes in intermittent gusts of fragrance. Ellen almost forgot her anxiety as she picked the red-toned fruit and listened to the drawling voice of Kayak Bill describing a cordial he had once made from the berries – a liqueur so subtle in its effects, so delicious and so warming that it had melted even the heart of a revenue officer sent up from Sitka especially to investigate him.

Later when they returned to the tents with lupine-laden arms and hats full of berries, there was in the air the good camp smell of frying bacon, warmed over brown beans and bubbling coffee. Boreland, apparently in the best of spirits, was setting out the dishes on a clean piece of canvas spread on the sand.

"Get a move on, gang!" he called. "Come and get it – my stomach's fairly cleaving to my backbone!"

As the adventurers ate, the sun, going down on the other side of the island, tinted the sky with shades of wild rose and forget-me-not. A cluster of tiny golden clouds floated high in the blue. As the trembling pearl of twilight came on, an occasional belated gull flew overhead with a single, gently sad question. The wind died away and the song of the surf mellowed to a croon.

After the dishes were done, Ellen and Jean put Lollie to bed in the blankets spread in the larger tent while Boreland and Kayak Bill, smoking and discussing the possibilities of the sands of Kon Klayu, squatted about the driftwood fire. Presently Jean left her sister and stepped out into the gloaming. She turned toward the south and walked along the edge of the sea drift. The smooth hard beach was a lure to her feet.

She lifted her chin, breathing deeply and swinging her arms free as she walked. The air was faintly cool with the smell of the sea and with it mingled the multi-scented breath of northern Indian summer: lupine, sun-dried sand, beach grass and celery bloom. Soft and dim and strangely lovely dreamed this island of the ruby sands. From a shadowy alders grove inland came the three plaintive notes of a sleepy golden-crown sparrow voicing the beauty, the mystery, the gentleness of the North. Enchantment broods in the twilight of Alaska nights. Jean had felt it many times during the summer, and loved it – the vague, wild sense of romance in its dusks. Tonight the thrill and promise of life seemed more poignantly sweet than ever before. She longed suddenly for someone to share this hour with her.

At last she reluctantly turned from the dim beckoning distance and retraced her steps.

As she neared camp, Kobuk, yawning, rose from his post by Ellen's tent, to greet her. Boreland and Kayak Bill had gone to bed in the smaller tent, and about the greying embers of their bonfire, rubber boots stood, like grotesque plants, each one drying upside down over a stake driven into the sand.

Jean undressed and slipped between the blankets beside her sister. The clean, fresh smell of trampled rice grass drifted about her pillow. The murmur of surf on the distant shoals was soothing as a cradle song as the tide came in, and the girl, with a tired sigh, adjusted her body to the unyielding, sandy bed, and drowsed off into slumber, unaware of the peril that was even then creeping nearer and nearer to the sleepers on the beach of Kon Klayu.

Courtesy University Alaska Fairbanks

Natives, trappers and prospectors extensively used sheet-iron stoves, called Yukon stoves, like the one shown here at a fishing camp in Alaska in the early 1900s.

13

THE CABIN

It was long past midnight when Jean was startled into wakefulness. Kobuk was barking with the queer, short woofs of the husky, and outside the tent Ellen's voice, fraught with fear and anxiety, was calling.

"Shane, Shane! Wake up! Quick!"

There was a stealthy sound as of lapping water close at hand. Then Boreland shouted.

"For God's sake, Kayak, get up!"

Jean, now fully awake, ran out into the grey that precedes the dawn. There was not a breath of wind, and the sea, glassy and as grey as the sky above, was smoother than she ever saw it afterward on Kon Klayu. There was something sinister in the gently heaving stillness of the vast body of water, for not ten feet from the flap of the tent tiny ripples of the incoming tide were swallowing at the dry sand with sibilant softness. One end of the pile of provisions just below the tent was already a foot deep in the advancing flood.

There was no thought of dressing. The race with the sea began at once. No one knew when the tide would be full, but each realized that should the provisions be ruined or swept away by the water, slow starvation would terminate the quest for the gold of Kon Klayu. Every moment counted. Every hand must help.

Grim faced and silent, Boreland and Kayak Bill drew on their tremendous reserve power, and during the next few hours performed almost super-human feats of strength and endurance in transferring the provisions to safety. Ellen and Jean, regardless of unbound hair and thin night robes, dashed out time after time into the ever rising tide to snatch up sacks of flour or boxes of canned goods, running with them far above the beach line. In the face of the threatened catastrophe they were hardly aware of wet or cold or the weight of objects. They were small women, but in the peril of the moment they carried backbreaking loads that would ordinarily have taxed the muscles of a strong man.

Even Lollie, after the first look of sleepy wonder, became alive to the situation when he saw his new pet, the pigeon, clutching the top of its cage above six inches of water. He rescued the bird, and while the others were busy with the outfit, rolled up the blankets one by one and carried them beyond danger. Before he had finished, the relentless tide had crept up about the stove, the box where all the cooking utensils had been placed, and the four rubber boots drying on their stakes. The little fellow, looking absurdly baby like in his nightgown, for all his eight years, splashed out to rescue the threatened articles. Later, at a word from his father, he gathered some high-thrown driftwood to make the fire, by that time sorely needed by all.

The sun was coming up radiantly over the edge of the ocean when they finished their labors. Though nothing had been carried away, the tide had risen two feet after discovery and got a third of the provisions wet. Silvertip, in his haste to get away from the island, had landed them on the tidelands. They later learned that only one or two tides a month reached that particular level, and the Borelands had encountered one of them. Had there been any sea whatsoever that night, everything would have been swept away, leaving them destitute, even if they had escaped with their lives.

The sun and a good, hot breakfast warmed and cheered everybody. Besides there was little time to discuss their escape, since every wet luggage bag and box had to be unpacked and the contents spread out in the sun to dry.

In making her round of the salvage, Jean came upon the box containing the old magazines and books from the collection of Add-'em-up Sam. It had been wetted on one end. She took off the top layer of books and then paused over the tattered volume of *Treasure Island* to put into place a crumpled paper that protruded from beneath the cover. She saw it was the crude drawing of Kon Klayu that she had hastily thrust back into the book that afternoon at Katleean when the quill-filled Kobuk had come cowering to her feet in the store.

"Shane," she called, waving it in front of her, "here's a little map of Kon Klayu. Maybe you might find out about the cabin from this."

Boreland strode over to her and glanced at the paper. Then he took it in his own hands and scanned it more closely. He then began looking up at the landscape, the sea, and the shoals off which they were camped. Suddenly his hand fell to his side, and with a great oath he began to pace up and down the sand.

The others, dismayed, gathered about him.

"Why, Shane! What is the matter?" cried Ellen.

"Matter?" Anger flared in his brown eyes and his hand closed on the map as if it had been the throat of an enemy. "Ellen, Silvertip lied! That pale-eyed son of a sea cook has landed us on the wrong side of the island. He was too much of a coward to take the *Hoonah* around the shoals. Look at this, Kayak." He smoothed out the paper so that his partner could see the lines." According to this, the cabin is all of three miles from here on the other side."

Kayak Bill took the map in his hands and held it for a long moment before his near-sighted eyes.

"By ... hell!" The words came slowly in a sort of whispered shout.

Then, as if unable to declare himself in the presence of the women, Kayak, with a suspicion of haste in his going, sauntered off to the far side of a sand dune. There he sat down, and in the manner of the true Alaskan, drew heavily on his stock of profanity to express his opinion of all Swedes, Silvertip in particular, the country, and the blind providence that could create an island without a harbor.

The situation forced upon the party was a serious one. It involved transferring the entire outfit three miles to the cabin – if indeed there was one – over the soft beach sand that made their only means of transportation, a wheelbarrow, utterly useless. There were but a few days during the year when a small boat, such as the whaleboat, could safely circumnavigate the shoals at the north end and the reef-sown waters about the island. Since this means could not be relied upon, the two men were confronted with the necessity of packing on their backs to the cabin every pound of provisions. And with the equinoctial storms close at hand, every day counted.

Boreland bit his lip in an effort to control the anger that burned within him. He realized that a month or six weeks must be spent in transferring the provisions. He also knew there was no time to lose in cursing the absent Silvertip. Immediate action counted and he was never one to let misfortune weigh long upon him.

Noting the worried look on Ellen's face, he crossed over to where she sat upon the opened box of books and put his arms about her.

"Never mind, little fellow. We'll come out all right. The darkest hour always comes before the dawn," he said, laying his rough cheek against her hair.

Despite her anxiety, a smile stirred the corner of Ellen's mouth as she heard this familiar bit of sentimental philosophy. During the ten years of her married life, Shane always had been ready with these words, no matter what crushing calamity came upon them. She patted his hand as she would have patted that of a child.

Loll, with his fingers under Kobuk's collar, had been looking on, his little face unconsciously assuming the seriousness of those about him. He turned now to greet Kayak Bill, who, apparently calmed and refreshed, was wading out of the rice grass. The old man's sombrero was cocked at a militant angle, his long rawhide laces snaked along behind his boots and clouds of tobacco smoke enveloped him.

"Well," he said gently, "I reckon there ain't no useless good vocabulatin' about that varmint, Silvertip. I should a-known better'n to trust a man o' his moth eaten morals, anyhow."

Ellen stooped down to pick up the map, which had fallen unheeded to the sand. For a moment she traced the beach line with her forefinger, reading the penciled names from the paper. "Sunset

Point … Skeleton Rib … Well, at least we know where to look for the cabin, Shane." She looked up decisively. "Let's find it before anything else happens to us."

Ten minutes later, the two men had disappeared behind the western sand dunes, and as if to assure them of his confidence in the future, Boreland's voice raised as a quavering Irish melody floated back to the camp where Ellen and Jean were spreading the blankets upon the sand. They were weary from their night's work.

With Kobuk on guard, they curled up beside Lollie. Lulled by the faraway calls of the gulls and the ceaseless chant of the sea, they soon were fast asleep.

The "hoo-hooing" of Boreland and Kayak Bill two hours later awakened the sleepers before the men reached camp.

"Everything is lovely and the goose hangs high!" Boreland cheerfully told them. "We found the cabin all right, and tonight we all sleep in our own little nest!"

The pale-green combers that were breaking for miles out on the shoals, made it impossible to think of using the whaleboat. Therefore, immediately after lunch, the party started on the three-mile walk, each one carrying a pack. Jean, with her violin and a scarlet blanket strapped across her strong young shoulders, stopped in the trail again and again to laugh at her smaller sister, nearly obliterated under two feather pillows.

Loll, important as the head packer of a government party, carried a pot of cold beans in his hand, and encouraged Kobuk, whose packsaddle was filled with necessary odds and ends for the night's camp. The sheet-iron stove, with food and cooking utensils inside, made a noisy, rattling pack on Boreland's back, leaving his hands free for his shotgun, which he carried for the ducks that were flying south. Kayak Bill shouldered a roll of blankets with an ease that many a younger man might have envied. He was balancing the broom across his palm when his eye fell on the pigeon. He picked up the cage with his free hand.

"Beats all get-out what women will get a man into."

A quizzical smile crinkled the corners of his eyes as he "hefted" his burdens. "Here's an old sourdough like me hittin' the trail with a broom in one fist and – by he-hen – a dicky bird in the other!" Occasionally it appeared to dawn on Kayak that his expletives were not exactly suited to the ears of women and children, and he seemed to be doing his best to modify them.

Boreland, whistling, led the way. Despite the discouraging events of the night and morning it was a cheerful little party that started out for the cabin. It is only in civilization that trouble and calamity eat into the heart. The wonder of the wilderness lies in that sense of adventure just ahead, which brings forgetfulness of the hardships left behind.

Shane and Kayak tramped down a trail across the sand dunes, through patches of purple wild peas and tall rice grass, whose silver-green heads nodded heavily against the travelers as they passed. Wind, spiced with seaweed and flowers, blew across their faces. They came out on the west side of Kon Klayu in a field of blossoming lupine that sloped gently downward to the sands, and beyond, the sea dashed in foam shot emerald against a ragged reef.

Loll's flower-loving soul looked out of his eyes an instant; then with a shout he abandoned Kobuk and the bean pot for the moment. Scattering the red-vested bumblebees, which were avidly working for honey in the lupine flowers, he began gathering a bouquet for his mother.

The warm August sun coaxed tiny whiffs of vapor from the long grey beach that curved southward toward a distant bluff. Sky and water met far out on the rim of the world.

Scampering ahead along the wave-washed margin, Loll excited Kobuk to laughter-provoking antics, as the dog, trying to play with him, swung along with his ungainly pack. The boy made frequent dashes up to the high-tide line, where Indian celery lifted creamy, umbrella-like blooms. From the beach line the vivid green of the tundra, patterned with daisies, stretched away to meet the alder bushes growing thickly where the land gradually rose toward the center of the island. A small lake here and there reflected the sky.

It was in one of these lakes close to the beach that a flock of mallards alighted, passing so near that the travelers could see the iridescent green of the drakes' heads catching the sun. Boreland slipped off his pack, and creeping toward the lake, soon disappeared in the Indian celery.

There was a moment of breathless waiting. Then a loud report and a scattering and whirring as the flock flew away toward the hill. Boreland, wet to the knees but grinning, appeared holding aloft three birds.

The tide had been coming in for some time, assaulting the shore with ever nearing combers. As the party neared the bluff around which they must pass, the wash of extra large breakers licked the base and in the wake of each receding wave the wet sand mirrored the steep, rocky wall above it. At such times it was necessary to wait until a wave had run out before they could hurry to a place of safety farther on.

"I ain't no nature for this place a-tall," said Kayak Bill, when they had safely dashed over two hundred feet of this sort of going. "There'd be hell apoppin' if a fella'd get caught there in a high tide."

"The cabin lies just beyond," Boreland announced.

The bluff sloped down to a tall bank topped with green, having a beach below it.

Following the sands for a short distance, they turned into what had once been a trail. The party halted, looking upward to the place that was to be their home.

A mere thread of a footpath, almost blotted out by tall grasses, led gently up the slope for sixty yards to where, above a natural hedge of celery blooms, a little cabin of weather-beaten drift logs cuddled at the foot of a steep, green hill. A porch jutted out in front, spindling uprights supporting the slanting roof. To the right, farther down and half hidden in the grass, lay the remains of a board shack that had fallen in.

There was a sound of trickling water in some hidden place. The sun fell warmly in this sheltered nook, bringing out the scent of green things; and over all was that melancholy stillness that envelopes human dwellings long deserted.

The boom of breakers far out on the reefs was hushed to a soothing hum, and faintly, from the reedy little lake farther down on the southward slope came the quacking of wild ducks. To the north and south and west lay the open sea, and as far as the eye could reach was no sight of land.

Jean broke her wide-eyed silence with a whisper.

"It's under a spell, Ellen, sure as you live."

She then found her voice and continued: "Look at that quaint old latch on the door – made of a piece of driftwood. And see the … Oh! Shane!"

Incredulity and fear shrilled in her voice.

"Shane! Why, it's moving!" She grasped her brother-in-law's arm as she pointed to the door of the cabin.

It was true. The door was opening slowly, jerkily, in a way that hinted of fearsome, unknown things. The next instant there stepped out of the opening a tall, shock-haired young man, naked, except for some tatters of an undershirt and a piece of old canvas wound about his hips after the fashion of a South Sea pareu.

Courtesy University Alaska Fairbanks

Many cabins, like the one in this story and in this photograph, often were hastily constructed and not built for comfort but to shelter adventurers from Alaska's harsh climate.

14

THE CASTAWAY

"By the roarin' Jasus," said Kayak Bill, the first to find his voice, which trembled with enormous astonishment. "If it ain't young Harlan!"

"My God, Gregg, has anything happened to the schooner?" shouted Boreland, his long stride covering the distance to the porch.

"Not a thing that I know of, Skipper." The young man, with a weary gesture, brushed the hair back from his forehead upon which blood from a slight wound had dried. "But you see, I left her before she started back to Katleean."

In answer to the quick questioning in the five pairs of eyes raised to his, he stammered: "I ... I ... wanted to come ashore for a few minutes, and the current carried me onto the reefs at the south end, and I wandered in here a little while ago."

Bruises and deep scratches marred the whiteness of his slim body and bore evidence of a desperate struggle with the sea and rocks. He was the last person in the world that Ellen would have chosen to be thus romantically cast up on the shores of Kon Klayu with them, but woman is potentially a mother and even her heart was touched by his plight. For Harlan, trying – and failing – to appear nonchalant and at ease in his embarrassing situation was boyishly appealing.

"Why, Shane, then the poor fellow hasn't had a bite to eat since yesterday," she exclaimed practically, while preparing to divest herself of her pack. "Everybody get busy here and we'll get him some lunch. Shane, you and Kayak see what you can spare in the way of clothes, and in the meantime, Mr. Harlan," her conventionally polite tone as she turned to that young man caused Boreland and Kayak Bill to exchange an amused wink. "You may take this blanket that Jean has wrapped about her violin and put it around you."

A few minutes later, Kayak Bill filled the coffee pot from a small crystal spring that trickled from the hillside into a sunken, moss-grown barrel, and placed it over a bonfire Boreland had made. Ellen left the old man to prepare lunch for their unexpected guest, and followed Jean and Lollie into the cabin that was to be their home.

The close, musty odor of decay smote her unpleasantly as she crossed the threshold. The room had one tiny, cobwebbed window through which the north light filtered. In the center a rough, homemade table, with one leg slanting inward, supported some battered cooking utensils now green with a fungus-like mold and disagreeably reminiscent of hunters who had last camped in the place, no one knew how long ago. In the corner, where a stove had once stood, was a pile of damp soot and ashes, and the floor was littered with decaying woolen socks, old papers and rubber boots from which the tops had been cut to make a house shoe known to Alaskan miners as "stags." Here and there daylight showed between the uncovered log walls, and great cobwebs wavered in dusty festoons from the chinking of brown peat. An infirm ladder leaned against one side of the room evidently for the purpose of mounting to the loft indicated by the black opening that yawned in the ceiling.

Ellen had no inclination to follow her sister into the little room that opened off the right. She was appalled at the amount of work to be done before the musty squalor of the place could be banished and the cabin made really habitable. For a moment she even considered the possibility of living in the tents until the White Chief brought the winter provisions, by which time she hoped she might be able to persuade her husband to leave the island.

Boreland, coming into the room with the broom on his shoulder, interrupted her gloomy thoughts.

"Pretty snug little place, eh, El?" he said cheerfully, looking about him and lunging for the nearest cobweb with his broom. "The roof is good, and when we get another window here facing the sea, and fix her up a bit, we'll be cozy as bears in a cave."

He filled his pipe, still warm from the last smoke, and lighted it. Going to the opening leading to the next room, he called: "Clear out now, young ones. I'm going to start things going in here pretty pronto!"

Through the open cabin doorway Ellen could see Harlan sitting by the bonfire in a borrowed undershirt and the scarlet blanket. He seemed refreshed and strengthened by his lunch and was telling Kayak Bill of his failure to swim back to the *Hoonah,* and his subsequent landing on the south end of the island. Though all but exhausted by his battle with the waves, he had managed to dig himself into the dry, sun-warmed sand and had slept heavily for hours. When he awoke, the position of the sun told him that it must be morning. Then, after washing the blood and sand from his scratches, he had set out to find the camp of the Borelands.

Harlan did not give any reason for his apparently senseless determination to swim ashore at the last moment, nor was any expected. On the frontier it is actions, not the reasons for them, that are of moment. At the risk of appearing a fool, Harlan kept silent on the subject. If he told now what he had heard of Kon Klayu that night he had lain in the top bunk at Silvertip's, there would be nothing for the Borelands to work for, nothing to hope for, during the time that must elapse before the *Hoonah* returned with the winter stores. The truth now would only arouse bitter thoughts of revenge in the heart of Boreland, who must chafe inwardly at his helplessness. There was time enough for the truth when the schooner returned to Kon Klayu.

"Over there on the east side of the island, almost directly opposite to this point, I think, I found a sort of Eskimo hut made of whale ribs and peat and drift," Harlan was saying as Ellen came out of the cabin. "It isn't half bad, and with a little work, I can make it fit to live in."

The young man saw Ellen and came to his feet.

"I honestly don't know how to excuse myself for being here, Mrs. Boreland," he said. There was a hint of wistfulness in the deep dark eyes he bent upon her. "But ... I am here and dependent on your generosity until the schooner comes back. I'll try to be as little of a bother as I can. I was just telling Kayak about the hut I found on the other side of the island. I'll live there."

Ellen's mind had already been busy with the problem of housing her unwelcome guest. She had not been blind to the interested and welcoming look Jean had given the young man as she greeted him half an hour before. She was aware of the almost inevitable result of propinquity. She looked up now with relieved interest, and despite herself, with faintly quickening approval. By living on the other side of the island, Harlan would in part solve the problem. She could then see to it that he saw little of Jean. If it were not for her sister, she might find it in her to like him – though she could never approve of the good-looking young ne'er-do-well. Through Kayak Bill she had come to know part of the truth about the death of Naleenah, but like most good women, she could not bring herself fully to exonerate one who had been so compromised. Potentially, if not actually, Gregg Harlan was to her a cad, and most certainly he was a drunkard.

"Well, Lady, me and him's goin' down to the North end of the island for another load o' grub and camp gear," drawled Kayak Bill as he finished scouring out a burned place in the frying pan. "You can't tell a speck about how long this here weather's goin' to last and we want to get under cover soon as possible. Besida's ...," "the old man said as his eyes twinkled, "Gregg here looks too durned ladylike in this la-de-dah outfit." He pointed to the scarlet blanket. "What he needs is a pair o' pants. Pants, I claim, has a powerful civilizin' and upliftin' influence on the mind o' man. Take the heathen now. They don't wear none, and see what ..."

Kayak's threatened monologue was cut short by Boreland, who, having attacked the dirt and debris in the cabin appeared now and began to pile some of it on the fire.

After the old man and Harlan had gone, Boreland swept down the cobwebs and made the cabin ready for scrubbing. That sense of satisfaction and happiness that comes to those in the process of homemaking in the wilderness, found expression in his rollicking Irish melody.

The legless Yukon stove was set up after the fashion of the country – an old packing box, found at the cabin, being filled with gravel and the stove put on top of it. A few minutes later there was a crackling fire of driftwood and every pot and kettle brought from the camp that morning was full of heating water.

The floor of smooth boards was unbelievably dirty. The lack of soap at first caused Ellen to despair of ever getting it clean, but Loll, who had watched Senott at Katleean cleaning her house, solved the problem by pouring sand on it while Boreland scrubbed with the broom.

Two hours later, the clean bare floor was drying rapidly from the heat of the stove before which Ellen stood stirring a savory pot of duck mulligan for an early supper.

It was late afternoon when Kayak and Harlan returned with their loads. As they turned in from the beach to the little grass-grown trail, Kayak stood a moment looking up at the silver smoke floating against the green hill. Jean, more starry-eyed than usual, was singing as she arranged the dishes on a canvas spread upon the floor of the porch, and at her direction Lollie was painstakingly placing some wild flowers in a tin can for a centerpiece. The two looked up to wave a welcome to the packers as they approached.

"By hell," said Kayak with slow appreciation. "It beats all creation how quick women folks can make a home out o' nothin'."

After supper the men sat on the porch smoking and discussing ways of transferring the provisions from the north end of the island.

"If we ever get a day calm enough so that we can use the whaleboat, it won't take long to get the whole business down here," Boreland said. "But we can't depend on that. I don't think the sea will get smooth enough this fall for us to bring the boat around the north shoals. We'd better skid it across to this side of the island – it can't be over a quarter of a mile wide there – and pack the grub over, too. When a favorable day comes we can load her up and it's only a few miles down here. It's lucky for us, Gregg," he added, placing a hand on the young man's shoulder, "that we have another strong back to depend on."

Evening closed in as they talked. From the alders on the hillside came the plaintive night song of the golden-crown – the three notes of poignant beauty and mystery that were linked indissolubly with the summer twilights of Kon Klayu. Out over the reefs the sun had gone down splendidly into the sea. Broad ribbons of clear jade streaked the primrose of the sky. Beneath, bands of amethyst, amber and rose merged slowly into a flame of crimson, and while the violet dusk crept over the sea, the stars came out. Blowing across the bare brown reefs, the night wind brought the scent of kelp and the muffled boom of surf.

The peace and promise of the sunset soothed all into silence for a time. Ellen, Jean and Lollie, sitting close together on the bottom step of the porch, watched in reverent wonder as the colors changed. At last, the boy lifted his eyes to his mother's face.

"God smiles, Mother," he said simply, resting his tired head against her shoulder. Jean leaned across to her sister.

"Ellen," she said quietly. "I think I love best of all the evening time of things, don't you? The fall of the year, the end of the day … I wonder." A wistfulness crept into her voice. "I wonder … I hope … no, I *know* that when it comes, I'll find that the sunset time of life is the most beautiful!"

She turned instinctively to look at the old man on the porch above her as she finished speaking. He was the only one of them whose slowing feet had turned into the Sundown Trail. Kayak's hand, loosely holding his cooling pipe, rested on his knee. His sombrero backed his strong, bearded face, which had taken on the serenity of the evening. His deep eyes were calm with revery. As she gazed, the girl's heart was flooded with a pitying tenderness for him, for Kayak Bill – who, because of something buried deep in his past – faced the sunset of life alone.

She turned her face away and met the warm young eyes of Gregg Harlan bent upon her. Suddenly she was glowingly happy because she was still young.

15

THE GIANT BALLS OF STONE

It was not yet five o'clock the following morning when Loll, from his blankets on the floor of the cabin living room, raised his tousled head and looked cautiously about him. His big, grey eyes were alive with eagerness and expectation. The strangeness of his surroundings thrilled him with possibilities. Through the window the sun-flooded world called him to adventure.

Again he glanced speculatively at the sleeping forms round him and then eased warily out of bed. With a pudgy finger on his lips, and with long steps of stealth so exaggerated that his balance was threatened at every move, he tiptoed to the corner where his shoes lay. Then without stopping for any further addition to his toilet, Lollie slipped out the door in his nightgown.

He avoided the blanket-cocooned figures of Kayak Bill and Harlan on the porch and continued a short distance down the path to the chopping block, where he sat down to pull the shoes on his little bare feet.

Kobuk, returning from some early morning adventure on the beach, espied him, and with a red-mouthed husky smile, came bounding up the trail, wriggling an extravagant and clumsy welcome. With loud whispers hissed through fiercely protruding lips, Loll tried to shoo him away, but the dog only whirled about, thumping him with a joyously wagging tail and poking a cold damp nose down the neck of his nightgown.

After fastening the top button of his shoes, the boy stood up and looked about him. The wonderful sunniness of the world thrilled him. Soaring gulls called to one another from the blue sky, and the sunlight poured down on the silver-green ocean and the little lake to the south. Faint breaths of air stirred the scent of green things, and everywhere was that exhilarating freshness of late summer that has in it the hint of autumn frosts.

The youngster waved his arms and danced from sheer joy in living, and with Kobuk at his heels, ran down off the trail through the damp grass toward the lake.

About a hundred yards from the cabin, hidden in a clump of alder bushes, he came upon a low hut built of drift logs. Half the roof was gone and pieces of decaying seal hide and a ragged red shawl embedded in the dirt floor hinted of the visits of long-ago Native otter hunters.

Interested in his discovery, the little fellow was peering cautiously in, when, with a sudden bound, Kobuk dashed by him nearly knocking him over. There was a whirr of wings overhead, sounds of bird alarm, and half a dozen swallows circled wildly about the frantic Kobuk before finding a place of escape through the hole in the roof.

"Gosh, Kobuk, I was pretty near scared," admitted the youthful explorer, looking up at the rafters under which several nests made clay-grey splotches.

Swallowing hard a time or two he buttoned up the neck of his nightgown. Outside the hut again he slanted a discreet glance back in the direction of the cabin to assure himself that everyone still slept, and then with a whispered whoop of invitation to the dog, skipped down toward the beach.

The cabin stood well back on the bank off the center of a small crescent cove, flanked on the north by the bluff around which the party had come the day before. Toward the south the beach curved to what was marked "Sunset Point" on Add-'em-up's map. Loll tucked his nightgown up under his arm and headed for that unexplored territory, talking to Kobuk as he skipped along.

The tide was falling and screaming gulls rose and fell over the rocks as they fed on shellfish among the seaweed. Far out on the water great flocks of black sea parrots floated, and overhead these stocky little birds flew in hundreds, their huge, crimson beaks thrust determinedly out before them, their round, white-ringed eyes showing plainly, and their wings, seemingly too small for their pudgy bodies, beating the air in a hurried manner, as they attended strictly to the business of feeding their young. Unlike the lazy gulls, they took no time to loiter along the way.

The boy, looking up at the busy black workers, little dreamed of the vital and spectacular part both he and they were to play later in the struggle for existence on the island of Kon Klayu.

The weed-covered boulders of Sunset Point drew him, but though he felt strongly the fascination of the ocean bed now becoming uncovered by the tide, for some indefinable childish reason he hesitated to go down among the rocks in his nightgown. So, whistling an unidentifiable tune, he rounded the point, Kobuk trotting on ahead.

Here the character of the beach changed, and the high-tide line, where the rice grass began, was piled with a crisscross confusion of bleached drift logs thrown up by the mighty surf of storms. Mounds of old kelp lay drying in the sun, and the unforgettable odor of decaying sea things mingled with the freshness of the morning.

Absorbed in the delights of discovery, Lollie poked about in the tangled masses finding strange, beautiful shells and sea flowers fragile and delicately colored as the heart of a rose. He gathered his nightgown up into a pocket in front of him in which to carry home some of the damp and none-too-fresh treasures of the beach.

Sea figs in tan and orange and vermilion made splashes of color among the wet piles of shiny brown kelp brought up by the last tide, and small dead starfish turned pale stomachs to the sun. Grotesque, bulging seaweeds stirred him to laughter, and after untangling one – a head-like growth that seemed to grin sociably at him from a tail twenty feet long – he tied the thin end about his waist. The bulb wriggled along behind him on the sand, alternately piquing and repelling the curiosity of the sniffing Kobuk.

Another point ahead lured him on. Clouds of sand fleas rose in rustling hops as he ran along. Here and there monster jellyfish glistened in the sun. With a continual "Oh" of admiration and wonder, the little fellow squatted repeatedly to gaze at the exquisite geometrical designs in their crystal depths; but after one or two half-hearted attempts to pry them apart to see how they were made, he contented himself with adding one to his already overburdened nightgown. Even in the thrill of discovery, he had an instinctive antipathy against marring a beautiful thing.

Kobuk, running on ahead, had found something that interested him. He stood looking back, woofing impatiently as if urging the boy to hasten and see what it was. Loll came nearer. Then he shouted in astonishment, increasing his gait with difficulty because of the impeding pocket in front of him. What he saw was a head of some great sea monster, perhaps twelve feet long. The dark skin was streaked with dull red and purple, and where the head had been severed from the body, the sea had whitened it to sand-encrusted tatters. The huge mouth lay open and twisted, and from the lower jaw protruded two rounded tusks, nearly a foot long.

There was a contemplative moment while Loll's eyes opened wide.

"Golly, Kobuk," he said with reverent awe. "Bet-cha that's the whale that swallowed old Jonah!"

There was a singular fascination about the battered remnant, far gone in decay. But the stench from it finally proved so overpowering that, despite his intense desire to linger near his discovery, Loll was obliged to move on.

He turned to the upper beach line for further explorations. Across a narrow strip of tundra-like land lay the small lake visible from the cabin porch. On the edge of the rice grass he stumbled against a boulder that was as remarkably round as if it had been shaped by human hands. He stopped in delight at the great stone ball and tried to move it with his one free hand. Farther on he saw more of the curious spheres. Some were two feet and more in diameter.

"Maybe giants played ball with 'em once," he whispered to himself, with a cautious glance about him.

He headed for the tundra and was startled by coming suddenly upon the skeleton of a whale whitening in the sand where an extra high tide had thrown the creature long ago. Purple wild peas and blue beach forget-me-nots blossomed between the monster ribs, and the huge vertebrae, scattered here and there, were half hidden by the grass. It was from this relic, no doubt, that the point opposite derived its name — Skeleton Rib.

Lollie's father later utilized several of these vertebrae for stools, but seeing them for the first time, the little fellow looked down at them respectfully, hushed into silence by vague, sea-born feelings. Far down the beach to the southward rose the cliffs where thousands of seabirds swarmed in the sunshine. Their screaming, softened by the distance, came to his ears with an eerie wildness. All at once he felt very small and alone among alien creatures. Kobuk had turned back without him and was bounding out of sight around Skeleton Rib. The giant balls of stone suddenly took on fearsome suggestions from the realms of fairy tales.

The dog had disappeared now. The plaint of a high flying gull drifted down to the boy. A breath of wind whispered in the grass about the whitening bones.

Suddenly he was flooded with a very panic of loneliness. Grasping the folds of the nightgown more tightly before him he set out as fast as his little bare legs would carry him toward home, the trailing kelp attached to his waist bounding wildly along behind him.

It was thus that Ellen, white-faced with anxiety, met her returning son as he rounded Sunset Point. She clasped him frantically to her to assure herself that he was indeed safe and sound, and then held him off at arm's length, surveying the havoc to his nightgown and preparing for the admonishing that was due. But Loll had already learned to divert many a mild scolding by the relation of some startling discovery. He launched forth now on the subject of the whale's head and the stone balls that giants must have played with, giving embellishments so amazing that his eyes stood out in growing astonishment as he talked.

Out-maneuvered, Ellen led him to breakfast where he took his

THE GIANT BALLS OF STONE

place still holding forth on the wonders of his adventures. Kayak Bill regarded him with an appreciative eye.

"Son, you sure do vocabulate most as well as a sourdough," he finally drawled, then paused to take a long, slow swoop of coffee and wipe his mouth with his red bandana. "The whale's head that et Jonah ain't so bad – but them giant hand balls o' stone sounds phoney ... you know there seems to be somethin' about this durned country that just nache'ly makes white men not lie exactly but sort o' put trimmin's on the truth. I recollect a couple o' yars back when I'm hibernatin' one winter up on the Kuskokwim River with a bunch o' white trappers and prospectors...."

Kayak paused long enough to scrape with a spoon the bottom of his empty coffee cup to get every unmelted grain of sugar that lay there.

"The next summer, I'm a son-of-a-gun, if them Injines up there ain't callin' that place by an Injine name that means 'The Valley o' Lies' ... I've sort o' got it figgered out like this ... this doggoned Alasky land, bein' so big and magnificent like, a man just feels plumb ashamed to tell of some little meachin' thing a-happenin' in it – he feels downright obliged to fix things up so's they'll match the mountains and the rest o' it."

And drawing his corncob from the pocket of his hair-seal waistcoat, Kayak Bill shuffled off into the cabin to light it from a splinter thrust into the round draft hole of the Yukon stove while Boreland and Harlan made ready to leave for the provision camp at the north end.

The weather continued clear for five days after their landing on the island, although the sea never became sufficiently smooth for a trip with the whaleboat. Each day the men of the party went down to the first camp to pack provisions across the island to what they called the west camp, the place from which they expected to load them into the whaleboat and take them by water to the cabin. When the entire outfit had been packed across, the whaleboat also was skidded over on small drift logs. By this means they avoided the long shoals that ran so far out into the sea.

"Now for a few days of smooth water," said Boreland, when the job was completed, "and we'll be able to take everything down to the cabin by boat. We must have this grub under cover before the autumn storms set in. The rougher the sea, the better chance for gold, so Silvertip – damn his cowardly hide – told me. Kilbuck said old Add-'em-up used to send his woman out patrolling the beach after each storm, and she usually found patches of black or ruby sand that carried considerable gold ... it seems reasonable enough, Kayak, for it's the same with all placer diggings along the sea."

The three men seated themselves on the upturned boat to eat their lunch. Boreland, whose mind was ever dwelling on the time when he should be free to begin his search for the gold of Kon Klayu, talked on. Harlan listened in silence to the other's eager plans.

"But of course it's the *source* of the gold we want. Silvertip thinks it is thrown up out of the sea by the action of the waves. Kilbuck imagines it is washed down from the banks, although all the prospecting done by the fox-farmers revealed nothing. But gold is where you find it, and I mean to leave no stone unturned while I'm here.

"Speaking of stones," he went on after a moment's silence. "Loll was right about his giant balls of stone. Have either of you noticed here and there along the beach, especially toward the south, small, perfectly round boulders? By thunder, they look exactly like cannon balls!"

Harlan, though he had at first attended the others' speeches, had gradually become immersed in his own thoughts. Each day, while his muscles ached and the desire for stinging liquor flamed like fire in his veins, he had worked with Boreland and Kayak Bill at the north end of the island packing provisions across on his back. Though he still ate his meals with the Borelands at the cabin, almost immediately after supper he took the mile and a half trail across the island to the hut, which he had found on his landing. Intuitively, he knew Ellen Boreland's opinion of him. He smiled sometimes at the grim humor of the situation. He, who had tried to get away from the society of women, found himself now on the mercy and generosity of a woman

THE GIANT BALLS OF STONE

who did not like him. He was dependent on her, by Jove, for every stitch of clothing on him, for even the soap that he used – for his very toothbrush. Soon, he knew, she would be giving him provisions so that he might cook his own meals on the other side of the island. She didn't want him around her, or her sister. It piqued him to be felt unwanted and aroused in him a desire to show her.

His innate honesty compelled him to admit that Ellen knew him in no hero's light. Still he could not help a feeling of bitterness at the relieved look that came, unconsciously, to her face each evening when he turned, reluctantly, from the homelike group on the cabin porch, to take the lonely little zigzag trail up the hillside.

His mind went back now to a scene of the evening before, when after supper just as he was preparing to leave, Jean had taken her violin from its case.

"I'm going to play, tonight, Mr. Harlan. Are you too tired to stay a while?" she asked, looking at him with friendly eyes.

Too quickly Ellen had interrupted.

"No, no, Jean. Don't keep this poor, tired fellow from his bed. I'm sure he wants to go to sleep as soon as possible. And here, Mr. Harlan," she said, as she advanced toward him and thrust a blanket and a pillow into his arms. "I found this extra bedding for your bunk today … there now, tuck it under your arm, like this. Goodnight – sleep well. *Goodnight.*"

Her voice was kind as she smiled up into his face, but there was no mistaking her meaning. With shame and resentment in his heart he had turned up the hillside trail.

On the brow of the hill he had stopped and flung the bedding angrily on the ground, himself upon it. Was he a criminal that he should be debarred from an hour's pleasure in the society of the only other human beings on this island? Suddenly he felt that he hated Ellen Boreland. He hated all women. He hated all the world. The longing for strong liquor swept him, shaking him like a leaf. He could feel his chin under his soft young beard quiver. He despised himself for being a weakling and a fool. He tightened the clasped hold of his arms about his knees and dropped his head upon them. The thought that had been tormenting him since the first day he began transferring the provisions, came back now with an added urge. At the west camp were flour, sugar, cornmeal and dried fruit.

With those ingredients he could make himself the stuff that his system craved – make it as the Natives made it, with two kerosene cans and a long piece of hollow kelp. In his hut on the other side of the island he could, undetected, heat the fermented mash in a can, attach the piece of kelp to the top and immerse it in cold water until the condensed steam came out at the other end in the form of Tlingit *hoochinoo*.

As he huddled there on the brow of the hill he cradled the thought in his mind, planning in detail each step of the distilling. With provisions so low it would be impossible to take enough from the cache to make any quantity – but he might make sufficient to ease, just once, the intolerable thirst that possessed him. It might be six weeks before the *Hoonah* returned … six weeks of torment and loneliness.

Another thing had been troubling him of late, too. His thoughts had been returning to stories he had heard of Add-'em-up Sam who had died of delirium tremens at Katleean. Silvertip, when in liquor, was fond of detailing the last, violent days of the old bookkeeper. Sometimes, Harlan fancied, he, too, was beginning to see those fearful shadowy images that dance on the borderland of insanity. How else could he account for that spectre of the tundra that he saw, sometimes, as he went home in the dusk – that dark, almost imperceptible figure far off toward the south cliffs where the lone tree of Kon Klayu stood on the brow of the hill? Was he, too, going the way of Add-'em-up Sam?

As he sat there, he cursed himself for ever leaving the *Hoonah* and risking his life to help a woman whose kind, polite aloofness irritated his drink-shattered nerves as an open declaration of hostility could not have done – a woman to whom he was merely a foolish young man who had chosen to get himself marooned, and whose presence forced her to calculate more closely the alarmingly depleted store of provisions left after the wetting of the tide.

Suddenly, in the midst of his bitter reverie, he raised his face from his clasped arms. Up from the cabin below floated the faint, pure harmony of violin strings. So exquisite, so lovely sounded the notes in the wide, wild loneliness of the evening that Harlan sat for a moment with suspended breath. Gradually, under the spell of the music, he became aware of the beauty of the world about him. The after-sunset sky was a vast expanse of tender rose and blue deepening into violet on the long encircling horizon line. Below lay the wine-dark sea fringing with pale foam the sands of Kon Klayu. The noise of breakers on distant reefs was like the wind in the eucalyptus trees of his California home.

A flood of homesickness dissolved the resentment in his heart, and gradually the old fears and haunting troubles faded from his lean young face. The low, vibrant tones of Jean's violin brought him comfort. The soft, rippling notes breathed in him confidence, and the silvery chords lured him into the promises of the future. He felt equal to noble and heroic deeds – to fighting and conquering. From a sense of being outcast and alone, he felt a sudden warming kinship with the world. With his heart expanding, he came to his feet to better catch the harmony.

The time and air had changed into something vaguely familiar. With a glow of pleasure he recognized it – the lament of the funeral canoes at Katleean, but with something else added, something that made him feel the mystery and the weirdness and the elemental call of the North. It was almost as if she played to him, comforting him with promises of this clean, new land of beginnings.

Abruptly, he remembered, the music had broken off. There was a moment's silence. And then there had drifted up to him Jean's invariable goodnight to the deepening twilight. Sweet and clear from a long-drawn singing bow it came – a commingling of love and peace and beauty he had once heard a great contralto sing:

"In the West
Sable night lulls the day on her breast.
Sweet, goodnight! ... "

He had longed to throw back his head and sing these words to Jean's music, but he had shaken himself. No. That was a song for a lover.

The young man again found himself musing about Jean and her violin music the next day.

"Son, are you plumb dead to the world?" Kayak Bill's words roused Harlan from his dreaming. He sprang up and began stacking provisions inside the tent. He realized as he worked, that today no tempting thought had come to him of secretly distilling hootch from stores he might take from this camp. The enormity of such an action struck him for the first time. This food meant life on Kon Klayu – and there was little of it.

A few hours later, as he headed down the long stretch of beach toward the cabin, he squared his shoulders under the heavy pack he bore and joined in with the voices of Kayak Bill and Boreland who, with lusty incongruity, were singing the whaling song of the trading post.

"Up into the Polar seas
Where ice is delivered free,
And a man don't have to hustle
Like a blooming honeybee!"

Work was hard in this country of the Last Frontier, but men had more time, more inclination to sing, he thought.

As he swung along the hard sand, in his heart was a sense of expectancy – for what he did not know.

16

THE STORM

The following morning was sunless. The air was still and heavy with foreboding. Leaden-colored waters heaved under a gloomy sky, and though the sea appeared smooth to the eye, the hollow roar of distant surf sounded louder than usual. There was a strong smell of kelp and salt brine, and a new, wild note in the cries of the gulls.

"I say," Boreland called to Kayak Bill, who was tying back the flap of the tent in which he slept. "It looks as if there's a storm brewing. But I never saw the sea smoother. I think, if we're quick about it, we can get a boatload of grub down here before she breaks. What you say, Kayak?"

Kayak spread his legs and leaned back to take a long look at the sky, just as Harlan came down over the hill and joined them.

"I'm yore man, Boreland," he said at last. "But we'd better be spry about it, for it'll be Davy Jones' locker for us if we get caught in a gale off the reefs."

A hasty breakfast over, Ellen joined the men and the four left for the west camp to select the most important things with which to load the whaleboat.

They worked swiftly once they reached their destination. Ellen made her selection of necessities while the men skidded the boat down to the water's edge. It was soon loaded. A small pile of lumber from Katleean for making sluice-boxes and furniture was made into a raft to be towed.

"About three more trips with the boat, and we'll have everything down at the cabin," said Ellen, as she tied the flap of the provisions tent. She had noted that while he worked, Shane had glanced uneasily from time to time at the grey sky. It was rapidly taking on a purple tinge, though the sea was still as oily smooth as it had been early in the morning.

When the last sack had been stowed away, and the raft made fast to the boat, Ellen saw Harlan call her husband aside. She heard him make some suggestion in a low voice, which Boreland dismissed with a gesture.

"Thanks, old man, but this is a job for all three of us," he said and then turned to join Ellen who was standing at the edge of the water. "We'll be home in time for supper, El," he said, with forced cheeriness. "Don't worry, now mind!" And he patted her hand reassuringly before he turned to the boat.

As she watched the craft slip away from the shore, she conquered a wild impulse to reach out and drag it back again. Shane and Harlan shoved on their oars with long, slow strokes, as they faced the reefs that lay between them and the open sea. Kayak Bill steered.

Ellen watched them move in and out between the protruding rocks. On the grey slope of the sullen swells that rose and fell unbroken about them the raft in tow shone wetly yellow. From time to time she caught glimpses of streaming tangles of kelp that somehow suggested the floating hair of dead women.

The boat crept offshore to get outside the most dangerous of the reefs, and once free, Boreland, small now in the distance, looked back to wave a hand at her. At last, having seen the craft swing and move slowly southward on the home stretch round the island, Ellen sighed with relief, and turning away from the sea, started down the beach toward the cabin.

Across the dark pall of the sky in the southwest clouds began to form in heaving somber masses. A breeze, coming at first in scarcely perceptible breaths, freshened almost in a moment, until the glassy surface of the sea was wrinkled and streaked far out with black. It was impossible to see the whaleboat now because of the barrier reefs. Ellen's heart grew heavy with foreboding. The wind – remembering the tales of quick-rising wind and sea, she prayed that these fitful puffs might not be the first breaths of a homing gale.

She found Jean and Loll on the beach below the cabin. They had felt the danger of the coming storm and were looking out anxiously for a first glimpse of the boat. Only rearing waters and lowering sky bounded their vision.

The wind increased.

Silence grew upon them.

The cloud banks in the southwest separated in the weird-shaped masses that detached themselves and began to travel swift and low toward them across the sky. Some menacing quality in this relentless, headlong rush increased Ellen's fears, and in growing alarm she watched the tiny whitecaps that were beginning to form on the waves.

As they hurried down to the point off the bluff to command a wider view of the waters, the wind whipped their skirts about them and tore at their hair.

Three grey gulls flew swiftly overhead with plaintive, long-drawn cries quite different from their usual raucous screams. In her anxiety, Ellen remembered that these wild birds of Kon Klayu had as many moods as the sea and were prophetic of them. Loll, holding tightly to his mother's hand, looked up at her with grave eyes.

"Mother," he said. "Senott told me one time that seagulls are the souls of little dead Indian babies and they always cry for their mothers before a storm. Hear them now?"

Immeasurably sad and longing, the birdcall struck through the sound of increasing surf. The whole sky was a mass of swiftly moving clouds. The wind increased steadily.

Another dragging hour went by with no sign of the whaleboat. With the incoming tide the wind had risen until Ellen's heart quaked with a great fear for the men who must row against it. Her senses tingled with the welter of torn, tempestuous sea and clouds that seemed to mingle and snatch at her with stinging, salt fingers. Her straining eyes smarted from the high flung spray of increasing combers.

Bracing against the gale, she suddenly found herself aching from the stress of trying, by sheer will, to keep back the force of the storm. Some pagan thing within her had endowed the elements with a godlike personality. She caught herself praying, beseeching the sea to rise no higher; to be kind to her loved ones tossing somewhere on its seething bosom. Both wind and tide were against the whaleboat now, and looking out across the rearing waters it seemed to her that no small craft could live in such a sea.

A few drops of rain stung her face. Far off from the southwest more was coming. She turned hopelessly from it – then almost at once her dull misery was changed to joy.

Half a mile out a blurred, dark thing rose for an instant on the crest of a billow. She started to point it out to Jean, but simultaneously the rain squall struck her, drenching, stinging, cutting off for a moment her view of the sea. From under the grey curtain of the driving rain, combers of muddy green raced in, spouting high in wind-torn fury against the rocks and rolling swiftly toward her to fling themselves roaring at her. Again in a lull she caught a glimpse of the boat tossing skyward ... dropping from sight ... rising again and creeping slowly, slowly onward.

Boreland and Harlan, hatless and coatless, were standing in the bottom of the boat shoving on the oars with every ounce of their strength. Twice she saw the younger man take the oars alone while her husband bailed. Kayak Bill, rigid, watchful, sat in the stern, his hand on the tiller, ready with the instinct that comes of long experience for every motion of the sea.

Inch by inch they battled their way around the point in the face of flying spray and driving rain. Behind them, like a live thing tugging on the rope, the raft rose and fell on the combs of the dark swells. Pathetic and tear compelling was the courage of these three men pitting their puny strength against the pitiless violence of the elements. Once the little boat seemed to stand still a long time, swashing up and down in the hollows of the waves, while over it the chop of the sea splashed in a spiteful fury. At last it advanced again slowly and Kayak swung broadside, turning in toward the beach on which the anxious woman stood.

A gust of wind caught viciously at the tarpaulin spread over provisions in the stern. It carried its fluttering blackness straight back into the white and green of a giant comber directly behind. The onrushing breaker reared its cruel head. Then just as another rain squall broke, hiding it from view, it curled down swift, terrifying, and the whaleboat disappeared in its foaming maw.

With a cry of despair, Ellen rushed to the very edge of the surf, straining her eyes over the wild sea. Had the force of the breaker swept everyone from the whaleboat? Had the canvas stretched tightly over the provisions been sufficient to keep the water from filling and swamping the boat? Would the violence of the tide and wind bring them in if … if Kayak Bill had not been torn from his post?

Suddenly she knew that on Kayak depended everything – Kayak Bill, who had once been a pilot at surf-bound Yakataga; Kayak Bill, who had run the raging bars of the delta-mouthed Copper River. Would he be equal to the surf of Kon Klayu? Could he keep his hold on the tiller? Oh, if the rain curtain would only lift! If she could but see out there in that foaming, roaring swelter of water.

She dashed a hand across her face, tearing aside the wet hair that flattened itself against her eyes. The squall was letting up. She could see now, but there was nothing, nothing but breakers. A sob tore itself from her throat. She started to turn away. Then dimly, she saw something.

Low in the water, veiled by flying whitecaps, they came – Boreland and Harlan bailing desperately, and in the stern Kayak Bill, his hand still on the tiller, keeping the oar-less boat steady atop the swift, rushing wave that was sweeping them on to the beach.

With outstretched, welcoming arms Ellen waded out into the foam of the spent breaker that grounded the whaleboat almost at her feet.

That evening the adventurers sat in the warmth of the crowded cabin living over again the events of the day. Every available corner was piled high with the wet provisions that had been unloaded from the whaleboat that afternoon, but contrasted with the gale outside the place was satisfyingly snug and comfortable. Still lingered in the savory aroma of the duck mulligan that had been their supper. In the Yukon stove the fire roared and crackled as if in defiance of the terrific blasts that shook the cabin. The sense of kinship that comes to those who have fought their way together through some great danger was strong upon them all tonight.

"Holy Mackinaw, boys!" Boreland emphasized his remarks with the stem of his pipe. "I wouldn't have given a hoot in Hades for our chances when that wave broke. Thought it was all day with us then. Kayak, Harlan, a fellow never realized what small potatoes he is until he looks up from the hollow of a wave." He stretched his long arms comfortably and laughed. "But ... after you've been up against a proposition like that, and come through, it certainly makes a man feel like a *man*."

"It certainly does, Skipper!" Harlan's eyes glowed. He appeared more alive than at any other time since his landing, beginning to understand, evidently, something of the hard freedom of the North, for which men must either fight or die.

Of the three men, Kayak Bill alone had been silent concerning his sensations. Ellen thought that the praise of the others had smitten him with a strange shyness. Loll was sitting astride the old man's knees, questioning him about that moment when the giant breaker had engulfed the boat.

Determined on an answer, the boy was urging for the fifth time.

"But, Kayak, what did *you* feel like?"

"Wall, son," Kayak said, as his hazel eyes twinkled. "I just couldn't figger out for a minute whether I was a clam ... or a pond lily."

In the laugh that followed, Harlan took up a roll of blankets and went into the other room. There was no thought of his crossing the island tonight. Kayak Bill's tent had blown down during the afternoon and he was, as he put it, "forced to seek better anchorage." He and Harlan were to spread a bed on the floor of the adjoining room.

Kobuk, with appealing whines and tentative pawing at the door, had finally won an entrance and was curled up in front of the stove. Shane had come in just before supper lugging the pigeon's cage, which he placed carefully on top of a tall packing box. Ellen felt the bird's presence in a way that was beginning to trouble her. Tonight it seemed to wear a sullen and dejected look, unlike its usual bold air. All evening it had sat motionless in the bottom of the cage. The only sign of life it displayed was in the deep orange pupils of its eyes, which she was sure, followed her about wherever she went.

She forced herself to look away from the cage. A hush had fallen on those in the room. The shrieking of rising wind challenged attention. Ellen listened with a feeling strangely compounded of delight and terror.

Never before had she known such a wind. It swept down on the roof of the cabin in woolies, threatening to blow it in, and then seemingly sucking it out again. The log walls quivered. Every joist and board creaked and strained. The box on which the lamp stood vibrated, and the flat yellow flame flickered. The air reverberated to the thunder of surf that crashed against the hundred reefs on Kon Klayu. Ellen had a feeling that the little island trembled in the splendid abandon of wind and sea – trembled, yet exulted in the freedom of the elements. She found herself paradoxically fearing, yet hoping, that the next blast of the gale might be heavier.

"Skipper," Harlan said after he had finished spreading the blankets in the other room. "I've been wondering how the whaleboat is doing. Before we turn in, I think I'll go down and see that we made the old girl fast." He took up his oilskins from the floor and slipped into them.

When the door had closed behind him, Kayak Bill looked and Boreland and nodded.

"I make affirmation," he drawled, "that there's a pay streak in any man who looks first after his hoss – or his boat."

While the significance of the old man's remark was dawning on Ellen, there was an odd lull in the storm. Surprisingly a new sound came to them. It was a sound blown from the south cliffs; a sound that was, yet was not, of the storm; a hollow reverberating roll that was deep and mellow, thrilling and strange. Boreland and Kayak rose simultaneously and looked questioningly into each other's eyes.

"What ..." Boreland's words were cut off by the flinging open of the door.

White-faced and dripping, Harlan staggered in, slamming the door to shut out the driving rain. He leaned heavily against it.

"God, Skipper," he gasped. "The whaleboat ... it's gone!"

At that moment, like a happening in a sinister dream, Ellen was aware that the pigeon perched high on the packing box had suddenly come to life. It was flapping its wings diabolically, exultingly.

Courtesy Anchorage Museum Rasmuson Center

Natives used whaleboats, like the one in this story, to go hunting in Alaska waters. This photograph shows men in two whaleboats – with another man standing between the boats on a whale they harpooned – after a successful hunt near Barrow in 1920.

17

THE MYSTERIOUS PRESENCE

The loss of the whaleboat was a calamity staggering in its magnitude. It meant that every pound of provisions left at the west camp must be packed on the backs of the men to the cabin. Not only that, but they were now without any means whatever of leaving the island. Nothing but the direst necessity could have forced Boreland to seek the mainland in the frail craft, but, remembering that the Natives of the coast had been known to journey the hundreds of miles from Sitka to Kodiak in open canoes, there had been a certain feeling of assurance in the thought that with the whaleboat there was at least a chance of bringing help to the island should it be necessary.

Boreland was the first to recover from the blow. The morning following the loss the three men were discussing it.

"Well, these postmortems get us nowhere," he said at last as he rose and prepared to stow the provisions away in the loft. "We'll tackle the job on hand now. After all, Kilbuck will be here with the *Hoonah* soon, and we can get another boat from him."

All that afternoon, while the gale tore at the corners of the little cabin and the sea beat with increasing violence on the beach and reefs, the men worked with hammer and saw, putting up shelves, making a table and a bedstead, and erecting two bunks for Jean and Lollie, one above the other in the adjoining room. Because he would so soon be leaving, Kayak Bill decided to pitch his tent again in the lee of the cabin as soon as the storm permitted, and occupy it until the *Hoonah* came.

The storm lasted three days. The second day the roof began to leak. The third day the rickety little porch blew down on one end and much of the chinking came out from between the logs of the cabin.

When, on the fourth morning, the wind died away and the sun burst out brilliantly upon a tumbling, muddy sea and rain-drenched landscape, Boreland's first thought was of repairing the house.

"We're in a devil of a stew here," he exclaimed after breakfast. "We'll have to get this place fixed up right now. Still, some of us ought to go down to the west camp and take a look at the cache. Luckily there are no animals on the island, so we have nothing to fear from that source."

"Why can't Loll and I go down to the camp, Shane?" broke in Jean. "Then all you men can get busy on the house. The poor, little old thing looks as if it had a black eye, with the porch battered down over the door."

Boreland was at first not in favor of the idea, doubting that it was safe for them to go alone. At last, however, he consented.

"Keep to the upper beach line," he cautioned, as the two started out. "And remember, if the sea is breaking near the bluff when you come home, wait on the other side until the tide drops before you attempt to cross."

Jean was as delighted as her capering little nephew to feel again the freedom of the beach after the long confinement in the crowded cabin. In spite of all the hardships – perhaps because of them – she was growing to love the sands of Kon Klayu and to look upon this incalculable ocean as a sort of fairy godmother, who, with every tide, brought up something different to lay at her feet. She never started out for a walk along the sea without experiencing that delightful, childish sense of expectancy that is so keenly a part of the life of Alaska.

While Kobuk trotted on ahead, she and Loll – remembering the talk of beach mining to which they had so often listened – scanned the way for ruby sand, the carrier of gold. But this morning the beach was untidy with great masses of fresh kelp and seaweed from the deep, torn by the storm and scattered everywhere.

"Oh, look, Jean! The gulls have found something," Loll said as he pointed ahead at a cloud of screaming, white-breasted birds that were rising and falling on slate-tipped wings over some object below them. "Let's hurry and see what it is."

But Kobuk was before them. Dashing on ahead he plunged into the melee, frightening the gulls from their find so that they flew shrieking into the air as the girl and her little companion ran up to discover the remains of a large fish on the sand. It was a halibut nearly six feet long. With the exception of the bones, only a small portion and the head remained, for the birds had been gorging on it for some time. The flesh, however, looked fresh and firm and white.

Jean regarded it thoughtfully. "If we had nothing else to eat, Lollie, we *might* eat a fish like this – that is if we got it before the gulls had been at it."

In an emergency even a great storm might be made to serve, since its very violence flung up from the deep such fare as this. At any rate, the gulls appreciated it, for even as Loll and Jean stood there, the birds had flown back, settling upon their find, their strong, lemon-colored, crimson-splotched beaks tearing greedily at the flesh. In their eagerness they flew thrillingly close, cold, gold-ringed eyes staring fiercely into the faces of the two, powerful wings fanning their cheeks. Loll, seeing Jean shrink away from an overly bold bird, took her hand and tugged her away from the discordantly screaming mass.

"Gosh, Jean, if those fellows were very hungry and I was alone, I bet they'd take a peck at *me!*"

Jean recalled a day at Katleean, when she had stood by a creek watching the salmon struggle up through the shallow water, while screeching gulls swooped exultantly down on the helpless creatures and gouged the eyes out of the living fish. Jean shuddered and quickened her steps.

They approached the tent cache at the west camp. It appeared intact. The wind, being from the southwest, had struck with full force on the opposite end of the island. Jean untied the flap of the tent and went inside. The provisions were piled up nearly to the ridgepole at the back.

Lollie, poking about, came upon a piece of rope, which, boy like, he took outside and wound about his waist. Jean heard him stumbling over the guy ropes at the side. Then from the back came his call.

"Jean! Come here!"

The girl ran out and joined him. He was pointing to the back of the tent. The pegs that had fastened it to the earth were uprooted. The canvas swung free. But what filled her with momentary conjecture was that which lay at her feet. A sack of flour evidently had been dragged out from under the wall of the tent and ripped open, for the sand was whitened with the doughy mixture resulting from the rain.

At this moment it did not occur to the girl to be frightened. There were no tracks in the sand other than hers and Loll's. Evidently, she thought, in the haste to load the boat before the storm, the men had dropped the sack and it had burst open.

"But how careless of them, Loll, not to peg the tent down again," she said.

Loll, however, was already headed for the first campsite made when landing on the northeast side of the island. Her call brought his eager answer.

"Aw, come on, Jean, I want to see how drowned we'd be if we'd stayed there during the storm."

Smiling to herself at the boy's love of dwelling on their narrow escapes from death, real and imaginary, the girl turned, picked up a stone and drove in a few of the tent pegs before she followed him.

On each side of the trail great patches of rice grass had been flattened from the force of the wind and rain, and the air was filled with the sweet smell of vegetation drying in the sun. As she approached the other side, the blue sky curved down to meet the ocean on a far straight line. The yellow-green of the sea was set off by astonishing areas of clearest cobalt blue, and the flying spray from combers breaking for miles out on the north shoals, caught the sunlight in a glory of rainbow mist.

THE MYSTERIOUS PRESENCE

"See, I told you, Jean," Loll said as he nodded sagely and pointed ahead when she overtook him.

A hundred feet above the place where the first camp had been, Jean saw that the rice grass had been torn out by the roots and whitened drift logs and kelp were massed confusedly.

In silence the girl stood looking at the spot. Emotions of fear, thankfulness and something of reverence swept over her. Lollie, looking down over the freckles on his nose, rested the lower part of his face in his hand in a manner reminiscent of Kayak Bill.

"Escaped, by hell, by the skin of our teeth!" he gloated.

The tide had been coming in fast during the past half hour. Jean, noting it, suddenly turned back, and with uneasy haste began the homeward journey.

Opposite the little lake where Boreland had shot the first ducks, Loll insisted on running up to the beach line to look over and see whether there were any more birds feeding there. Jean, waiting for him, watched him make his way through the short grass to the narrow, sandy lakeshore, and then stoop to look at something. All at once he raised his head, and with a strange, blanched look on his little face, glanced quickly, fearfully behind him into the tall alder thicket toward the hill. Then, wide-eyed, he sprang toward her without a sound.

"Wha ... what is it, Loll?" she gasped.

The boy's eyes shone with excitement. "It-it-it was a wild beast's tracks, Jean. This long ...," he said as he measured off about twelve inches between his trembling hands. "And it had claws – big ones that digged deep into the sand!"

"But there are no beasts on the island, Loll. You must be mistaken."

"No, no!" Loll's face quivered in his anxiety to convince her of the truth of his statements. Knowing the youngster's unconscious tendency toward exaggeration, she was doubtful. There could be no animal on the island. But ... to make sure ... she herself would go back to see.

She looked about for Kobuk, but the dog had gone on toward the bluff. Impressing on Loll the necessity of remaining where he was until she came back, she turned toward the lake again, running.

As she drew near the margin, unreasoning terror of the unknown began to take possession of her. Every pile of driftwood, every alder bush became alive with sinister possibilities. She drove herself forward. She could see the stretch of sand where Loll had stood. She could see that there were marks of some kind upon it. Trembling, fearful, her heart beating like a hammer in her breast, she pressed forward and looked closely at the marks. Loll was right. Here on Kon Klayu were monster tracks – of what she did not know.

She wheeled swiftly and ran back to where the boy waited. Without a word she snatched his hand and fled with him down the beach toward the bluff and home.

Kobuk, far in advance, was picking his way along the bluff, and now as they ran Jean became aware that a new danger threatened them. The tide had come in so far that even from a distance she could see the foam of spent breakers washing up against the rocky wall ahead. Boreland had said to wait until the tide fell before attempting to pass the bluff, but with the new, strange terror behind them, she had no thought of obeying. The sea, roaring almost at her feet, seemed kinder and more to be trusted than the unknown beast lurking in the alders, or perhaps slinking along, even now, above the beach line, watching, waiting to spring out at them any moment.

Upon arriving at the bluff she saw, with dismay, that the backwash of breakers licked all along the base. She stopped, tightening her hold on Loll's hand. She looked a long moment at the huge rollers of the incoming tide that crashed so close to her, and then back from whence she had come.

Loll raised his sober little face to the sky.

"God," he said, conversationally, "I guess *you'll* have to take a hand."

Jean slipped the rope from about his waist. She tied one end to him and the other about her own body in clumsy, womanish knots.

"Lollie," she said, and despite her efforts of bravery, her voice quavered. "We're going to run for it. Cling tightly to my hand, dear."

At that moment a wave receded. They ran dizzily forward in the shifting, wet gravel of the beach. When the next incoming comber was beginning to curl down from the top, Jean dashed to the bluff. Shielding the little fellow below her, she clung to the uneven shale of its base, presenting her back to the billow that crashed with a deafening roar just behind her.

Swift, terrifying, the wash of the breaker boiled and foamed about their feet, to their ankles, to their knees. It made Jean's head swim. It paralyzed her power of thought, leaving her with only the instinct to cling.

She had to wait while two more breakers rolled in and broke before she saw a chance to stagger to the next point of safety. It seemed to her that hours passed thus while she and Loll struggled, wet and battered, onward.

They had gone but two-thirds of the way when, glancing at the incoming wave to calculate how far they might run, she became aware of a mountainous unbroken roller immediately behind it – a watery monster that humped its back into a ragged, dancing crest high above her head. It advanced in eager, liquid blackness. She knew it must break nearly against the bluff where they stood.

Her desperate eyes espied a rough ledge just above her. With the strength born of despair, she caught up her nephew and tossed him to safety. Frantically she herself tried to climb the bluff.

She thought she heard a man's voice shouting to her. There was a moment when Loll's white face looked down at her through a haze – a moment when his little hands moved swiftly taking a turn with the rope about a ragged, upstanding piece of rock. Then a boiling, roaring sound filled her ears. An avalanche of dark water crashed down upon her, freezing her, smothering her, crushing her. She felt her body thrown high against the stony wall.

As she was whirled, choking, into darkness and oblivion there flashed through her mind the thought:

"This, then, is how it feels to die."

18

THE PERIL OF THE SURF

A fter Jean and Loll had left for the west camp that morning Harlan, Boreland and Kayak Bill set to work repairing the roof of the cabin and the porch. From his position astride the peak, Harlan could hear Ellen busy at her tasks indoors. As the tide began to run in, he saw her come to the door from time to time and walk down onto the beach to look for the absent ones. Apparently she was vaguely uneasy. The island's possibilities for good or bad were yet unknown to her and she was evidently never quite secure in her mind when any of her household was out of her sight. After one of the last excursions to the beach, she had spoken of the fact that the waves had reached the base of the cliff.

"They won't be able to come now for a while," she said, addressing the men on the roof. "Could two of you give me a little help inside, Shane? I need to move the bed," she added.

Kayak and Boreland accordingly slid down from the ridge and followed her into the house.

Harlan paused in his work of nailing tar paper over the boards and stretched wide his arms. He was taking a cursory glance toward the incoming tide when his attention was attracted by the figure of Kobuk ambling up the trail from the beach. The dog was dripping wet, and at intervals he stopped to shake himself violently. Kobuk must have been playing along the edge of the surf, Harlan thought.

And yet, he must have crossed the sands below the bluff ... and the tide was only an hour from the flood ... but of course Jean would not dream of attempting a crossing now. He took up his hammer again. Suddenly he hooked it over the ridge. At any rate, he decided, he would go down and make certain.

Slipping off the roof, he ran down to the beach. There he sped along its curve until his eye could command the length of the bluff. He stopped aghast. Midway Jean and the boy were coming on, stumbling across the sand left bare by a receding wave, dashing to the ragged base of the cliff and clinging to it while the incoming comber broke and seethed about them, then rushing on again. Owing to the storm of the past days, the billows were higher than usual. Also there was yet the most dangerous portion of the way to be traversed.

With a call for help, Harlan started racing toward them as the breakers ran out, and climbing the cliff out of their reach as they broke.

He shouted to Jean to attract her attention. If he could only sign to her to ascend the bluff and hold fast till he came. Vainly he tried to make his voice heard above the deafening roar. She neither heard nor saw him. Desperately he plunged on, not taking time now to climb up for his own safety, but plowing through the onrushing waves. Once a crashing comber caught and threw him flat on the shifting gravel.

Before he could right himself, it had sucked him almost into the maw of the next down-curling sea. Fortunately, it was a small one. He was able to regain his feet and stagger to a hand hold.

Then at the same instant that Jean's eye caught it, he became aware of the huge, unbroken billow advancing toward the struggling figures of the girl and boy.

He saw her snatch up the child and toss him to the safety of the ledge, saw her ineffectual efforts to follow ... then the dancing crest broke and Jean became but a formless dark object tossed like a drift log on the foaming waters that spouted against the foot of the bluff.

With a despairing cry, Harlan plunged forward, and as the great wave, the first of three, receded, he reached her.

Limp and unconscious she hung from the rope that bound her

to the terrified small boy above, and he saw that the little fellow had taken a turn with it about a jagged rock. But for this timely precaution the girl must have been drawn back into the sea and the child with her.

An extra long recession of the water gave him time to lift the inert body and throw it across his shoulder, and thus, while the second giant roller broke at his back he gripped with his torn hands into the sharp shale and held on. As it ebbed he hoisted her to the ledge above him.

From the temporary safety of this narrow shelf he considered their chances. It was impossible to scale the face of the bluff above him, yet the tide would not be full for an hour. Owing to the enormous sea, they would all three be swept into the ocean if they remained where they were. There was but one thing he could do.

He laid a hand on Loll's quaking shoulder.

"Pal," he said quietly, "will you be afraid to stay here while I carry Jean to the other side of the bluff?"

The boy looked down at the clamorous, booming tide and hesitated. He swallowed hard, blinking. Then he looked at the inert form of his aunt, and meeting Harlan's eyes, shook his head bravely.

"Good! Hang on tight then, old man, and I'll be back for you before you can say 'Jack Robinson'!"

He cut the rope about Jean's waist, and backing down from the ledge, took her again across his shoulder. As Lollie's hand reached out and began coiling the rope, he turned to watch the breakers so that he might time the first dash of his flight back to safety.

The tide was higher now, the combers nearer, and he had but one free hand with which to cling to the base of the bluff when the enveloping waters rose about him. He plunged. He staggered. His senses after a few moments were bludgeoned into numbness by the roar of the sea; his body was sore from the impact of beating water and stinging gravel. He struggled on step by step, feeling his way along the shifting beach, until only the primal instinct of self-preservation was guiding him in the grim game with the tide.

At last he reached the other end of the bluff. He reeled up to the dry sand and let the body of the girl slip from his shoulder. As he did so he heard a shout. Boreland and his wife were running down from the cabin trail. He did not pause but plunged back again through the drenching maelstrom.

In a moment their frantic calls were swallowed up in the deafening roar of waters. Would he have strength to fight his way back? Would he find the boy where he had left him, or had a comber swept him off the narrow shelf? Harlan was unutterably weary now. He longed to let go his hold on the rocky wall, to cease fighting, and let himself be taken out into obliteration; but he drove himself on ... and on. After a long while he gained the perilous perch where Loll bravely awaited him above the roar.

He rested a moment. The little fellow's absolute faith in him gave him the will to fight his way back again. He took the child on his shoulders and once more plunged into the watery hell.

How he returned to safety he never knew. He was conscious only of reaching the place where Jean lay ... of asking whether or not the girl was still alive ... then the great weariness overpowered him. He sank down on the sand beside Jean. Then Lollie's glad shout as he was clasped in his mother's arms floated through his mental numbness like a clear toy balloon drifting up in a fog.

Three hours later Harlan was resting on the bed in the living room. In the adjoining room, where Jean lay in her little bunk, he knew that the girl was hearing from Ellen's guarded lips the story of her rescue. On recovering consciousness she had tried to rise, but one side, where she had struck against the rocks, was bruised and so painful that, though she rebelled, she would be obliged to remain in bed for the remainder of the day at least.

Loll had already told the story of the mysterious animal tracks by the lake, and the scattered flour at the cache. Boreland had taken his rifle and gone down to the place as soon as the tide permitted. As Harlan lay there thinking, he was filled with an intense relief – he knew now that the spectre of the tundra that had so worried him was no creature of his own disordered brain. Whatever it might be, it was of flesh and blood. He could speak of it now.

Boreland returned about suppertime.

"Did you see 'em, dad?" shouted Loll as his father came in the door.

"What was it, Shane?" Jean called from the other room.

Boreland replaced his rifle in the rack over the head of the bed.

"Bear tracks," he answered succinctly. "Hind foot measures fourteen and a half inches!"

Courtesy Wildpedia

Kodiak bears, a subspecies of brown/grizzly bears, are the largest bears in the world and live exclusively on the islands of the Kodiak Archipelago. They may grow to more than 1,300 pounds and stand more than 10 feet tall.

These bears have been isolated from other bears on Kodiak's islands for about 12,000 years, according to Alaska Department of Fish and Game experts.

19

HOMEMAKING

"I figure that the Kodiak cub the Alaska Fur and Trading Company brought over here as a pet is now wandering about the island a full-grown grizzly, instead of being in bear heaven as the people of Katleean thought," said Boreland, as they all sat about the supper table. "Confound it, it makes it mighty bad for us, with all that grub down there at the west camp! If the beast takes a notion, he can go there and raise the very devil."

Harlan spoke up and offered to help.

"I'll take my blankets down there tomorrow and guard the cache until we get the provisions transferred," Harlan said. "I'd like to get a shot at a Kodiak bear."

"Son, I ain't a-castin' any asparagus on yore shootin' ability, but I claims the right to shoot that anamile myself!" Kayak Bill exclaimed.

"Funny!" Boreland said with a laugh. "I had the same idea myself."

After supper they discussed the problem of getting the remainder of the provisions down to the cabin at once. It was decided that each man should take a turn guarding the cache. Boreland finally left the conversation to Kayak and Harlan while he sat at the table silent, one hand clutching his hair, the other drawing queer-looking cartwheels and figures on a paper before him. Just before the others started to leave for the night, he sprang up with an exclamation.

"By thunder, I've got it!" he announced enthusiastically. "Fellows, we're going to make a nautical cart and sail her on the beach of Kon Klayu."

The nautical cart, when completed, proved to be a hybrid contrivance with two large wheels. The wheels had a cumbersome appearance, owing to the double rims that were tired with barrel staves cut in two and nailed crosswise to prevent sinking into the sand. The top of the cart was a platform eight feet long and four wide with two handles projecting at each end. Rising from its middle was a mast for which Kayak Bill rigged up a sail from a tarpaulin.

Boreland stood off and regarded the finished child of his brain. Beside him, Kayak eyed it for some minutes in admiring silence.

"By hell!" he drawled at last. "Sired by a whisky barrel, spawned by a stretcher and a throwback to a Chinese sampan."

Boreland laughed. "I got my idea for this little beauty from something I read once about the sailing wheelbarrows used by farmers in the interior of China, Bill. I'll bet you, with a fair wind, we can make all of five miles an hour with her on the beach."

The cart exceeded even its builders' expectations. Steered to the west camp the next afternoon it was loaded with provisions and the sail hoisted. With Harlan between the two front handles, and Boreland at the rear, the odd vehicle then headed toward home. The sail, twice as large as the cart, strained at the mast from the force of the wind behind it, and to the men between the handles, the load seemed hardly to matter at all. Barefooted, with trousers rolled up to their knees as in boyhood days, the two men found it a new and distinctly pleasant sensation to be swept along thus before wind.

In a few minutes, Kayak Bill, smoking placidly before the provision tent, was left far behind.

Remembering the backbreaking loads he had carried to the cabin, Harlan grinned back at the bellying sail behind him as he sped along.

"This is child's play, Boreland!" he shouted to his partner. "The problem of transportation is solved – if there's one thing we never lack on Kon Klayu, it's wind!"

And so it came about that, thanks to the nautical cart, which though the subject of much jesting, did the work, a month from the time of landing found all that remained of the adventurers' outfit transferred to the cabin. Not once during this time was the bear seen in the vicinity of the cache, though sometimes fresh tracks appeared on the margin of the little lake – now christened Bear Paw Lake – where Loll had discovered them.

With the boards taken from the tumbledown shack, an extra shed had been built near the cabin, and the porch repaired and strengthened. Harlan found time to make a much larger cage for the pigeon. As he told Ellen, the bird, confined in such close quarters, might not thrive.

Harlan noticed that despite Ellen's determination to leave the island on the coming of the *Hoonah,* she took a woman's delight in doing her best to make life comfortable with the few things at her command. Since it was the dictum of fate – if she would be with the man she loved – that she must spend so much of her married life in tents along new trails, floating down rivers in flatboats or wayfaring in trappers' cabins, she sooner or later accepted those conditions. Doubtless, many times she rebelled in her heart. Any woman would. But, he fancied, she was the kind who would chide herself for the momentary disloyalty to Shane and with an increased tenderness, set her capable, feminine touch to perform some new marvel of transformation in each wild place of the moment.

In the cabin on Kon Klayu she accomplished much. With newspapers and magazines found in the box of books from Add-'em-up Sam's collection, she papered the rooms. At the new windows that framed a wide expanse of ever-changing sea, giving a sense of space and freedom to the living room, she hung cheesecloth curtains. The folds of these draped a bookshelf beside the window, supporting few books but holding in its empty space the gold scale, unused as yet on Kon Klayu, and glinting newly as it caught the light on its polished surface. In a corner of the room the bed was gay with Native blankets and bright cushions. The homely cheer of a red tablecloth was reflected in the bright nickel of the shaded lamp on the table, and on the white, sand-scoured floor a long strip of rag carpet from Ellen's old home in the States made a note of old-fashioned, comforting cleanliness. On the Yukon stove the kettle sang cheerily to the pots and pans hanging in a shining row on the wall behind, and the room was pervaded by the faint, clean smell from the wood box piled high with newly split wood that had lain long in the sea.

Harlan followed Boreland into the house the day Ellen finished her curtains. He came upon the big prospector standing with his arm across his wife's shoulders.

"I'm blessed of the saints, entirely," Shane was saying, as he bent to lay his cheek affectionately against her hair. "God love you, Ellen, little fellow … you could make a home out of a dry goods box."

After the rescue of Loll and Jean at the bluff, Harlan noticed that Ellen's silent gratitude found vent in a dozen little ways, though he was aware also that he never had an opportunity of seeing the girl alone. Since the *Hoonah* was expected any day now, Ellen had suggested that the young man bring his blankets across the island and "bunk" with Kayak Bill until their departure. Had it been offered three weeks earlier, this arrangement would have been eagerly accepted. But the young man's attitude toward life on Kon Klayu had changed. It was still changing.

He was now cooking his own meals at the hut, clumsily it is true, since his unaccustomed hands had never before held a frying pan. But he was learning, and he was surprised to find himself taking pleasure in the experience. He thanked Ellen for her invitation, but refused it. He would not have been human had he not felt a certain satisfaction in doing so.

He wondered tentatively if Kayak Bill had suspected the struggle that was going on within him during his first days on the island – the fear of delirium tremens, the fight he was making to conquer the craving for liquor that continued, intermittently now, to torment him. The old man said nothing on the subject, but on one pretext or another Harlan noticed that Kayak managed to spend much of his leisure time at the hut.

Often, if the night were fine, he would roll up in a blanket before the fire and stay there until morning.

Kayak Bill's sauntering feet had followed Dame Fortune over every gold trail from Dawson to Nome, and there was no trick of Alaska camp life that he had not learned. He never tried to force his knowledge on the younger man, but casually, in the course of his slow, whimsical monologues, he taught Harlan much that was of inestimable value to him. Indeed, if it had not been for the old man, Harlan might have been forced to swallow his pride long before and ask for shelter at the Boreland cabin, for despite his brave talk of living in the hut, it was a shelter of the rudest type, built, probably, as a feeding station by the experimenting fox farmers.

Its structure interested him. It was made by standing whale ribs up on end about two feet apart in a circle. The spaces between were filled with turf, which abounded all over the island, thus making a wall two feet thick. Harlan had repaired it, and in the words of Kayak who helped him, had "rigged" himself up a stove from kerosene cans. It was the old hootch-maker who showed him how to arrange stones to form a crude, open-air fireplace in front of his door for use in fine weather. It was Kayak Bill who taught his blundering hands the trail way of stirring up a bannock and baking it in a frying pan propped up before the blaze.

Harlan now had less time to think about himself. The little can stove required much finely chopped firewood to keep it going. The open-air fireplace consumed large quantities of driftwood, which he had to chop with an axe, since the one saw on the island was needed at the cabin. After his day's work with Boreland, he had his meals to prepare. There were brown beans to clean and cook, and sourdough hotcakes to set for the morning. Kayak had taught him to prepare his sourdough – a resource that was to become the food mainstay of all on the island. Harlan learned from the old man that the sourdough hotcake, or flapjack, is as typical of Alaska as the glacier. The wilderness man carries, always, a little can filled with a batter of it; with this he starts the leavening of his bread, or, with the addition of a pinch of soda he fries it in the form of flapjacks. So typical a feature of Alaska is the sourdough pot that the old-timer in the North is called a "Sourdough."

Harlan grew to have a real fondness for his hut, the only home he had ever made for himself. Its very primitiveness endeared it to him. He grew also to look forward to the fine evenings when he and Kayak stretched before the open fireplace with their backs to a bleached whale rib, smoked and yarned and sang while they watched the leaping driftwood flames.

Strange, picturesque characters of the Last Frontier stalked through all Kayak Bill's tales – reckless bonanza kings of Klondike days, buying with their newfound gold the love of painted women; simple-hearted, gentle Aleuts kissing the footprints of skirted, bearded Russian priests; pathetic, gay ladies of adventure; half mad hermits of the hills; secretive men who took Native wives, and wistful, emotional people of mixed race – all these Kayak Bill made to live again in the glow of the evening fire.

In his quaint, whimsical way he told of the prospector, that brave heart who makes gold but an excuse for his going forth to conquer the wilds. Harlan came to understand them, the lure of gold and their slogan: "*This* time we will strike it." Through Kayak Bill's eyes he saw them aged, broken by the rigors of many northern winters, but with the indomitable spirit of youth still in them, a recurrent yearning that defies age, rheumatism and poverty, and sends them with their grubstakes out questing into the hills. He saw them with picks and gold pans wandering happily during the wonderful Alaska summer and fall. And when the frost paints the green above timberline with russet and gold and the Northern Lights beckon them back to the settlements, he saw them arrive, tired, penniless, perhaps, but satisfied, and already planning the next trip into the magnetic golden hills.

One night, being in a pensive mood, Kayak told of a partner of his, the Bard of the Kuskokwim, an old northern poet unknown except in the Valley o' Lies, who had put the prospector's soul hunger into verse.

"We yearned beyond the skyline,
With a wistful wish to know
What was hidden by the high line,
Glist'ning with eternal snow.

And we yearned and wished and wondered
At the secrets there untold,
As the glaciers growled and thundered,
Came the whisper: "Red, raw gold!" *

As if he feared Harlan might think him sentimental, Kayak Bill finished his recital with:

"Yas, son, that old cuss partner o' mine was always recitin' them poetry sayin's o' his. Durned if he wouldn't vocabulate to the trees or the hills when there warn't another soul nearer to him than a hundred miles!"

But of Kayak Bill, himself, Harlan noted, there was never a personal thing. In all his tales the old hootch-maker was ever the spectator, amused, kindly, philosophical.

Sometimes the two were silent – with the companionable silence that the campfire instills. Leaning back against the whale rib, while the embers died in the fireplace and the sea below took on its veil of twilight, they mused and listened to the universe. It was at such times that Harlan began to feel, though faintly, the healing, vibrant energy that comes to those who live close to Mother Earth. Katleean and the bunk full of liquor that at first had occupied so much of his thought, occurred to him less frequently. The States – and all that had happened to him there – were becoming a dream. He began to feel as though he had always lived as he was living now. To his surprise, as the time drew near for the arrival of the *Hoonah,* he found himself unconcerned, indifferent. Like Kayak Bill, he was learning to face life serenely, undisturbed as to the morrow, but doing his best today.

* From the unpublished poems of Edward C. Cone, Bard of the Kuskokwim

20

GOLD

T oward the end of September another heavy gale swept the island. This time the little party was snug and warm in the cabin with the provisions under cover, and while the storm raged outside, Ellen and Boreland climbed up into the loft and made a list of the supplies on hand. In the log, which Ellen had begun to keep the day they landed on Kon Klayu, she made this entry:

"Heavy gale blowing from the southwest. We hear again that strange rolling sound from the south cliffs. Discovered today that all rolled oats and flour is musty from being wetted by the tide when we landed, and much of it is spoiled. Fortunately the flour caked on the outside and the inside is fairly well preserved. We used the last of our butter today. We have sugar for one more week."

Though she said little, her growing anxiety communicated itself in some occult way to the other members of her household, even to Loll, to whom she gave daily lessons in reading, writing and arithmetic. The little fellow was at this time moved to write and illustrate a book on some discarded letterheads of a defunct life insurance company. Ellen breathed a prayer of thanks that he so well entertained himself on stormy days.

On the first page of this work appeared the text of Old Mother Hubbard written in the boy's large, childish, downhill hand with spelling of distinct originality. Above it in a flaming red wrapper a lady with a large bust and impossible tiny feet, slanted tipsily toward some shelves – conspicuously empty – while in the offing quite aloof from the lady a lean, pale-green animal stood with despondent drooping head and tail. Other nursery favorites that had to do with eating and food, followed. They were illustrated in red and black and green. The red was made by a crayon pencil, miraculously produced by Kayak Bill; the green was obtained by the simple expedient of chewing up rice grass. Toward the end of the book were many of Lollie's own poems, composed for his mother, and beautified with marginal decorations of flying gulls, sailing ships and fat button-eyed daisies, all bearing evidence of repeated erasures with a wet little finger.

"The red sun sinks down in the sea of the West,
The wind goes to sleep.
Seagulls flies homes to their nests.
And the gold stars their watches keeps.
I think the weather will be fine.
So the Hoonah can come in.
If she don't we will be out of grub.
And O, what will we do then."

Thus Lollie indicated the unspoken thought that underlay all the activities of the Boreland household now. They were subconsciously counting the days until the White Chief should come to the island with the *Hoonah* and, while they counted, they were beginning to fear.

During the time of this second great gale Boreland and Kayak Bill made ready for mining by making a gold-saving device called a rocker. It was a box-like affair four feet long, eighteen inches wide and the same dimension in height. The front end was open, as well as the top, and it was mounted on rockers like a cradle. Over the back end was a sieve or hopper, and immediately beneath slanted a frame covered with blanket cloth. The pay dirt was to be poured into the hopper and running water turned in on it. While the cradle was rocked with a jerky movement, the sand sifted down through the hopper to the slanting apron.

Much of the gold, Boreland explained, would be caught in the nap of the apron, and in the little sag at the bottom of it, but the sand would flow on out over the bottom of the rocker that was also lined with blanket cloth held down by cleats nailed crosswise at intervals. The sand, being lighter than the gold, was washed on down the length of the rocker floor and thence out on the ground, while the cleats and the rough nap of the cloth caught any further yellow metal.

With his Irishman's gift for seeing life through childish eyes, Boreland made a small duplicate of the rocker for his son's use, a gift that, in a way, was for the purpose of distracting Loll's mind from a misfortune that had befallen Kobuk during the storm.

The dog, while playing about the shed where the men were working, had knocked down the long crosscut saw, and the sharp teeth had fallen with full force across Kobuk's right foreleg, cutting it cruelly – and it was feared, cracking the bone. Shane had cleansed the wound with the last bit of antiseptic and bound it up in splints, but Kobuk's limping had brought forth Loll's extravagant proffers of sympathy.

The first receding tide after the six-day storm found the whole party on the beach. With the provisions under cover, and the cabin repaired, all was clear for the mining. They were patrolling the beach for prospects.

Kayak Bill and Gregg turned southward toward Skeleton Rib, as Harlan's growing interest in the round boulders of that vicinity often drew him there. Shane and his family took the beach around the bluff toward the north. Ellen carried the rifle, for though there had been no time yet to hunt, especially for the great bear that roamed Kon Klayu, she was always on the alert. Boreland, happier than he had been since his landing, was at last outfitted with a shovel and a gold pan, emblems of his romantic calling.

Each storm that tore the island produced a different effect on the beach. When they rounded the bluff this morning, instead of finding piles of seaweed and gravel tossed up as they had after the first great gale, they were surprised at vast areas of bedrock from which every vestige of sand had been swept away. Tiny rills of water, drainage from the tundra banks above the beach line, flowed down the shallow crevices of the very hard substance.

Jean, who had never seen a nugget in its native state, was excitedly searching for pieces of gold. Ellen smiled to see her, with Loll at her heels, running hither and thither, expecting any moment to come upon large, brassy-looking lumps resting like eggs on the hardpan.

Boreland skirted the edges of the bedrock.

They had reached the vicinity of Bear Paw Lake when abruptly he dropped to his knees and looked keenly at the formation beneath him. In an instant they were all running toward him.

He raised his face, transfigured with an eager joy.

"Gosh all hemlock!" he exclaimed. "Here it is at last! Ruby sand – *kon klayu* – look, El! Jean!"

The women saw the edge of the bedrock dark beach sand was mixed with minute garnet-like particles that imparted to it a tinge of ruby. A first glance revealed nothing but rills of water running down through the sand carrying it through the depression in the bedrock. Like live things, the atoms crawled slowly along the seam. Suddenly each watcher caught her breath. Amid the shifting flow there came a glint ... then another. A second later, in the roughened surface of the bedrock lay flakes of virgin gold.

Gold!

No thrill that gold can buy ever equals the wild ecstasy experienced by those who find it. Jean threw her arms successively about her happy sister and brother-in-law, and finished by capering over the bedrock with Loll as a willing partner.

When the first excitement had spent itself, Boreland sent the boy to Kayak Bill and Harlan with word to bring shovels and the wheelbarrow. It was necessary to gather and convey the pay sand to a place of safety before the next tide covered it, as the surf of Kon Klayu was too heavy to permit surf mining. Marking the spot with a piece of driftwood, Boreland continued down the beach with the others.

They followed the shore as far as the site of the west camp looking for further patches of ruby sand, but found none.

Having learned that by the aid of a hairpin and Boreland's knife they could pick up the colors of gold that were caught in the crevices, Ellen and Jean were on their knees examining the seams in the bedrock when Kayak and Harlan arrived. The particles of gold were extraordinarily flat and thin, and the largest flakes only could be seen with the naked eye. There were few of these, but no miner was ever prouder of his spring cleanup than was Jean of the ten colors she collected in her drinking cup.

Harlan could hardly credit his eyesight when he beheld the yellow flakes Jean showed to him. Gold on the island of Kon Klayu after all! Then he recalled that on that memorable night of the potlatch dance the White Chief had admitted there was gold, but while the tides occasionally uncovered pay sand rich beyond most placers, there would follow months when not a single color showed up in the sands of Kon Klayu. It was not a paying proposition. This deposit of ruby sand must be what Kayak Bill called a mere "flash in the pan." Though he tried not to let his coworkers become aware of it, Harlan was filled with doubts.

All that day, while the tide permitted, the men wheeled pay sand to a place of safety above the high-tide line and the following morning, the cart, speeding before a spanking breeze, carried all the mining outfit, including Loll's rocker, down to the pay dirt. Ellen, because of household duties, was the only one to remain at the cabin.

Once more the night tide had shifted the sands, and they found no trace of any gold carrier. The bedrock that had been bare the day before now lay under several feet of gravel. The complete change in the topography of the shore was almost weird. It filled them with wondering and a strange respect for the mysterious workings of the sea.

The rockers were set up on the beach just below Bear Paw Lake, and with a flume made of a series of boards nailed together in a V-shape, water was conveyed to the hopper of the rocker. Jean and Loll, before beginning their own preparations, watched while

Boreland and his two helpers rocked out the first gold. After glints of yellow began to appear in the nap of the cloth apron, they turned to their own outfit.

Harlan solved their water problem by digging a hole below the large rocker and catching the waste after it had done its work above. Long before the pool was completed he and Jean were on terms of laughing friendliness. This was the first time he had been with her, without being uncomfortably aware of the watchful and disapproving eye of Ellen. He felt a distinct exhilaration.

He poured sand into the hopper while Jean rocked and Loll, detailing much little boy wisdom, dipped up the water from the hole beside them.

Though it was her first year in the North, Jean, he thought, had fallen into the ways of the country with the natural ability that marks the young seagull launching out on the deep. Evidently she had dressed hastily that morning. Her khaki flannel shirt, belted loosely with green leather and worn like a Russian blouse, lay open at the throat. Her mass of dark hair was tucked under a green tam o' shanter perched at an unconsciously rakish angle. Unframed by her hair, her face had a piquant, boyish look, and her wide-set hazel eyes seemed larger than usual. There was a ghost of a golden freckle or two on the bridge of her straight little nose. From her green tam to her stout leather boots, Harlan could find no evidence of a single feminine artifice – not a thing, perhaps, that might have appealed to him a year ago – yet he was conscious of a stir of pleasure as he looked at her.

He placed a shovel of sand in the hopper, spilling half of it on Lollie who was at the same moment pouring in water. The girl laughed at his clumsiness as she loosened her hold on the rocker handle and straightened, tossing her head so that the tam assumed a different but equally alluring angle. Her sleeves were rolled to the elbow. She had the lithe slimness and the greens and browns that suggested the outdoors. When she turned away from him presently to look out over the sunlit sea, Harlan rested his shovel in the sand to watch her.

"I wonder where my Kobuk is this morning?" The remark came

from Loll, who was squatting at the edge of the waterhole waiting for it to fill again.

Neither answered him.

"Have you noticed how clearly, on days like this, one can see the mainland, though it is ninety miles away?" Jean asked, her mind apparently intent on the far horizon. "There seems to be something in the atmosphere that brings it nearer."

"I whisht I knew where my Kobuk is, I do," murmured Loll plaintively. The youngster was evidently getting tired of work. He was filling the pail listlessly, emptying the contents over his own red little hand.

Jean's eyes roaming out over the shining ocean spaces rested upon a spot in the northwest. Very low on the rim of the sea lay a mountain range, its purple and white ethereal in the distance.

"I *said*, I whisht I knew where my Kobuk is!" There was a slight belligerent tone in Lollie's voice that Jean, doubtless, failed to catch, for she mused on.

"Though I know that coast over there is practically uninhabited, it always gives me a feeling of being closer to people when I can see it – and a sense of delightful unknown things lying just there beyond the range." She paused as if contemplating some illusive thought.

Harlan, looking at her profile, became aware that her chin, while of an engaging firmness, had that impalpably soft texture that suggests the powdered wing of a creamy butterfly. He was surprised that he had never noticed it before. The tam slanted obligingly to the other side and left exposed the lobe of a small ear that was as rosy in tint as the delicate tiny clamshells he occasionally marveled at on the beach. The curve at the back of her neck had the look that invites kisses in a very little girl who has her curls knotted up on the top of her head. He found mining a distinctly agreeable occupation.

"You are like a soft, cool breeze from the sea after a hot day in the city," he was astonished to find himself saying. But his statement was lost in a verbal explosion from the enraged Lollie.

"Gosh darn it! *Nobody* listens to *me*!" The little fellow was looking up at Jean with petulant indignation. "I'm going to find Kobuk!"

He flung his pail to the sand, as if casting all thought of fickle women from him, and ran off down the beach toward the cabin, deigning not to hear Jean as she called to him.

"The poor little man," Jean said sympathetically as she looked after the flying figure of her nephew. "I know he must feel lonely sometimes with no one of his own age to play with."

"It's a feeling he shares, then, with some of us older ones."

Jean glanced at Harlan quickly. "Then why ..." she began, and checked herself.

Courtesy Alaska State Library

Ancestors of Alaska huskies like Kobuk date back thousands of years before Russians and Europeans came to North America. Anthropologists believe domesticated dogs accompanied waves of people migrating from Asia across the Bering Sea Land Bridge more than 20,000 years ago.

She wanted to ask him why, if this were so, he had buried himself in the isolated post of Katleean. She wanted to know why he, young, educated, brave, with the world of opportunity before him. had immersed himself in the lazy, dreamy life of an Alaska trading post. Was he of the stuff that Silvertip was made? Silvertip who was content to do odd bits of work for the White Chief at Katleean, for which he took his pay in tobacco or some other luxury necessary to his own comfort, while the energetic Senott kept his house, gathered and chopped his wood, salted fish, canned berries, dried clams and put down seagulls eggs in salt for the winter? Was this good-looking young creature a womanizer of Native women at heart, if not in reality?

She was intensely interested in those strange members of the white race who go Native. She had been raised to believe that races should not mix, although she did not have the contempt for those who took Native wives that Ellen felt. She had only a kindly desire to understand their point of view.

In a way she could account for the White Chief. Katleean was his wilderness kingdom where he ruled white and Native alike by sheer strength of arm and will. Silvertip, ignorant, lazy, weak, she could also understand vaguely. But there were others. She recalled a day on the beach at the trading post when she had met a tall, blond man. He was sitting on the edge of his canoe nonchalantly smoking a cigarette, while his Native wife and their four biracial little children dug clams a few feet away. One minute he had talked to her of the effect on character of the geographical aspect of the country, sprinkling his remarks with "Schopenhauer maintains" and "Nietzsche says." In the next breath he had informed her proudly that he and his children were of the eagle totem – claiming it by reason of his Tlingit wife's clan.

The incident remained vivid in her mind, setting up never ceasing queries. *Why? How?* Neither Ellen or Shane encouraged her attempts to discuss these conditions.

Jean's thoughts wandered on. It occurred to her that Ellen seemed to be changing, too. There was not the old freedom of speech between them that had always existed prior to their coming to Kon Klayu. Perhaps it was her own fault, for lately, especially since the day at the bluff, she had resented Ellen's attitude toward herself and Gregg Harlan. There were many things she wished she might talk over with the young man. Her interest in how white men went for Native women, for instance. But of course that would be impossible, she reminded herself. She had nearly forgotten – there had been that Native girl, Naleenah.

As if in answer to her unspoken thought, Harlan turned to her impulsively.

"There's something I want to tell you, Miss Wiley, about ... about that little Indian girl." He stopped, his tanned face flushing. It was as if he had no words to express himself in terms that she would understand.

"You see I ... I ..."

"Ahoy, there, Gregg! Jean! A ship! Look, it must be the *Hoonah*!" Boreland's joyous call broke in on them. He had run down from his own rocker and was pointing far out where the sunlight fell on the sails of a vessel heading directly for the island of Kon Klayu. It was the first sail sighted since the schooner went away.

"Hurrah boy! She's coming with the provisions!" Boreland tossed his cap into the air. "Jean, run down to the cabin and tell Ellen the glorious news!"

The girl looked at the approaching ship a moment. Happy as she was at the sight, she could not help wishing that Boreland had discovered it a few minutes later. She leaned toward Harlan.

"Tell me some other time," she said softly, and with a word to Shane started for the cabin.

She found Ellen, who never threw anything away that might later be used for food, rolling some hard, sea-soaked lumps of flour beneath the rolling pin trying to crush them fine enough to use.

"Oh, angel child, you won't have to save that stuff now!" Jean shouted, bursting in upon her. "The *Hoonah's* coming! We sighted her!" She caught Ellen about the waist and whirled her madly over the floor, releasing her suddenly to dash out the door with a "Come on, Sis!"

The two arrived breathless on the point of the bluff from whence the ship was visible, and whence the men had gathered. Jean began eagerly pointing out the sail, but even as she did so, she faltered. She turned and caught the sickening look of disappointment on the faces about her. A thin line of smoke was now trailing out behind the vessel. It was not the *Hoonah*, but a steamer. Also it had swerved in its course and now, broadside to the island, it was headed south.

"Oh-oh-oh!" With a world of hopelessness in her voice Jean uttered the sound and threw her arm about Ellen's waist. Together they watched the departing vessel with that desperation of heart that hopes, even while the brain knows there is no hope. A quarter of an hour passed, but the ship did not change its course.

They turned from the sea to find that the men had begun to gather up the tools and the cleanup from the sand.

"It's a cannery steamer, El, with the sail up, going to the States for the winter," Boreland said, dully. "The salmon run is over."

Ellen was not listening. She had taken her eyes from the fast vanishing steamer and was looking anxiously down the empty beach toward the far away rockers.

"Shane ... Shane . . ." she faltered now. There was a queer, frightened tone in her voice that sent a chill to the hearts of her listeners. "Where is Lollie?"

Boreland wheeled about.

"Why, he went home to you two hours ago, El ... haven't you seen him?"

"No!" Ellen's alarmed gaze sought his. Forgotten was the ship, the gold, the people about them; forgotten was everything else in the world but the soul-gripping parental fear they saw reflected in each other's face.

"The grizzly!" The mother's white lips whispered the words the father dared not utter. "Oh, Shane, come! Quick! We must find him!"

21

KOBUK

B oreland and Kayak Bill searched the beach below the cabin for footprints while Harlan took the trail across the island toward his hut. Ellen and her sister, hoping that the boy had returned during their absence, ran home to look into every nook and corner. The silence drove them once more into the open.

Ellen, her throat tightening with unshed tears, stood on the porch and called for the boy.

"L-o-l-l-i-e! ... S-o-n!"

The only answer was the mocking cry of a gull floating high in the sunlight.

Boreland came hurriedly up the trail from the beach.

"There are no tracks in the sand toward Sunset Point, El, but Kayak is going along Skeleton Rib toward the cliffs."

At the stricken look in the mother's face, Jean turned quickly to her brother-in-law.

"He must have found Kobuk and gone off adventuring again, Shane ... but he can't have gone far with the dog so crippled. Perhaps he's picking flowers," she suggested hopefully.

Ellen had started down toward the dilapidated hut where Loll had surprised the swallows on his first morning exploration. Lying on the doorsill she found some fragrant spikes of late-blooming orchids tied with a grass blade. Calling to the others, she picked up the flowers. Boreland answered her with a gesture, and after running back into the cabin for his rifle, followed.

"He loves the yellow flowers best, Jean," Ellen said thoughtfully. "Perhaps he has gone to the gulch where they grow thickest."

Toward the steep depression in the hillside some two hundred yards distant the coarse grass of the tundra was flattened in spots as if something had passed that way. The women seized upon this clue and eagerly followed the signs.

Where the land sloped upward toward the hill they came upon a grave. It was old, so old that the Greek cross at the head was moss-grown, broken and decayed.

Ellen and her son had stood there once before, touched with the gentle speculative melancholy that a wilderness grave always brings. Before leaving they had placed a cluster of flowers upon it in memory of the bold Russian sailor of long ago, whose body lay beneath. Now there was a fresh bunch of blossoms at the foot of the cross. At the sight of them quick, hot tears welled up in Ellen's eyes. It hurt her to remember Loll's quaint way of talking to the flowers he had picked.

Boreland, rifle in hand, overtook them just as they entered the gully that ran upward to the flat top of the island.

During the rainy season the gulch undoubtedly cradled a small stream of water, but now it was only slightly damp, and on each side, untouched yet by frost, grew a golden profusion of flowers. Here and there freshly broken stems indicated that Ellen had not been amiss in her surmise as to the boy's route.

Halfway up they came upon Loll's cap swinging from a dried celery blossom. With a cry Ellen caught at it and clasped it to her breast while she called his name again and again. Jean joined her. Then Boreland took up the name.

There was no answer.

When the voices died away at last it seemed strangely, ominously still in the sunny, flower-scented hollow. With a sickening fear that she might never hear her boy's call again, Ellen continued to stand straining her ears for the sound of it. On either side of her a wall of yellow bloom arose, shutting her in. A breath of air stirred the fragrance of it – clean, sweet. Suddenly, on its scent, there flashed before her baby pictures from the realm of her mother memories. Loll, curly-headed, grey-eyed and laughing, holding out chubby arms as he took his first unsteady steps; Loll's plump, diminutive legs, dancing "tippytoe" with comical baby joyousness before he would consent to be buttoned into his nightie; Loll asleep, his little tousled head on the pillow beside that of "Shuteye," an absurd and dilapidated doll dear to his infant heart. And once, when she had impatiently slapped his fat little hand as it closed on a forbidden object, Loll's baby face looking up at her with hurt, astonished eyes and quivering chin. This last thought stabbed her with poignant regret, wounding her heart with such anguish and self-reproach and longing that she burst into sobs as she climbed blindly to the top of the gulch.

On the crest of the hill all three stopped for a moment, out of breath from the steep ascent.

Spread out like a vast beautiful meadow the top of the island lay flat as the palm of a hand. The tundra, softly green and brown, was splashed with the yellow and rose and purple of late blooming wild flowers.

Small brown pools of water bordered with moss were sunk here and there. To the north and east not a tree or bush broke the level, but southward the tundra rose gently toward the top of the cliffs a mile or more away, where the air was thick with seabirds. A narrow path, suggestive of heavy padded feet, ran from north to south along the edge of the hill.

Despite this gentleness, this softness of contour characteristic of the tundra meadows of the North, there was a feeling of wind-swept spaces. The air was exquisitely pure. Jean, looking about her, involuntarily drew a deep, long breath. Midway between her and the edge of the distant cliffs stood the one lone tree of Kon Klayu – a small gnarled spruce, its branches all growing from one side of the trunk, bearing mute testimony to the velocity of the prevailing gales. There was about this tree an air of almost human loneliness and waiting. On the brow of the hill it faced the sea like a woman with long, windblown hair. Near it rose a dome-shaped mound like a Native hut in form but many times larger.

As the girl's eyes followed the trail south she suddenly became aware of a small, slowly moving object … then another.

"Oh, Ellen!" There was glad relief in her voice. "*There* he is! There they are! Loll and Kobuk! See – their heads are bobbing just above the grass toward the tree!"

At the first exclamation, Boreland had started hurriedly along the trail. The two women followed him, calling to the boy as they ran. But Loll, evidently deeply interested in his own small adventures, did not hear their shouts. Kobuk was now hobbling on ahead, and despite his bandaged leg, was tacking hither and thither woofing in the manner of the husky when he wishes to bark. As Loll neared the tree, they saw him branch off the trail and a few minutes later disappear around the hummock.

But Kobuk did not follow.

With short staccato woofs he was limping forward toward the crest of the hill and back again. There was a strange note in the sound. Presently he stood still, his long nose raised, wolf-like, as if to catch a scent.

At this point Boreland stopped in the trail.

"El," he said hurriedly, "you and Jean stay right here. I'm going to make a shortcut to the hummock. I'll bring Loll back. Mind what I tell you, stay here!"

He started swiftly across the deceptively smooth-looking tundra, his face drawn and ashen. While Jean watched him, he slipped his rifle to the hollow of his arm. The movement brought the thought of the bear to the girl. Her heart thumped against her side. She glanced at Ellen, but her sister was standing with hand-shaded eyes following the progress of Shane, who had covered nearly half the distance to the mound. Jean turned again to the crest of the hill where Kobuk had been. He was hobbling toward her. Even as she looked, the dog stopped, glanced behind him, then stiffened, every hair along his neck bristling. He stood as if sniffing the wind that was blowing toward her.

Then he came on.

"Kobuk, what's the matter, Kobuk ..."

The girl broke off with a gasp of terror. In a fascination of fright her gaze became fastened on a spot beyond the advancing Kobuk.

Out of the bushes that crowned the edge of the hill a great, hairy head was slowly rising. Followed by the massive arches of shoulders, then the whole powerful body.

An instant later the vast bulk of a Kodiak bear, with low-hung swinging head, was outlined against the growth behind. A moment it stood, looming huge, brown, fearful – the most dangerous beast that roams the Alaska wilderness. Then deliberately it came to its haunches, its immense paws dangling in front, its monstrous head and neck turning from side to side. Dropping to earth again, it slouched heavily in the direction of the hummock where Lollie had disappeared.

Jean turned swiftly to see if Boreland was aware of the proximity of the creature, now making for the opening to its den on the other side of the mound – a den that Loll no doubt was at that moment exploring. She saw her brother-in-law was preparing to spring across one of the little brown pools. Then, to her despair, he stumbled, and one leg went down in the soft muck of the farther edge. As he fell, he tried to throw his rifle to the bank, but the heavy, metal stayed, butt jammed against his hand.

Jean held her breath. For a long moment he did not move. Had he broken his leg? Had he ...? She then sobbed with relief when she saw him beginning to struggle out; but, even in her excitement, she noticed that he did not use his right hand. It hung limply from the wrist.

Ellen must have seen the beast as soon as Jean, for as her husband fell she was dashing away across the tundra to him. Jean's mind wrestled with the situation. With his right hand useless, Boreland, good shot though he was, could never send the single bullet that must kill the grizzly. They could risk no fight at close range with a wounded and infuriated Kodiak bear. Jean remembered her sister's unusual skill at target practice on the *Hoonah*. Jean herself was a good shot but Ellen could, unfailing, hit a bull's eye at twenty paces, though she could never be persuaded to shoot at a living thing. Would she have the courage, the coolness, to face the monster in that critical moment that meant life or death to her son? Would she *be* in *time*?

Now the bear had traversed more than half the distance to the hummock and was still lumbering along. She must stop him, must at least delay him – she and Kobuk – so that Ellen might reach the other side of the mound before him.

She ran to meet the dog. Snatches of hunting tales Kayak Bill had told came to her, tales of northern huskies hamstringing wild beasts. She did not know what the term meant, but Kobuk could do it. Kobuk, the powerful, the swift, the beautiful … then she remembered that Kobuk's right foreleg was crippled and still tightly bandaged ... Kobuk crippled stood no chance against a Kodiak bear!

She came up to him. At her approach, as though reinforced by her presence, the dog turned clumsily on three legs to face the beast. Low, savage growls issued from his throat. His lips curled away from his sharp fangs; spasms serrulated his nose; the hair along his spine rose and fell.

Jean patted his side. Sick at heart she urged him forward. She pointed desperately to the monster.

"Mush, Kobuk! Sick 'em, old boy!" She forced enthusiasm into her tones. "Go head him off!"

The dog limped a few feet. He looked back at her, his ferocious look softened. His crippled leg hung useless. He raised clear, questioning eyes to her face.

"Oh, Kobuk, darling, I know … I *know* …" the girl's voice broke. She knelt and threw her arms about him. "But you must do *something*, Kobuk, you must!" She pleaded with him as if he were human.

Once more the dog looked at her, his dark, intelligent eyes fearful and sad. He gave a half-hearted little woof, shifted on his three legs and rested his head a moment against her knee.

She sprang up and ran a short distance ahead of him. Again she pointed to the bear.

"Mush, Kobuk! Oh, go after him, boy!"

He started. Once more his hair bristled ferociously. Then suddenly, to Jean's dismay, he turned and instead of heading the bear off, began to make a detour behind it. Forgetful of all else but the necessity of delaying the beast, she ran after the dog shouting encouragement.

As he left her behind he gathered speed. He swerved, making straight for the back of the bear. His woofing sounds had ceased now. He was grimly silent. The instincts of his wolf ancestors at the sight of quarry must have awakened in his heart making him forget his bodily pain, for as he sped on in his desire to maim and kill, he put his bandaged leg to the ground with increasing frequency. By the time he reached the animal, gone was the friendly and gentle Kobuk Jean had always known. In his place rushed a new and terrible Kobuk – a snarling, leaping devil-dog, with blazing eyes, white fangs gleaming in a dripping mouth, little ears laid back against a lean, wolf-like head.

He attacked the bear from behind, nipping it slightly. The huge beast stopped and whirled in clumsy astonishment. For a moment it looked almost curiously at the white-fanged fury leaping away. Then turning, it lumbered on again toward the mound. The monster had lived so long on Kon Klayu undisturbed by man or beast that it was apparently indifferent to both.

But Kobuk, cripple though he was, would not be ignored. Again he dashed at the bear, seeking to nip it from the rear. Again he retreated. Repeating these maneuvers he kept on, until suddenly Jean saw the beast whirl viciously. Its cumbersome bulk stiffened, its little eyes gleamed with rage. It rose on its hind legs, its monster head swaying from side to side. Then the girl stopped, horrified, dazed at the unequal battle that ensued.

She had a confused memory of a huge upstanding creature laying about it like a fiend with great furry arms. She saw her dog, crippled, but dauntless, ever dodging, wheeling, leaping, circling and attacking from behind the moment the bear's back was toward him.

She saw Kobuk catch glancing blows from the mighty claw-barbed paws and roll five feet, ten feet. She saw him battered, bleeding, panting, struggling to his feet again and again to renew his losing fight. Backward and forward over the tundra they fought, swiftly, savagely, yet despite it all, ever nearing the mound. Then all in a moment they disappeared around the edge of the hummock. To the girl it was as if the earth had swallowed them. She stood for a moment bewildered. But remembering, she turned to where she had last seen Ellen and Shane. Her sister was not in sight, but Boreland was limping around the opposite end of the mound. He carried no gun. Then he, too, disappeared. A second later a shot rang out – then another. After that was silence.

The sound of the rifle galvanized the girl into action. With wildly thumping heart she sped toward the scene of the shooting, dreading what she might find there. Rounding the hummock she stopped, staring at the scene before her.

A few feet from the cave-like opening in the hillock, lay the great bear, dead, but with limbs still twitching. It had been shot fairly through the shoulder and into the heart. Ellen, the rifle at her feet, stood sobbing against her husband's breast. His sound hand patted her back mechanically, but his eyes were fixed on something beyond.

Jean's followed them.

Loll was sitting flat on the ground beside the prostrate body of Kobuk, holding the dog's head on his knees. Kobuk's great dark eyes, swimming in tears of pain, were raised to the child's face, in a look so sad, and withal so full of love that Jean started forward, a cry breaking from her heart. From shoulder to thigh the dog was a bleeding horror where one whole side of his faithful body had been raked by the deadly claws of the bear.

"Oh, my Kobuk! My dear doggie!" The little boy sobbed and laid his cheek against Kobuk's head.

The dog moved slightly, and his pink tongue went out weakly to lick his small comrade's face.

"I won't let him hurt you no more now, Kobuk," crooned Lollie.

Jean sank on her knees beside him.

"Kobuk … dear old Kobuk …" she murmured brokenly, stroking a limp, hot paw.

The dog's dimming senses must have caught the sound of his

KOBUK

name, for his tail moved feebly as if, with the last beat of his brave heart, he was trying to wag goodbye. He lifted his head … a shudder passed through him. Then he lay still, his wide, glazing eyes fixed on the little boy's face.

Jean buried her head in her arms, oblivious to everything but the wild grief that shook her. But Lollie, not realizing that Kobuk was dead, sat patting the relaxed bandaged leg, while he whispered childish words of comfort in the unheeding ears.

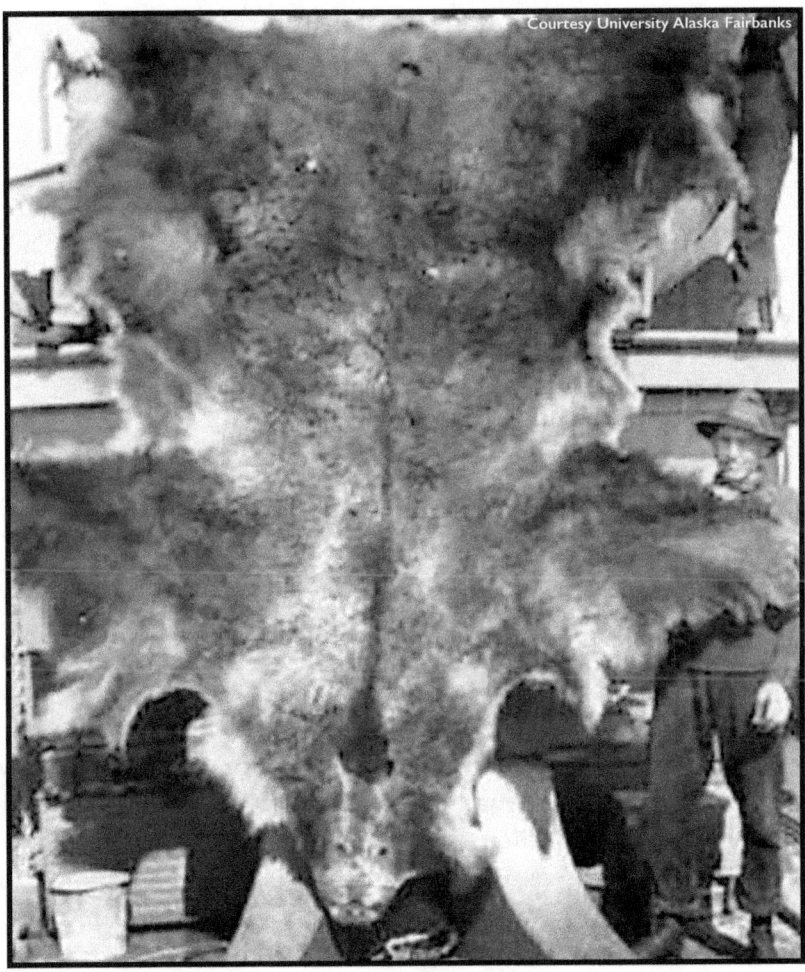

Courtesy University Alaska Fairbanks

A huge Kodiak bear, like this one, could provide a lot of meat for a family.

22

AT THE LONE TREE

That evening they buried Kobuk on the brow of the hill near the lone tree of Kon Klayu. At sunset time Loll sat by himself on the cabin steps. His chin was in his hand and his wide, grey eyes were fixed on the clear rose of the western sky. It was the first time that death had come near to him and the mystery and loneliness of it filled him with strange, new thoughts.

For a long time he looked into the fading glow. Then he shook his head slowly, reproachfully.

"God," he said, in the uncanny way he had of seeming to converse with Deity. "God, how can you smile so, when my Kobuk is dead?"

The purple dust of twilight sifted down on land and sea ... at last, awed by the unanswerable mystery of life and death, the little questioner turned in to the cabin, where his mother sat sewing in the soft, yellow light of the shaded oil lamp.

Breakfast the next morning was an event. Harlan had accepted Ellen's invitation to be present, and as he entered the cabin, the air was permeated with the delicious smell of frying steak. With the exception of ducks, the party had eaten no fresh meat for a month before coming to the island, and the recent daily breakfasts of musty oatmeal and hotcakes was becoming monotonous. Despite the tragedy of Kobuk, it was a grateful family that gathered about the big platter of bear meat and steaming cups of black coffee.

"This ought to tide us over nicely until the *Hoonah* comes," said Boreland as he helped himself to another piece. "A fine breakfast, El! Upon my word, it couldn't be better if we were in the States ... still, I'd like a bit of butter – real, honest-to-God cow's butter — on my hotcakes."

"Wall," mumbled Kayak with his mouth full of steak. "Sugar and like sweetenin' hits me where I live. I used to think if they took away my sugar I'd just as lief die. But now that there ain't any, I'm scratchin' along tolerable wall. But I'd give my hat for somethin' tasty to smear on these here sourdoughs!"

"Go on with you, Kayak! With El's sourdoughs, you don't need sweetening," Boreland said with a laugh. "We can use bear fat instead of butter now, for that old devil certainly was fat. We'll try some of it out. Of course we won't need much, for the schooner will be in any day now. We'll smoke part of it and put the rest down in salt." He leaned back in his chair and drew contentedly on his pipe.

"By hen, a smoke does taste mighty good after high-toned grub like this," drawled Kayak, surrounding himself with a cloud.

"You men smoke too much," Ellen broke in. "Sometimes I'm convinced that pipes bear the same relation to men that pacifiers do to babies. At the rate you three are going, you'll be out of tobacco in no time. If the *Hoonah* doesn't ..."

"Holy mackinaw, El! You're eternally seeing the hole in the doughnut lately," her husband interrupted somewhat testily. "Of course she will be along right away. No man would leave us on this island long without provisions. It wouldn't be human. And about smoking," he waved an airy hand, "why I can quit any time I want to and never miss it."

"Same here," Kayak said as he puffed out another tobacco-scented cloud. "I'll tell a man no measly habit ever got a strangle holt on me."

Harlan said nothing.

After breakfast the cleanup from the rockers was panned and freed from sand. Boreland weighed the dust in the new gold scales.

"Four ounces," he announced, as they balanced. "That ought to bring us about sixty dollars. Not bad for one day's work. If we can only find enough of that sand we'll make a stake here, boys. Gad, I wish the *Hoonah* would get here so we could establish ourselves permanently." Boreland had been trying to induce Kayak to remain with him on the island.

The remainder of the day was spent in getting the bear meat to the cabin and preparing it for preservation. The Native hut where Loll had surprised the swallows was cleaned out and fitted up as a smokehouse. Harlan cut and brought in several backloads of alder to furnish hardwood smoke to cure the meat. The women were busy indoors trying out the fat.

After the fire in the smokehouse had been going some time, Kayak Bill sauntered in with a can full of ashes.

"These here's hardwood ashes, Lady," he told Ellen. "We ain't got no white man's antiseptic medicine now, and I reckon we better make some o' the Injine kind. Put warm water on these and let 'em stand overnight. You'll have an antiseptic then that'll be a ring-tailed wonder, Lady."

As they worked about the house that morning Ellen and Jean discussed the shooting of the bear. It was the sight of the monster tearing her dog from shoulder to thigh that had calmed Ellen. Her fear was swallowed up in a gripping desire for revenge that made it possible for her to take careful aim and fire. Jean knew that Ellen had experienced none of the thrills that come to the hunter of big game. She was a domestic woman, a homemaker, thrown by circumstances into situations where she was forced to do things she never dreamed she could do – things she shuddered over afterward. Even as she told of the incident it seemed to both women like a tragic and terrible dream – a dream whose influence would not leave them.

On this day the sisters were heartily sick of life on the island of Kon Klayu.

Jean's depression continued all day long. The thought of Kobuk never left her. She found herself recalling his friendly, wagging ways; the feel of his muzzle nosing her hand; his soft eyes looking up at her from attentive, side-turned head. She found herself regretting that Kobuk was not there to share the fresh meat with them.

Several times during the day she stopped in her work to lift her head, listening. She kept fancying she heard Kobuk's husky woofing. Once she went to the door and looked out to convince herself that he was not there. Down at the smokehouse, Lollie, whom she had expected to be loudly inconsolable at the death of the dog, was helping the men. He had his old revolver tied to his waist and was shouting lustily. Jean felt a pang of disappointment in her nephew. She would have had him come to her and talk of the dog. Womanlike, she wanted to comfort him for the loss and in so doing ease her own grief. Kobuk had been her dog and Loll's.

She stepped back into the living room.

"I suppose it's the nature of the male to forget quickly," she said.

"Forget what?" Ellen asked, the word "male" causing her mind to fly at once to Harlan.

"Oh, nothing."

While the girl was doing up the supper dishes she heard Loll go whistling down the trail. When she had finished she took her violin from its case and stepped out on the porch. Kayak and Boreland were engaged in a close game of double solitaire. Ellen, with a headache, was lying down in Lollie's bunk. Harlan had gone across the island to his hut. It was very lonely.

She put down her violin.

"I'm going for a walk, Shane," she called through the open door.

Down past the smokehouse and the Russian sailor's grave she went; then up the gulch that led to the top of the hill. There were no animals to be afraid of now.

On the crest she turned her back on the flat lonesomeness of the tundra and looked down on the wide expanse of ocean spread below. The day was dying in soft flushes of amber and rose and lavender. Life on Kon Klayu was hard, but she never tired of the soothing beauty of its nights.

Her eyes followed the trail to the solitary tree facing the sea like a waiting woman with long, wind-blown hair. In the fading light its human aspect brought a sense of comfort to the girl. It made Kobuk's grave seem less lonely. She wished Loll were with her, she would go then and see how the men had left him. Poor Kobuk, with his dear, friendly ways! Everyone but her seemed to have forgotten him today – even Loll. Suddenly she decided she would go by herself.

She was startled by the sound of a step behind her. Glancing over her shoulder she saw Harlan coming from the north along the bear trail that skirted the bushes at the edge of the hill. She waited for him.

"I was headed there, too," he said simply, indicating the tree down the trail.

They walked silently in single file along the narrow path. The sweetness of a long sunny day came up from the grass that brushed Jean's skirts. For many minutes the new mound they were approaching was screened by the tall growth, but when they saw it, Jean stopped abruptly, her finger on her lips. From the grave came to them a muffled sound.

Loll was there before them.

The little fellow, oblivious to everything but his loneliness and his loss, lay across the fresh turned earth. His bare head was buried in his out-flung arms. One hand fiercely clutched a few bruised flowers and his small body shook with long, slow sobs.

Jean's throat tightened and tears of sympathy flooded her eyes. With outstretched arms she started impulsively forward to comfort him, but before she had taken a second step Harlan laid a detaining hand on her arm.

"Not now," he whispered. "Come." He drew back along the trail. Wondering, she followed until they were out of earshot.

"We'll wait for him here at the top of the gulch, Jean." It was the first time he had called her that. Each was aware of a sudden, warming sense of comradeship – a sense of sharing something tender, sad.

They sat down on the crest of the hill, so close that only a single tundra daisy nodded between them in the deepening twilight.

"Why – why did you do that, Gregg?"

He did not answer at once. Up from the sea came the susurrous voice of the reef whispering its eternal questions.

"Because ... men, real men, bear their grief silently, and alone," he said at last. "It is their way."

Jean thought of the little fellow, so childish in many ways, but silent all day on the subject of his loss. He had gone to cry out his grief, unseen, on Kobuk's grave. Suddenly she loved him with a tenderness she had never known before, but ... with it came a new loneliness. It was as if already his boyish hand had shut her, a woman, from that place in his heart that only men might know and understand.

She rested her elbows on her knees and cupped her chin in her hands.

"Oh," she said, reflectively. "I did not know. I did not dream that men were like that." The hearts of men ... it was strangely sweet to know what lay hidden in the hearts of men.

The faint, disembodied cry of a seabird keened across the dusk. Formless waters stretched away into the wide, beckoning dimness. The twilight wind was pungent with the strange awakening smell of the sea. Forgotten now was the depression of the day; it had no place in the romance, the mystery, the promise of the northern night. She became suddenly conscious that there was something sublimely beautiful in life that she had never yet experienced, something that unknowingly she had been waiting for; something that must come to her at last. She wondered if the young man sitting so close to her was ever stirred by such rapturous, intangible thoughts. With quickened interest she turned to look at him and met his deep eyes intent on her face.

Somewhat confused, he snapped off the head of the daisy between them.

"I ... I was just wondering what you were thinking about, Jean."

"I was thinking about you," she answered candidly. "I was wondering ..."

There came the sound of little running feet on the trail near them, and the girl rose hastily, calling Loll's name.

"Don't be afraid, honey. It's Jean."

Breathless, but relieved at the sight of them, the boy joined them and the three went slowly down the gulch toward the cabin.

Before the porch Harlan stopped.

"No, I won't go in now," he said in answer to her question.

They stood a moment, a sudden shy silence falling upon them.

"Good night, Jean." Slim and tall, he stood looking down at her, holding out his hand. Hers went out to meet it and the pressure of his strong, slender fingers sent a thrill to her heart. She was stirred by the magic of his nearness.

"Good ... night," she whispered wonderingly. She longed to linger there in the dusk with him, but because of her desire, she turned and ran up the steps to the cabin.

Ten minutes later she stood in the twilight on the bank below the cabin. The sea, the night, the world seemed to hold out loving arms to her. A feeling tremulously new and enchanting had come to her. She tucked her violin beneath her chin and drew her bow softly across the strings. This night she could play as she had never played before.

This night she must play.

The music floated up through the dusk with dreamy, questioning sweetness ... time slipped by. At last she drifted into the notes of her goodnight. She felt that there was a special tenderness in the chords from her long-drawn singing bow tonight. Lost in the harmony of her own creating she hardly knew when the voice – his voice – from the hilltop took up the strain. So softly was it done that she was not surprised. The words came down to her now clear, mellow, thrillingly masculine, and ... did she only imagine there was something personal in them?

"In the West
Sable night lulls the day on her breast.
Sweet, goodnight! ... Love, goodnight!"

23

ELLEN

The days passed. They were growing noticeably shorter now and provisions were getting low. The trail up the steep hillside behind the cabin became hardened by the feet of the watchers alert for the expected arrival of the *Hoonah*. At the top, which they all had come to call the Lookout, every hour of the day found someone of the party anxiously scanning the ocean toward Katleean.

Many cannery steamers and whalers on their way south were sighted, but all gave the island a wide berth. The hundred reefs of Kon Klayu had no lure for sailors of the North Pacific.

Boreland, who never failed to patrol the beach daily, found one more patch of ruby sand, which the three men rocked out. He weighed the gold after the cleanup.

"This sand is richer than the other batch, El!" he exclaimed enthusiastically.

For a moment, Ellen eyed the yellow gleam of the dust without interest. Then she leaned over and dipped her fingers into the golden flakes, letting them fall slowly back into the scales.

"Shane, Shane," she said, and then turned away and patted his arm maternally. "You are like a little boy playing with wooden money." What value had gold on the island of Kon Klayu, she thought, where it could not buy an ounce of food?

To Ellen Boreland these were days of anguished conjecture, of harassed indecision. As they passed with no sign of the *Hoonah,* she began to recall her last week at Katleean. On the screen of her mind appeared over and over again the White Chief's dark face, in her ears the voice of memory repeated his softly spoken, enigmatic words: "Remember ... you'll want me ... the pigeon loose, comes back ... I will understand."

The *Hoonah* was overdue. Was this then what he had meant? Was he now holding the schooner believing that in her anxiety for the safety of her loved ones she would release the bird? Was he trying to force her, at such a cost, to buy from him the lives of those dear to her? Had he planned this thing from the beginning? Was he even now at the post waiting – certain that eventually she must release the pigeon? The picture unnerved her to the point of panic. And yet she tried to reassure herself. No man, however cruel and pitiless, could deliberately plan so monstrous a thing. She tried to find excuses for the non-arrival of the *Hoonah.*

Perhaps the fall steamer had not come in on time. Perhaps some accident had happened and the White Chief was having the schooner repaired. Surely he would come, if only to ascertain the fate of his bookkeeper for whose safety Silvertip must account. But Silvertip ... had the Swede told the truth? Might he not have said that young Harlan had preferred to stay behind and had been safely landed with the party? Then it occurred to her with a fearful knowledge that to the White Chief of Katleean the life of a man meant nothing.

While she went about her household duties she remembered again and again the sound of the white trader's sardonic: "I have presented your son with a pigeon." Not to her, nor to Jean had he given the bird, but deliberately he had made a present of it to her little boy that Loll might innocently love and care for the thing designed to be the symbol of his mother's shame!

To her harassed mind the bird came to have a hideous vitality. There was something uncanny in the way it thrived in its captivity, as though it fed on her distress. And almost like a conspiracy was the determination of her loved ones to preserve it. Loll was devoted to it, especially now since the death of Kobuk. It was his only playmate.

Shane was particularly zealous in his care of it, exercising the bird by means of a long string, since Loll would permit no one to clip its wings. Even Kayak Bill was always bringing it green stuff to supplement its diet of rolled oats. Only Jean appeared indifferent to the bird – Jean, always tender of dumb things. She had remarked, once, that its smoke-grey color reminded her unpleasantly of the eyes of the White Chief.

Sometimes, in a kind of fury, Ellen wondered if the pigeon bore a charmed life – if it could not die. Dead, her problem would be solved for her. Yet she dared not let it die – not while there was a chance! Standing before the cage day after day, Ellen would torment herself with a thought. If she should leave the door unlatched, so that it would jar open ... if, of its own accord, the bird should fly away. Then, when the White Chief came she could disclaim all knowledge of its going. But there was the lock of her hair, about which she had lied to her husband. It was still in the possession of the trader who, secure in his power over everyone in his wilderness kingdom, was capable of any melodramatic folly, of any false tale. And Shane, hotheaded, protective – she shuddered. In her overwrought imagination she saw her husband's hands stained with another man's blood. No, the bird was a kind of thing fastened upon her that she could not, must not in all conscience lose.

Torn by these conflicting emotions, and sick with foreboding, she would turn away from the cage. Tomorrow ... she would wait until tomorrow. Perhaps the *Hoonah* would come tomorrow. Perhaps it was even in sight now! With hope and longing so intense that it bordered on despair she would leave the cabin and climb to the Lookout to scan the empty sea.

One sunny afternoon she was standing alone watching a dark streak of steamer smoke move slowly southward. Below her, stretching away to the wide horizon lay the sea, its great, smooth swells heaving jade green in the sunlight. Autumn color lay over the tundra moss, the rice grass, the short alder bushes. Autumn, a soothing autumn was in the air, promising the northern world of growing things a long, snow enfolded peace; but herself and her little family – what?

For some time she half-consciously had been aware of a strange encircling hush. She looked about her and realized that nowhere was a seabird of any kind. Then far out, a dark mass, like a fallen cloud, challenged her attention. Even as she wondered it rose into the air and began to advance swiftly toward her – it resolved itself into thousands of small black birds.

"The sea parrots!" Ellen exclaimed. "They must be going south." She had not known that this would happen. She felt a dull regret that it should be so.

With crimson beaks pointed south they came nearer and nearer, until, flying directly overhead, they cast a shadow as if a cloud had passed over the sun. The sky was black with them. Noiseless on the wing, there was something ominous in the sea parrots' silence during the quarter of an hour in which they flew steadfastly over the island on their course. Ellen watched them with an interest divided between wonder and awe.

Before they had passed, an increasing wild chorus came to her ears. She turned to face the north again where another cloud, grey-white, was coming. She knew it to be composed of her noisiest neighbors, the gulls, bound also for southern shores.

Over the island these birds sailed with gay squawking, their wide wings seeming to wave a contemptuous goodbye. It was as if they scorned, yet pitied the human creature below who must stay behind because she had no wings to bear her away.

The last call dimmed and died. Despite the lazy swash of the swells on the beach below the sunny afternoon was heavy with silence. Ellen's eyes swept the vast circle of the distance. The smoke of the southbound steamer was no more. Far down the tundra toward the cliffs stood the one lone tree of Kon Klayu facing the sea like a waiting woman with long, windblown hair.

An appalling sense of loneliness flooded Ellen. A sudden, overwhelming need for human companionship swept her. She turned hastily into the trail that led down to the cabin, and then checked herself as the sound of someone whistling came to her. She glanced back.

Walking briskly toward her along the tundra trail that led from his hut to the Lookout came Gregg Harlan. He must recently have borrowed Shane's razor, for the soft, dark beard that had shadowed his face was gone. Bareheaded, he advanced vigorously, his chin up, his whole figure the personification of youth, confidence and a new strength. For the first time Ellen was glad to see him.

As she waited for him to approach, she studied him with interest. He had changed much since his landing on Kon Klayu. Under the rigors of hardship, of physical labor, of abstinence, he had developed a clean-cut masculinity that was strangely reassuring. She remembered how unconsciously, during these past weeks, she had turned to him for the steadiness that others had lacked; how instinctively she had counted on him for a perception of the little things, the smaller needs, which are so often the greater ones. After all, she reminded herself, in the day-by-day stresses of life, it was this gift of understanding, of sympathy with the innate needs, that counted so tremendously.

She pictured Jean, with her wane emotions, her love of the finer beauties of life, thrown into the rough and changing currents of existence as the wife of a man older, sturdier, perhaps, than Gregg, but without his steadier gentleness. Ellen shrank instinctively from the thought. And Gregg had changed – of that there was no doubt. There was no longer a sign of his old subservience to the poisonous brew of Katleean; instead there was every evidence that he was not another man, but in a greater, stronger way, the man he had once been.

After all, Ellen thought, who was she to determine for Jean the sort of man the girl should choose? She who had permitted herself compromising entanglements with such a one as the White Chief! With Gregg, Jean was safer at that moment than was she in her own tragic situation ... safer and cleaner in her motives! With something of appeal for the steadying power of his friendship in her need, whose eventualities would be as vital to Jean as to herself, Ellen turned with a new warmth in her manner to greet the young man. Discussing the phenomenon of the bird migration, she went with him down the trail to the cabin.

As they approached the house, Lollie came rushing up from the beach, holding something tightly in his little hand. He was shouting excitedly, and at his urging the family gathered curiously around him to find themselves electrified at the disclosure of what the youngster held. It was a nugget, fully an ounce in weight. He had found it, he explained, on the bedrock below Bear Paw Lake.

Boreland went off immediately to prospect with Kayak Bill and Harlan. Contrary to all previous experience, this gold had not been uncovered by a storm. There had been no storm. Then there must be a place where the yellow metal lay otherwise revealed. Somewhere on the island must be a mine of gold. Harlan, who had spent an inattentive year at a school of mines before he was requested to leave, began to take an interest in the situation.

Shane returned that night, long after the others, without having found another sign. Nor was he any more successful, when day after day he continued to patrol the beaches, though his faith in the sands of Kon Klayu remained unshaken.

Ellen and he were returning one afternoon from Skeleton Rib where they had gone to look for pay sand. He had recovered the use of his sprained wrist and had brought along the shotgun. Opposite the little lake in this vicinity they turned in from the beach.

A drizzling rain had begun to fall. The dead yellow grass lay flat on the ground. The bare brown branches of the alders were hung with globules of water that fell, wetting Ellen as she brushed through them. Out on the lake she caught glimpses of a flock of belated mallards, but since there was now no upstanding vegetation, it was difficult for the hunters to hide their approach. Crouching low behind an alder, Ellen watched Shane creep up within shooting range. Since the gun was an old thing held together by copper wire, and went off at the slightest jar, it was impossible to carry it loaded. Shane paused, inserted the shells, raised the piece and took careful aim. There came a loud report, a whirr of wings, and the next instant Shane fell backward, one hand flung upward to his head.

Ellen sprang to where he lay motionless, blood streaming down one side of his face. Even in her anguish she noted that the gun barrels had burst from the force of overloaded shells. Swiftly she plunged her handkerchief into the water, and uttering incoherent entreaties and endearing names, began to bathe his face, which already was beginning to swell.

For what seemed a long time, Shane did not move. Frantically she tore a strip from her long chemise and bound up his head to stop the flow of blood. Then with all her strength she sought to raise him from the grass. His head fell limply back exposing his bare brown throat to the falling rain.

"Shane ... Shane ... Oh, help me, dear! Please!" Cold fear gripped her and made her voice tremble. She struggled once more to raise his heavy body. She was unable to lift him. Calling him, imploring him, she tried again and again, until at last he sat up slowly, groaning and putting both hands to the bloody bandage about his head.

"Come, dear," her voice broke as her shaking hands tried to assist him. "We must go home, Shane. Come now." As if he were a child, she coaxed and encouraged the stunned man until he rose painfully, swayed, and steadied himself against her. After a lurching step or two he managed to keep his feet, and in silence that struck to her heart, he suffered her to lead him along through the soft, drizzling rain.

Ellen found only Harlan at the cabin. Without a question the young man sprang to her assistance. He helped Shane into the house and to bed.

The last of the antiseptic had been used for Kobuk, so Ellen ran for the clear water from the hardwood ashes – the Native antiseptic that Kayak Bill had induced her to make. Then while she held the basin, Harlan washed the blood from her husband's face. The sight of the wound sickened her. Just below Shane's right eye was a livid gash two inches long.

What could she do? In some way stitches must be taken to draw the edges together, but how? She had nothing but ordinary needles and thread. She blamed herself bitterly for leaving Katleean without a medicine chest. A moment she thought of that one, ordered from the States, which was to arrive on the *Hoonah*. Then again she set her mind to the solution of the problem before her. It came to her in a flash, one of Kayak Bill's tales of a Native woman's ingenuity!

"Gregg." She spoke firmly. "Hand me the scissors." She took the hairpins from her hair and it fell in a heavy coil to her waist. Harlan eyed her as though he feared she had suddenly gone insane when she cut a strand of hair and held it up to him.

"We'll boil this and some needles, Gregg," she continued quietly. "And when they are sterilized, you must help me put the stitches in this wound."

Half an hour later it was over. Shane lay back on his pillow. Ellen watched beside him stroking his hand that lay twitching on the coverlet. Something in the outline of her husband's long, still body under the blankets chilled her with foreboding. Heretofore the thought of hunger only had been with her. Now, should sickness or further accidents come upon them ... should Shane develop blood poisoning . . .

Like one doomed, Ellen's eyes sought the wall calendar. NOVEMBER 1 met her gaze with the force of a blow. The *Hoonah* was already two weeks overdue.

Suddenly she bent and rested her head against the blankets, pressing her quivering lips fiercely, passionately against her husband's thin hand.

Tomorrow ... tomorrow she must – she *would* release the pigeon.

24

MAROONED

Six hours later, Kon Klayu was cowering in the blasts of the most terrific storm yet experienced by the adventurers. The fearful velocity of the wind and rain made it impossible for Kayak Bill to keep his tent erected. In the middle of the night he was forced to move his bedding into Jean's and Lollie's room, where the sisters helped him screen himself off by tacking up a tarpaulin.

After Jean had slipped back into her bunk, she was surprised to hear her sister discussing, almost wildly she thought, the possibility of a bird's flying against such a gale; and after everyone else had settled down again for the night, she could hear Ellen pacing the floor of the living room. Poor Ellen, thought the girl, she was all unstrung over Shane's accident and frightened at the thought of blood poisoning.

But Shane was feeling much better next morning, though he kept to his bed all day and for several days after. He was unusually silent, realizing, perhaps for the first time, the gravity of the situation, for the storm did not blow itself out in three or six days, as storms had always done before. It lasted twelve days and increased in violence until near the end.

During this great gale Jean sought her bunk early each evening and lay there between sleep and wakefulness listening to the wind and sea. She was thankful that this was not a snow storm, since snowfall on Kon Klayu did not come until later, owing to the proximity of the

Japanese current, but she found herself concerned for Harlan alone in his hut on the other side of the island. When it became apparent that Shane's cut was healing as it should, the girl found her thoughts lingering on Gregg. She missed him more than she cared to admit, even to herself.

Before Shane's accident with the shotgun it had fallen to Gregg's lot to hunt the ducks and geese, which were by now an important part of their food. There was little ammunition and every shot must be made to tell. With the makeshift shotgun it was impossible to hit anything on the wing, and though it was evident that Harlan's sporting instincts revolted against slipping up and pot shooting birds on the water, the scarcity of shells compelled him to do it. Kayak Bill flatly refused to handle anything but his .45, confessing to a casual scorn for what he termed a "shootin' iron that spewed its durned in'ards all over the range." In the growing anxiety over the non-arrival of the *Hoonah*, Ellen had relaxed somewhat her vigilant attitude toward Harlan, and so Jean had come to join the young man on his hunting expeditions.

Recalling them now she glowed at the memory of those past October mornings, when, leaving the rest of the family sleeping, she had slipped out of the cabin and met the waiting hunter. She had grown to love the hunt – the early sun sparkling on the yellow of frost-coated grass, the green of the ocean, the tonic of the sea air and the swift, never-to-be-forgotten creak-creak-creak of flying wings close overhead. There was a thrill in the cautious creeping toward the lake wreathed in the gossamer mist of the autumn morning, and the wriggling through the stiffened yellow grass, and a pang of delighted wonder at coming so close to the wild, winged things, squattering and making soft duck chattering in the shadow of the reeds.

But duck hunting days were over now, she reminded herself regretfully. The shotgun was useless.

Shane's wound continued to heal without complications, but still after everyone else had long been in bed, Jean could hear Ellen pacing the floor nearly every night. This increased the uneasiness that had been growing upon the girl. She wished Ellen would confide more in her. She was finding it very hard for her to understand her sister these days. Ellen had not been herself for weeks. The girl recalled her curious and changeable attitude toward the pigeon the White Chief had given Loll. From at first ignoring it, Ellen had suddenly begun to manifest a lively interest in its welfare. The best of the rolled oats went to feed it. Owing to the occasional frosts Ellen had moved the cage into the shed, and she herself had solicitously covered it nightly with an old blanket. Sometimes she had stood for ten minutes at a time looking in at the smoke-grey bird.

One incident stood out clearly in Jean's mind. She had come upon Ellen musing thus beside the cage. Her sister had just washed her hair and it hung about her shoulders in lovely, golden-brown profusion. There was a look on her face – Jean, thinking of it, shook her head to banish the memory of that look. Presently Ellen had reached up, and with a trembling hand gathered together the short tresses that marked the place where she had foolishly, Jean thought, cut off the lock of hair in Katleean. Ellen's fingers slipped over the severed ends, and then flattened themselves forcibly over the latch on the pigeon's cage. "No! No!" Passionately the words had escaped her as she turned her back on the cage. Meeting Jean's questioning eyes, she had flushed and gone on into the house without speaking.

Always, at night, as Jean lay thinking, this incident drifted with curious insistency through her mind.

As the storm continued through dreary days, blowing always from the southwest, the strange, reverberating roll from the south cliffs came more loudly than ever before. Listening to it sometimes, Jean would shiver at the hint of the supernatural in its cadence.

The continual thundering of the surf on the beach and the trembling of the cabin in the rainy blasts of the gale finally began to tell on the nerves of those confined in such small quarters. Gradually the talk at the table grew less. Even Kayak Bill ceased his monologues. He and Shane smoked more than ever and buried themselves in the reading of the old magazines and papers. Ellen seemed more affected than any of them. Her face had become drawn and haggard. She was so inattentive to Loll's questions when the daily lessons were in progress that the little boy grew impatient and asked Jean to help him instead. Then, too, Ellen's strange solicitude for the pigeon increased until it was with difficulty that Shane could prevent her bringing the bird into the cabin during the gale.

One night Jean woke from a troubled doze. Everywhere was a strange, arresting stillness. She realized in a moment that the wind had gone down. The roar of the breakers, which had been so loud and constant, now sounded muffled. Her first feeling was one of intense happiness and relief. The storm was over at last – the longest storm she had ever known. Surely, now, she thought, the *Hoonah* would come.

Though she knew it must be after midnight, there was a murmur of voices in the living room. A chair scraped along the floor. Then came Kayak Bill's tones, distinctly and with a gravity that sent a chill through her. He was evidently concluding some argument.

"But I'm a-tellin' you, Boreland, that there's nary a Injine or a white on the Alasky coast that'll venture nigh the island o' Kon Klayu after November first –"

"Great God, Kayak!" Boreland's protest cut him short. "Kilbuck *knows* we haven't enough grub for the winter ... he wouldn't leave us here to starve, especially two women and a child, after he has put us here himself! He's *promised* to bring us provisions. Given us his word. To go back on it would be a violation of the law of the cache. Why, the man has my schooner, and he hasn't paid for her yet. No, no, Kayak. Kilbuck will come ... by God, he's *got* to come!"

There was slow finality in Kayak Bill's answer.

"Boreland, he's waited too long. He can't come. It's the thirteenth o' November. No one can come to Kon Klayu now till the breakup o' the winter. The White Chief's staked the cards on us, son. We're up against it."

P A R T   I I I

25

ON RATIONS

After the great November storm was over, Ellen realized that her problem – for the present – had been taken out of her hands. Even if the pigeon were sent now, the White Chief would not risk bringing a schooner to the island of Kon Klayu; there was no boat built that could make a landing on its reef-guarded shores during the winter season. It was too late. They were marooned until spring at least. She would keep the bird until then. Further than that she refused to think.

As she accepted the inevitable, she felt a sense of peace settle upon her, and with it came new strength. As Kayak had said, they were up against it, and knowing now what she had to fight, she was ready.

Her mind turned at once to the pitifully meager supply of provisions. With all the shrewdness of a general preparing to withstand an indeterminate siege, she planned her rations so that they might last the longest period of time. If the party could exist until spring, a cannery boat, a whaler, a ship of adventure, might call in and get them, even though the White Chief did not come. Ellen made a mental vow that they would live until spring.

On the fourteenth of November she made the entry in her log.

We have the following provisions on hand:

Flour - damaged - enough for eight months

Bacon, 1 slab

Dried onions, 1 pound

Beans, enough for five months if we have them once a week

Rice - damaged - for five months, once a week

Lemon Extract, 1 bottle

Salt and Pepper

Worcestershire sauce, 1 bottle

Dried bear meat

Bear fat, rancid

Rolled oats - moldy - four months

Tea and Coffee

Three boxes candles

Two jars canned plums from Mother's

That afternoon, on a pretense of his looking for pay sand, she sent Loll down on the beach, and, calling the others together, summed up the problem that confronted them. She read her list of provisions and set forth her plan of rations. In conclusion, she urged that each one take a tum hunting for seafood on the rocks and stranded fish on the beach. If they could supplement their ration thus, they might, by confining themselves strictly to it, exist until some boat came in the spring. Harlan, she decided, must take his meals at the cabin.

"Jean and I will begin gathering shellfish tomorrow, while you men start to lay in a supply of firewood for the winter months," she finished.

Even Shane agreed that existence, now, instead of gold, was their main concern on the island of Kon Klayu, although his was the logic that still insisted that their desertion by Kilbuck could not be true simply because it seemed so intolerable.

Strange to say, after this frank facing of their difficulties, every one of the party felt more cheerful. There came a letting down of the tension, a relaxation of the nerves, which had made their storm-bound days so trying.

The following morning found Ellen and her sister in rubber hip boots, belonging to their men, headed for Sunset Point. They were equipped with pails and case knives.

The sun shone bright, although there was little warmth in it. The air was sharp and exhilarating and wonderfully pure after the great wind. The thunder of surf on a hundred reefs spoke of the storm of yesterday.

They soon found themselves down among the great boulders amid tangles of brown seaweed, where the shallow pools left by the outgoing tide were alive with strange and interesting sea life. Here, more than in any other place on Kon Klayu, they were conscious of the air, the sound, the whole enchanting spell of the sea. The bottoms of tiny sea pools were dotted with red and yellow starfish. Entrancing rose and purple sea anemones blossomed like thistles on the water-covered stones, but at a touch, a sound, folded their delicate beauties into tight buttons hardly to be distinguished from the base to which they clung. Comical, tiny iridescent fish, with eyes of bulging astonishment, and thorns on their backs, darted about the women's feet and went into hiding under floating russet seaweed. The big boots lumbering into the shallow water caused sea eggs of green and lavender to move solemnly on the bottom with ray-like prickles erect.

"We'll try the sea eggs later on," Ellen said, as she watched them. "Senott told me at Katleean that all Natives eat them."

The boulders were encrusted with great, grey, open-mouthed barnacles. Periwinkles, like tiny purple snails, clustered on the weeds. These were so numerous that the sisters could not step without crushing them. The crunching sound at first filled Ellen with repugnance for her task, but necessity forced her on. And before she had filled her pail with them, she had become accustomed to it.

As they moved farther out to where the waves of the ebb tide were creaming against the rocks, the dark seamed sides were painted a delicate sea pink by a lichen-like growth. Above their heads these boulders rose and all about them was the soft, seeping sound that sea things make when the tide is low.

Kayak Bill had often described what he called a "gumboot," remarking that the name was bestowed locally because of the toughness of this aquatic animal when cooked. From the old man's description Ellen had thought they might be limpets. Since there were no clams on the beach of Kon Klayu she had concluded to try them.

Now, suddenly, she came upon them, their cone-shaped shells adhering to the rocks. When she and Jean tried to pick the small creatures from their abiding places, the least touch or sound caused them to tighten to the boulders. It was impossible then to dislodge them without smashing the shell.

"We'll have to sneak up on them, El," whispered Jean, suiting her actions to her words, and with a sudden, swift movement sweeping half a dozen from their support. It was then that the sisters began to experience the thrill of anticipation, the fascination of uncertainty, which comes to those forced to hunt their food in wild places.

The tide came in flooding the pools in which they were standing and warning them that it was time to leave. With full pails they hastened to the cabin eager to try their new food.

Periwinkles, boiled, had not an unpleasant taste, but because of their likeness to worms, neither of the women could eat them. It fell to little Loll to extract them from their small shells by means of a pin. This was a slow process, and after the novelty wore off, the youngster gave utterance to loud lamentations over Kayak Bill's fondness for periwinkles.

The "gumboots" were also boiled, and found to be as rubbery as the name implied. Chopping them fine, Ellen made a hash of bread crumbs and fried the mixture in bear fat. Afterward she sometimes added a small bit of chopped bacon, considered a rare treat since the bacon was hoarded for flavoring beans, which they were permitted but once a week.

In putting her family on rations, Ellen noticed that each one's appetite increased tremendously. Only by exercising the most rigid self-control could she keep herself to the portions she had allotted. The sight of Lollie scraping his plate for the last morsel of food, and then looking up at her expectantly, was the hardest thing she had to bear. She soon began, surreptitiously, to put aside a portion of her daily share for him.

For a time, food was the all-absorbing topic of conversation. The men found a certain grim amusement in sitting about the table talking of the kind of "grub" they would order if they were in the States. They could go into such detail as to taste and smell of certain appetizing dishes eaten in the past that often Jean laughingly stopped them.

"By Jove!" Harlan would say. "I know a little place in San Francisco where you can get a beefsteak Bordelaise that would *actually* ... "

"Um-m, yes," Shane would follow, "and don't you remember that little Italian dump on Columbus where they serve spaghetti with a gooey stuff filled with chicken livers and mushrooms – oh ... man!"

"One time up on the Kuskokwim I snared me a cutthroat," Kayak Bill would drawl, and then, with an angler's delight, proceed to describe every wiggle of that super fish until he landed it, and every phase of campfire cooking, until, crisp and bacon garnished, he ate it from the frying pan.

Jean's longing for fruit, especially bananas, was so intense that she used to wake up at night thinking about them. She dreamed of bananas smothered in cream. When she closed her eyes sometimes during the day, bunches of the yellow fruit dangled enticingly in her mental vision. She tried to reread *Pickwick Papers*. The hungry Fat Boy at first appealed to her, but Dickens' masterly descriptions of the nourishing food of old England filled her with such a hunger that she put the book aside.

December proved to be a month of snow and blizzards, but despite the faithful patrolling of the beach, nothing in the way of pay sand came to light. Whenever the weather permitted, everyone sought shellfish among the rocks, as it had become necessary to gather a quantity sufficient to last during storms. The prickly sea eggs were now added to the fare. Often however, when the wet snow was hurled unceasingly against the windows for days, the supply of seafood gave out. Then, for hours, there was hunger in the little cabin on Kon Klayu.

Jean noticed that her nephew, in some manner, had come to know that it distressed his mother to speak of being hungry after he had eaten what she had to give him. It was seldom now that he mentioned it. His little mind appeared to be taken up with speculations as to Christmas.

Jean had often listened to Kayak Bill prefacing his tales with: "I'm a-tellin' o' you, you never can tell a speck about a man till you 'cabin' with him a-durin' o' one winter." She was beginning to understand what the old man meant by it now. She was growing to appreciate Shane's irrepressible Irish cheerfulness that always rose above hunger, accident and the nerve-trying confinement of the cabin in stormy weather. Because of him, the storm-bound hours, despite the food situation, were for the most part times of storytelling and exchange of reminiscences. For Shane, with a strange faith, still clung to the thought that the White Chief might bring the *Hoonah* to the island before the end of the year.

As Christmas drew nearer, however, with one storm succeeding another, a change came over him. He began to sit beside the table in silence, his head in his hands, his brown eyes looking off into space.

One night when the house trembled in the grip of a blizzard and the unexplained reverberating sound from the south cliffs came louder than usual, he sat thus while Kayak Bill played a game of solitaire on the opposite side of the table. Lollie had established himself in his mother's bed. While he turned the pages of a fairy tale book, he pointed out the pictures to Jean.

That day there had been no shellfish to supplement the scanty allowance of food and the little fellow lingered hungrily on the colored pictures depicting bountiful tables of feasting kings; jolly fat cooks basting roasting ducks in the kitchens of queens; little Jack Horner pulling a ripe plum from a pie. Finally he turned a page, which disclosed the Queen of Hearts holding out a pan of delicious, brawny-crusted tarts. The crimson jelly at the centers seemed almost to quiver.

"Oh, Mother, Mother, I'm so *hungry!*" he burst out.

Ellen laid aside her sewing. And going to the cupboard, she then brought out a tiny dish of rice and gave it to him. Jean saw Boreland's eyes follow the movements of his wife. She wondered if he, like herself, suspected that the dish contained over half Ellen's portion for that day. There was a tenseness about his jaw, a smoldering light in his eye that sent a queer chill over the girl. A few minutes later he rose and climbed up into the loft. When he descended he held a revolver in his hand.

The weapon was one he had carried since boyhood. Its history belonged to an old-time Native scout, a friend of Boreland's father. On its handle were three notches. The last time the girl had heard the story of those three notches was at Katleean when Shane, pointing them out to the White Chief, had told him that each one stood for a man who deserved and met death at the hand that held the gun.

She grew inattentive to the questions of Loll as she watched her brother-in-law at the table oiling and polishing the old revolver. He spent much time at his task and when it was finished sat thoughtfully, his thin fingers slowly passing over the notches as if he were counting them for the first time. After some minutes he leaned across to Kayak Bill.

"Kayak," he said so softly that the girl could scarcely hear, "*if* I get back to Katleean in the spring *there will be four.*" He tapped the notched handle of the revolver significantly.

A sudden chill of foreboding, doubly terrible because at first so vague and incomprehensible, swept her. She saw Kayak's eyes looking into Boreland's. They were tense, half-closed and glittered coldly, not at Shane, but at some vision induced by Shane's words. Then the old man nodded twice, slowly, approvingly, decisively.

As the days of December went by everyone on the island, with the exception of Loll, asserted often that of course there could be no Christmas. Despite this, however, as the date drew near the holiday spirit hovered persistently over the camp. Mysterious things were going on. Kayak Bill withdrew himself behind his curtain very early each day, and tantalizing sounds of whittling came from his corner. Boreland and Harlan shut themselves up for hours in the shed.

The day before Christmas came white and still with great soft snowflakes falling until noon.

"Santa Claus weather! Santa Claus weather!" sang Lollie, dancing up and down before the window. "He'll surely come now – if there is one," he added for Jean's benefit. The girl had tried to explain the spirit of Christmas to the youngster, but he still clung to his early conception of the good old saint.

There was a party that night on Kon Klayu. Jean had never admired her sister more than when she saw Ellen rise above the haunting fear of starvation, and with the few pitiful things at her command, create the cheer of Christmas Eve. And there was no lack of presents – homemade gifts that had cost their donors much thought and hours of labor – gifts, some of them smile-provoking but bringing with them a sense of warmer friendliness, a touch of tenderness that enhances the spirit of fellowship that comes to those who share the hazards and adventures of the North.

Loll, with one lump of hoarded sugar, two full-rigged schooners, a Native war canoe and a new blouse sewed by Ellen's fingers, was supremely happy. For the men were mittens made of a blanket, scarves knitted from the unraveled yarn of two old sweaters, and – even on Kon Klayu – the male members could not escape the inevitable Christmas necktie, for Ellen had produced from the bottom of her trunk three brand new ones purchased for Shane before she sailed from the States.

Kayak Bill looked his over a few minutes and then disappeared behind his tarpaulin screen in the next room. When he emerged it was with one hand holding aside his bushy beard. The new necktie, impaled with a large nugget pin, hung low on his blue flannel shirt.

"I ain't wore one o' these dude halters for ten yars, Lady," he drawled, hitching his shoulders with an air of being pleased with himself. "But I ain't forgot how they goes."

There were two beautiful caps for Ellen and Jean made of the iridescent necks of mallard drakes, carefully prepared and sewed by Kayak; a dustpan made of a kerosene can; a calendar ruled off on the letter paper of the defunct life insurance company, and to their genuine delight, two paper knives carved from the tusks taken from the sea monster's head that Lollie had discovered. Adorned with the emblematic figures of the Thunderbird and the Wolf, they were in their way works of art, and Ellen, reading the penciled greeting on the paper attached to her gift, could not keep the look of surprise from her face as she thanked Harlan for it. It occurred to her that this young man was continually and agreeably surprising her lately.

After the distribution of the gifts, and the old-time stories told in the candlelight, Jean, by the magic of her violin, coaxed them all into singing the Yuletide songs fraught with memories of the homeland – all that is with the exception of Kayak Bill. The old man, his high forehead shining from his recent ablutions, his bushy beard hiding his new tie, sat silent, even wistful, stroking the homemade gifts that lay upon his knees. Jean, as she played, wondered what long ago memories were misting his hazel eyes.

When the singing came to an end, little Loll, without an invitation, rose and announced:

"*Now*, I'm going to speak my piece."

He walked to the middle of the room and made a low, circular bow. In the effort to recall that "piece" he had spoken the year previous in Sunday school, his brow puckered and his grey eyes took on a look of intense thought. His emphasis fell in strange places:

" 'Twas *the* night before Christmas
An' all *through* the house
Not-ta creature ... was ... was *stirring*
Not-teven a mouse ... not-*teven* a mouse ...
Not-teven a *mouse!*"

All efforts to remember further having proved vain, Lollie, far from being embarrassed, bowed low again with the poise of one who has recited brilliantly, and took his seat amid the applause.

Harlan rose at last to say good night. From Loll's bunk, where she was helping the sleepy boy to bed, Ellen called after him her Christmas wishes. Jean slipped into her coat and followed the young man out to the porch.

The night had turned wondrously clear, but it did not seem cold to the two who stood silently looking out on its beauty.

"Never was there such a night for Christmas carols, Gregg," said the girl after some minutes had gone by. "Wait."

She darted into the cabin and returned almost immediately with her violin tucked beneath her coat.

"I may never have a chance like this again. I'm going up as far as the Lookout with you. Come."

They climbed up through the white, starlit silence to the top of the hill. From the height they looked down through the weird half-light reflected from the snow. The formless waters kissed the ermine-wrapped shores of the island. The sweet, hoarse voice of the sea had in it the cadence of happy child calls. There was an effect of illimitable space, of wonderful freedom. Up from the north into the night-blue bowl of the sky mystic lights unfurled themselves in pulsing, wreathing chiffon-like streamers of changing rose and violet, green and amber, red and gold unfurled ... trembled ... rippled into opal splendor, and then swiftly and softly swept across the heavens and entangled themselves in the calm, friendly stars that looked down on Kon Klayu.

Jean caught her breath.

"The Christmas lights of God," she whispered. "I have never been so near to Him before." She lifted her violin to her shoulder and began the opening bars of "Holy Night." Gregg's voice joined the instrument, reverent, worshipful.

As she played there beside him the girl knew that they were sharing something never to be forgotten by either – the magic of a moment of perfect accord, a moment of beauty that transcended earthly things and left them but two souls worshipping together beneath the softened glory of the Northern Lights.

26

WINTER DAYS

It had taken Gregg Harlan some time to realize fully that mere existence on Kon Klayu was an all-absorbing problem. But when he did so the primitiveness of it stimulated and intoxicated him, not as liquor had once done, but with a freshness that cleared his brain and sent his blood racing through his veins. Every cell in his body tingled with life. He felt this exhilaration in his swinging stride, his uplifting chin. By Christmas he was no more tormented by a craving for liquor. On the contrary, he was nauseated at the memory of his stupid, sodden days at Katleean. Alaska, the Great Country that either makes or breaks, had challenged him to prove himself a man – and he had accepted the challenge. Kon Klayu, island of mystery and beauty, had laid its charm upon him, for despite the hardships it was a place where romance and adventure were the realities of life.

For the first time in his twenty-five years he felt the spur of responsibility. He was filled with a desire to fight, to conquer, to do something to try his new strength and to earn favor in the eyes of Jean – and Ellen. He grinned boyishly to himself, sometimes, when this mighty urge to noble deeds resolved itself into the accomplishing of prosaic tasks, such as getting in firewood and hunting shellfish.

In the matter of clothes, Boreland and Kayak were the only ones who were in any way prepared for the cold weather. Ellen had cut up a scarlet blanket to make Harlan and Loll winter coats. Jean had fashioned for herself an attractive mackinaw from a small white blanket, and the young man was not blind to the picture she made, red-cheeked, laughing, trotting along beside him on the beach as they looked for seafood.

One windy day Kayak Bill came in from the beach without his cherished sombrero.

"The got durned breeze snatched it offen my haid and lit out with it for foreign parts," he drawled sadly as he smoothed down his wildly blown locks. Despite Ellen's anxious protests he went bareheaded after that, although he wound his scarf about his ears on extra cold days. His hair continued to grow unchecked also, for after watching Ellen earnestly manipulating an inverted bowl and a pair of scissors while she trimmed her protesting husband's hair, Kayak spoke with slow conviction:

"I hearn tell o' lady barbers down in the States, but I ain't no nature for 'em a-fussin' round my noggin. My kin folks drug me to the Methydist meetin' house once a-fore I stampeded from Texas, and the sarmon teched on a long-haired pugilist, Samson, what was trimmed by a lady barber by the name o' Dahlia."

For some time Kayak and Boreland had been trying, as they put it, to "taper off" on their tobacco. Harlan, when he found that the *Hoonah* was not coming, had given up smoking so that the older men might longer enjoy what tobacco was left. After days of silent, mental wrestling with his desire, he reached the stage where he had successfully downed the craving, and he watched with grim amusement, and no little sympathy, his partners' vain efforts to limit themselves to one pipe after each meal.

There finally came a day when Kayak and Shane sat at the supper table lighting their farewell pipes.

"Goo' bye, lovely Lady Nicotine!" Airily Boreland waved a hand through the smoke. "I bid thee farewell without fear and without regret. As a matter of fact, Bill, I've intended to quit right along, and this makes it easy. Filthy habit, anyway, and I don't want to set a bad example for Loll."

It was from Jean that Harlan learned the details of the following dismal day. It was so stormy that the men could not go out to work. After breakfast Shane and Kayak had risen from the table and, pipes in hand, instinctively sought the tobacco box in the corner. Their fingers met on the bare tin bottom. With blank looks they faced each other.

"Hell, Kayak, I'd forgotten!" Boreland grinned sheepishly. "Now begins the battle of Nicotine – buck up, pard!" He forced a cheerfulness into his tones as he slapped Kayak's shoulder.

Kayak Bill looked down at the empty pipe cupped lovingly in his hand. With a sound between a grunt and a groan he put it back into his pocket and dawdled dispiritedly off into the other room to his bunk behind the tarpaulin.

Shane thrust both hands deep into the pockets of his overalls and shifted his weight alternately from heel to toe. Then crossing over to the stove where his wife stood, he bent upon her a wistful, little-lost-dog expression, so ridiculous in a man of his size that Ellen burst into laughter.

"Poor little thing," she sympathized, patting his cheek. "It's lost its pacifier, it has!"

With a sickly grin Shane turned to the window and dully watched the slanting sleet blown by the gale. Kayak's puffing snore came presently from the other room. Boreland wheeled about, glaring.

"By thunder! To think that old cuss can *sleep* at a time like this. The man must have a heart of stone. For two cents I'd go in there and ... "

He paced the floor, his hands fidgeting.

"Are you *sure*, El, you didn't save out a box of tobacco on us, just to give us a bit of a surprise now?" he asked hopefully for the third time that morning.

In the days that followed, Harlan could not make up his mind who suffered most during the "battle of Nicotine." Shane or Kayak Bill or Ellen. He grew to feel a bit sorry for Ellen. He found himself gradually assuming the duties neglected by the other two men during their period of misery. Boreland lost much of his good-natured cheerfulness. He was inclined to view the food situation with increased alarm. He often spoke sharply to Lollie, and sometimes to his wife. But invariably after an irritable outburst he sought to make up to the boy with some homemade toy, or a new story of adventure. With Ellen his method of apology was different. He would put his arm across her shoulders and look down at her whimsically.

"I swan to goodness, little fellow, if I wasn't an angel I couldn't live with you at all, at all, you're that peevish since I've stopped smoking." Then with his most wistful Irish look he would add, "Be patient with me El. I'm having a hell of a time."

As Harlan watched the struggles of his partners, he grew to have a better opinion of his own power of self-control. Jean was responsible for this in a way.

Sometimes on stormy days when it was impossible to go outside, the patience of the whole family would be sorely tried by the actions of the older men. They would research every nook and corner of the cabin, go into the pockets of every garment and even rip linings in their efforts to find some overlooked bit of tobacco. After just so much of this, Jean would turn on them scornfully and compare their childish actions with those of Harlan when he was undergoing the same deprivation. Undoubtedly this holding him up as a good example had the opposite effect to that hoped for by Jean, but it nevertheless caused a warm glow to encircle his heart.

One day Boreland made a great discovery. By pulverizing the old nicotine-laden pipes, of which there were over half a dozen, he found that the resultant mixture could be smoked. He and his partner in disgrace did no work that day. In disgust, Ellen banished them to the woodshed to do their smoking. From this place of refuge Kayak Bill's drawling tones of immense satisfaction floated out at intervals.

"Honest to grandma, Shane, I'm a-feelin' like a new man."

By the time the corncobs had all been pulverized and consumed, and but one cannibalistic pipe, itself pared down until it held but a thimbleful, was left between them, all the other members of the party had arrayed themselves against the sufferers. By persisting, even though sickness was often the penalty for smoking an extra strong pulverized pipe, they had forfeited the sympathy of all hands.

Matters came to a crisis one afternoon, when Boreland, taking a candle, crawled up into the loft to make one more search among the provisions.

Suddenly there was heard a great commotion overhead – a beating and a floundering about.

"Hey! Get some water up here quick," came Shane's alarmed shout. "I've set the bloody place afire!"

Half an hour later the fire was out, thanks to the efforts of the bucket brigade that rushed water from the spring, but in the roof was a gapping hole, and much of the outfit stowed away in the loft was wet again.

Boreland came slowly down from above. He was besmudged, apologetic and sheepish. Ellen was waiting for him. She looked him over from head to foot, her blue eyes snapping, scorn and supreme disgust radiating from her. Next she turned to Kayak Bill and took him in with the same look.

"Now, men, listen to me," she said sternly, as they both started to slip toward the door. "I've reached the limit of my endurance." She emphasized her next remarks with a decisive finger. "The *very next one* of you who mentions tobacco inside this cabin will be banished to the smokehouse to live by himself. I mean every word I say!" With hang-dog looks, the culprits turned away and disappeared through the door. Ellen, with business-like brevity, climbed up into the loft to investigate. Harlan followed.

He found a roll of tar paper with which to mend the hole in the roof and helped Ellen shift the luggage bags that had been wetted by the water. They worked in silence for some time.

Suddenly Ellen stopped in her operations. She rested her palms on the floor and looked up at Harlan. In the candle-lit gloom of the loft he could see that her eyes were twinkling. A new friendliness was in the ingenuous smile she gave him.

"Gregg," she said in a tone that finally admitted him to her friendship. "Remember – there isn't a man living who cannot be benefited by having a good, sound scolding once in a while."

And so the days passed until the end of January. They were

stormy ones for the most part, yet no ruby sand showed on the beach of Kon Klayu. One clear, cold morning Harlan and Jean were gathering shellfish among the boulders on Sunset Point. The air was strangely still and under the pale sunshine the sapphire waters were tinged with rose and lavender. They had long been accustomed to those tricks played with sea and clouds by the magician Mirage, and today the crest of each billow was magnified until, on the horizon the points seemed to leap up into the sky. Above a lucid space in the southwest a mass of silver and amethyst tinted clouds moved slowly and spread out like a platform.

They sat on a flat boulder to watch the changing beauty of the colors. Their daily forays for shellfish had deepened their love of the sea – its ways of mystery that were ever bringing to their attention some new loveliness of form and tint. Now, before their incredulous eyes there appeared rising from the cloud bank the illusion of graciously rounded domes, spires, minarets, and the next instant they were gazing on a city of enchantment softly reflected in a pearly sea – a silvery city of fantasy like an exquisite shadowy drawing of some foreign land. They sat silent, entranced. How long the vision lingered neither of them knew. Then a breeze fanned their faces, and in a twinkling, the city of dreams vanished.

They raced back to the cabin with their news but found the others on the porch. They too had witnessed the phenomenon. Kayak Bill alone showed no surprise.

"That's what sourdoughs up here calls 'The Silent City,'" he drawled. "Alasky folks have been seein' it for yars. One time I saw it above Muir glacier, and one time when I was a-crusin' in the Bering Sea. Sailors calls it a mirrage. If I don't miss my guess, there'll be hell a-poppin' in the way of a storm purty soon."

Kayak was right. Within twenty-four hours the worst southwest gale they experienced racked the island. The strange reverberating roll from the south cliffs beat with weird insistence on their ears for three long days and nights. When the weather cleared, the immediate need for shellfish sent Jean and Harlan out among the rocks again.

They were coming home from Skeleton Rib with their pails full of "gumboots," making a desultory search for pay sand, which no one had seen for weeks. They left the beach and turned toward the little lake visible from the cabin porch. The storm had shifted the cannonball-shaped boulders that characterized that part of the shore, stripped the tundra of every sign of vegetation and exposed the brown turf beneath. Harlan, in restoring his knife to his pocket, dropped it. As he stooped to pick it up a look of astonishment crossed his face. He sank on his knees and eagerly scanned the brown surface beneath.

"Jean!" There was excitement in his voice as he beckoned her. "Look!"

The girl rushed to his side. She bent to look and caught her breath.

The dark surface of the turf was flecked with glittering colors of gold.

Courtesy University Alaska Anchorage

Sometimes miners found gold near lakes, perhaps like this one in southcentral Alaska.

27

Spring

Once again gold cast its magic spell over the island of Kon Klayu. The daily food hunting was alternated with preparations for mining the gold-bearing turf – the top of which had caught, like the nap of a blanket, the flakes of yellow metal washed up by the storms of years. Though the men knew they had not yet found the source of the island gold, they were confident there was a small fortune in sight.

In his enthusiasm, Boreland put behind him for a time the growing hatred for the White Chief of Katleean that was slowly eating into his heart, and with Kayak Bill and Harlan went about the "dead work" that preceded the actual mining. There were puddling boxes and sluices to be built at the edge of the little lake off Skeleton Rib, and the top of the gold-carrying turf was to be cut up into squares and piled like cord wood until they were ready to shred it and run it through the sluices.

While the work went on, everyone kept a sharp look out for cannery ships going west, for along the Alaska coast the first sign of spring is the coming of the fishing fleet from the States.

"Of course, February is a month too early," said Harlan one evening as they sat about the supper table discussing the possibilities of rescue, "but we ought to have some way of attracting attention. We might put up a flagpole on the Lookout, but," he shrugged his shoulders, "we have no flag."

"If you men get the pole up, I'll see that you have a flag," Ellen promised.

No one had been well supplied with clothes in the beginning of the island adventure, and gradually Ellen had used every available piece of cloth to eke out the worn and patched garments, which, despite all her efforts, turned her family into tatterdemalions. But she took what was left to put together her flag – some flour sacks, an old blue shirt of Shane's and a red blanket that could hardly be spared. The men hunted for days among the driftwood of the beach before finding a log the proper length and shape for their purpose, but at the end of a week the pole was in place.

The hoisting of the flag for the first time was made an event that demanded the presence of every member of the party on the Lookout. Sudden, poignant emotion stirred the six tattered figures that stood about the pole as the crude banner unfurled its stars and stripes to the strong breeze. Homemade and heavy it was, but it fluttered above them, the emblem that has ever stood for hope, for freedom, for justice, and there was that in the sight of the flag that caused the men to stand with bared heads, while Ellen and Jean viewed it through a mist of tears.

"Oh, surely, *surely* now, some ship will sight it and come in!" proclaimed Jean, as she turned to scan the sea, her face alight with the faith inspired by the faded colors.

It was the latter part of March before the smoke of the first cannery boat was seen moving slowly to the westward. Though the vessel was so far away the watchers knew their low island could hardly be seen from its deck, the mere fact that ships were beginning to navigate the northern sea promised well, and the flag was kept flying from the Lookout day and night, its stars turned down as a sign of distress.

It was decided that Jean and Harlan should attend to the evening signal fires. There was little darkness in the nights, for already the long Alaska daylight had set in, but by placing half-dry seaweed on the driftwood flame a great smoke resulted that, it was hoped, might be seen by passing vessels.

It was good to sit about the fire looking down on the sea while the dusk crept in, and now that Ellen had, to some extent, modified her opinions regarding Harlan, there was nothing to hinder the growing of a delightful, outdoor companionship that made the hours pass with miraculous rapidity for the two young fire tenders. Past hardships and hunger were forgotten up there on the Lookout. The evenings became hours of confidences when they discussed their plans, their dreams, their budding philosophies of life. They came to know each other's moods and each other's thoughts and that magic of shared adventures that can be more binding than love.

One night Gregg told her of his early ambition to be a mining engineer, his year at a Midwestern school of mines, where his studies were terminated, he admitted with entire frankness, by a request to leave. He told her also of his return home to San Francisco, and the subsequent years of aimless drifting that ended in the final break with his father.

"I can see now," he concluded, "that poor old dad had good reason for disappointment. As a last resort he sent me to Katleean hoping that I'd get some sense jolted into me – but – well, I didn't, Jean, until ... until the *Hoonah* put into the bay. I've been wondering what he is thinking now. He hasn't had a word from me since August, although, of course, he hears from Katleean." He checked himself, pausing a moment as if he were on the point of telling her something else. Then continued. "Dad is – he's interested in the Alaska Fur Trading Company, you know."

But Jean's mind was already intent on the young man's future.

"Now you *are* going to wake up and do something, though," she declared with a decisive movement of her little head. "I don't care much for what you've told me of your past, Gregg," she admitted frankly, "but ... ," she waved her hand with a gesture of dismissal, "up here it isn't yesterday that counts, it's today and tomorrow. This is a wonderful new land to begin in . . . ."

"And you just watch me do it, Jean!" he interrupted her enthusiastically. As if he already felt the need of action he rose from the ground, and thrusting his hands in his pockets, began walking up and down before her. "I've done a lot of thinking over there in my little hut – a *lot* of it, and I know this country has gotten a hold on me, some way. It's mine from now on. There's something about it that makes me feel alive. I want to get out and hustle like the dev ... dickens. Honestly, if it wasn't for you and Ellen and Loll, I could be glad we have been put up against it here on Kon Klayu – I've actually enjoyed the fighting for food and warmth and shelter! We'll all have a good stake when we leave here, Jean, but already I'm planning to come back. I have a few ideas about mining that I'd like to try out."

The girl looked up at him, her eyes glowing with interest. Encouraged, he took his place once more by the signal fire and began to detail his plans for the further prospecting and development of the island.

But not all their hours on the Lookout were spent in the discussion of mining. They seemed to have the whole world to themselves up there – an enchanted world, cool, redolent of hidden sprouting green things and the smell of driftwood smoke; a world tinctured with a sheer beauty that neither of them had ever known before. They had reached the stage in their companionship where sometimes they sat silent for long minutes, only occasionally looking across the fire at each other with the smile of understanding that is often better than speech. Sometimes they laughed together as only youth can laugh, over inconsequential things, and sometimes he sang to her – songs of the sea, men's songs at first, but these gave place later to the songs of sentiment that may, when the singer choose, be made more intimate, more tenderly personal than the most personal spoken word.

Jean, after she had gone down to her little bunk at night, often lay there wondering how, under the circumstances, she could be so happy, especially since the food situation was becoming more desperate each day. But, with the exception of occasional lapses into acute anxiety, she was strangely content and confident for the future.

One morning she was awakened by Loll's excited whisper.

"Jean! Oh J-e-a-n! Do you hear anything?" The youngster was standing beside her bunk, the early light falling on his red head, his ear raised alertly after the manner of the little dog in a famous phonograph advertisement. She roused herself drowsily and sat up to listen. Above the sound of the surf on the beach came the faint wild call of gulls.

"Oh, Loll, winter's gone!" she exclaimed just above a whisper. "The birds have come back to nest!"

She bounded out of bed and a moment later the two slipped quietly out to the porch. The light fall of snow had already been gone for weeks. It was a glorious morning of sunshine and sparkling sea. Looking up she saw against the cobalt sky the white wings of sea gulls – the harbingers of spring.

Her happiness in the sight was somewhat lessened as the sound of coughing came from inside the cabin. Everyone but Ellen appeared to be standing well the enforced diet of bread and shellfish upon which they were now living. Sometimes Jean was worried over her sister's condition. She suspected that never from the first had Ellen eaten her full share of the food, even when they had had beans and rice and oatmeal. Her sister could not eat the tough "gumboots" and her only nourishment was obtained from bread and black coffee. Ellen still went about her household tasks, but it took her longer to do them now and it was evident to Jean's critical eye that her strength was waning. Meat – meat was what she needed, the girl thought. The pigeon – once she suggested to Ellen that it might be killed, but her sister opposed the idea so violently that Jean never mentioned it again.

One day Harlan brought down a seagull with a stone. Jean hopefully cooked it, but the flesh was so tainted with fish that no one could eat it. The sea parrots had returned to the island, but these wary little birds kept far out over the water.

There came a morning when Ellen did not get up for breakfast. The men left early for the lake. They were devoting all their time to their mining, and secure in the thought that they had struck something rich, they were eager for the cleanup; but to Jean, stepping quietly about her household tasks, gold did not seem valuable now. It made no difference how much they found – it would not buy them one ounce of nourishing food – and nourishing food was what Ellen must have, and soon.

The girl tiptoed to the bed and looked down at her sister's face, white and thin against the tumbled mass of golden-brown hair. There was something small and very girlish-looking about Ellen as she lay there – and something suggestive of a great weariness. Jean felt a sudden tenderness for her – a desire to clasp her sister in her strong young arms and shield her, from what she could not tell. She stooped and softly kissed the small, work-stained hand that lay outside the blanket.

As she continued her work, the plan that had often before suggested itself to her, now returned. Ellen's peculiar conduct in regard to the pigeon precluded her mentioning it to her sister. She took a sheet of thin paper and in painstaking, minute characters wrote a message. She would attach it to the pigeon and turn the bird loose. Perhaps it might fly back to Katleean, and then, surely, if the White Chief found her message he would make an effort to come at once.

Half an hour later she had the pigeon on the beach below the cabin. She was urging it to fly, but the bird merely spread its wings and fluttered about. Fearing that the long confinement had deprived it of the power of flight, Jean was redoubling her efforts, when Loll came running along the sand.

"Gee whiz, Jean!" he yelled, "What-cha doing with my pigeon? Can't you see he can't fly good yet? Dad clipped his wings that time one of them got caught in the hinge of his cage." And Lollie, with coaxing noises and terms of endearment proceeded to gather his pet into his arms.

Obliged by Ellen's illness to assume the responsibilities of the larder, Jean was surprised and dismayed at the small amount of food that was left them. She tried to banish the fears that this knowledge brought her by talking cheerfully of the certainty of procuring seabird eggs.

Spring had the effect of coming suddenly. The yellow grass and bare branches that had greeted them for so many months changed seemingly overnight. The adventurers awakened one morning to find that the alders had burst into pungent, sticky little green leaves and the tundra had taken on a tinge of emerald. When the Indian celery had grown a foot in height, Jean and Loll brought an arm load to the cabin. The girl remembered that Senott at Katleean had told her "him plenty good eatin' when salmon run." Everyone craved something green, and though the celery was hollow-stalked, very watery and of a strong musky taste and odor, they ate it, because, as Loll put it, it felt like green stuff going down, anyway.

Ducks and geese flew over the island so low that the sibilant sound of their wings could be heard from the porch. Shane often tried to kill one with a stone, but without success. He and Kayak Bill had long ago used all the ammunition for their revolvers endeavoring to shoot hair seals off the south end. Shane's revolver finally disappeared entirely. One day, however, after he had stood long by Ellen's bed, he went out to the shed. Jean coming upon him there had found him thoughtfully twirling the weapon on his finger – his trigger finger as he had often called it. Although he announced that there were no more cartridges for it, the girl later came upon five wrapped in a bandana handkerchief.

When at last the flowers began to bud, Jean and her nephew climbed the gulch trail to the top of the island where Kobuk lay under the tundra on the crest of the hill. The lone tree had lost one of its branches during the winter gales, but it still stood, as if looking out across Kobuk's grave to the far-away, illimitable skyline; ever looking, Jean thought, as she was, for a ship that never came.

She and Lollie made Kobuk's resting place a bed of transplanted violets and iris and dogtooth lilies. When the work was finished, Lollie stood leaning on the club he had begun to carry, as his one desire in life at this period was to emulate Robinson Crusoe. He looked thoughtfully down at the grave for some time.

"Perhaps, after all, Jean, it's better that Kobuk died," he said at last. "We'd have nothing to feed him now, poor old Kobuk, and he'd be hungry, like us." He raised his thin little face to watch a sea parrot fly overhead with a fish in its bill.

Jean leaned against the tree, one of her recurrent floods of hopelessness sweeping her. Far down the tundra toward the north she could see the flagpole on the Lookout. The tattered homemade flag hung dispiritedly in the still sunny air, and the smoke of the signal fire was a mere straight-rising wisp. The calls of happy mating gulls came to mock her– gulls replete with the bountiful food of the sea. Today she was hungry, so hungry that every atom of her body cried for food, hot, nourishing food that she had not known for months. And Ellen, back there at the cabin, was growing weaker and weaker each day.

The girl's eyes dully followed the low-flying sea parrots. In a half conscious way she noticed that many of them came toward the crest of the hill and disappeared. Sea parrots were not as fishy tasting as gulls, as she had heard Kayak Bill say. If only they had some way of killing these birds, perhaps the broth and the flesh might bring back Ellen's strength.

"Jean, isn't that the place the old bear came up the hill?" Lollie's voice broke in on her thoughts. He was pointing to the scrubby growth on the brow of the hill where she had first seen the bear of Kon Klayu. "Let's go over and see."

As they walked toward the ridge their feet made no sound on the soft tundra. They peered downhill into the shady recesses under the stunted alder and salmon berry bushes. Jean's nostrils twitched as there was wafted up to her the strong, acrid odor that lingers about the places of nesting birds. As her eyes became accustomed to the dimness, she ventured a remark that died abruptly as she caught her breath. Beneath the low canopy of branches the ground was bare of vegetation, and on the cool brown earth, packed hard by the patter of webbed feet, a dozen or more sea parrots were sitting not fifteen slanting feet below.

At the sight of them, Loll dropped to his hands and knees and, club in hand, crept cautiously down under the low-growing bushes. Inch by inch he drew nearer to the birds. Then, with a swift movement, he was in the midst of wildly flapping wings, clubbing fiercely at crimson-beaked heads.

Jean, fearing that he was in danger, threw herself on the ground and tried to wriggle forward to him, but the low growth made the passage of her larger body impossible. She drew herself back and called frantically to the boy. She could hear the commotion and see the parrots one by one flying clumsily out as they escaped from the spot where he fought. With a shout of encouragement to him she made another attempt to crawl under the brush. At that moment Loll's freckled face was thrust through the undergrowth. He turned to tug at something, grunting and straining as if trying to free it from the tangle.

"Jean! I've got 'em! I've got 'em!" he yelled.

A second later he was standing before her, breathless, his blouse torn from his shoulders, his face scratched. In his bleeding little hands he held five dead sea parrots. "Killed 'em with my club, Jean, just like Robinson Crusoe, 'cause they can't fly away quick under there!" he explained. "They've all got little tunnels under there, too – nests I think they are, but I couldn't reach the end of 'em when I put in my arm!"

An hour later Jean was attending to the cooking of the birds. When skinned, only the breast was found to be edible. The meat when cooked was coarse and dark red, but it was a palatable sea parrot and dumpling mulligan that the girl evolved.

When the men returned from Skeleton Rib that night there was more rejoicing over the food than there was over the fact that at last everything was in readiness at the lake for the first cleanup. Three puddling boxes stood full of the soft brown muck that had once been turf. The sluices were in place ready for the water that would be turned into them the following day, and the tools, wheelbarrow and the cart had been drawn aside, clearing the space for action.

"Tomorrow, boys, we'll be bringing home *ki-yu* gold!" Shane asserted confidently at supper. "And before the end of the week, we'll all have enough to go anywhere we wish. Now that we are certain of plenty of birds, sure our hearts should be – light as feathers for a boat will surely be along soon!"

On the Lookout that night Jean said goodnight early to Harlan. As she came down the hill to the cabin she stopped to look at the wide-spreading ocean.

The sun had gone down in a strange sea mist and below her the waters heaved dim and vast and ghostlike in the twilight. There was a hushed feeling in the air. It may have been that she was more tired than usual, for when she slipped into her little bunk she fell into a heavy sleep almost as soon as her head touched the pillow.

It was Shane's incredulous shout that awakened her.

"Kayak! Come here!"

She could hear Kayak Bill moving quickly toward the door in the living room.

"Ellen, you come out, too!" It was evident that Shane was laboring under an intense astonishment.

The girl clambered out of her bunk, and flinging on a kimono, started for the porch. Before she reached the door, Kayak Bill's unbelieving exclamation sounded.

"By hell! The lake . . .," he paused in sheer leaden amazement. "The lake is *gone!*"

Courtesy University Alaska Fairbanks

Miners poured water into sluice boxes like this to find gold in the sand.

28

THE CLEFT

On the porch all eyes were turned toward the south where the silver of the little lake off Skeleton Rib had always glimmered through its screen of alders. There was no friendly sparkle of water this morning, and gone were the trees that bordered the shore nearest the beach.

Instead, a strange desolation, more noticeable because of the brilliant sunshine, hung over the spot, which now showed a vague reddish brown in the distance. It had the sickening effect of an empty socket from which the eye has been torn.

The bewildered look on Kayak's face was slowly changing to one of enlightenment.

"Folks," he said quietly. "We're lucky to be alive this morning. There's been a tidal wave!"

His eye was taking in the length of the beach that lay between the cabin and the lake. There was a weird look of alteration about it, as if a giant hand had tampered with it during the night. Piles of drift logs were stacked up far inland, and the vegetation on the banks above the beach was flattened, and in many instances swept completely away. Close at hand – not twenty feet from the cabin – lay windrows of seaweed, left there by the spent wash of the great wave. Death – swift, sweeping and terrible – had been diverted only by the high bank that stood below the cabin.

It seemed incredible, monstrous, that they all should have slept peacefully while the mass of water was rolling in on them from the deep. Kayak Bill, who had once seen a tidal wave on Bering Sea, pictured it advancing in the grey unnatural night from the far reaches of the ocean, growing larger and larger as it neared the shallows off Kon Klayu, and then, tossing its dancing crest to the sky in gigantic abandon, curling down from aloft in green-white crushing splendor and flinging itself far over the beach line in its endeavor to encompass them all.

Without waiting for breakfast the men went down to the spot where the little lake had been. Nothing but a dark ooze remained. Every block of gold-carrying turf, every puddling box, sluice and tool had been carried out to sea. The work of weeks had come to naught. Their last hope of gold was gone.

During the gloomy fortnight that followed it was the food supply, however, and not the calamity of the tidal wave that was subject of the most discussion. With the exception of flour there was little left of the outfit that had been landed on Kon Klayu, and to the consternation and chagrin of the men, they discovered that Loll was the only one who could slip up on the sea parrots and kill them with a club. Shane, Harlan and even Kayak Bill tried it repeatedly with no success. They were unable to creep down under the low-growing brush in a manner stealthy enough to reach the birds. Even Loll found it impossible to approach them in the open, and they grew more wary day by day. Six people depended on the child for nourishing food, and Lollie, after that first wild morning when he had discovered his ability to kill the birds, found his tender heart revolting against his bloody task.

Ellen, slowly recovering her strength now that sea parrot broth had been added to the daily fare, had become painfully intuitive in the matter of all those phases of the situation that Shane and the others clumsily tried to keep from her. Though apparently asleep, she knew the instant that Shane crept from his bed in the very early mornings before the sun had dried the dew on the tundra. She could hear him tiptoe toward Lollie's bunk, and with forced lightness, call softly.

"Come, Loll, son. Hop up now. We must be after the birds this fine morning."

"Oh, Dad! I don't want to kill any more – I can't do it, Dad ... let this morning go by ... please!"

"Whist, lad, your mother'll hear you. Come along now, son, we'll talk it over on the outside."

"Oh, please, *please*, ..."

Quickly Ellen would put her fingers over her ears that she might not hear the beseeching little-boy voice, but she knew the moment Shane lifted the reluctant child from his warm bunk, and she knew, too, that Shane's heart must be aching with the pity of it, as was her own.

One morning, thinking they had gone, she raised her head to note the hour. There was the sound of a quiet step on the porch outside.

"Oh, Dad!" came Lollie's pleading tones, and Ellen knew just how his grey eyes, big now in his small thin face, were raised to his father's. "Dad, if you could see them down there under the leaves, strutting so cute-like and innocent in front of their little tunnel nests getting ready for their babies!" Then with passionate intensity: "Today ... couldn't you just let me off for today, Dad?" Inspired, perhaps, by some shade of feeling in Shane's eyes he went on with hurried, promising emphasis.

"An' *tomorrow,* maybe tomorrow, Dad, I'll feel like getting lots of 'em. Honest, maybe I will!"

Ellen, with a moan of mental anguish, buried her face in her pillow and covered her ears to shut out the rest. That her boy, friend and lover of all wild things, was obliged, against his will, to slaughter birds in order that they might live seemed more than she could bear.

And as if to add to the hopelessness of the situation, daily now steamers and sailing vessels passed far out on the North Pacific, but none swerved in its course. There was nothing to hinder the *Hoonah's* coming, nothing but the word of the White Chief of Katleean. Ellen chafed inwardly as the long, light days and nights dragged by. Help must come soon, and for some time she had been counting the hours until the pigeon's wing feathers should grow out again. As soon as the bird could fly she was going to take it to the Lookout and speed it on its way with her message of capitulation to Paul Kilbuck.

The long sunny days of May passed, turning Kon Klayu into a garden of wild flowers. It was violet time with great bunches of purple blossoms nodding against the hillsides. Above the beach line rice grass waved luxuriantly. Indian celery thrust its graceful, creamy parasols above beach forget-me-nots, strawberry blooms, black lilies, blue geraniums and thick carpets of delicate wee flowers that have no names. The green of the tundra on top of the island was splashed with yellow buttercups and pink and lavender daisies, and on every little brown pool and lake floated golden lilies.

The warm salt wind from the sea stirred the fragrance of it all – the flowers, the moist tundra, the sun-warmed sand into a perfume that is the breath of Alaska – a clean, invigorating perfume that once known can never be forgotten. It is charged with that indefinable charm, that hint of promise, which is so much a part of the great North Country.

To Jean and Gregg, racing along the beaches on their various hunts for food, it brought a joy of spring that, when they were in the open, made them forget completely the growing seriousness of their situation. Nearly every day now the air was softly, embracingly warm, and owing to the scarcity of garments, no one was wearing more than was necessary. The men had long been going barefooted, and Jean, as soon as the weather and the nature of her work permitted it, put her only remaining pair of worn shoes in the loft against the day when she should leave Kon Klayu. She, too, went barefooted for the most part, delighting in the feel of the cool sand against her feet, but she carried with her the hair-seal moccasins given her by Add-'em-up Sam's widow at Katleean. These she put on to walk over stones or along the tundra.

As the sea parrots were daily growing more wary, and Lollie had now to exercise the greatest caution to get near enough to club them, the need of eggs became imperative. One day Jean and Harlan were racing along the beach headed for the south cliffs to make their accustomed search. A rope coiled about the young man's waist held to him a bucket that dangled and bobbed as he ran. The afternoon was sunny and a fresh sea wind lifted the hair on their bare heads. The surf ringed the grey sands at their feet with long foaming lines.

"It's so beautiful, so beautiful, this land and sea, Gregg, that I feel today must bring us some good luck," said Jean, who – out of sheer exuberance – was skimming along ahead, her arms outspread, her chin high, as she dipped and leaped in imitation of Senott's seagull dance that she had seen at the potlatch.

"Wait a minute, wild girl," called Harlan, endeavoring to accomplish the feat of rolling up a trouser leg as he hobbled. "Come back here!" His voice took on an exaggerated tone of threat. "Don't you realize that a woman's place is three steps to the rear?"

In answer to his shout, she turned and laughingly waited for him. He advanced, suddenly assuming the slouching, shoulder-swinging gait of the "bad man," his brows drawn and fierce, his chin thrust out.

"Don't cross muh, woman," he hissed, melodramatically. "I tell yuh, I'm rough, an' I'm tough, an' I'm from Katleean. Muh bite is poison, an' muh s-s-s-ting is d-e-a-t-h. To the rear, I say!"

Quick as a flash the girl bent, and catching up a long streamer of damp kelp tossed it about his neck, retaining her hold on it as she ran ahead.

"Speak not to me of the rear, man," she intoned boastfully. "I am Xun, the Unfettered. Xun, the Woman of the North Wind. Men move not in the North except by my will. My breath in their lungs brings oblivion. My voice in their ears – and the trail – is empty. Come!"

Laughing derisively at his pawing efforts to dislodge the clammy kelp, she drew him along until the streamer broke. Then, still talking their happy nonsense, they trotted side by side toward the cliffs.

Half a mile farther on Jean sat down on a spherical boulder and donned her moccasins. Afterward they turned in from the beach, crossed a flat sweep of tundra and ascended the hill to the top of the island. As they walked toward the edge of the cliffs the shrill chorus of thousands of seabirds grew louder.

"Oh-oh-oh!" there was a little bell-like shiver in the girl's voice. "There's no sound in all the world so wild, so suggestive of the mystery of the untamed, as the calling of nesting gulls, Gregg."

They stood on the promontory with the winged things dipping and swirling all about them. Jean continued slowly, as if trying to put into words some illusive feeling. "Sometimes it frightens me – I don't know why – and at the same time, it fills me with such a sense of freedom and lightness that often, just for a little moment, I almost believe I, too, might rise into the air and balance myself against the breeze with them."

Harlan had never seen the nesting grounds of gulls in season, but Jean, before coming to Kon Klayu, had once gone ashore on a gull island during laying time.

"For weeks afterward," she told him, "every night when I closed my eyes I could see the green waving grass and grey sand dotted with hundreds and hundreds of crude nests. Each nest contained from one to three eggs, larger than duck eggs, and of a Nile-green color closely speckled with brown, yellow and lavender. Why, they were so near together, Gregg, that it was difficult to step without crushing the eggs."

With the memory of the gull island in her mind, she started with Harlan to traverse the stretch of green back of the promontory.

Back and forth for a square mile they went, searching the flat above the cliffs. Gulls, flying above, eyed them curiously, making strange human sounds. Occasionally one alighted on the ground. As often as this happened they raced hopefully to the spot but found nothing but grass blades bending from the wind.

"It's no use, Jean," Harlan decided, after two hours' vain effort. "It's too early for them to lay. Let's go back to the edge of the cliffs. The shags lay earlier, I believe, only their nests are so blamed hard to get at down there."

Jean was not enthusiastic about shags' nests.

"They fill me with melancholy – those long-necked, black creatures, Gregg," she said uneasily. "Lollie and I call them witch birds. I remember last fall we used to sit on the porch steps in the afterglow, watching them – strings of dusky, witch birds, speeding silent and low over the darkening water to the cliffs. But if you wish," she added, "we'll go and see."

They headed for the windy heights overlooking the ocean, where nodding tundra grass fringed the space beyond. Harlan took her hand as they crept close to the edge. They peered down through the cloud of wild fowl that swarmed in uncounted thousands before their eyes. Three hundred feet below, deliberate blue rollers, with spray-laced tops swept in and broke against the rocks, the impact sending whitened water high into the air. The face of the cliff was plastered with seabirds: murres, gulls, sea parrots and cormorants, which some called shags. Harlan threw a stone down and the air became black with them, leaving the numbers in the rocks apparently the same. Sea parrots flew in from the water and disappeared under the overhanging sod at the top. Mingled with the breath of the ocean was the wild, unforgettable odor that clings to the places where seabirds roost.

Suddenly Harlan spoke. "There *are* shag eggs down there, Jean, but the cliff right here is too steep for us to get them. I couldn't even let you down over the edge on the rope. But I'll tie one end to you and we'll go along here until we find a place from which I can descend, perhaps."

They drew back from their perilous position, and after making fast the rope about Jean's waist, proceeded, stopping at intervals to lie flat and look down over the rim of space.

They were feeling their way along the highest part of the island, when suddenly at their feet the tundra opened in a deep cleft not over five feet wide. It began six yards or more back from the edge and led down between crumbling, rocky walls at a fearful incline, to a ledge thirty feet below.

Jean drew back with a cry at the sense of peril that came over her, but Harlan looked eagerly down.

"By Jove, there are a *lot* of eggs on that ledge," he announced enthusiastically, "and we can get them!" He hesitated a moment, considering. His eyes sought hers. "You're not strong enough to lower me down to the ledge, Jean, but – would – would you be frightened if I should let you down to them?"

For one awful moment the sea and sky and birds swirled together as the girl stood, steeped in fear. Then the raucous cries of the gulls penetrated her consciousness like shrieking voices calling: "Coward! Quitter!"

Harlan was saying convincingly: "I wouldn't let you fall, Jean. My arms are strong as a blacksmith's," he said as he flexed the muscles beneath his thin shirt. "And see, there's a depression here at the head of the chasm. I can stand in it and brace myself!"

Ten minutes later Jean, with her heart beating fearfully, stood facing Harlan, as she prepared to back down the steep rocky slide.

Shag's nests, or cormorant's nests, with eggs – like these on an Island In Southwest Alaska in 1919 – helped many people survive in Alaska's wilderness.

29

The Secret of the Cliffs

As she felt herself going down step by step, Jean kept her eyes resolutely shut. She steadied herself with outstretched arms and hands just touching each wall of the cleft. The rope tightened about her, as inch by inch Gregg let it out from above. Gradually, as all went well, curiosity overcame her fear and she opened her eyes. At that instant there came a whirr and a flapping of wings that set her heart thumping again, and out from the overhanging tundra on top of the cliff an astonished sea parrot flew, so close that the tip of his wing stung her cheek. She could hear other birds below and about her beating their wings and hurling themselves in alarm from their resting places. Far beneath the billows exploded against the crags. With hands and feet now she clung to the rough juttings of rock as she was being lowered. Harlan's voice, shouting encouragement, gradually became fainter. At last she felt her feet strike the flat of the ledge.

With a gasp of relief she straightened and turned to look about her. She stood high on a narrow shelf thrust out from the sheer-rising cliff. Before her face swarms of birds fanned the air, their wrangle and jangle sounding almost in her ears. The wind stirred the acrid smells about her. At her feet were several crude nests of sticks. They contained eggs smaller than hen's eggs and of a pale greenish color. They were the first she had seen for nine months and the sight sent a thrill through her. With a little laugh at her own enthusiasm she untied the bucket at her waist and carefully worked her way from nest to nest as she gathered them.

Jean, not being one of those who find themselves affected by heights, quickly became accustomed to her perilous shelf above the sea. After tucking a large silk handkerchief about the eggs to insure their safety, she sat down on the ledge to look about her. Every nook and cranny in the surrounding rocks was alive with birds. Close to her, long-necked shags on widespread wings balanced with dusky gracefulness before sailing away through the myriad screaming gulls. Dignified murres, their backs to the sea, sat soldier-like in the crevices like plumb bobs from their perches. Huge beaked sea parrots squatted with comical solemnity or flapped quickly away toward the outer reaches of the ocean where thousands of their kind floated on the water like a black cloud. These were the love days in bird land – the mating time for all feathered things. Sitting there, the girl felt a sudden kindred friendliness for all these small creatures – a feeling of at-one-ness and sympathy with their little lives and nest-making ambitions.

As she became more at home on her ledge she began to look about her with a view to exploring further. She lay flat on the rock and peered down. Below her on the floor of the sea, now exposed by the falling tide, she saw dozens of the strange, perfectly round boulders that had become so familiar to all on Kon Klayu. They were of assorted sizes, and where they lay thickest there was no seaweed or kelp. After some minutes she became aware that from one end of her ledge where it joined the cliff, and running parallel to it, rough, out-jutting rocks slanted downward in a crude, natural stairway, almost to the beach. With care, she told herself, after a long scrutiny, she might make the descent. The rope about her she knew could not reach to the bottom of the cliff. She would untie it and trust entirely to her clinging hands and prehensile moccasined feet. She stood up, suddenly confident of her own powers in this element. Cupping her hands about her mouth, she shouted to Harlan, informing him of her intention. Evidently he did not hear her, or else she could not hear his answer. After waiting a few minutes, she untied the rope from about her and cautiously began the descent.

Very slowly and carefully she lowered herself, her feet and hands clinging tenaciously. The keen salt wind ballooned her ragged skirts about her. Occasionally when her foot slipped and showers of loosened particles rolled down startling birds from their perches in screaming clouds, she could feel the blood pounding in her temples in momentary fright. At first she marveled at her own daring – then she reveled in it.

As she descended she began to experience the thrill that comes to those who tread where no other human foot has trodden, who look on scenes no other human eye has seen. She felt sure she was the first to visit this part of Kon Klayu, for the steep cliffs at the south were inaccessible both from the east and from the west side of the island, even at the lowest tide. And in all the tales of Kon Klayu she had heard, no one had ever mentioned the chasm down which she had come to the ledge. In this section of tidal waves and occasional heavy earthquakes it was possible that the cleft had opened up recently.

At last she felt her feet on the beach below. She straightened and turned to face the ocean. The waters were sewn with jagged rocks and long-running reefs. Sleek-haired seals bobbed up to look humanly at her. A thin, high-rising jet of water afar out bespoke the presence of a whale. Back of her loomed the precipitous wall of the cliff. She gasped at her own daring as her eye followed the rough stairway down that she had descended. A moment she wondered, with dismay, if she could possibly climb back again; a moment she pictured her plight should she be caught here when the tide came in and covered the narrow beach; then her attention was drawn by something that lay farther along. She ran forward, wending her way in and out between the giant balls of stone that lay about her.

At the base of the precipice just ahead of her, and level with the sea floor, she saw a huge opening. As she approached, it widened, grew higher, until she found herself peering into the yawning mouth of a sea cavern fifty feet wide and half that in height. Like monster peas in a giant's open mouth lay the spherical boulders on the bottom of the cave.

She was frightened, yet fascinated by her discovery. She hesitated a moment then advanced slowly into the cool dampness of the place. As far ahead as her eye could pierce the dimness, the balls of stone lay catching the light on their rounded surfaces. The walls closed in about

THE SECRET OF THE CLIFFS

her as she walked. Water dripped on her. Her feet splashed through puddles in the uneven, hard bottom, but here there was no trace of the seaweed that draped the rocks in all other parts of the island.

The sound of breakers booming against the reefs came to her in the cavern with a strange reverberating effect. The underground way ran on apparently with an upward slant as far as she could see. She longed for a light so that she might explore farther. After some minutes advance into the deepening gloom, a feeling of timidity began to assail her. She paused, leaning against a lopsided boulder. The absence of life, the stillness, the Stygian darkness ahead seemed suddenly ominous. She turned and saw the mouth of the cavern far back of her. Like an oblong frame it enclosed a small bright picture of beach and sunlit sea. Undoubtedly, she thought, when the tide was full, the ocean rushed in along the floor of the cave. Perhaps, when it was stormy, it rolled the giant balls of stone backward and forward.

Once more she glanced toward the unknown inner recesses of the cavern; then, with a little shiver, began making her way back toward the light again.

Her foot went down with a quick splash into a water-filled depression, and in shaking the drops from her moccasin she noted that the strings were untied. She stooped to fasten them; her eyes now perfectly accustomed to the dim light, caught a dull gleam at the edge of the pool. She was conscious of a wild thumping of her heart – an eager trembling of the hand she instinctively reached forward.

"No, no! It *can't* be," she temporized aloud, as if to fortify herself against disappointment. She forced herself to finish tying her moccasin, and even looked to the security of the other one before she hesitantly reached over and put her fingers on the object that had attracted her. She held it up to the light.

"Gold! Oh, it *is* gold!" she breathed.

In her hand lay a flat piece of yellow metal, smaller than the nugget Lollie had found, but of the same character. She dropped to her knees, and with unsteady eagerness searched the bottom of the shallow pool for other nuggets. Her trembling fingers encountered another one, and still another! Then her luck seemingly came to an end.

The floor of the cave was strangely worn and filled with numerous depressions into which the sand had settled. Jean finally dipped her hands into the pool again and brought up perhaps a cupful. She ran with it out to the beach and spread it out over a boulder. It was black, showing tiny garnet-like particles, and here and there the sun glinted on colors of gold.

She gathered the precious sand together again and stuffed it into the pocket of her shirt, then swiftly set off toward the spot where she could ascend the cliff.

Suddenly she remembered Gregg waiting for her at the top. She gasped, dismayed by the knowledge that she had been totally unconscious of the passage of time. Had she been gone an hour, two – or perhaps more? What was he thinking? Perhaps he had tried to descend the cleft after her and had fallen. Perhaps he was even now lying on the ledge broken – dead.

Trying to shut out these unwelcome thoughts that took away all the joy of her discovery, she hastily began scrambling up the steep incline.

She had gone only a few feet when a shout halted her. Glancing up she saw Gregg's relieved face above her.

"Thank heaven, you're safe, Jean!" he shouted, and with reckless disregard of consequences, he began to slide from the ledge toward her. "I thought you'd fallen down the precipice when I pulled on the rope and found you not there!"

He landed on the beach at her feet. The tense look on his face faded as his eyes devoured her.

"Lord, girl, whatever made you do such a thing? I rushed back toward Skeleton Rib and met Kayak Bill coming this way. He let me down to the ledge for I couldn't get down any other way. He's up there now waiting for us. Doggone you, anyway, you little rascal." he said with a shaky laugh, grasping her by the shoulders. "You nearly scared me to death!"

"But just see what I've found!" Jean opened her hand suddenly, and with the three nuggets lying on it, raised it toward his eyes. Then without waiting for him to look at them, she thrust them into his hand and began to drag him toward the mouth of the cave.

Half an hour later, two wild, troglodytic figures were giving vent to their joy by capering and dancing about the floor of the cavern.

"Jean, you've struck it rich – you've found the source of the gold of Kon Klayu!" Harlan shouted for the fifth time. "It's better than beach mining – it's better than Shane ever dreamed! I know enough to venture that this whole blessed little isle must have a base of igneous rock and the formation of this south end, especially, is impregnated with a network of gold-bearing dykes. Why, anyone could see that by the walls of this cave!" He bent, scooped up a handful of sand, and with eager, shining eyes watched while he spread it over his palm.

"Just imagine this hollow during one of our terrific sou'westers, Jean," he went on, looking about him. "The monster billows crashing into this cavern, rolling the boulders along the bottom, grinding them along this gold-bearing formation. By Jove, the action is the same as

Sometimes the source of gold nuggets found on beaches was traced to caves, like this one pictured in Southeast Alaska in the early 1900s.

that in a stamp mill, almost. The gold is freed, becomes mixed with the sands, and sooner or later is carried out and concentrated along certain zones on the island."

"But away goes all the mystery of our island, too, Gregg," Jean said, her voice carrying a hint of regret. "That accounts for the strange, rolling sounds we used to hear during the storms, and for the giant balls of stone, and for everything."

They filled their pockets with samples of the sand to take home to Shane and ascended to the ledge. From thence, with the assistance of Kayak Bill and the rope, they mounted one after the other to the top of the precipice.

The old man listened to their story of the cavern in silence, though his eyes were glowing.

"By Hell, from what yore a-tellin' 'o me, children, you sure have struck it rich!" he drawled at the end.

Jean threw her arms impulsively about his neck and landed a kiss on his ear.

"We all have struck it rich, you old dear! We'll stake the whole little island of Kon Klayu, and if we can ever get to the States to get an outfit, we'll come back here and work it."

Jean knew that any show of affection caused Kayak acute, wriggling embarrassment. He backed away from her now, his cheeks fiery red. To cover his momentary confusion, his hazel eye impaled Harlan's ragged back, which was showing the effects of his rapid slide down the cliff.

"Young man," he declared with slow solemnity. "The bosom o' yore pants is showing conside'ble wear an' tear." Gregg whirled to face him, but before he could utter a word, Kayak, now master of himself once more, drawled on: "It never rains but it pours, I reckon. I plumb forgot to tell you, Gregg, that just a-fore you drug me up here this afternoon, me and Boreland was a-mouchin round just south of Skeleton Rib and durned if we didn't come across the old whaleboat, high and dry with celery bushes a-growin' up around her. She's stove in some, but we can fix her, and I reckon we'll be settin' sail for the mainland in a couple o' weeks!"

THE SECRET OF THE CLIFFS

30

THE PIGEON'S FLIGHT

Wonderful as it was, the discovery of the gold took
second place with the finding of the whaleboat. Gold
had no more value than sand on Kon Klayu, unless the
adventurers were rescued, and the whaleboat meant at least a chance
of rescue, provided it could be made tight enough to float. It is true
that with summer coming on there would be an abundance of eggs,
sea parrots and later on berries, for already the north end of the island
was white with strawberry blossoms – but flour and coffee were now
all that remained of the supplies, and the flour was low in the barrel.
Help must come before another winter set in.

Ellen, in her first joy over the discovery of the whaleboat, had
joined eagerly in the plans that the three men discussed at the cabin.
She saw herself freed at last from the terrible necessity of summoning
Paul Kilbuck. The pigeon could fly – she had tested it. In another
week she would have sent it with the message that meant life to her
family, but death to her own peace and happiness. But now, in her
relief, the last vestige of her illness fell from her. She felt strong again,
ready to take up her work about the cabin. She found herself, for the
first time, able to look normally on the smoke-grey creature, seeing it
as a bird, and not as a hated, yet horribly cherished representative of
the White Chief of Katleean.

It was slow work putting the old and battered whaleboat in repair.

Ellen had not seen the craft since its recovery, but Shane had told her that every seam needed to be recaulked. There was no oakum for the purpose, so she tore up some garments that neither she nor Jean could spare. He spoke casually of a cracked plank or two that would be strengthened by tacking pieces of canvas and tin both inside and out.

After several days Ellen noticed that Harlan and Kayak Bill ceased to talk of the proposed trip, although Shane still kept up a brave front and spoke confidently, in her presence at least, of landing at Katleean. She began to feel vaguely uneasy.

One morning when Jean and Lollie had gone off to gather gull eggs, which were now found in small quantities, Ellen decided to take lunch to the men who were working on the whaleboat a mile and a half away.

As she approached the spot she saw the upturned hull of the boat lying upon the sand. No one was in sight. She gasped as she saw the battered condition of the craft. One end seemed splintered and a jagged hole showed plainly in the bottom. Three other holes had been mended with tin. The next instant she was aware that the three men were sitting on the other side of the whaleboat, resting probably. Their voices floated out to her distinctly.

"We mout as well face the music, boys," Kayak Bill was saying. "We're up against the damn'dest bit o' coast in Alasky, and in a rotten tub like this it's a ten to one chance we're takin' but ..."

At this point, to Ellen's vexation, the paper containing the lunch burst apart letting half a dozen gull eggs, which formed the principal part of it, fall to the sand. Instinctively she stooped to gather them. The next words that came to her told her that Shane and Kayak were discussing the unwritten law of the North – the law of the cache. In a land where food is the god supreme, this law has made itself. White and Native alike bow before it. It means life. The food cache, no matter where found, is inviolate. There is no more foul or cowardly crime than robbing a cache. And ranked with the cache robber is the man who goes back on his promise, or fails, through neglect, to furnish food to those who depend on him. Death, Ellen knew, is the penalty for both crimes in the remote places of Alaska. As she went forward she heard the White Chief's name and some words that were unintelligible to her. Then Shane came to his feet. He was speaking in a voice toneless, dispassionate, but weighted with finality.

"I'll do it, but I don't need a gun, by God!" From his pocket he drew his revolver, which he had taken that morning in the hope of getting a seal. He laid it across his other palm. "I have five shots left, but I'm going to do it with my hands on his throat!"

As he finished speaking Harlan and Kayak Bill stood up also. The young man turned and saw Ellen coming toward them. There was a moment's dissembling as Shane returned the pistol to his pocket, then he greeted her with a cheeriness that in no way deceived her.

She said nothing that might betray her comprehension of the situation, but as soon as she could, retraced her steps to the cabin.

She knew now that while it was in her power to prevent it she could never allow her men to put to sea in the unseaworthy whaleboat. One chance in ten, Kayak had said. Even during the best weather they had known on Kon Klayu she herself had seen a gale blow up in two hours. One chance in ten. The words repeated themselves in her brain. And if they did make the mainland, what then? "I don't need a gun ... I'll do it with my hands on his throat."

The clash between Shane and the White Chief was inevitable now, no matter how the meeting came about. She was enough of a frontier woman to appreciate this. She would summon Kilbuck at once, before her men had a chance to risk their lives, and when she had sent her message, she would tell Shane her whole miserable story beginning with the night of the potlatch dance. He might lose faith in her. He might despise her. But she knew that he would fight for her.

She took out pen and paper and sat before the table to write her message to the White Chief. She must make it so urgent that he would come at once before the whaleboat was launched again. She wrote several, but discarded them. At last she was satisfied. Folding the paper tightly she slipped it into the little finger of a thin kid glove she had cut off for the purpose. Then she went out to the pigeon's cage.

With the fluttering bird in her arms, she ascended the trail to the Lookout. At the top the homemade flag flung its tatters out in the sunshine. Ellen noted that it blew toward Katleean. The wind, then, was favorable. The trader should have her message by morning. And in two more days ... she shook her head, not permitting herself to think further.

A few minutes she stood looking seaward. Then she held the bird out in both hands and with all her strength tossed it into the air.

Fluttering wildly, it recovered its balance, circled narrowly, rose a few feet and then settled down on the tundra before her. It took a few limping steps. Ellen was puzzled at its behavior. Perhaps she had tied the message too tightly about its leg. She would readjust it and urge the bird to flight again.

With outstretched hands she advanced toward it and tried to imprison it between her hands, but the pigeon flapped along ahead of her just out of reach. After some minutes running back and forth over the short grass she caught it, and with her back to the flagpole, sat down on a piece of firewood to loosen the string about the creature's leg. So intent was she on her work that she did not at once hear the sound of approaching footsteps. When she did turn her head quickly it was to look up into the anger-lighted eyes of her husband.

He reached roughly across her shoulder and with one hand grasped the pigeon by the legs. With the other he thrust toward her two pieces of thin writing paper.

"Now, perhaps, you will explain these ...," he said in a voice that fluctuated strangely from his intense effort to control himself.

Dazed by the unexpected turn of affairs, Ellen rose and mechanically took the sheets. They were two half completed notes to the White Chief – notes she had discarded. She must have overlooked them when she burned the others. What had she said in her anxiety to bring Kilbuck immediately to Kon Klayu? What had she said to arouse Shane's sleeping devil of jealousy that she had known often during the first years of their married life? "*Paul Kilbuck,*" the words stood out black in her large handwriting. As she read the words she slipped the other paper over them. "*I want you now –*"

"So you want him *now*, do you?" Mocking fury sounded in Shane's voice. "You want him now, this fine, womanizing lover of yours who left you to starve! God, what a blind fool I've been – but I can see it all now. I remember his whisperings to you that day we left Katleean." He snatched the papers from her hand and thrust them into his pocket with a bitter laugh. "I'll deliver your loving message myself just before I choke him . . ."

"Stop, Shane!" Suddenly Ellen was herself again. She knew nothing that had happened between her and the White Chief was one tenth as dishonorable as the things Shane's jealous imagination pictured. She stepped over to him and laid a hand on his trembling arm. "I *can* explain these half written notes," she said quietly. "I can explain everything, Shane."

She looked up into his tense, passionate face. He must have seen something in her blue eyes that calmed him, for he asked more reasonably: "Tell me, then."

Beginning with her distrust of the trader she did tell him. She ended with her attempt that afternoon to send the pigeon with a message urgent enough to bring the White Chief to their rescue before Shane and his partners had sailed away in the leaky whaleboat.

When she finished, Shane made no comment. She waited. Was it possible he did not believe her? A long minute went by ... and then another. Obeying an impulse she did not understand she swiftly took the pigeon from him and tossed it once more into the air.

It readjusted itself and rose confidently. There was a swift movement as Shane whipped his revolver from his pocket. Before the bird had flown twenty feet he fired. The first shot missed, but the second brought the smoke-grey pigeon to the ground.

A moment later Ellen felt her husband's arms about her.

"God love you, little fellow." There was tenderness, contrition and a great relief in his tones as he laid his cheek against her hair. "Sure, nothing matters now that I know it's myself you're still in love with and not that damnable blackguard in Katleean."

For an hour they sat on the log below the flagpole, explaining, mutually forgiving, planning. Shane, with Irish logic, chose to see in the death of the pigeon a riddance to all adverse circumstances. He seemed suddenly endowed with a new faith concerning the trip in the whaleboat and succeeded in imparting some of his enthusiasm to his wife.

"Luck is with me, El. I tell you I can feel it in my bones. The devil himself can't keep me from making Katleean now," he declared confidently as they walked hand in hand toward the trail that led down to the cabin.

As if fortune had at last decided in their favor, the days went sunnily by. Gulls began to lay by the thousands. Loll was relieved of his hated task of killing sea parrots, for Harlan discovered that when the birds began to lay, he could urge them from their tunnel nests with a long stick and capture them. The whaleboat, repaired and recaulked, was launched and brought down to the beach before the cabin. All was in readiness, at last, for the journey.

The evening before they were to set sail Jean went up the hill to the Lookout to help with the last signal fire she and Gregg would build together. The night air, soft and scented, was like a caress to the senses.

Sea and sky were luminous with the rose and amethyst tinting of Alaska nights. The three plaintive descending notes of the golden-crown sounded from the alders along the crest of the hill.

When she reached the top she found a campfire glowing above the ashes of past flames. Gregg had preceded her and at her coming he tossed his old blanket coat to the tundra for her to sit upon. He took his place beside her. Their usual gay exchange of badinage had failed them tonight. For a time they sat silent, with arm-clasped knees, looking into the vermilion heart of the fire. All day the shadow of approaching separation had weighed the spirits of each with heartache and anxiety. Yet each knew that in this hour tonight there was some potent quality, some indefinable magnetic thing that seemed to charge the air with sweetly mysterious emotions.

People of the cities, worn with the artificialities of civilization feel the need of some powerful stimulus to arouse emotion: Love is often born of the wine cup and a dusky, cushioned corner; of music; of the dance. When the glamour of these is removed, love dies. But inborn in the heart of every man is a love dream – a dream of some day finding that mate who shall battle cheerfully side by side with him against environment; that mate whose courage, whose understanding, whose faith shall enable him to laugh at the buffetings of Fate and go unafraid down the years with the light of dreams in his eyes.

Perhaps with Jean and Gregg it was the subconscious knowledge of the fulfillment of this universal dream that kept them happy during all the lean months on Kon Klayu. They had shared elemental things. Together they had hunted food that they might live, battled against storms and endured hardships. Together they had sung and laughed and made a playtime of it all, and slowly there had grown up between them a love as clean and wholesome as the summer winds that swept the tundra of their island. Hitherto they had felt no need of caresses or words to express their joy in one another. They had been happy as children are happy, with no thought of tomorrow. They had parted each night knowing that morning would bring them together again. But now. ...

Jean, looking into the flame of the fire, dropped her chin in her cupped hands. Incongruously, it seemed to her, at that instant there flashed into her mind the memory of a day on an island trail, when she and Gregg had come suddenly on a sea vista of heart-stopping beauty. His eyes had sought hers in quick, silent appreciation of it. She could not tell why this simple incident should suddenly seem so intangibly beautiful, but she knew now that it was a moment out of life that they two would share forever. There had been other times when they had sung together under the golden winter stars – fleeting, rapturous spaces when she had been conscious that not only their voices, but in some way their spirits blended. But now ... he was going away into the gravest danger – into death perhaps. ...

She overcame a quick impulse to reach out, to feel him under her hands, to hold him back.

Gregg rose to place another log on the fire. He brushed his hands one against the other and thrust them deep into his pockets. She felt his dark eyes compelling her own and raised her face from her hands. Neither spoke, but for a long tempestuous moment they looked at each other. Something perilously sweet and magnetic drew her. Even as she rose Gregg was at her side. She felt his arms close about her with eager tenderness. She stood against him within his hold, tremulous, thrilling to his nearness, yet even in the ecstasy of it, realizing that their separation was now made more poignantly unbearable.

"Jean … ,"a little hoarsely he said her name, and she was aware that his heart was beating as wildly as her own. "Jean, you – you are so dear to me. When I come back, could you … will you marry me?"

His arms tightened about her as his head bent to hers. In answer she raised her face to his, and in the first joyous enchantment of young love met his kiss.

Two hours later she lay in her little bunk steeped in glad tumultuous memories of those last moments on the Lookout. Her spirit fared forth on the wings of her love into the future – a future made beautiful beyond her girlish dreams. She told herself it was not possible that other men and women loved as she and Gregg; not Ellen and Shane … not anyone. All at once she became conscious that in the living room her sister and brother-in-law were still talking, though everyone else had long since gone to bed.

The indistinct murmur of their voices mingled with the metallic clicking sound that informed her Shane was again oiling his revolver. Then his words came to her with low distinctness.

"El, I'm going to leave this with you. There are three cartridges left in it, and if … if I don't come back, and no help comes to you before another winter … you know, little fellow, you know what to do."

31

THE JUSTICE OF THE SEA

Because there is no night in the Northland in June, dawn on Kon Klayu was but a tender merging of golden twilight into amber and rose and blue, with the sun reappearing within an hour of its setting, kissing the summer sea into sparkling sheets of silver and jade.

The little green island with its girdle of creaming surf had never seemed so beautiful as in the early morning of the day Shane, Kayak and Harlan sailed away in search of help. The electricity of adventure, of hope, was in the air and the wind was as soft and balmy as a breath from tropic seas.

After the last goodbye had been said, Ellen, Jean and Loll stood on the beach below the cabin watching the little whaleboat riding the long, gentle swells just outside the line of breakers. The tin patches on the frail sides glinted bravely in the sunshine, the mended old Christopher Columbus sail caught the breeze, and slenderly outlined against it were the forms of Shane and Harlan waving a cheerful farewell to the watchers. Kayak Bill, his hand on the tiller and his face turned resolutely away, headed the pathetic craft out into the treacherously smiling North Pacific and laid his course for Katleean.

The boat was slowly lost in the sunny silver distance, and the sisters, arm in arm, turned and listlessly followed the trail back to the cabin. Lollie, walking on ahead, brushed the tears from his eyes and squared his narrow shoulders as if already he had assumed the responsibilities of the man of the family.

The door of the cabin stood open and the sun made a great rectangle of light on the floor. It was very quiet – and lonely. The loneliness was new to both women and it hurt like a pain in their souls. It seemed impossible that nowhere on the island were the men to whom they were so accustomed.

Ellen began picking up the dishes that were standing as she had left them after the early breakfast. Jean helped her. When the work was over there seemed nothing left but the aching emptiness of waiting.

The long day wore away at last. Tomorrow, if the wind held favorable and all went well, Ellen and Jean assured each other repeatedly that the whaleboat would reach Katleean, and in two more days a ship might come for them.

At twilight Jean climbed alone to the Lookout. The sunny day had faded in a grey mist. Afar down toward the south cliffs the tree, so like a waiting woman, stood out against it in weird, life-like appeal. The flat desolation of the plateau was marked by the tundra trail that led across the island to the hut – the trail along which Gregg had so often come to meet her. She had not dreamed that life could hold so much emptiness nor that longing for a loved one could be so intense as to be almost a physical pain. She sank down beside the dull ashes of last night's fire. The loneliness was almost unbearable.

From the pocket in her blouse she took a folded paper that Gregg had pressed into her hand as he left that morning. She unfolded the sheet and saw it was a verse from some poet unknown to her. "Read it when I am gone," Gregg had whispered to her.

"When I am standing on a mountain crest,
Or hold the tiller in the dashing spray,
My love of you leaps foaming in my breast,
Shouts with the winds and sweeps to their foray;
. . . I laugh aloud for love of you,

Glad that our love is fellow to rough weather
No fretful orchid hot-housed from the dew,
But hale and hardy as the highland heather,
Rejoicing in the wind that stings and thrills,
Comrade of the ocean, playmate of the hills."

Before Jean had finished, her shoulders had straightened. She felt strangely comforted, lifted out of herself. Surely, she thought, nothing but happiness could come of a love like this. Even the elements must be kind to one who loved so. Back in her little bunk she thought of him out on the dark sea in an open boat with only the night for a covering. To calm her fears, she repeated over and over again the words of the verse he had left her.

Her faith was sorely tried the next morning when she woke to the old familiar roar of wind and wave, and felt the cabin trembling in the blasts of a gale. She saw, with alarm, that Ellen was not in her bed. On investigating, Jean found her out on the beach standing bareheaded while the wind wound her garments about her, loosening the strands of her braided hair and pelting her with rain and flying spray. Ellen was gazing, in a fascination of dread, at the green-back waves humping their backs like fearful monsters, chasing one another in to the line of foaming breakers that spent themselves at her feet.

Jean slipped her hand into her sister's and drew her back to the cabin. When they entered Loll was up making a fire in the Yukon stove.

The day wore on. The storm increased, though it never became as violent as some they had experienced during the winter. The direction of the wind was favorable to their sailors. Both women knew that no makeshift craft could live in such a sea, yet they hoped with intensity akin to despair that Shane had made the shelter of Katleean Bay before the full fury of the storm was reached.

Night came on darker than usual, low scudding clouds and flying wave tops seeming to mingle. Waves sheeted with foam faded ghost-like into the tossing greyness. Drifts of rain blew stingingly in from the sea. Cruel and cold the waters appeared now to Jean's anxious eyes, and she found herself repeating again the lines of Gregg's verse, as if it had become the tenets of her faith.

The second day of the storm passed, as did the first, except that evening brought an end to the rain. The clouds in the west began to lift. The sisters, drawn closer by their common, mounting dread, slept together that night, one on each side of Loll.

It was long before sleep visited Jean. But presently she was dreaming that she dangled at the end of a rope over the cliff above the cavern, trying to snatch nuggets from the rocky ledges. The wind blew her body hither and thither, as she clutched the jutting crags.

She tried vainly to secure a foot or hand hold. From above, Gregg's voice was calling, calling her plaintively, weirdly. She tried to make out his words – but could not. The wind blew them far away, and only a faint, wild "Awh-hoo-oo-oo-oo!" came to her. Then her rope began to slip and she was falling, falling interminably past the face of the precipice, past shags' nests, past thousands of flapping birds that shrieked tauntingly at her. With a convulsive movement she tried to spring to the rock shelf below her – tried so hard that she woke trembling and in a cold perspiration of dream-fear, with her heart pumping so loudly that she could hear it.

The wind had died down and only the muffled beating of the great combers on far seaward bars was audible, but of a sudden she was bolt upright in bed, listening with every sense alert. On the island, where they three were the only human beings, someone, something was calling. Above the sound of the sea it came – the haunting, long-drawn cry of her dream.

"Awh-hoo-oo-oo-oo! Awh-hoo-oo-oo-oo!"

But this was no dream. The cry came again, one minute apparently from the depths of the ocean, then from the Lookout above the cabin. It came nearer, growing more appalling, more mysterious in its possibilities. It filled her with fearful, inchoate imaginings.

In an agony of terror she reached out and shook her sister's shoulder.

"Ellen! Ellen!" she whispered tensely. "Listen! Someone is calling!"

Ellen, awakened out of a belated sleep, raised up on her elbow and tossed the long loose hair from her face.

Again came the unearthly: "Awh-hoo-oo-oo!" rising thin and high and dying away on the falling inflection.

Ellen's face went pale as she listened. She lingered a moment, then sprang out of bed. Slipping her hand beneath her pillow she drew forth the revolver and started for the door. Jean crawled gently over the sleeping Lollie and followed.

They stood on the porch in the freshness of the dawn searching the familiar landscape for some sign of life. The storm had cleared away and long scarf-like clouds streaked the intense blue above. Once out in the open Jean's mind was cleared of its phantoms. But a sudden shock went through her when, from just over the bank, the call came again.

Almost immediately there appeared in the trait the strange, tottering form of a man. He advanced haltingly, as if spent from some long struggle, his bare, black head sunk on his chest, his damp garments clinging to him.

"Stop!" Ellen's voice rang out. "Tell me who you are and where you are from!"

The man raised his head. At the sight of the two women standing in their white robes, their loose hair floating about them, a spasm of mortal terror crossed his dark face.

"*Kus-ta-ka! Kus-ta-ka!*" he yelled, at the same time throwing up his arms and turning to run weakly down the trail.

Ellen covered the staggering figure with her revolver, but Jean caught her hand. "Don't, El! Be careful," she cried breathlessly. "Can't you see? It's our old friend – it's Swimming Wolf from Katleean!"

She sprang along the trail after him, calling, "Wolf! Oh, Swimming Wolf! Don't run away from us! Don't you know your friends?"

The man terrified by something, she knew not what, kept up his feeble running gait. She overtook him and grasped his shirt. The big Native collapsed on the sand. His hand closed painfully over her arm while his wild black eyes searched her face. At the touch, his look gave place to one of relief.

"Ugh! Little shaatk' with white feet!" he gasped. "Swimming Wolf think you all the same dead – think all you people dead. Long time you have no grub."

He pinched her arm again as if to reassure himself that she was flesh and blood and not the *kus-ta-ka*, the ghost he had thought her.

"Long time now, Swimming Wolf no grub, too," the Native continued. He opened his mouth and pointed a shaking finger down his throat. "No grub, no water, no sleep, t'ree day." He held up three fingers as he turned his head slowly from side to side. "T'ree day lost. Plenty tired."

His voice was weary, plaintive, as only a Native voice can be. Jean wondered how she had for one instant attributed his cry to supernatural powers – she who had often heard him calling to members of his tribe along the shores of Katleean.

Noting his weak condition, the girl checked the eager questions that rose to her lips, and when Ellen came up, between them they managed to get the worn man to the cabin. They fed him bread and hot sea parrot broth. He ate ravenously as much as Ellen thought good for him, but when she tried to induce him to lie down in Kayak Bill's bunk, he shook his head, and started unsteadily for the door.

"No, no!" he said sharply. "You come along. Other man with Swimming Wolf."

They followed him down the trail to the beach and turned with him toward Sunset Point. He paid no attention to their eager questions, but suddenly stopped and pointed ahead. In the maw of the surf inside the Point a whaleboat was churning. At the sight of it cries of alarm broke from the women's throats, but again the Native shook his head.

"Him not there," he assured them. "Him up *there*." He indicated the high-tide line. He lurched along beside them, intent on taking them to where his friend lay.

They saw the still dark form lying prone on the edge of the rice grass where Swimming Wolf had dragged it. Ellen, with a bottle of water and some bread in her hand, ran forward toward the prostrate man.

Within a few feet of him, Jean saw Ellen check herself and shrink back. Then, reluctantly the girl thought, she went on. Jean quickened her pace.

As she approached, Ellen turned swiftly to her.

"Jean," she said hardly above her breath. "Look!"

Jean gazed with incredulous eyes into the face on the sand. The black beard was matted with seawater. Below the bandaged forehead two weary grey eyes opened. A faint look of surprise crept into them for a moment. Then they closed again and the man lay still as death.

"Oh-oh-oh!" Jean's voice held an uncontrollable quiver. "Oh-oh-oh! It's the White Chief of Katleean!"

Courtesy University Alaska Fairbanks

Vicious storms are not uncommon in Alaska. Oftentimes winds and waves toss a wide array of wreckage on to the beaches, as the aftermath of the big 1913 storm near Nome shows in this photograph.

32

BENEATH THE BLOOD-RED SUN

A week had gone by since the day the White Chief and Swimming Wolf had been cast up on the shores of Kon Klayu. The women, with the help of the Native, had lifted the inert form of the dazed man to a mattress at the spot where they had found him, and dragged it literally inch by inch along the beach to the cabin. They put him to bed in Kayak's bunk in the little room off the living room.

For Ellen and Jean the days were filled with intangible doubt and mounting fear, for no sail whitened off Kon Klayu. Added to the acute anxiety in regard to their men was now the problem of the White Chief of Katleean. What queer twist of Fate had tossed the trader, helpless and without food, on the island where his very life depended on those he had left to starve? And, if their men were lost at sea, what would happen to them when Kilbuck recovered his strength?

Gradually, from the disjointed utterances of the superstitious Native and from their own knowledge of the trader, they were able to piece together the story of the White Chief's mishap – not the story as Swimming Wolf knew it, tinged with eerie Tlingit superstition and mystery – but the prosaic version of the white man, who sees everything through logical eyes and is ever explaining away all that is mysterious in life and much that is interesting.

The White Chief, sometimes going for months without liquor,

had, as they knew, periods when he drank as no other man in all Alaska. Curiously enough, he never gave way to his desire while at Katleean, but with one faithful Native to attend him, he would go aboard some visiting vessel, and there sink himself into the oblivion brought about by quantities of hootch.

It was in the latter part of May that a schooner, the *Silver Fox*, came to anchor in the Bay of Katleean. The owner and captain was a German, bound for Cook's Inlet with a load of gasoline and enough equipment to start an illicit still at Turnagain Arm. Paul Kilbuck, after nearly a year of abstinence, succumbed to his craving, and with Swimming Wolf, sought the cabin of the *Silver Fox*. After two days of the German's liquid hospitality, he was ready for any mad adventure. Doubtless the thought of Ellen and her family must have been with him during the winter. Perhaps he had some inchoate drunken plan of seeking her when he put to sea with the potvaliant captain of the *Silver Fox*; but six hours from the post he collapsed in a stupor on the captain's bunk.

Tales of the North are replete with instances of the incredible recklessness of men drunk on the pale liquor of that land – men who, sailing along the dangerous coast, lash the wheels of their vessels, and leaving all sail set, go below for a day's carousal; men who drain the very liquid from the compass to satisfy their burning thirst when hootch is gone. So it was no surprise to the women to learn that the storm that swept the island so soon after the departure of the three men, had broken upon the *Silver Fox* when all hands, except the faithful Swimming Wolf, were too far gone in drink to man the craft. As he talked, the Native, with expressive eyes and hands, acted out each step of his story. He told how the wind increased; how he lashed the wheel, and all alone tried to reef the bellying canvass, letting it fall as it would at last. With a few words, and many dramatic gestures, he made known how the trader, roused from a two-day stupor by the pitching of the vessel and the banging of the boom sticks, had staggered up out of the cabin, and been struck by the heavily swinging boom of the mainsail.

The captain and the three sailors crawled to the deck soon after, where the freshness of the rising gale undoubtedly cleared their brains somewhat. They tried to make things shipshape to weather the storm. The captain was just about to cut the towline that still bound the trader's whaleboat to the stern of the *Silver Fox*, when suddenly volumes of black smoke came pouring out of the cabin.

Swimming Wolf was never able to give a white man's reason that would explain the fire that started in the hold of the schooner where the gasoline was stored. He swore it was the *kus-ta-ka* who kindled the flame, the *kus-ta-ka* who knocked the White Chief on the head and made him fall "all same dead." That he finally got the trader into the whaleboat and escaped the burning vessel, while the crew departed in their own small boat, was evident. There was but one oar, and the craft was blown hither and thither on the tossing sea at the wind's will. In the dawn of the third day, Swimming Wolf had been able to beach it on the rocky shore off which he found himself.

The Native had no idea where he was landing, and when he saw the white-robed figures appear on the rickety porch of the cabin, it was not surprising that he thought them ghosts.

Further questioning of Swimming Wolf revealed the fact that at Katleean, two drunken sailors had run the *Hoonah* ashore in the lagoon on one of the highest tides of the fall. Though uninjured, it would have required some work to get the little craft off again; so there, evidently, she had remained.

"But Swimming Wolf, why didn't the White Chief get another boat and come with our provisions? Why didn't the Natives come for us? Didn't anyone care whether we starved or not?"

The Wolf looked at Ellen with that stolid, blank expression a Native assumes when he does not wish to be questioned.

"Me dun know. Me dun know." He shook his head. "Indian have no boat. Kilbuck, he Big Chief. He all time say: 'Mind you business or Indian get no grub. Tomorrow I go." He all time say 'Tomorrow.'"

Tomorrow! From the lips of Kayak Bill who knew his Alaska, Ellen and Jean knew what tragedies lie behind that word. From waiting on wind and tide and the next steamer to go someplace, from waiting on summer or winter to do something, from waiting on an indifferent government to act on something, people of the North have found that Alaska has become essentially a Land of Tomorrow! A month in Alaska becomes as a day in the States.

Humanity demanded that the two women do their best for the man who had brought about their present perilous situation, though he had forfeited all claim to womanly sympathy. Ellen could not bring herself to go near the White Chief after he was placed in Kayak's bunk, but she directed Swimming Wolf, who nursed and fed him. At first Kilbuck lay in a stupor, but suddenly, at the end of twenty-four hours, he came out of his daze. Jean, going into his room, encountered his narrow grey eyes looking up at her with their normal expression.

He recovered quickly from the blow on the head, and on a diet of bread and broth rapidly regained his strength. The women avoided him whenever possible, but Loll, on whom once more they were dependent for sea parrots, found time to sit beside him, asking about his friends at Katleean, and in turn telling the trader all his small affairs of the day. As time went by he must have given the man a fair idea of the struggle for existence during the winter on Kon Klayu.

Kilbuck, for the most part, was silent. He made no effort to explain his failure to keep his promises. His strange, grey eyes, whenever it was possible, followed the movements of Ellen and Jean. Sometimes the women could hear him, indistinctly, questioning Lollie.

The fourth day Swimming Wolf assisted him to the porch where he sat looking a long time at the sun-kissed sea. The fifth day, with the Native's help, he took a walk on the beach. What he thought of the situation Ellen and Jean had no means of knowing, but as they watched him rapidly regaining his old arrogant manner, vague fears crept insidiously into their minds. At the end of the week he was issuing his orders to Swimming Wolf with all the ease and certainty of one in supreme command.

One afternoon Ellen sat on the porch trying to piece together the remnants of a little shirt for Loll. Jean and the boy were off with

Swimming Wolf gathering food. The White Chief had gone to his room some time before. Ellen's heart was heavy with anxiety for her husband. If he were alive, he should by now have returned to her. If he were dead. . . .

For some minutes she was oblivious to all about her as she strove to thrust this thought from her mind. The incipient menace of the White Chief's presence hovered about her, though so far he had never by word or look betrayed any sentimental interest in her since his advent on the island. Perhaps by now, she told herself hopefully, time and his illness had changed him for the better. Perhaps.

Something caused her to turn her head toward the cabin door back of her. Against the portal stood the White Chief. His hand was hooked beneath his scarlet belt in the old familiar manner. His narrow, pale eyes were fastened upon her in a way she had known in Katleean. She felt suddenly that he had taken in every detail of her appearance – her heavy braided hair, her worn and faded blouse, her short ragged skirt, and her feet incased in homemade moccasins of canvas. She felt a rush of hot blood rising to her hair. He noted it and smiled, his sardonic, thin-lipped smile. The peculiar warmth that crept into his eyes caused Ellen's heart to contract with a realization of appalling possibilities. A small, inward panic took possession of her.

She rose abruptly and ran swiftly up the hillside trail to the Lookout. She knew now that she was not dealing with a sick man. She and her sister were practically at the mercy of Paul Kilbuck.

She resolved to keep her suspicions from Jean as long as possible, but that evening as they were sitting together in the living room, after Lollie had climbed into bed, the girl kept glancing apprehensively toward the closed door that shut off the sleeping place of the trader.

"Ellen," she said, hardly above a whisper. "I don't think he's as ill now as he would have us believe." She nodded toward the closed door. "We ought to ask him to move over to the hut with Swimming Wolf now. ... Ellen – I'm growing dreadfully afraid of him. ... Oh!" She started nervously at a sound from the other room.

"I wish we had some way of locking that door."

In a low voice Ellen thus admitted her own uneasiness, while her gaze wandered about the room. "We might put the table in front of it, and then if he did try to come through in the night, we would hear him."

Cautiously the two women lifted the table and placed the inadequate barrier across the door.

"From now on, Jean, only one of us will sleep, while the other watches – just to be ready, you know. If he makes one suspicious move . . .," she broke off and patted, almost lovingly, the revolver she had drawn from an inside pocket of her blouse.

Noting the look of fear that had crept into Jean's eyes since her suspicions had been confirmed, Ellen added: "But it won't be much longer, Jeanie, this waiting. Surely Shane will come in a day or two. It's nearly the twenty-first of June."

The twenty-first of June, the longest and most beautiful day of the year in the North, was also the anniversary of Ellen's wedding. Never during the last ten years had Shane forgotten it. Never had he failed to bring her some little surprise, to arrange some extra pleasure for her. For the past two weeks this thought had been with Ellen constantly, comforting her, promising her. By some complex, womanish process she had come to believe that on the twenty-first of June Shane, if alive, must come to her. As she and Jean lay awake whispering during the long, light nights, she had instilled some of her faith into the girl's mind. If they could but keep the trader from any untoward action until then, they both felt that all would be well.

During the days that followed the sisters never left each other's side. Swimming Wolf and Lollie procured the food. The Wolf chopped the wood and attended to other like duties about the cabin. The White Chief did nothing, except lounge on Kayak's bunk. In response to Ellen's suggestion that he move to the hut on the other side of the island he had merely looked into her eyes and smiled.

Since recovering his strength he had begun to take long walks about the beaches. Ellen feared that sometime he might come upon their cavern and learn the secret of the gold of Kon Klayu, but Jean assured her that there was no approach from either side of the precipice. The only way to the cave lay by way of the cleft.

As time dragged on the strain of uncertainty became almost more than the women could bear. Sometimes as they sat about the table eating the wild food that was their only sustenance now, Ellen could hardly control her impulse to hurl at the enigmatic man opposite her the questions that rose to her lips. Why was he so silent? For what was he waiting? What did he think of their situation? What did he mean to do with them?

She realized that they could not go on indefinitely as they were now. *Something* must happen to relieve the tension. She had reached a point where any word, any action that might give her a clue to the trader's intentions, was welcome. She began to long intensely that he might do something that would give her an excuse to use the revolver she carried constantly beneath her blouse.

But beyond looks, and an occasional cryptic smile, he did nothing to alarm either of the women. Yet his very silence and inaction were more ominous than threats. He instilled in them a crawling dread, a growing terror and uncertainty that was worse than anything they had hitherto known.

The twenty-first of June dawned beautiful and clear. It had been Ellen's turn to watch all night and she was a-stir early, happier and more cheerful than she had been for months. Today – today Shane must come. She was sure he would come. He had never failed her. She woke Jean and Loll, and with that undying instinct that prompts every true woman to make a feast for her returning man, Ellen prepared an extra amount of the poor fare at her command: gumboot hash, boiled eggs and sea parrot.

Shortly after the midday meal the White Chief, now fully recovered, went off with Swimming Wolf in the direction of the south cliffs. Ellen, with her sister and Lollie, climbed hopefully to the Lookout to begin their watching.

In the bright sunshine the sea below heaved gently and stretched away to the horizon where, today, the dim outline of the amethyst range showed. Afar out the smoke of a westbound steamer smudged the sky faintly, lending a suggestion of human nearness to the scene that cheered the waiting ones. Nearly three weeks had gone by since the men had left the island, and the weather, with the exception of the one storm, had been calm. Today, certainly, Shane would come if he were alive.

Eagerly, hopefully, they talked of his arrival as they sat scanning the ocean toward Katleean. The soft breeze died away. The sea took on the smooth shimmer of undulating satin. From afternoon down to sunset the day grew in beauty.

Time went by and the passing of each hour lessened somewhat the measure of their blind faith and hope. Their talk became desultory. The blue and silver of afternoon gave way to the blue and gold of approaching evening. The tide came in and the amber sky took on the luminous tints of rose and jade, cobalt and orange. The heaving, chameleon sea, unruffled by a breath of wind, gave back the colors quivering, burnished, opalescent, like the bowl of an abalone shell. They, on the Lookout, felt themselves alone inside the tinted bubble of the world. Ellen's day was waning in an enthralling splendor that rendered the watchers speechless; it numbed them by its exquisite beauty so incongruous with their own growing sense of hopelessness. Ellen's day was waning, and yet there was no sign of Shane.

From the pole on the Lookout the homemade flag hung in pathetic bleached tatters, like lifeless grey hair down the back of an old woman. Beneath it, on driftwood left over from the signal fires, sat the watchers. A faint breath from the dead ashes mingled with the freshness of the evening air and added an indefinable touch of loneliness.

Little Loll, tired out from his long, vain watching, curled up against Ellen's knee and went to sleep. Shags, dark and witch-like against the glowing sky, flew in long, low lines toward the cliffs. There was no sound except the eternal murmur of the surf.

The opal tints deepened, then faded to a dull amethyst. Just above the line of the sea the blood-red sun stood out against the haze like an immense weirdly luminous balloon. The women watched it sinking ... sinking. It seemed pregnant with awesome, universal mysteries, this dully growing crimson ball of the sun whose descent marked the close of the day.

"Oh, Jeanie, Jeanie!" Suddenly the low cry quivered on the hush of the night. Ellen's brave spirit had succumbed at last to the awful, beautiful, loneliness. She sank her head on her sister's shoulder and clasping her arms about Jean, vainly tried to still the surge of grief that shook her.

"Jeanie!" she sobbed. "He's dead. Shane – my husband – is dead! If ... if he were living, he would have come to me today!"

The tattered flag on the pole above stirred to an awakening breeze. The midnight sun touched the rim of the sea, and lingered to kiss with blood-red lips the cruel waters that have taken many men. Then it doubled back on its track and slowly, perceptibly, rose again, as if reluctant to lose sight of the lonely Lookout where Lollie, fully awake now, was trying to gather two sobbing women into his thin, little-boy arms.

33

ANCHORS AWAY

An hour later, Ellen, worn out by the vigil of the night before and the long watching on the Lookout, lay on the blankets of her bed fully dressed. Lollie slumbered beside her, his tumbled red head in the crook of his arm. It was Jean's night to watch, and she sat before the table, the revolver ready to her hand. Her shoulders drooped and her eyes were heavy-lidded and swollen from weeping. She rested her elbows on the table and dropped her face in her hands. Numbed by their grief and disappointment, both women for the time being had relaxed their caution, and for the first time in days, the table had not been placed across the closed door of the White Chief's room.

For an hour the girl sat immovable. Then she glanced up at the clock. It had stopped. Ellen had forgotten to wind it. Jean wondered dully how they were now to tell the time. There was no other timepiece on the island. But time didn't matter. Nothing mattered now. She dropped her face again in her hands. Her head was very heavy. Her arms slipped slowly until they rested on the table. Her head settled forward until it lay upon them. There came a long, tired sigh, and then the regular breathing of the sleeper.

The sun of late morning was streaming in through the little north window when the door off the living room softly opened. The tall figure of the White Chief stood a moment as he looked in at the quiet forms before him. A gleam of triumph showed in his narrow eyes as they came to rest on the pistol lying before the dark bowed head of the girl at the table. His nostrils twitched and his lip lifted in his wolfish smile. He tiptoed cautiously until his avid hand closed on the weapon.

In the middle of the room he paused, and with an air of satisfaction, turned it over and over in his hands. There was a movement on the bed in the corner, and abruptly Ellen sat upright, her wide gaze on the man before her.

"Good morning," he said, smiling at her derisively. His instinct for effective poses asserted itself as he began showing off his aptitude with the revolver. He twirled it, with elaborate carelessness, on his trigger finger, and with one movement of his wrist, stopped it, at the same time drawing a bead on the shining gold scales above the window. "I've been trying to get my hands on this for days," he said conversationally, turning to her again. "Your aim is a little too sure for me to take any chances." He looked at the weapon in his hand. "You know, my dear, I have never really believed in that popular fallacy concerning women and force – that a club and long hair go together. Still, you never can tell ... as a persuader this is a bit better than a club, but ... ," he said as he shrugged his shoulders contemptuously, "I'll not need it – here." He extracted the three cartridges from the revolver and tossed it easily to the bed.

"Oh-oh-oh Ellen!" Jean's despairing voice struck through the room as she woke and found the pistol gone.

The trader glanced from one to the other. "I am indeed a fortunate man," he said with a laugh, "to be cast upon an island with two charming women. Some might think it an embarrassment of riches – but I. ... " He allowed a significant silence to sink in.

Ellen had risen from the bed and stood beside her sister, a hand resting protectively on the girl's shoulder. The White Chief crossed to the table and seated himself on the edge of it, one foot swinging free.

"You're both going to think a lot of me before we're taken off Kon Klayu," he told them. "Oh, yes, we'll be taken off, my dears, but not by your husband, Mrs. Boreland." He ignored Ellen's cry and proceeded. "I was a little afraid the first week that he might, by sheer Irish luck, have escaped the storm and be turning up here – but it's too late now. I'll wager you're a widow."

He seemed to be enjoying himself immensely as his pale eyes lingered first on one and then on the other woman before him.

"The pale white rose, and the dewy red bud," his vibrant voice went on mockingly. "Oh, do not be alarmed," he said as they both shrank back. "I'm not going to be crude. I have plenty of time – plenty of time. Oh, you would, would you!" He broke off with a sudden snarl, as Ellen, infuriated by his manner, snatched up the empty revolver and hurled it with all her strength at his head.

He dodged, and with one panther-like movement, leaped at her, his arms closing like a vice about her shoulders.

As if maddened by her struggles, he crushed her to him and grasping her wrists in one powerful hand, he embedded the other in her loose hair and brutally drew her head back until her face was upturned to his. A moment he bent above her, crouching, feral, then he thrust his dark bearded face against hers and shut off her screams.

At the first intimation of the man's violence Jean had rushed to her sister's aid and was beating him with wildly impotent hands, calling despairingly to Lollie, to Swimming Wolf, even to Gregg. Then like a young tigress she sprang at him from behind trying to get a hold on his neck so that she might drag him from Ellen.

But the man was impervious to everything outside the circle of his arms.

"Oh, Swimming Wolf! Oh, help! Help us!" Jean's desperate screams rang out again as she heard the sound of hasty footsteps on the porch outside.

She leaped for the door, but before her hand touched the latch it was flung open and against the blinding sunshine loomed the tall figure of Shane Boreland.

With one bound he crossed the living room. There came the sound of a blow ... struggling ... a sudden choked cry ... and Shane's gasping words.

"God ... you cur ... come out in the open ... I'll kill you!"

Two writhing, panting figures reeled about the living room. They broke. Then Shane, livid with rage, sidestepped, and with the agility of a wildcat leaped again at his adversary. His arm encircled and tightened about the trader's neck. Kilbuck turned in the grip, and chest to chest they swayed, strained, their tentative blows rendered impotent by their very nearness to each other. With twisting of legs and sudden sagging of bodies they sought to get each other prostrate. The hot breath whistling from their gaping mouths made the only human sounds. Wheeling, lurching, they fought swiftly about the room, knocking over chairs ... the table ... sweeping the stove from its foundation. Then Shane's ankle turned as his foot encountered the fallen revolver, and he lost his balance.

In that instant the trader had him down – was upon him, slugging viciously with both fists. From the first there was no science in the fight. Both men inflamed, one with a long-denied passion for revenge, the other with hatred for one he had wronged, had reverted to the primitive lust to gouge, to claw, to kill with bare hands. They rolled about the floor, first one on top, then the other, striking, tearing at each other's throats, their very blind fury defeating their purpose. Again a turn found them on their feet, and like snarling beasts they bounded back to the attack. Shirts were torn from their backs, warm, gummy blood on their sweating bared bodies rendered their grips insecure.

After what seemed to the watchers a frenzied eternity, their efforts began slowly to slacken. Their grips became more feeble, their hoarse rasping gasps for breath more labored. The Chief attempted groggily to dodge a blow. Shane recovered his balance, rushed him low, and closed. A moment they swayed together, then slowly the trader was lifted off his feet. A sudden twist of Shane's shoulders, a heave, and the Chief was slammed against the edge of the overturned table, his arm striking heavily. Even as he went down, Shane was on top of him, his hands fastened in a death grip about Kilbuck's throat. The man's face began to tum purple, his pale narrow eyes widened slowly, horribly until they seemed starting from the sockets.

Then Jean screamed.

"Gregg! Kayak! Stop him! Don't let him commit murder!"

The sound of the girl's voice broke the spell that had bound the spectators standing in the doorway. Kayak Bill and Harlan strode into the cabin, and between them tore Boreland from his enemy and placed him on the bed in the comer, where Ellen and Lollie took charge of him. The insensible White Chief was carried into the next room and put in Kayak's bunk. Breathing heavily from exertion, Kayak Bill stepped back to look at him.

"That lyin' skunk's so crooked he cain't lay straight in bed, Gregg. I was honin' somethin' powerful to horn in on that little shindy – but I reckon Shane's bunged him up conside'ble," he drawled with immense satisfaction, as he leaned over and felt the trader's arm. "'Pears like he's got a busted flipper, and I know his noggin is sure addled. Get some water, Gregg. I mout as well bring the durned pirate back to life, 'cause when he's well again, I aim to knock hell outen him myself. ... "

Kayak turned to find that his remarks had fallen on the empty air, for Gregg and Jean, standing amid the ruins of the dish cupboard, were oblivious to all the world except each other. His hazel eyes roved to the bed where Ellen and Loll were welcoming Shane as if he had returned from the dead. Kayak stood a moment.

" 'Pears like I'm playin' a lone hand here," he said wistfully as he started for the water that was to revive the White Chief.

"Oh, Kayak! Kayak!" came Lollie's shout as he burrowed out from between his parents. "It's your turn now to get some lovin'. Wait a minute!" And the little fellow sprang from one end of the bed into Kayak's arms. A second later both Ellen and Jean were welcoming him with a warmth of affection that sent his new sombrero flying and made his old hair-seal waistcoat slip halfway off his shoulders. Delighted, but unprepared for such demonstrations, Kayak was at a loss how to meet them. His cheeks turned fiery red, and though his eyes were glowing, he backed away the moment they released him and began earnestly to readjust his worn waistcoat.

"By he ... hen, Lady," he managed to say with some semblance of his old nonchalance, as he fumbled with a torn buttonhole. "I ... I," he glared accusingly at the hair-seal garment, "I believe this durned thing is ... is ... is a-sufferin' from poverty o' the buttons, or — or maybe enlargement o' the buttonholes!" And in the laughter that greeted his statement, he went off to care for the White Chief.

Joy in the reunion and an hour's rest put Shane on his feet again. While the women gathered up their few belongings, they learned how the old whaleboat in which the men had left Kon Klayu had held together, seemingly by a miracle, during the first part of the storm, but later had been driven out of its course. When Shane finally landed at a cannery fifty miles from Katleean, the boat was abandoned and they were taken to the trading post in the canoes of some fishing Natives. There they learned of the White Chief's trip on the *Silver Fox* and set about getting the *Hoonah* off the beach at the lagoon. The tides of June being higher than usual they had little trouble, but it took days to caulk the seams and put the schooner in shape for the trip.

"We were within fifty miles of here yesterday when the wind died down, El," Shane told his wife, "and myself doing my best to make it on our wedding anniversary. I knew you'd be expecting me, little fellow!" He patted her hand. "Well," he continued after some strictly personal remarks, "I suppose we'll have to take Kilbuck to a doctor before we go to Katleean—damn him, I ought to kill him, though. There's an M.D. at the cannery this summer. I want the blackguard fixed up so I can settle with him later." He drew a new corncob from his pocket, and cramming it with tobacco, lit it. "But I tell you, girls," he went on between puffs of the keenest enjoyment, "Kayak and I had the biggest surprise of our lives the day before we left Katleean." He turned to Gregg and made a ludicrous confidential attempt to wink a swollen eye. "A cannery steamer put in and landed no less person than his royal nibs – the president of the Alaska Fur and Trading Company!"

This announcement was received with no particular enthusiasm by either of his listeners.

"We got close as paving bricks right off the reel, and he's going to finance the mining of Kon Klayu!" he said, and then stopped to note the effect of this statement. "We left him at the post looking into the business methods of the White Chief. The cannery steamer will be back in ten days, and we'll all strike out for San Francisco together and get our outfit. We'll be back here at Kon Klayu this fall to begin operations."

There was a dismayed exclamation from Ellen, a delighted one from Jean.

"Oh, cheer up, El," he said to his wife. "You and I won't have to come unless we want to. We've already appointed the old man's son resident manager. He wants the job – is crazy about it in fact. Turn around girls, and I'll present him to you: Mr. Gregg Harlan, ladies!" With a grand flourish, Shane indicated the flushing young man.

"Why he chose to keep it a secret all these months, he hasn't told us yet, but – perhaps Jean will find out!" Laughing at the incredulous look on Ellen's face, he limped out to the shed where Kayak Bill was doing up samples of ore to take aboard the *Hoonah* lying just off the bluff.

At midnight the schooner was rippling gently over the long swells into an atmosphere of golden sunset light that flooded the sky and crinkled along the wave tops in shimmering, mellow orange. Up in the bow of the *Hoonah*, silhouetted against the glow, old Kayak Bill stood alone. In his hazel eyes was the wistful look that crept there sometimes when he watched the domestic happiness of those about him. Atop the cabin by the main mast Jean and Gregg stood looking back over the lengthening stretch of water. Kon Klayu lay, an oblong of jade in the amber light, ringed with a wreath of foam. A single gull winnowed across the vision calling a wistful question, and from the Lookout the tattered flag flung itself out on the breeze as if in farewell.

Jean's happy voice came to him from where she snuggled in the circle of Harlan's arm.

Kayak Bill let his gaze wander to the stern where Shane and Ellen stood together at the wheel: Despite Boreland's battered countenance, his chin was up in his old jaunty and debonair manner. The wind ruffled the hair on his bare head. One hand managed the steering gear. The other arm lay across his wife's shoulders.

Kayak, watching, shook his head gently.

"I always hearn tell," he spoke softly to himself, "that the only difference a-tween happy marriages and unhappy ones is that the happy ones keeps their bickerin's private like ... but I don't know. I don't know."

A moment more he looked at the prospector and his wife, then he turned away and his old eyes gazed out across the tinted ocean spaces to that something that had always seemed to beckon him from beyond the sunset glow. Lost in his dreaming, the old man did not hear Shane's eager voice as he released the wheel a moment and pointed off the bow to where, beyond the rim of the sea, lay the northwest coast of Alaska.

"It's up there in the Valley of the Kuskokwim, El. They've made a brand new strike and are getting ten dollars to the pan!" He looked down at her and went on in his most coaxing Irish way. "Darlin', when we get Loll in school, and Jean and Gregg and Kayak safely settled on Kon Klayu ... , " he hesitated. Then finished eagerly, "Sure El, it would do us the world of good to go up there, little fellow ... just to take a bit of a look. " He straightened, his eyes alight with the old questing expression, his face turned to the northwest, his spirit already faring forth across sea and land to the beckoning Valley of the Kuskokwim.

THE END

ALASKA'S FIRST OFFICIAL AUTHOR

FLORENCE BARRETT WILLOUGHBY

BY LAUREL DOWNING BILL

Many Alaskans recognize Florence Barrett Willoughby as the Last Frontier's first official author. While other writers brought stories of the Great Land to the rest of the world in the early 1900s, none actually lived in Alaska for any length of time.

Robert Service, who penned poetry and prose about the Klondike gold rush era and made famous such ballads as "The Cremation of Sam McGee" and "Dangerous Dan McGrew," never lived in Alaska. The Englishman stepped off a steamer in Skagway in 1904 and promptly boarded a White Pass and Yukon Railway train bound for Canada's Yukon Territory. He lived in Whitehorse for a couple years, where he wrote *The Spell of the Yukon*, his first major publication. He wrote several more manuscripts after moving to Dawson City and then left Canada in 1912. He moved to Europe and died in France in 1958.

Jack London traveled Southeast Alaska's Chilkoot Trail in 1897 and headed on to Dawson City to seek his fortune in gold country. But he only spent a few months in a cabin in the frigid Yukon before heading back to California in June 1898 – with only scurvy to show for his troubles. He later had better luck mining tales of gold, however, including *The Call of the Wild* and many other stories about the North Country. He died at his beloved Beauty Ranch in California in 1916.

And Rex Beach, famous for writing *The Spoilers* in 1906 – a story of the Nome gold rush that included crooked judges, con men and miners – spent parts of five years prospecting in the north. He then returned to Florida where he penned his tales of fiction. Other notable stories he wrote about Alaska include *The Silver Horde*, *The Iron Trail* and *The Winds of Chance*. Beach died in Florida in 1949.

Florence Barrett Willoughby lived the adventures about which she later wrote. Born in Wisconsin in 1886, she spent more than 20 years in Alaska after her father, Martin Barrett, brought the family north in 1896 on board a schooner named *Leslie*.

Martin Barrett, born in Ireland in 1846, partnered with three other men to purchase and outfit the ship in hopes that they would find their fortunes in gold, according to an article titled "Martin Barrett's Experiences" published in the *Cordova Daily Alaska* on Nov. 30, 1912. Along with a Capt. Lyons, Barrett and his family left the shores of Washington state and prospected along the coast of Alaska all the way up into Cook Inlet.

The group became marooned in September 1896 on Middleton Island, about 90 miles southwest of Cordova in the Gulf of Alaska. Martin Barrett and Capt. Lyons wanted to prospect for gold on the island and had sold their schooner with the understanding that the ship would come back and pick them up after a period of time. The ship never returned.

Middleton Island, seen here, is a low-lying, unforested island 50 miles south of Prince William Sound. It is about 4,300 years old and a Registered Natural Landmark.

Other ships avoided the dangerous waters around the island, so it took about 10 months for the family to be rescued. *Where The Sun Swings North* is based, in part, on Florence Barrett Willoughby's experiences as a 10-year-old struggling to survive on that barren, storm-racked island.

No animals and only a few birds inhabited the 1-by-4-mile-long strip of land. That made for a long, lonely and hungry winter for the family, which included mother Florence, born in Germany in 1867, older brother Lawrence, born in Wisconsin in 1884, and younger brother Frederick, born in Washington in 1892. The group survived on the few rations they had packed for their short trip, along with water-damaged flour and limpets – a small marine snail – until they were rescued by a cannery tender in June 1897.

Following their rescue, they heard the news about a major gold discovery in the Klondike. So the Barretts moved on to Dawson City, Yukon Territory. On Sept. 14, 1897, Martin Barrett filed a claim on Victoria Gulch, according to Canadian placer mine documents. The Barretts apparently stayed in Dawson for several years, as their names appear in *Polk's Alaska-Yukon Directory* in 1901-1902, with Martin being listed as a miner. Other sources indicate that the couple spent the winters "Outside" and summers mining near Dawson while children Florence and Lawrence attended Catholic boarding schools near Seattle.

When Martin Barrett decided to follow the lure of copper, oil and coal in the new community of Katalla, the family moved to Prince William Sound in southcentral Alaska. Interest in the rich resources of that area predated their arrival by seven years after one man literally stumbled upon a pool of oil.

Trapper Thomas White was hunting bear in the Controller Bay region near what became Katalla, about 50 miles southeast of Cordova, in 1896. While tracking a wounded animal, he fell into thick, black mud seeping up from the ground.

After cleaning his gun and himself, he tossed a match into the pit "to see what would happen," he later said. The pool burst into flames and burned for a month.

By 1903, when the Barrett family settled in Katalla, several oil derricks, cabins and pipelines dotted the hillside.

It became the first producing oil field discovered in Alaska, and in 1901, the Alaska Development Corporation – known as the English Company – drilled its first well. It brought in the first gusher the next year at the mouth of the Bering River, about 15 miles from actively producing coalfields. *The New York Times* printed an overly optimistic report of the find:

"Oil stands in pools and small lakes all over the surface of the lowlands lying east of Copper River. ... In places there are lakes of oil covering acres."

The hillside near the discovery site soon blossomed with oil derricks, drilling equipment, cabins and pipelines. Workers dug deep pits in the bog to temporarily store the crude.

Thus Katalla was born in 1903 and soon more than 5,000 people were enjoying the amenities provided by hotels, banks, stores and a newspaper. Enthusiasm in the new settlement ran so high, that the banner of that new newspaper, *The Katalla Herald*, proclaimed:

"Katalla, The Coming Metropolis of Alaska, Where the Rails Meet the Sails."

This optimism was dampened as time marched on, however,

ALASKA'S FIRST OFFICIAL AUTHOR

due to the nature of violent storms that often prevented ships from loading and unloading at its shore. But when Martin Barrett bought into the dream in 1903 and became the owner of a hotel, restaurant and general store, he and many others indeed thought that Katalla would become a major city in Alaska.

By all accounts, his then 17-year-old daughter loved living in Katalla. That's where the seeds of her writing career may have taken root, too. An announcement appeared in the *Catalla Drill* in December 1903 that read:

"We understand Miss Florence M. Barrette [sic], professional stenographer and typewriter, is preparing to do work in her line for those requiring her services. She can be found at her father's restaurant on D Street."

By the fall of 1904, business was booming for most entrepreneurs in the new town. There were 15 holes down or drilling, including two at Katalla, two at Strawberry Harbor and nine between Katalla Slough and the Bering River. And these early successes drew another

Courtesy Anchorage Museum Rasmuson Center

A raised walkway and wooden road graced Katalla's main thoroughfare in 1907. Several businesses, including Barrett's store, also were located on this street.

adventurer to Katalla who would become a part of young Florence's life.

Oliver L. Willoughby, a newspaper publisher from Port Townsend, Washington, came north to learn about land and mineral possibilities, according to biographer Nancy Warren Ferrell in her book, *Barrett Willoughby Alaska's Forgotten Lady*. He then introduced potential investors to areas that showed promise, and he later got into the lumber business.

It is not known what drew Florence to Oliver, whom she called Ollie, but the 21-year-old married the then 38-year-old Willoughby on January 24 1907. The couple settled into married life and soon Florence became pregnant. Sadly, she gave birth to a stillborn baby on December 23, 1907, just a few weeks before her first wedding anniversary. That was her only child.

Newspaper social accounts indicate she turned her interest toward attending and hosting parties and events in the bustling town. And although terrible storms in 1907-1908 prevented many ships from docking at Katalla, the community continued to have high hopes for oil production.

Enthusiasm began to wan, however, after railroad operations to haul resources to tidewater were moved to Cordova. When *The Katalla Herald* ceased operations in 1909, most hope died and many people left the community to seek fortunes elsewhere.

The Barretts and Willoughbys did not want to give up on Katalla. But eventually Oliver Willoughby began spending more time in Washington as he tried to lure investors south, leaving Florence to handle business affairs in the dying Alaska town.

Katalla had a bit of good news in 1911. A small experimental refinery, the first in Alaska, was built on Katalla Slough – a short distance from the oil field – and some oil was refined. Expansion of the refinery was accomplished the following year. It then went into regular operation producing gasoline and other products. That offered work to some Katalla residents, although most of the refinery products were used in Cordova.

On Nov. 23, 1912, disaster struck the Barrett family. Martin Barrett,

ALASKA'S FIRST OFFICIAL AUTHOR

66, died of a heart attack. Then Fred Barrett, 21, died of tuberculosis a few months later.

About four months after Martin Barrett's death, Florence's mother married Oliver Willoughby's brother, Charles. Apparently young Florence approved of this union, according to biographer Ferrell. The marriage meant that Florence became her mother's sister-in-law in addition to being her daughter.

It was about this time that Florence began testing the literary waters. She earned 50 cents for her first sale of a household tip and soon became a correspondent for *The All-Alaska Review*. She sold short pieces to several other publications, as well, including *Sunset Magazine*, *Seward Gateway* and *The Alaska Times*. One story printed in *Boy's World* earned her $2.50 in 1915 – more than $60 in 2018 dollars.

Her reputation as an up and coming writer began spreading to a few other Alaska communities. On Sept. 16, 1916, *The Alaska Times* of Cordova reprinted an article originally published in the *Seward Gateway* that announced she was visiting friends in Seward. In part, the article stated:

"… Mrs. Willoughby is a clever writer, whose work appears often in outside publications. She has a very successful future ahead if she continues the work…."

While Florence was seeing some success as an author, she was not having much success in her love life. Her relationship with husband Oliver did not withstand the test of distance or time. The couple divorced in April 1917, but they continued to correspond with each other throughout their lives.

Less than three months after her divorce, Florence left Katalla to marry Roger Summy, who had worked for Oliver in the coalfield business. The couple moved to Anchorage, where Florence's brother Lawrence and his family lived. However, the Barretts soon took off for Casper, Wyoming, which at the time was booming with oil.

Unfortunately, Lawrence had an eye for the ladies and one of them followed him to the new boomtown. On October 16, 1917, "Seattle Bessie" Fisher shot Lawrence at a Casper restaurant. He died the next day, according to an article in the *Anchorage Daily Times*.

In five years, Florence had lost her father, younger brother Fred and older brother Lawrence. She also had lost a marriage, quickly remarried a man who enjoyed liquor too much and was unhappy. She separated from Summy in May 1918, officially divorcing him that October, and decided to go to school in Tacoma, Washington.

It was during this time period that a friend convinced her she should pursue her talent for writing and move farther south. So by January 1920, Florence was settled into her new home on Bush Street in San Francisco to begin her writing career, according to Ferrell.

Florence went to work as a secretary for Frederick O'Brien, author of books such as *Atolls of the Sun, Mystic Isles of the South Seas* and *White Shadows in the South Seas.* O'Brien encouraged Florence with her writing. She soon was putting in a full day's work and then writing about five hours every day.

A couple years later, she sent her manuscript for *Where The Sun Swings North,* based on her family's experiences while stranded on Middleton Island, to George Palmer Putnam. The publisher decided to take a chance and agreed to print it.

Barrett Willoughby's first book, *Where The Sun Swings North,* was released in October 1922.

Putnam advised Florence to use a masculine pen name, however. While women were beginning to have a few more choices than their female ancestors, they still faced sexism and prejudice in the 1920s. Many people didn't think that women should have a place in the literary world.

So Florence chose her masculine-sounding maiden and married names to create Barrett Willoughby. *Where The Sun Swings North,* which first appeared in serial form in *The Chicago Tribune,* came out as a book in October 1922. It was the first of many successes for the young author.

On June 24 that year, shortly after the serialized version began appearing in the Illinois newspaper, the *Cordova Daily Times* reported:

"It is claimed that Barrett Willoughby is the first real Alaskan novelist."

Following publication of that first story in serial form in the *Chicago Tribune*, Florence set out for Alaska to do research for more stories about her beloved country. Her goal was to share the real Alaska with readers. While other authors, including Service, London and Beach, spun stories of rough adventurers who tackled a cold, isolated, unforgiving land, she wanted to tell tales of romance, endurance and a landscape teaming with life.

An article titled *Noted Writer Visits Sitka after Data*, printed in the *Sitka Tribune* on June 23, 1922, reported:

"Frances Barret [sic] Willoughby, noted writer, sourdough and Alaskan musher spent the past week visiting Sitka gathering material for an all Alaskan novel....

"Leaving on the steamer *Queen*, Mrs. Willoughby and her friend are now on their way to Kodiak where they plan to remain for two months or more, gathering information on fox farming, fishing, and other northern industries."

Courtesy Alaska State Library

Throughout her career, Florence continued to travel to Alaska and immerse herself in research and adventures in order to write with authority about the landscape, as well as her heroines, heroes and flawed characters. She went to Fairbanks and flew with famous Alaska aviator Carl Ben Eielson in his open-cockpit biplane;

Barrett Willoughby traveled to various parts of Alaska in steamers like the *Queen*, seen here.

she spent time in Juneau investigating its gold mining history; and she studied the salmon industry's history and practices on a trip to Sitka. During a radio interview in the early 1930s, she said she had covered 6,000 miles in two months "using steamers, railroads, cruisers, canoes, automobiles and airplanes," according to biographer Ferrell.

But she never wrote her novels while on these trips. She only amassed material for her stories and then wrote her tales once she returned to California. Sources say she wrote about 2,000 words a day in order to capture everything around her while on her exploratory trips north. She always had her journal near at hand, too, following the advice of early mentor Frederick O'Brien, who told her to keep a diary and always to be herself.

While visiting Juneau in July 1936, Florence explained to a reporter for the *Daily Alaska Empire* why she could not write her novels while she was in Alaska.

"Barrett Willoughby has a home in San Carlos, California, and a studio in San Francisco. She stated here today that she would live in Alaska permanently were it not that she finds she can't write of Alaska at such short range; she needs to be farther away to obtain a proper perspective on her subject matter."

Following the successful debut of *Where The Sun Swings North*, Florence wrote three more books over the next few years.

Rocking Moon, set on an island off Kodiak Island, involved Russian influence in the area, romance and the fox farming industry. It first was serialized in *The American Magazine* in 1924-25, released in book form in April 1925 and made into a movie that same year. It was the first time a major production from Hollywood came north to film a movie in Alaska, although the producers chose Sitka instead of Kodiak as the backdrop. The *Sitka Tribune* reported on September 24, 1925:

"The first big motion picture company from Hollywood to film scenes in Alaska arrived in Sitka on the *Virginia* today, where they will spend three weeks making scenes for *Rocking Moon*, a romance of the land of long shadows, on the actuat [sic] locations of the story."

Based on the success of these first two novels, publisher Gosset and Dunlap of New York printed *The Fur Trail Omnibus*, which contained both *Where The Sun Swings North* and *Rocking Moon* in 1925.

Next came a nonfiction book titled *Gentlemen Unafraid*, published in 1928, where Barrett Willoughby narrated stories of six Alaska pioneers, including Martin Barrett, her father; Alexander "Sandy" Smith, an early trailblazer; Allan "Scotty" Allan, a sled-dog racer; George Evans, an expert in coal fields; Sydney Barrington, a steamship captain; and C.C. Georgeson, a plant expert. She decided to include more than 75 black and white photographs in this book, which helped bring the history of the men alive. It worked so well, that she included photographs in all her future nonfiction projects.

In 1929, *The Trail Eater: A Romance of the All-Alaska Sweepstakes*, debuted. This novel, first serialized in *The American Magazine*, featured romance set amid dog mushing activities in Nome. Florence also wrote myriad stories during this time period for publications like *Sunset Magazine*, *The All-Alaska Review* and *The American Magazine*.

While her literary endeavors brought her much success, the same cannot be said for her love life. With two failed marriages behind her, Florence entered into matrimony for a third time on October 19, 1927, when she married University of California engineer Robert H. Prosser. Although sources say it was a happy marriage, it was short-lived. Eight years her junior, Prosser died on June 9, 1928 – less than nine months after the wedding – from complications incurred during a sinus operation.

Florence did have family to help her during this difficult period of her life, however. Sometime during the mid-1920s Florence's mother and stepfather gave up on trying to make a living in Katalla. The town's population, which had nosedived to only 50 souls, could not sustain businesses so the couple moved in with the now-successful author in California. The elder Florence, who died sometime between 1945-1956 according to biographer Ferrell, took over management of her daughter's house. Her husband, Charles, started a silver fox ranch venture that was staked by his stepdaughter.

The world was introduced to two more of Barrett Willoughby's

SPAWN OF THE NORTH

BARRETT WILLOUGHBY

Critics said Barrett Willoughby's book, *Spawn of the North*, published in 1930, was full of swift action.

works in 1930. *Sitka: Portal to Romance*, a historical nonfiction book that included elements of a travelogue and romance, and *Spawn of the North*, a fictional novel with lots of action that revolved around the fishing industry in Ketchikan. Paramount Studios made this novel into a motion picture, released in 1938, with famous actors of the day, which included Henry Fonda, Dorothy Lamour, George Raft and John Barrymore.

A review in the June 11, 1931, *Cosmopolitan* magazine, which had printed *Spawn of the North* in a serialized form before the book's publication, stated:

"The swift action takes place during the brief, intense summer season when the salmon surge up from the sea to spawn in their natal streams; when air, water, forests, all are vibrant with the stir of procreation, and when, according to Alaska tradition, men and women too, go a little mad with love."

It appears Barrett Willoughby also went a bit mad with love again after she met boat operator Earl Bright while on a research trip to Wrangell. Bright, also a writer, used the pen name Captain Larry O'Connor, and eventually began using that name for everything. The couple's marriage certificate, dated July 17, 1935, in Reno, Nevada, recorded the nuptials with the names of Larry O'Connor and Florence Prosser, according to biographer Ferrell.

During this time period, Florence produced two more works.

A nonfiction book published in 1933, titled *Alaskans All*, featured biographical sketches of five Alaskans, including aviator Carl Benjamin Eielson, Skagway entrepreneur Harriett Pullen, pilot Louis Lane, priest and geologist Bernard Hubbard and the infamous Klondike-era pioneer newsman E.J. "Stoller" White.

Her fictional novel released in 1936, *River House*, told a tale of adventure and romance at a hunting lodge near the border of Alaska and Canada in southeast Alaska. *River House* was another resounding success, appearing in *The American Magazine* as *The Captive Bride* before the book was published. The novel then was reprinted three times during April 1936 following its release. Perhaps it was during her research for this book that she met O'Connor in Wrangell.

By all accounts, the author and her new husband were well suited. In a 1939 radio interview, Florence said that they enjoyed criticizing each other's works and acting out their stories. They loved to travel, without any plans, after finishing major projects – letting "the gods of chance decide our itinerary," according to biographer Ferrell.

Courtesy Alaska State Library

Florence Barrett Willoughby met her fourth husband, Captain Larry O'Connor, in Wrangell.

The gods of chance, or perhaps change, continued to whirr around Florence's family and finances. Her beloved stepfather, Charles Willoughby, died of heart failure on January 13, 1938, which meant that she would never recoup what she had grubstaked him to start his silver fox ranch. Charles was not much of a businessman, it seems, so that business went bust.

Florence dove into her writing and produced another successful novel, titled *Sondra O'Moore*, the year following Charles' death. Set in Sitka, this story was sprinkled with smuggling, spies and romance and earned high praise from the Sept. 28, 1939, issue of *The Alaska Weekly*:

"Once again Alaska's favorite writer hits the bull's-eye with a stirring tale of old and modern Sitka ..."

The American Magazine changed the title to *Lover Come Back* and serialized the story with its dedication to "Larry O'Connor – with laughter."

However, it turns out that laughter and home fires were not burning brightly on Florence's true-life love story. Her charming husband, who began charming other ladies, was quite adept at convincing Alaska's first official author to spend money on his failed ventures. He even managed to liquidate money she had set aside for her golden years and eventually ran off with the bookkeeper of his failed furniture business. Florence divorced him in 1942.

As she had done in the past, the author pored herself into writing one more nonfiction book and another successful novel. The nonfiction work, titled *Alaska Holiday*, chronicled some of Barrett Willoughby's adventures while in Kodiak with a friend and other narratives of Alaska that included totem poles, lighthouses, sourdoughs and more.

Her fictional tale, *The Golden Totem*, later serialized and syndicated by *The Chicago Tribune*, was reprinted four times within several months of its 1945 publication. It was to be the ticket to recouping her finances following her stepfather's death and her failed fourth marriage. Set in Juneau, the story revolved around gold mining, adventure and her trademark – romance.

Courtesy Alaska State Library

Barrett Willoughby's last novel, *The Golden Totem*, was set in Juneau and revolved around gold mining. The mill for the Alaska Juneau Gold Mining Company is seen along the mountainside in this photograph.

Barrett Willoughby did not write any more adventurous books after *The Golden Totem*. Although she wrote a few articles for publication, collaborated with some people on other projects and continued to take writing classes up until her death from heart failure on July 29, 1959, at age 73.

Herb Hilscher, a longtime friend, offered this insight into Florence's success as an author in her obituary printed by the *Anchorage Daily News* on August 7, 1959:

"Many have been affected by the geography, the people and the texture of Alaska, and will readily tell you why they came and why they stayed.

"But there are few persons sensitive and skillful enough to capture this mood and translate it into literature. Most critics agree that Florence Barrett Willoughby was one of those rare people."

* For a full account of Florence Barrett Willoughby's life, I highly recommend the book, *Barrett Willoughby Alaska's Forgotten Lady*, written by Nancy Warren Ferrell, published by University of Alaska Press in 1994. It is an easy, entertaining and factual read about this prolific writer who produced seven novels, several nonfiction books and two dozen articles centered around the Alaska she loved.

Florence Barrett Willoughby, seen here in 1903 Katalla, wrote seven novels, a few nonfiction books and a couple dozen articles set in Alaska.

LIST OF WORKS
BY BARRETT WILLOUGHBY

NOVELS
Where The Sun Swings North (New York and London: Putnam, 1922)
Rocking Moon (New York: Putnam, 1925)
The Fur Trail Omnibus – Includes *Where The Sun Swings North* and
   Rocking Moon (New York: Grosset and Dunlap, 1925)
The Traileater: A Romance of the All-Alaska Sweepstakes (New York:
   Putnam, 1929)
Spawn of the North (Boston: Houghton Mifflin, 1932)
River House (Boston: Little Brown, 1936)
Sondra O'Moore (Boston: Little Brown, 1939)
The Golden Totem: A Novel of Modern Alaska (Boston: Little Brown, 1945)

NONFICTION
Gentlemen Unafraid (New York: Putnam, 1928)
Sitka: Portal to Romance (Boston: Houghton Mifflin, 1930)
Alaskans All (Boston: Houghton Mifflin, 1933)
Alaska Holiday (Boston: Little Brown, 1940)

ARTICLES
"Interesting Westerners: George Watkins Evans" (*Sunset Magazine*
   February 1916)

"Interesting Westerners: Alice Anderson" (*Sunset Magazine* March 1916)

"Katalla Revived" (*The All-Alaska Review* June 1916)

"Interesting Westerners: George Barrett" (*Sunset Magazine* June 1916)

"How Famous Ship Went Down" (*The All-Alaska Review* July 1916)

"Elias Light is Ready for Business" (*The All-Alaska Review* September/
   October 1916)

"Interesting Westerners: Mrs. C.W. Hammond" (*Sunset Magazine* February
   1917)

"Oil Development Work in Alaska Slow" (Oil Trade Journal May 1917)

"Interesting Westerners: Allan 'Scotty' Allan" (*Sunset Magazine* February
   1921)

ARTICLES - Continued

"Interesting Westerners: Father Andrew P. Kashevaroff" (*Sunset Magazine* February 1923)

"Interesting Westerners: Walstein G. Smith" (*Sunset Magazine* April 1923)

"The Law of the Trap Line" (*The American Magazine* November 1923)

"A Little Alaskan Schooner Was My Childhood Home" (*The American Magazine* October 1924)

"King of the Arctic Trail" (*The American Magazine* August 1925)

"Father of Pictures Captures the Spell of Alaska" (*The American Magazine* January 1926)

"The Passing Alaskan" (*Sunset Magazine* May 1926)

"Challenge of the Sweepstakes Trail" (*The American Magazine* July 1926)

"The Man Who Put the Midnight Sun to Work" (*The American Magazine* August 1928)

"Grand Ball at Sitka: When Alaska was Russian" (*The Century Magazine* April 1929)

"Moon Craters of Alaska" (*The Saturday Evening Post* December 1930)

"Lighthouse Keeper at the End of West" (*The Saturday Evening Post* January 1935)

"Log of the New Pioneers" (*The Saturday Evening Post* June 1935)

"Papa Came C.O.D." (*Good Housekeeping* July 1956

"The Silent City" (*The Alaska Sportsman* June 1959)

PROJECTS WITH OTHERS

"The Devil-Drum" in *The Best Short Stories of 1925*, edited by Edward J. O'Brien (Boston: Small, Maynard & Company Publishers, 1926)

"Volcanoes Packed in Ice" by Bernard Hubbard, edited by Barrett Willoughby (*The Saturday Evening Post* August 1930)

"I'm a Cream-puff Pioneer" by Mrs. Victor Johnson, edited by Barrett Willoughby (*The American Magazine* 1937)

"The Snow Woman and Mary Hewitt" by John Hewitt with Barrett Willoughby (*The Alaska Sportsman* December 1953)

Pioneer of Alaskan Skies: The Story of Ben Eielson by Edna W. Chandler with Barrett Willoughby (New York: Ginn & Company 1959)

BIBLIOGRAPHY

Anchorage Daily News, Aug. 7, 1959

Anchorage Daily Times, Oct. 28, 1917

Aunt Phil's Trunk Volume Four (Anchorage: Aunt Phil's Trunk LLC 2009)

Barrett Willoughby, Alaska's Forgotten Lady, Nancy Warren Ferrell, Univeristy of Alaska Press (1994)

Catalla Drill, Dec. 21, 1903

Cosmopolitan magazine, June 1931

Cordova Daily Alaska, Nov. 30, 1912

Cordova Daily Times, Sept. 16, 1916

Cordova Daily Times, June 24, 1922

Daily Alaska Empire, July 27, 1936

Grant for Placer Mining Application, Yukon Dept. of Tourism & Recreation & Culture, Whitehorse, Yukon Territory, Canada, Sept. 14, 1897

Polk's Alaska-Yukon Gazetteer (Seattle: R.L. Polk & Co. 1901 & 1902 Dawson)

Sitka Tribune, June 23, 1922

Sitka Tribune, Sept. 24, 1925

The Alaska Weekly, Sept. 28, 1939

The Katalla Herald, various

Thirteenth Census of the United States, Population Alaska, Second District, Katalla (1910)

MORE BOOKS FROM AUNT PHIL'S TRUNK

Winner of the Literary Classics International award for Best Nonfiction Series in 2016, the *Aunt Phil's Trunk* Alaska history series is filled with entertaining short stories and hundreds of historical photographs that share Alaska's colorful past!

"I sampled one before going back to critical activities, but it's like sampling a new flavor of a gallon of ice cream. 'Even a gallon is a sufficient sample,' you grumble as you try to get your face into the carton to lick the bottom." – Larry Winebrenner, reviewer

These history books are available for $19.95 each at www.AuntPhilsTrunk.com.

Volume One
Early Alaska up to 1900

Volume Two
1900 to 1912

Each book in this highly acclaimed Alaska history series shares easy-to-read short stories and dozens of historical photos that captivate readers from ages 9 to 99.

Be sure to check out specials on our website, AuntPhilsTrunk.com.

Volume Three
1912 to 1935

Volume Four
1935 to 1960

Volume Five
1960 to 1984

*Spell of the Yukon
and Other Verses*
$14.95

*The Call of the Wild
and Other Northland Stories*
$19.95

The Spell of the Yukon, by Robert Service, and *The Call of the Wild and Other Northland Stories*, by Jack London, both include short biographies written by Alaska author Laurel Downing Bill.

School curriculum now available!

Aunt Phil's Trunk of Alaska Trivia $9.95

How much did the largest gold nugget found in Alaska weigh? What is unusual about fireweed? Which Alaska glacier is larger than the state of Rhode Island?

You will learn the answers to these and many more questions when you get *Aunt Phil's Trunk of Alaska Trivia*. Its 104 pages are filled with fascinating facts and crosswords, word searches and sudokus that will tease your mind and broaden your knowledge of America's Last Frontier.

Sourdough Cookery $14.95

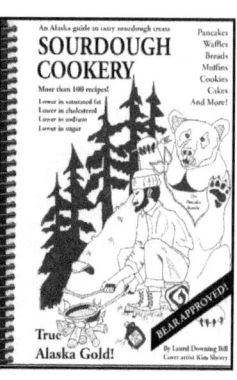

More than 100 heart-healthy recipes are featured in the *Sourdough Cookery* cookbook, which comes with authentic, 100-year-old Alaska sourdough starter!

Along with recipes for low-fat, low-sugar, low-sodium breads, biscuits and buns, you will find treats like Cranberry-Chocolate Cake, White Chocolate Cherry Muffins and Apple Pumpkin Bread – all made with egg, sugar and sodium substitutes. However, each recipe includes how many real eggs, how much sugar and other items are needed for those who want to bake with the "loaded" ingredients.

Muckluck, Alaska $14.95
Where Nothing Ever Happens

Muckluck, Alaska – Where Nothing Ever Happens, released August 2012, is written by Alaska author Lisa Augustine, edited by Laurel Downing Bill and published by Aunt Phil's Trunk LLC.

Readers will be enchanted as they travel through this 200-page fictional tale about life during 1930s-1940s in the Last Frontier. As told through the voice of 95-year-old Kate, a lifelong Alaskan, the stories ring true of small town Alaska in days gone by.

Alaska Children's Books

www.AuntPhilsTrunk.com

Raven's Friends $9.95
Alaska Animals Far and Wide

Raven's Friends, Alaska Animals Far and Wide, released June 2012, is written and illustrated by Kim Sherry. Children ages 3-8 will love this book as they follow its narrator, Raven, through 32 pages filled with colorful illustrations and poems that share facts about animals that call Alaska home.

Raven's Friends $9.95
Tails Along Alaska Trails

Raven's Friends, Tails Along Alaska Trails, released June 2013, is written and illustrated by Kim Sherry. Children ages 3-8 will love this book as they learn new things about animals that travel along Alaska trails. These 32 pages are filled with colorful illustrations and poems.

The Dragline Kid And Her Golden Wish $9.95

The Dragline Kid and Her Golden Wish, released July 2014, is written by Alaska author Lisa Augustine and beautifully illustrated by artist Melody Trone. Children ages 3-8 will delight in this story of a little girl who dreams of finding a gold nugget in Alaska's wilderness.